Garden Grove

By L.V. Gaudet

Copyright 2015 L.V. Gaudet
All rights reserved

ISBN 978-1-9992823-1-8
Library and Archives Canada
First edition published October 2019
Printed by IngramSpark

Cover by L.V. Gaudet

Discover other titles by L.V. Gaudet:

Garden Grove
The Gypsy Queen
Old Mill Road

<u>The McAllister Series:</u>
Where the Bodies Are
The McAllister Farm
Hunting Michael Underwood
Killing David McAllister

Acknowledgements

This book is inspired by actual events. No, it is not a based on a true story kind of book. All of the events and characters are entirely fictional and any perceived similarity to real persons or events is coincidental and unintentional. This story was inspired by actual frustrations endured at the seemingly endless and unavoidable noise of construction equipment at the start of a building project.

And the tractor. The actual tractor photographed for the cover photo had a hole in the windshield resembling a bullet hole, which was a big part of the inspiration for this story. The photo was altered to enhance that hole.

And now for a quick R.I.P. to the well-worn pair of runners who sacrificed their selves to the sole-devouring muck in order for this photo to be taken. You were a good pair of runners.

Table of Contents

1 - Garden Grove Vandalism

The last of the woods that once bordered this small town which my home has become are disappearing; those beautifully twisted old oak trees that filled this little piece of the world with their mangled skeletal fingers, clacking in the winds of the dark fall nights and offering protection from the strong prairie winds.

They are being ruthlessly knocked down by the big monstrosities of metal clearing sections of land to make room for more houses. Day by day, they are taking away those trees which once surrounded me and watched me with their stoic wooden faces, always watching while I can only helplessly stare back.

Their ruination is my salvation, their obliteration my release from their bony prison.

This land was once a mixture of woods and prairie, open land with farms and pastures surrounded by grassy plains and scattered woods on the edge of a scattering of new settlements that grew to call themselves towns. It did not take much to call a handful of buildings a town back then when the land was first being settled. And before that, it was a wild land of buffalo-filled plains and forests, home to a few indigenous tribes whose land had been taken over and colonized by the people of Europe, beginning the slow conquering of the indigenous people.

Now, generations later, those towns that started more than a hundred years ago as a scattering of farms and a small timber-walled fort has become a city surrounded by farm fields and cozy little bedroom communities only a short drive outside the city's borders. Bedroom communities like this one, that city people love to hate for daring to flaunt their small community lifestyle and yet continues to grow because city people move out to these little communities.

They assume I don't know all this because I am ancient by their standards. They think I sleep when I am really awake.

I think, perhaps, they have even forgotten I am here.

People think that somehow those little rural communities feel friendlier and safer than the suburbs within the city do.

They think the evils borne of crime and overcrowding are confined within the city limits.

Sometimes, in these sleepy little communities, evil just waits a little deeper.

Beep Beep Beep.

The incessant beeping and growling of construction equipment relentlessly fills the air, driving all the nearby residents to distraction.

Last night was Halloween, the kids are all over-tired and cranky and so are the parents, some of whom were up dealing with sick achy stomachs from kids scarfing down piles of sweet candy bliss.

The morning dew still sits as an icy crust on the grass and the orange glow of the rising sun still fills much of the sky, leaving remnants of the dark shadows of night clinging where they will.

Three deer jog across the road in single file. First one, who looks back to show it's safe, then another, and finally after a pause in the road the last one brings up the rear. They always come through at the same time. You could set your clock by it.

They are unusually alert and nervous.

The chill frost in the air seems to be making them uneasy, or perhaps it is the recent changes to their environment that has awakened their sense of danger.

Their usual winter trail has been irrevocably changed by the construction and the crispness in the air has urged them to turn to their winter habits despite the lack of snow on the ground.

Trees have been ripped ruthlessly from the ground and the topsoil scraped away and carted off to be sold back to the homeowners after the houses are built. Roads for new houses are being roughed in by the hulking metal monsters that roam back and forth growling and beeping.

Canada geese fly overhead, their flight patterns seeming to make no sense while they make their practice runs in preparation for the great migration.

They seem confused, or perhaps they too are agitated by unusual activity on the ground where they previously fattened themselves on the grasses.

Inside one of the houses bordering the construction area, a group of housewives hunch over their cups of hot coffee after sending their kids off on the school bus, plotting how they can silence those infernal construction tractors that are taking away the woods, desecrating the adjoining farm fields, and have destroyed the tranquility of their quiet community to build a new housing development.

The large billboard sign welcoming all to the new addition to the community taunts them with its artist's depiction of the perfect happy family and the large lettered words:

GARDEN GROVE MEADOWS

Where Families Come to Live

On the edge of the last small untouched part of the woods a lone figure stands silently, hunched against the cold in a thin worn jacket, watching the construction.

The old man shakes his head sadly; his leathery face is scarred with the lines of spending many years in the sun working the land. He turns and slowly shambles away on arthritic knees, muttering to himself.

The hulking front-end loader chugged weakly, coughed, and let out a final death rattle before lapsing into silence.

With a tired grunt, the driver climbed down out of the machine to the man waiting below, the foreman Stanley Rutthers.

"The old bitch is dead again," the driver grumbled.

"Vandals?" Stanley asked.

"Pretty sure."

"Damn, that's the third time this week."

"She's going to be out for a while this time to get fixed."

"Humph," Stanley grunted. "This job is getting expensive."

He took off his hard hat, ran a stressed hand through his hair, realized, and put the hat back on his head, giving it a meaty slap with his palm.

"I've got to go check out the rest of the site, see what else the vandals have been up to."

Stanley stalked away in a foul mood.

The ongoing vandalism at the worksite was only one of his problems.

A group of men in rough dirty clothes, heavy work gloves, steel toe work boots, and hard hats stood milling around, staring at a rocky pile of mud half spilled out of a large Cat front loader.

Stanley Rutthers approached the group, stopping to stand beside one of his most seasoned workers, Dave McCormack. The weather-lined look of their faces and over-worn work clothes made the two look almost like brothers.

"You check the plans?" Dave asked without turning to look at the foreman.

"Yeah," Stanley said. "They don't match up. Somehow our plans are different from what's at the office."

Dave looked at him in surprise. He wasn't really surprised, but you're supposed to look like it when these things happen. This whole job has been a bigger carnival of mistakes and screw-ups than usual.

He dutifully made shocked noises.

"The one in the office was altered?" Dave asked. "No surprise they forgot to send the changes somewhere again."

"That's what's strange," Stanley said. "The planners said they haven't made any changes. The copy filed with the municipal office doesn't match too. All three copies are different and none of the copies look revised. It's like the planners drew up new plans, each one a little different, instead of just making copies of the new revised plans. Except, there are no new revisions."

"I don't think anyone's finding that joke funny."

"No joke. The planners back at the office insist they only drew up one new version last month and made copies of it. They've had no changes to the plans since. The chief planner is right pissed about it."

"I bet he is," Dave said, almost amused by the thought of that gawky man trying to intimidate the other planners in the office.

"The municipal inspector is coming down on our asses too because the work doesn't match the plans that he has. He's threatening to shut down the whole jobsite," Stanley said.

Dave frowned. He needed that money. Shutting down the jobsite means sending all the guys home, and sitting on your butt in front of the television with a beer doesn't earn a pay check in this line of work.

"They're trying to figure out how this could have happened and which set of plans are the right ones," Stanley said. "Copeland is threatening to fire whoever's behind the prank."

He shook his head, at the insanity of the whole situation.

"If it was a prank, it was pretty well played out," he said. "The engineers seemed genuinely confused how this could have happened."

"Maybe they were forged," Dave said jokingly.

Stanley looked at him seriously. "I hope not. Only limited people have the skills to forge the blueprints."

"Nah, they couldn't be forged," Dave said. "Like you said, they would have to have the skills; but they'd also have to have access. None of our guys would dare cross Copeland on purpose, even for a joke. He does not have a sense of humor. It definitely has to be a big screw up in planning somehow."

"So, what's with the bucket?" Stanley asked; referring to why everyone was standing around staring at the large tractor's bucket.

"Some old bones turned up," Dave said.

"Damn," Stanley swore.

If they were just cow bones the guys would not be interested in them.

Finding bones was dreaded by anyone running a jobsite and by all the workers too. They were almost always just some kind of animal, usually cow, but every once in a while they turned out to be human. When that happened they all prayed to the construction gods that they were relatively new. The remains of a murder or accident victim could shut down the jobsite for weeks, but old bones possibly from an ancient settlement could shut down the site for months, or even indefinitely. That put men out of work.

Most bones were crushed beneath the machinery without ever being seen. The ones that were found were often just covered up, crushing them beneath the huge tires of the tractor without reporting them. Usually they had no reason to believe they would be anything but some animal. But boys will be boys and they all wanted to take a look with eager morbid fascination when something interesting was found.

And every now and then, they'd get a green guy on the crew who thought they should report the find just in case. This was one of those times.

"It's just some animal," one of the workers argued.

"I don't know," the young worker who uncovered the bone hesitated, "seems kind of big for an animal." He was new to both the crew and the construction field.

"It's a farmer's field; we're going to find cow bones. This is at least the eighth cow bone I've seen so far. They're scattered all over the place."

"Hey, we could make soup!" a jester from the crowd tossed in.

The young worker looked around.

"Looks like it used to be a wheat field to me."

"Barley actually I think," someone said.

"Whatever." One of the men was getting annoyed. "There used to be more dairy and beef farms around here. It's just a cow leg bone."

"We probably still should-," the young worker was interrupted by the shrill whistle of a Cat operator across the field.

A large Cat some distance off lurched to a stop, the driver jumping out and running around to dig in the mud turned over by the bucket.

He whistled shrilly to get the group's attention, proudly holding up his prize with a big grin.

"Looks like we've got more than cows!" he yelled to the crew.

Like a bunch of schoolboys trying to look too cool to be overly eager over someone else's gruesome find, the men shuffled and casually ambled their way over to check out the new treasure.

Stanley didn't have to see what it was. He had a pretty good hunch.

"Damn," he muttered. He turned away, feigning ignorance, and started walking back to the office trailer.

The Cat operator beamed as he showed off the yellowed scarred skull, a human skull. He hadn't decided yet if he would add it to his trophies of weird construction discoveries or crush and bury it like the usual bones.

He was genuinely dismayed and disappointed when that decision was taken out of his hands.

The new worker was determined this bone had to be reported. To him it was the right thing to do.

"We have to report this," the young worker said, becoming more awkward with the annoyed glares he received from the other guys.

"Just crush it," someone said. "Whoever it was died a long time ago. Won't hurt anyone."

"Nah, I think I'll keep it to decorate my bar," the finder said, proudly displaying his trophy.

The young worker looked around, distressed. He couldn't understand the other guys' reactions. This was a human bone! A real dead person!

"No, we have to report it," the young worker insisted, worried they would destroy it before it could be reported.

"Toss it back, crush and bury it and let's get back to work." There were a lot of assents to that.

The young worker turned away from the group, pulling out his cell phone and dialing. One of the guys made a half-hearted attempt to snatch it away but he managed to dodge him and make the call, the sounds of jeering and argument drowning him out so he had to talk loudly to be heard as he walked away.

A few hours later the bulldozers and tractors slumbered in the chill sunshine, the workers stood around sipping old thermos coffee and complaining about lost wages, and the jobsite was closed.

Yellow police tape fluttered in the wind and police cars sat idly by while a few of the uniformed officers wandered around the jobsite. The rest stood around in groups talking among themselves.

When the call came in that human remains were found, the police sent every available car to secure the scene until the crime scene investigators could get there. Until they knew otherwise, they would have to treat it as a crime scene. When they saw the aged condition of the skull, it became a waiting game. There would be no evidence to protect. They were now waiting for the go ahead to clear out all but a single car to watch the scene.

The crime scene crew coming to investigate the scene and arrange for the excavation in search of more human remains should be arriving sometime in the next few hours.

2 - Work Shutdown

I can see the tractors, the workers, and the great swaths of black ruined earth marring the weed infested tan stubble of the once cultivated fields. They have all come to a stop. The scene is partially obscured by the naked bony fingers of the twisted oak branches. They look arthritic and deformed. Despite the belief that oaks are very strong, their branches can be very brittle when they age and dry. Their gnarled rough-bark trunks stand misshapen and ugly in their own kind of beauty.

It was the nonstop growling of their tractors that woke me. The rumbling as they tear apart the ground, scraping and digging.

They haven't started ripping apart this last section of woods yet. But they will, sooner or later they will. And then they will dig up the ground because they don't know what is here.

The work will stop now, for a while. And then they'll come. They'll dig away the final barrier between me and the world.

News of their grisly discovery travelled quickly through the small community, as any dirty laundry or bad news does in the hornet's nest of gossipmongers that make up all communities. Ah, but what do they do, playing with those old bones?

Sigh.

Cold. I'm always so cold these days. My old home is so draughty. My prison.

The figure pulls the shawl closer about withered shoulders. The worn threads don't do much anymore.

One of these days, I'll crochet a new one.

The figure turns and shuffles away, receding into the darkness behind a veil of shadows, a faint smile at the corners of age-lined lips. They used to be full. Now they are a withered tight line, drawn together like a little drawstring bag even as they thinned with age.

They'll be back. The work will start again. The fools.

Some things shouldn't be dug up. This is one of them.

3 - Mrs. Crampchet's Pastries

The construction site was abuzz with activity. Already behind schedule due to a calamity of errors, and then from the site being shut down temporarily to investigate the discovery of the human skull, the workers were now scrambling to play catch up. Their boss, Bruce Copeland, was riding them, pushing them hard. He was even offering bonuses for meeting progress milestones, and Bruce Copeland never gave bonuses.

It was determined that the skull was old, but fortunately it was also determined from the lack of other artefacts found nearby and by its bone structure that it was likely the skull of an early settler and not that of a native inhabitant, and the location to have no significance. The other bone was determined to be part of a cow leg.

With no likelihood of an old burial ground, village, or other important find, the construction could continue around that one small section. They were keeping an area around where the skull was discovered off limits to the crew for now just in case there were more remains of that person to be found.

The area of the discovery is staked off into squares, a group of archaeology students from the local university and their professor having been given permission to continue excavating the site in search of any more discoveries as part of the agreement to allow the construction to begin again.

Bruce Copeland, owner of Copeland & Howe Construction, Excavation and Land Development, the company contracted to build the development, had argued against the archaeology dig and lost.

Noticing movement near the worksite entrance, a few of the construction workers gave a quick glance up the roughed in road that leads into the site and continued with their labor. Someone else would deal with their visitor.

Not far from the trailer that served as an onsite office, a group of men stood around talking.

A little old lady was very slowly shuffling up the dirt road. She had just passed the large billboard sign at the entrance announcing to the world:

GARDEN GROVE MEADOWS

Where Families Come to Live.

A couple of men standing by the trucks parked near the entrance glanced up curiously, wondering why this little old lady would be walking into a construction area. Not really caring, they went back to their conversation.

The old lady shuffles on past them, carrying a large heavily laden tray with both hands.

A big tractor drove out from between a couple parked tractors, swerving to miss the old lady that the driver saw almost too late, narrowly missing grinding her beneath its massive wheels.

The old lady shuffles on as if the tractor wasn't there, even as the driver stares down in shock at the little woman he'd almost ran over.

If it had been anyone else that stepped out in front of him he would have gestured rudely, yelled, and swore at them. But you don't gesture rudely, yell, and swear at elderly women.

As the old lady slowly draws closer to the group standing by the office, more men stop to stare, watching her painfully slow progress.

Dave comes out of the trailer office. Seeing them all standing around staring towards the road, he turns and spots the old woman with surprise. He pauses to stand with the men, curiously watching the old woman approach.

"What's this about," he asks.

One of the guys shrugs. "No idea."

The closer she got, the tinier and frailer the old lady looked. Her thin white hair was tied beneath a sheer flowered headscarf, her threadbare coat had seen much better days, and her shawl looked downright tattered. She was working on crocheting another, but her arthritic hands made the task difficult.

In her tiny hands, wrinkled and knotted like the old oak trees from age and arthritis, she carried a surprisingly large tray.

At last, she made it to the group of men who seemed to be doing little but standing around visiting outside the small trailer office.

She stopped before the first man, who towered over her shrunken stooped little frame, looking up at him solemnly with age-paled eyes.

Dave McCormick looked back down at her, unsure what to do. He knew he should be quickly escorting the little old lady safely off the jobsite. It had also taken her such a painfully long time to walk up the road that he honestly didn't think he could do it without breaking down in frustration and impatiently scooping her up to carry her off. He estimated her frail little frame wouldn't weigh much more than a child.

"You boys are working so hard," she croaked in her old lady's voice. "You look like you could use some nourishment. I made these myself."

She held the large tray out to him.

Dave glanced at the other guys, who smirked and tried not to snigger at him in front of the old woman.

He took the tray awkwardly.

The old lady's hands had the age tremble as she carefully peeled away the tin foil covering the tray to reveal its contents.

It was piled high with delicate little pastries that were hand made with great care.

Staring at the woman's trembling hands, Dave marveled at how such twisted and shaky arthritic-looking old fingers could have possibly created such delicate little treats.

He looked from her hands to the old woman's face, still feeling startled. It took a moment for his mind to register what she was saying.

She was angry about something.

"I said, your manners young man," she scolded, her face even more wrinkled with scorn, if it was even possible for it to be more wrinkled that it already was.

"Huh?"

The old woman looked like she was about to take him by the ear to go cut a switch out behind the old woodshed. At least, that's what went through Dave's mind that she was about to do right at that moment.

"Say thank you."

"Uh – thank you," he stammered.

"And don't forget to say your graces," she lectured, eying each man meaningfully with her rheumy eyes.

Without another word, the little woman turned and began the slow shuffle back down the uneven roughed-in road, humming happily to herself.

Dave stared after her in confusion.

The other guys couldn't hold it any longer and began sniggering at Dave, sharing a few good natured elbow jabs to the ribs with each other.

"Um, what about your tray?" Dave called after her.

She waved a hand noncommittally in the air.

She said something that sounded like, "Oh, you'll find me," her voice just as frail and shaky as her body. She continued her slow shuffle down the road, finally turning the corner and disappearing from sight.

The men eyed the tray of goodies hungrily.

Treats!

Ten minutes later, the first ambulance arrived.

4 - Sick Workers and Senility

Stanley Rutthers stood in his boss's office nervously gripping his hard hat in his hands.

His boss, Bruce Copeland, sat at his desk looking anything but relaxed.

"What do you mean they're all sick?" Copeland demanded.

"The whole damned crew had to be taken to the hospital," Stanley said. "They all can't stop puking. Most of them can't even stand up. Some of them are in intensive care."

"What the hell?" Copeland almost yelled it.

"Looks like some kind of poisoning," Stanley said.

"Poison? What the hell'd poison an entire crew?" Copeland demanded.

"Not what," Stanley said, "who."

Copeland just stared at him, dumbstruck.

"Dave said a little old lady gave them pastries just before they all started getting sick," Stanley said.

Copeland just couldn't believe it.

"First the site and equipment keeps getting vandalized," Copeland said angrily. "Then someone messes around with our plans, and I still think it was that damned Lezkowitz that somehow did it, he'd do anything to steal a job off me for his own company. Then we dig up some damned old skull. And now we have little old ladies poisoning an entire work crew? Shit, damn, and mother! What the hell is going on here?"

Stanley just shook his head. He was mystified.

"How long are they going to be off?" Copeland asked. "Any idea?"

"A few of them didn't eat too many, maybe a couple of days. Others-," Stanley shrugged, "I just don't know. A lot of the guys are in pretty bad shape."

"Damn!"

Copeland's mind was running fast, thinking hard. Somehow, this had to work out.

"Can we find guys from anywhere else?" Copeland asked. "Guys off injured? Pull some from other jobs?"

Stanley shook his head.

"Best we can do is pull a crew off the Anc-Chor project."

"No," Copeland said. "That won't do. We can't do that. That project is already behind with all the time wasted trying to fit things together and redoing them because of the project owner's secretiveness."

The Anc-Chor project is another of Copeland and Howe Construction, Excavation and Land Development's projects, and one that Bruce Copeland often wished he had lost the tender on despite the profits it was making for his company. The Anc-Chor Corporation is run by a single man, the majority shareholder and CEO, Mr. Chornelhus. The Anc-Chor project is a top-secret project that appears to be some large laboratory facility, although Mr. Chornelhus is completely secretive about the purpose of the facility being built.

He muttered something unintelligible to himself.

"Guess we'll have to hire a new green crew," Copeland sighed.

He was not happy about this. An untrained green crew would work much slower and make more mistakes, slowing down the already behind Garden Grove project even more.

"I think so," Stanley agreed. "It'll put us even further behind on the Garden Grove project."

"We have no choice."

"No, we don't."

At the hospital, men groaned in pain and thrashed on gurneys, rolling feebly to vomit furiously into too small jellybean shaped hospital blue plastic dishes. Even more disconcerting were the ones who just lay silently suffering as if they had given up, their eyes looking haunted in their emotionless faces.

They all looked like hell.

The men in intensive care looked even worse. Their ashy pallor left their skin grey looking and their blue-tinged lips were not a good sign. Hospital staff worked on them furiously, their anxiety making the seriousness of their conditions clear.

Dave was one of the lucky ones. He had mostly stood there holding the tray of pastries and thinking how strange it was that this little old lady brought them baking out of the blue, while the other guys eagerly grabbed handfuls of the delicate little pastries and wolfed them down with delighted noises of enjoyment.

Dave only managed to have one of the fluffy little treats, and had just taken a bite of it when the first men started to stagger weakly and vomit violently.

He had quickly spat it out before he had a chance to swallow.

Not knowing what they were poisoned with, the hospital staff had made a best guess and gave those who could manage to keep it down a foul tasting drink they hoped would counteract the poison or at least minimize the damage to their stomachs.

Dave looked around at the guys around him, his crew and friends, weakly trying to sit up, to roll over and vomit some more. They were so sick; worse than that time some of the guys had food poisoning after eating at that questionable little hole-in-the-wall restaurant, and that was pretty bad.

He wondered if some of the sicker guys would make it.

Poisoned! He could not believe it. The doctors were sure it was some kind of commercial poison, not just a simple food poisoning.

But they did not know what poison or why.

Was it an accident? Had the old woman just grabbed the wrong container of something, making a dangerous error because of her aging eyes or mind? She wouldn't have poisoned them on purpose, would she?

"Nah," he thought. "It had to just be a mistake."

A police officer knocked on the old lady's door. He waited, knocked again, waited. Constable Timothy Berkham is a young man and new on the job, having graduated his training only six months ago.

She didn't come to the door.

Constable Berkham walked around the outside of the little old house, looking in the windows, and saw movement somewhere deep inside past the old yellowing age-stained lacy curtain of one of the windows.

He went to the front door and knocked again, calling out.

"Hello!"

He knocked again.

"Hello, Mrs. Crampchet?"

He peered in through the window by the door.

"Mrs. Crampchet, I know you're in there," he called out. "I can see you."

He knocked again.

"Mrs. Crampchet, it's the police. Please come to the door."

He heard movement inside.

The old lady did not come to the door.

He tried the door. It was Unlocked.

The door creaked loudly when he opened it. The worn hinges were long overdue for some lubricating.

Constable Berkham took a step inside, nervous. He paused just inside the front door, looking around and leaning to look through an interior doorway to the rest of the house. The front door opened to the living room and from there he could see a short hallway with an entrance to the kitchen.

The idea of walking unwelcomed into the residence of a suspect and knowing they're in there but they won't come to the door made him very nervous. It's a dangerous situation where the suspect could be hiding anywhere, just waiting to strike before fleeing. It was his first time having to actually do it outside of a training exercise in his class. Normally he would have waited for backup.

But this was a different kind of nervousness and this is a wellness check, not a criminal arrest.

This is a frail little old lady, possibly a very confused old lady who may be in some stage of dementia. And, from the poisoning of the work crew, may herself have been poisoned by her own baking.

Young Timothy Berkham had never entered anywhere uninvited before. He felt like a burglar, an unwanted and unwelcome intruder, not a police officer.

"Mrs. Crampchet," he called out. "Hello? Mrs. Crampchet? Police. Can you come to the door please?"

He heard the sound of movement from another room, muttering, and then the heavy clunk of something being dropped. It sounded breakable and very heavy, china or some kind of pottery maybe. It didn't sound like it broke.

"Mrs. Crampchet?"

"Yeah, yeah," the old lady croaked back, her voice frail and wavering. "What do you want?"

"Uh, Mrs. Crampchet? I'm Constable Timothy Berkham. I just want to make sure you're ok."

"I'm fine, I'm fine."

She shuffled out from a bedroom in the back of the house. A large heavy vase lay on its side out of sight on the floor behind her where she had dropped it.

She moved down a short hall and through another doorway to the kitchen.

Berkham saw movement. The old woman appeared in the hallway where it met the living room and kitchen doorways and went into the kitchen. He could just make her out as she came and went from sight, doing something in the kitchen.

"Would you like some tea dear?" she called out.

"Uh, no thank you ma-am. Mrs. Crampchet? I'd like to talk to you. Can I come in?"

He paused.

She didn't answer.

"Mrs. Crampchet? I'm coming in."

One of the first things he learned was to always announce yourself before entering an uncertain situation. Do not surprise the occupants and do not make them panic. A panicked suspect acts without thinking, making the situation less controllable.

He approached the kitchen cautiously. She was out of sight now but he could hear the old woman moving around. He found her there preparing for tea.

"Mrs. Crampchet?" he said as he entered the kitchen.

"Hello dear. The water is almost ready for the tea," she said.

An old kettle sat on the burner of an old stove. The light isn't lit to show the element is turned on, but the knob is turned. The plastic covering the light is yellowed with age and turning brown, a sign it is likely burned out, charring the plastic when it went. A faint wisp of steam trailing up from the spout and the slow ticking and hissing of the metal kettle heating up told him the stove element is in fact working.

Delicate little teacups teetered dangerously on their dainty little saucers as the old woman shuffled to the little table carrying them. The cups rocked and tinkled against the saucers, almost tipping over as she put them down.

"Mrs. Crampchet, can you tell me about the pastries you brought to the men at the Garden Grove construction site?" Berkham asked.

She shuffled over to the cluttered counter, picking up a tin canister and spoon. She shuffled back to the table and struggled with the lid for a moment, paused, then held the tin out.

"Would you mind dear?"

He looked down at the offered tin before reaching to take it. He didn't move to take the tin.

"Uh, Mrs. Crampchet?"

"Hmm?"

"Mrs. Crampchet, that's not tea."

"Oh?"

She looked down at the canister in her hands, turned it over.

"Coffee" it said.

"Oh dear," she muttered, shaking her head and tut-tutting to herself.

She shuffled back to the counter and changed canisters, bringing back the one marked "Tea" this time.

After having him open the canister, complaining how hard it is with her arthritic hands, she spooned some of the loose tea leaves into the little cups. She shuffled back to the counter to return the canister to its place.

As he watched, Berkham wondered why she didn't use a teapot like people usually did with loose tea leaves. It couldn't be good with all the leaves in the cups.

"Mrs. Crampchet, I need you to tell me what you put in those pastries," Berkham said.

"Would you like some sugar, dear?" she asked, shuffling back to the table with another canister. Putting down the canister, the old woman carried the kettle to the table using an old folded tea towel and poured it into the cups.

The water had an unhealthy looking yellow color.

Returning the kettle to the stove, she shuffled back to the table, opened the canister, and started spooning the white powder into one of the little cups. The fine powder floated on top in a clump before finally beginning to sink.

"Sugar?" she asked, ready to spoon some into the other teacup.

"Uh, oh-no thanks Ma-am."

He looked at the canister she held.

It said "Flour".

"Mrs. Crampchet, about those pastries," he tried again. This was getting nowhere.

She looked at him as if he'd just shown up and she'd never seen him before. Confusion furrowed her brow. Then a smile creased her age withered lips.

"Johnny?" she asked, a little unsure. "Johnny? My Johnny!"

She rushed over as fast as her arthritic shuffle could and threw her arms around him, trying to pull him down to kiss him.

"Oh Johnny," she cried. "You're here, you're here!"

She looked toward the door, and then looked back up at him, clinging to him.

"Your father will be home any minute now Johnny."

He gently extricated himself from the little old woman.

"Uh, Mrs. Crampchet, I have to go now."

He made a quick getaway. His report would show that the poisoning of the men at the Garden Grove Meadows construction site was accidental in his opinion, based on the old woman's failing mental faculties.

A visit by a social worker would be requested to make sure the woman's needs were being looked after and to determine if she should be put into a care home.

Following the young officer to the door, she called out to him in her feeble age withered voice.

"Johnny, don't go. Come back Johnny, dinner is almost ready."

He looked back once at the confused old woman staring at him from the open doorway. Her look suggested she wasn't sure if he was coming for a visit or leaving. She gave him a little uncertain wave and he beat a hasty retreat to his car.

She closed the door behind him and turned, humming, and shuffled back to the kitchen to dump out the ruined tea.

A smirk creased her aged lips.

5 - The Coffee Clutch

I can see you out there, with your chainsaws ripping into the gnarled bark of the old oak trees, tearing their wooden flesh apart until they teeter and crash to the ground.

You just can't leave well enough alone, can you?

I'm so sleepy, so tired. I could just sleep again and might have, but you woke me again with all your noise, your activity.

The loud growling of chainsaws, banging of large metal tractor buckets against dump truck boxes, and the frantic pattering of terrified squirrels fleeing the roaring and trembling of their homes being felled.

They are cutting down more of my beautiful trees, my glorious prison.

The squirrels who I have been watching so frantically collecting nuts are going to have to start all over again.

They'll probably starve this winter.

The wild turkeys that come in the spring will have to find a new spring roost.

The calm solitude of the sound dampening trees will be gone. Soon the winds will tear through here like they do the empty fields surrounding this little piece of old growth woods.

And the secrets those gnarled twisted old trees hide won't be secret much longer.

Another round of coffee was poured in the little kitchen for the four women of the coffee clutch.

"I just can't take it anymore," Libby Waterbourne moaned. "The beeping and constant noise of the tractors first thing in the morning, I swear they start earlier every day and it goes on all day long."

"And the garbage," Mrs. Henderson complained. "Why do they have to just toss their garbage all over the place? Are they men or pigs?"

Mrs. Henderson was new to the group today. She's a long time resident of the small community, but not well known. Her regal bearing gives her an unapproachable feel and none of the other women have ever given her more than a self-conscious wave in passing. The kind of wave small town people give other small town people whether they know each other or not.

None of them wanted to come right out and admit to her face they didn't know her first name, and last names are just too formal for a cozy coffee chat. So, they just talked around not mentioning her by name.

"You should see the mess they left in front of my driveway," Barbara added, "big chunks of mud in the road. I had to move them just to get my car out."

"Are you sure they aren't just from your mudslinging with the neighbor, Barb?" Pamela joked.

"Funny." Barb eyed her levelly. She didn't think it was funny. She's had an ongoing feud with the neighbor beside her ever since their kid started walking the dog and letting it poop on her lawn last summer. The kid never picked the dog's poop up and it drove her crazy.

"Did you hear that old Mrs. Crampchet poisoned the work crew?" Libby asked.

The women all made the appropriate shocked faces and sounds, even though they'd all heard the story already. News like this travels faster than a cold virus in a small town.

"I heard they decided she just put something into the dainties by accident, that she has dementia."

"If that old Mrs. Crampchet has dementia, then I have six toes," Mrs. Henderson humphed.

They all glanced quickly at her socked feet even though they knew she meant it sarcastically.

They looked up at her face, wondering what she knew.

The constant growl and beep of construction equipment in the background never ceased. The incessant banging going on at the same time grated on the women's nerves even more.

Silence fell on the coffee clutch, but it did not last. They sipped their coffee and talked about old Mrs. Crampchet and the skull discovered on the jobsite. They all wondered the same thing, although no one voiced it.

Even though the authorities decided it was just an old relic from the days of homesteaders crossing the prairies, they could not help but wonder if it could really be a long ago victim of Mrs. Crampchet's pastries. After all, the woman is so old and has lived in her little home her whole life.

They lapsed into silence again.

"I wish there was something we could do to just shut them up," Mrs. Henderson said suddenly, breaking the silence.

The other women all tried to hide their smirks.

Libby stifled a giggle.

Mrs. Henderson looked around at them, suspicious.

"You know," Mrs. Henderson said casually, "I heard rumors there's been a lot of vandalism at the new housing development they're building."

She sipped her coffee, looking at the other women over the rim.

Pamela and Libby exchanged conspiratorial glances, trying to hide them from Mrs. Henderson.

"I think it's a bunch of kids," Mrs. Henderson continued, "teenagers probably, from the high school."

"Teenagers," Pam nodded.

"Definitely teenagers," Barb agreed,

"You know," Libby said thoughtfully, "I don't think the kids have done anything to their port-a-potties yet."

"That's good," Pamela said. "That would be terrible."

"Messing with a man's toilet," Barb agreed, "that would just be too low."

"Especially after eating old Mrs. Crampchet's pastries," Mrs. Henderson added, giving them a knowing look that did not crack her always serious expression.

They all turned to stare at her. She made a joke! None of them could ever imagine this stoic woman would ever crack a joke.

That night four figures skulked around the construction site in the cover of darkness, furtively running from the deep shadows of one hulking piece of equipment to another.

The stoic face of Mrs. Henderson was caught briefly in the pale moonlight as they fled the scene.

A figure prowled in the darkness by the entrance of the roughed in road leading into the Garden Grove jobsite, the shape revealed in the shadows of the trees and bushes by the light of the stars and moon and distant streetlights. The form was tall and wiry and appeared to be male. The figure came creeping up the road into the Garden Grove Meadows housing development, keeping to the trees and bushes along the edge to avoid being seen.

He paused outside the small trailer office, the mud-spattered light above the door showering him with speckled grimy light to reveal his identity.

It was Vern Lezkowitz, owner of Bruce Copeland's biggest competitor Lezkowitz & Sons.

There could be no good reason for Vern Lezkowitz to be skulking around Garden Grove in the night.

He grasped the padlock locking the door, giving it a tug. It is secure. He released it with a callousness that suggested the item had somehow insulted him.

He moved on to a group of tractors, one of a few groups of equipment parked on the hard mud of the ruined ground across from and near the corner of the office. He climbed up the outside of one Cat with a front loader bucket. Holding on with one hand, he reached down and started pulling a tool from the tool belt around his waist.

He froze, eyes wide as he looked around, listening.

Did he hear a sound?

A scrape, maybe a foot scuffing on the roughed in road.

A snap. A branch? He turned and looked in the direction he thought it came from. That way was houses, some with a line of bushes and trees blocking out all but the roof of the houses on the other side of the greenery.

Sliding the tool back down into its loop on his belt, he got down slowly, careful to be quiet. He had finally gotten up the nerve to do this and did not want to get caught. Vern Lezkowitz is not a man to take risks that would get him into a confrontation he was not guaranteed to win. It is one thing to bully the men working for him, employees too scared to stand up for themselves out of fear of losing their jobs. If he is caught skulking around the Garden Grove site Copeland and his guys will put the boots to him.

With both feet on the ground now, Vern moved to peer cautiously around the tractor.

He is sure he heard a noise again, but still can see nothing.

There, movement along the edge of the road; in the grass beneath the trees bordering a house.

"Someone is coming! Did Copeland hire security for this site?" he thought, feeling the rush of panic over the possibility of being caught.

With one last long look to make sure nobody would see him, he scampered quickly across to another tractor and from there went behind the trailer office.

He peered around the corner of the wheeled building before running across the field for the trees some distance behind it, the last stand of old growth forest separating the backyards of the old houses along that stretch of road from the new development.

He breathed a sigh of relief after reaching the shelter of the trees, stopping to look back at the construction site. He watched for a moment and was sure he saw movement. He counted them. One, two, three, four? He could not be sure just how many.

"Damned kids," he muttered, assuming now that it had to be local teens who were bored and looking to get into trouble. He half thought of going back and chasing them off, but did not want to be seen by anyone or deal with the confrontation.

He turned unhappily and started making his way through the trees and bush, the fallen leaves crunching under his feet despite his efforts to walk quietly. He swore an oath at the noisy leaves.

Vern could swear he heard another set of feet crunching in the leaves, following him. The sound matched his own steps but was off just a fraction, a weak echo of his own movements.

He stopped and so did the crunch of leaves beneath his feet.

Nothing. He listened to the silence, the breeze in the trees and bush, and the sound of a distant vehicle passing on the highway. He could see the headlights moving in the distance as if it passed through the edge of the field. That side was open field all the way to the highway.

He started forward again, the leaves crunching beneath his feet. After four steps, he was sure he heard it again; someone else's feet crunching behind him almost in perfect unison with his own.

Vern stopped again, looking around. He looked up at the sky through the trees with a frown. The night seemed darker somehow even though the moon and stars in the sky still put off the same light as a moment ago. He was in the middle of the small copse of trees. Ahead of him was a clearing where the trees seemed reluctant to grow. Around it, the old oak trees seemed more twisted than the rest.

Watching for whoever was following him, he moved forward into the small clearing. He looked at the strangely twisted trees, thinking how it looked like they were somehow dancing and frozen suddenly in mid movement by his arrival.

A cloud moving slowly across the sky finally covered the moon, making the night suddenly darker and the shadows deeper.

A chill crept over him and he shivered, the darkness of the night deepening further, seeming to close in on him. The rest of the world suddenly seemed unimaginably far away, shut off from him. The blackness engulfed Vern.

Vern felt dazed and confused, uncertain what had happened or why he is there outside surrounded by trees. He blinked as he looked around, trying to focus on his surroundings. It is dark and he can see the moon and stars in the sky where they peeked through the sporadic clouds. He is at the edge of a small clearing in the bush with no memory of how he got here.

Disoriented, he doesn't even know where here is.

He felt older suddenly too, drained, like something had just sucked some of the life out of him. He looked down at his hands and, for just a moment, they looked withered. He shook his head and blinked his eyes, looking at them again and they were normal, if a little thinner than he thought he remembered. His face itched and he raised one hand to scratch at it.

Vern looked up again, studying his surroundings to get his bearings. He can see a field through the trees. He made his way to the edge of the small copse of trees and looked around. He is on the edge of a small town. Headlights in the distance revealed the location of the highway. To his left across the field are the looming shapes of heavy construction equipment.

He realized now where he is. That is the Garden Grove site. Vern shook his head in dismay.

"Odd," he muttered and moved on through the trees to the crunch of dry leaves beneath his feet, moving away from Garden Grove and towards yards that he hopes will bring him quickly to the street. He has no idea where his truck is and can only hope he finds it quickly, assuming that is how he got here.

6 - Vandals Strike Again

As dawn broke over the horizon, adding an orange glow to the darkness, trucks and cars started lining up along the still unpaved road going into the Garden Grove site where new homes would soon start sprouting from the ground.

The large sign at the entrance announcing the coming of sleek and stylish homes and the promise of country-city living in the new Garden Grove Meadows development sported a new and rather rude crudely drawn caricature of what appeared to be intended as the foreman overseeing the job.

Stanley Rutthers stopped his truck to look at the vandalized billboard sign. He shook his head with a chuckle at the drawing of himself splashed across the sign in large swatches of paint in a color that suggested someone had bought the wrong paint and rushed to the store in horror for a new color, leaving the unused paint to eventually find its way here.

"Kids," he muttered.

Yelling from the site caught his attention.

He continued on into the jobsite to park closer, wondering what he will find this time. This constant vandalism has gone well beyond being tiresome.

He parked near the scene of the commotion where one of the men was pounding senselessly on the door of one of the blue plastic portable toilets and swearing loudly.

As Stanley got out of his truck, the man ran off down the road, jumped into a truck, and tore out of there, the truck's tires spitting dirt as he gunned the engine in a big hurry.

Stanley watched him go and stared down the road in mute surprise for a moment after he was out of sight before he turned and looked at the men standing around, their reactions ranging from laughter to shock and fear. It was obvious there was an issue with the toilets and the man really had to go.

He headed over to them to find out what is going on.

"The doors are all glued shut," one of the men said as he approached.

Stanley turned and walked away shaking his head. He did not know if he should laugh or cry.

He walked towards the little portable trailer that serves as a jobsite office, digging his keys out of his pocket on the way.

Stanley paused just before reaching the trailer, looking around. A chill feeling of dread ran down his back and the words of an old saying from his childhood, "someone just walked over my grave," came to his mind. He'd heard the phrase many times in response to that sudden unexplained shiver that sometimes takes people by surprise.

He has the uneasy feeling that someone is watching, and that it is not just a casual observer. He can feel the intent to harm in that stare and for just a moment he could not shake the feeling that he was the mouse the cat is about to sink its claws into.

Stanley turned and stared at the section of woods that they had not yet cleared. He has a sense he is being watched from there. He studied the woods, looking for any sign of movement. There is none except the muted shaking of the trees' branches in the wind.

The uneasy feeling would not go away.

He continued on and stopped at the trailer door, grasping the padlock in one hand and bringing the key to it.

The key resisted going into the padlock. The keyhole seemed to be blocked by something.

"Glue?" he wondered. If someone glued the toilet doors, they could have glued the lock too.

He knelt down, examining the lock. He thought he saw something pink inside it.

He tried shoving the key in again. There was resistance, but he could force it part of the way in. He could not get it even half way in.

He pulled the key back out.

Some kind of pink substance came out in small chunks, scraped out of the lock by the key.

He sniffed it.

Bubblegum.

"Shit!" he muttered.

Stanley is in a foul mood now as he headed back to his truck. He has to go to the company office for a pair of bolt cutters to cut through the padlock and a new lock.

"Hey, what are you going to do about the toilets?" one of the crew called after him.

Stanley paused and turned back to meet the expectant stares of his men.

"Hell if I care," he grumbled. "Cut the damned doors off."

He was turning away again and thought better of it. These guys probably would cut the doors off. He turned back to them again.

"I'll get the office to call the company to bring out new ones. They can cut their owned damned doors off."

He turned away and went to his truck, driving out of there a little too fast in his anger.

At the hospital, Dave McCormack and a few of the other poisoned workers are being discharged. Being the slow process that it is, the discharges ran over the span of a number of hours.

As the men left one by one, they stopped in to wave a goodbye and crack the usual jokes about hospital food to the other men sitting in their rooms dressed to go home with their hospital issue plastic bags holding their personal effects of cards, well wishes, and stuff that was supposed to entertain them during their temporary hospital incarceration. They made their rounds of the men who would still be in the hospital for a few more days or weeks, the ones who were allowed visitors anyway.

Dave was one of the earlier releases. He made his rounds with his worried wife at his side fussing over him and looking like she was going to cry over every man they visited who couldn't go home just yet.

Dave almost cried himself while he visited some of the men he'd worked with, spending long hours laboring and joking, the casual after work Friday beers shared, and now looking like death hovered within reach.

Two men who were supposed to go home in a few days had worsened and were moved into intensive care. It isn't looking good for either of them.

One of the men originally in intensive care had been moved to a regular hospital bed after improving considerably.

Another was taken off life support, his quality of life ruined and showing little brain activity. But his body is still too stubborn to pass away. His heart kept ticking, his lungs feebly collapsing and expanding. The doctors are sure he will not survive.

Dave walked out of the hospital into the bright cool afternoon with an exhilarating feeling of release mixed with a heavy heart. He feels like he has just been released from a prison, although he'd never actually had the prison experience to compare his feelings to.

He also walked with the weight of an entire injured crew on his shoulders.

He isn't the foreman. It is the foreman's job to take responsibility for the safety of the men on the crew. But he feels the guilt just the same. He is the most senior man on the crew after the foreman. He feels just as responsible for the men's safety, especially the green ones.

When Stanley returned to Garden Grove he went directly to the trailer office. Pinching the padlock loop just above the block shaped lock mechanism between the blades of the lock cutter; he squeezed the lock cutter arms together angrily with more force than was needed. With a little resistance, the blades pinched and cut through the lock, and the lock clattered to the ground.

He picked it up, removed the loop that still held the door latched, and went inside.

His snarl of outrage could be heard across the jobsite.

Inside the trailer was clear evidence someone had gained entry and gone through files. Files and papers had been scattered everywhere.

7 - Rusty Plowshare's Scheme

"So, the skull wasn't good enough, huh? Oh, I've got something better than that, much better," Rusty Plowshare muttered bitterly.

The old man nodded to himself. His chin, white with unshaven whisker stubble, caught and held a piece of loose straw in the stubble when he came away from the stacked bales of hay he was digging between. The straw bales were sagging with rot and greyed with age, their fibers breaking down over the years they had sat idle.

He turned away, rummaging through one pile and then moving on to another. Rusty moved with arthritic slowness, the skin on his thin arms sagging from age and loss of the underlying muscle mass of youth. His face, leathery from decades of working in the sun and wrinkled with age, gave him a crazy old man in the mountains look instead of wizened with age.

He was in the old barn, its interior packed with an amazing amount of clutter of every description. It is unbelievable the old man can even move around in there, much less search the place. The old packrat collected anything.

There are cats everywhere too, cats of every age and description, some looking very unhealthy, all feral strays that had made this barn their home.

"Now, where'd I put it?" he muttered to himself.

It wasn't in the narrow space of a double wall between two stalls. He moved on to search somewhere else.

"Maybe behind the loose board in the wall?" He pried the board off and looked.

"Ah, I know, under the floorboard!" He moved and stooped over a floorboard, pulling it up to look beneath. Most of the barn floor is an open dirt floor. However, one end of the barn, for reasons known only to the old man and his predecessors, has a rough floor of old two by fours that are now soggy with rot. One part of this section, in the dark shadowed recesses of the corner, hides a small makeshift cellar dug into the ground beneath the floor, the rest of it covering part of the dirt floor that makes up most of the barn floor. This particular floorboard covered a gouged out section of dirt just deep enough to hold its small treasures wrapped in rotting cheesecloth.

But what he is looking for is not there.

"Damn!"

"I know it's here somewhere," Rusty grumbled.

Noticing the carelessly dumped loose soil marking the spot where the skull had been dug up from, the old man reminded himself, "Got to stamp that down some, won't do to have anyone finding it."

The old skull had been buried in the barn for a very long time. Of course, the rest of the body was there too, along with the tool used to kill the man.

It's very possible the man buried so many years ago in the dirt of the barn was old Rusty Plowshare's great great grandfather.

He did not really know for sure. There was more than one body buried beneath the old barn through the generations of his family that lived here.

His great great grandmother's husband, the man whose family name he carried, did not really know for sure either when he bludgeoned the young man to death in a jealous rage in that year after the then young couple was married.

If the rumors spread that day so long ago by a group of busybody old women making trouble where they had no business putting their noses were true, rumors of the wife's alleged infidelity and possibly questionable pregnancy, then those were the remains of his murdered great great grandfather.

Or, the young man may have been an innocent victim of a husband's jealousy and a bunch of busybodies making trouble where there wasn't any.

Only his great great grandmother knew the truth.

She was buried beneath the woodshed some years later, after failing to provide her husband with an offspring that was undeniably his in his mind. She had given birth to more children after that first boy, but her husband could not let go of his suspicions.

There are many dark secrets in his family's history, and Rusty Plowshare knows where each one of them was buried.

It also could have been someone else. Rusty had heard stories passed down about his great great grandfather's violent temper.

"Ahh, there you are!" he cooed. "Beautiful." He pulled out a round wrapped bundle and held it up as if presenting it to the watching eyes of the dozens of felines witnessing his moment of triumph.

"I know just what to do with you. If you don't stop them from digging out those woods, nothing will," he said.

"I know just what to do with you," he repeated happily.

8 - Blueprint Errors

The building inspector is mad.

Maybe mad is sugar coating it. Willie Williams is well beyond mad, he is furious to the point his neck is red and his ears are turning purple. His face looks like it would explode at any moment like a cartoon teapot head with steam blowing furiously from his ears, eyes, and mouth.

It does not take much to make Willie mad when it comes to dealing with these construction workers. They all remind him of the boys who teased and beat him up regularly throughout his childhood over the unfortunate name his parents saddled him with; years of bullying abuse that helped shape him into the man he has become. It is a resentment he will take to the grave with him someday. He also feels he is superior to them in every way, more educated, more intelligent and, well, just superior.

He is jabbing his finger hard at the plans spread out on the table between Stanley Rutthers and himself.

Stanley had to refocus, bringing his attention back to what Williams is saying. He does not like the man or his overbearing attitude, as if being a building inspector made him a very important man.

Stanley is sure a lot of the other builders bribe Williams to overlook things that weren't quite done the way they should be.

He knows for a fact that his boss, Bruce Copeland, does.

This is part of the problem.

Stanley refuses to bribe Williams. Not out of any sense of right and wrong, he'd bribed many inspectors many times. Bribery is sometimes just one of the expected costs of doing business. He just cannot stand the man.

He'd prefer to deal with the other inspector who works out of this office, Samuel Watkins, despite his unfailing honesty and refusal to let anything slide or take a bribe. But Williams is the main inspector and Sam Watkins is the municipal engineer and fills in as a backup inspector only on an as needed basis.

"Here!" Williams jabbed the paper with his extended finger. "Right here! The road runs twelve feet wide of where it's supposed to. It's here on the plans," he pointed to the obvious road as if Stanley might miss it, "and you guys built it here!" He jabbed hard and angrily with his finger at where the road was actually built.

Stanley shrugged. What can he say?

"Yes, we know the plans we are working from are wrong. Mr. Copeland is looking into the problem," Stanley said. "But your plans are wrong too. See, here-,"

William's face twisted into a deeper scowl and he cut Stanley off.

"There is nothing wrong with my copy of the plans," Willie snapped. "We are going by my plans."

Stanley just sighed inwardly. William's plans are wrong too despite his refusal to accept that.

He tried to explain it again.

"Bruce Copeland has grilled everyone on the discrepancies in the Garden Grove plans and came up empty," Stanley said. "Nobody could explain to him how different sets of plans could have ended up in the different offices.

His chief planner swore that he had even double-checked the plans himself after the first incident and was positive the revised blueprints that were re-distributed were correct and all matched.

But it happened again. The different copies of the plans do not match.

Look Willie, I can't explain how it happened. We just don't know. But, somehow the copies got mixed up and they have errors."

Stanley knows there is only one explanation for this. Someone has to be deliberately forging and swapping out the blueprints. This goes beyond the petty sabotage that has been happening to the jobsite, or simple errors.

"I'm telling you, these are not the same plans that were handed to you," Stanley continued. "Someone has switched them."

Williams shook his head angrily.

"There is no way," Willie said. "Bruce Copeland handed the plans right to me. These are the plans he gave me. Nobody could have gotten into this office without any obvious break-in and swapped out this copy of the plans. My copy is correct."

He leaned over the blueprint on the table between them, staring Stanley down with a superior smirk.

"As far as I'm concerned it is nothing more than the incompetence of someone in your office or your crew. Either your people messed up the blueprint copies or your crew are not following your own plans, and you people are trying to cover it up."

Stanley gave up. It is no use trying to explain it. The inspector just refuses to see it.

At this point, they are not even sure which plans are right; or rather what items on each set are not wrong.

Until this mess is straightened out, who is to say that they put the road in the wrong place? His boss, Bruce Copeland, is not about to go to the expense of moving a road at his own cost if he can avoid it.

"And here," Willie jabbed at the blueprints angrily, "you didn't even dig down to bury the culverts. You just scraped the topsoil, laid them down, and covered them with fill! What the hell was that? Runoff can't go uphill over the culverts to get to the catch basins, and if any drainage water did get in there it would just freeze and block the whole damned system come winter. The whole damned development will be flooded in the spring."

"Yeah, we fixed that," Stanley said.

"You sure did," the inspector spit when he said it, getting even more red-faced. "I was just there this morning and it's still not deep enough. You're going to have to dig it all up and do it again."

"Shit," Stanley thought. His boss was going to be pissed.

"Ok," is what he said.

"And the catch-basin, here." Jab.

"Yeah," Stanley coughed, stifling a snicker, "that wasn't even in our plans. We put it in. I don't know how you guys missed that. Raising and levelling that ditch to match the surrounding ground level would've flooded all the pre-existing yards if you didn't catch that and add the catch basin to the plans."

"No it wouldn't!" Williams complained. This was a sore spot with him.

"Um, yeah. You had us replace the drainage ditch with buried culverts and level the ground, but there was no way for the water to drain into the culverts. That ditch was the only drainage for this whole back area here." He motioned to the section of woods and fields that would later be cleared and included in the construction. "And the houses here, along a strip adjacent to the development." He waved his hand over the area just off the blueprints.

"No it wasn't and they would have been fine," Willie insisted. "The only reason we added the catch-basin was because a bunch of residents that don't know what they're talking about kept complaining about it."

"Well, it's there now," Stanley said.

"Sticking four feet out of the ground?" Willie's tone had risen to the point of almost yelling. "There'd have to be more than four feet of water before it even started draining into the basin!"

Stanley could really picture steam pouring out of the man's ears now with a shrill whistling. He coughed to stifle a laugh again.

"That's what the plans showed," he shrugged.

"Are those guys working for you all idiots?" Willie demanded. "They didn't think something was wrong?" He wasn't about to take the blame for that error himself, not when he could project it on someone else. And it was too obvious a mistake to not have been caught immediately.

"It's a green crew," Stanley explained. "Just about the whole crew got sick. We had to hire a bunch of new guys. None of them have much experience. They just followed what the plans said."

"Well, you'd better fix that culvert and the catch-basin."

Williams started rolling up the plans roughly, his way of saying the meeting was over.

"And get your plans sorted out," Williams finished. "Figure them out or I'm shutting down the whole job permanently."

"Yes sir," Stanley said.

When Stanley finally got into his truck after the meeting, he tore out of there, his tires kicking up rocks in the gravel parking lot.

"Where the hell is everybody?" he grumbled. "I wasn't supposed to be at that meeting alone, not with so many problems with the job and the plans."

He barely looked and did not slow down as he careened out of the parking lot onto the road.

"Where the hell is Copeland's chief planner, Doug Walton?

Where the hell is Copeland?"

Stanley gripped the steering wheel so tight his knuckles were white and his fingers ached by the time he calmed down enough to relax his grip.

He found out when he got to the construction company's office.

The doors were closed and locked. Nobody was there.

"What the," he muttered, staring at the locked door to the building with a confused expression. "Where is everybody?"

That's when he finally pulled out his cell phone and noticed the missed calls. He had turned both the ringer and vibrate off while he was in the meeting with the municipal planner.

He checked his messages.

Two of the poisoned workers had passed away in hospital that day. The office and jobsite were shut down for the day out of respect and to let those who knew them grieve.

Stanley did not know what else to do, so he drove by the jobsite. The jobsite was deserted. He drove right up to the office and got out of his truck.

Stanley felt out of sorts and did not know where to go. There was just so much going on that did not make any sense. He felt the loss of his co-workers' deaths as a vague sense of being lost himself.

He looked around as if uncertain where he is, his mind feeling numb.

He wandered the jobsite, thinking back to the blueprint errors, trying to piece it together. Why is someone doing this? What can they possibly gain from it? This isn't even one of the better money makers as far as jobs went.

Stanley noticed a pair of deer crossing along the far edge of the field. The two does watched him warily but without much concern. It is apparent they are used to people and have no fear, but do not trust them.

He watched the does walk and then speed up to a jog, their heads held mid-point between high and low, relaxed. Their trajectory will bring them along the edge of the last remaining stand of old growth woods that will be torn down later in the development process.

They closed the gap and paused just before reaching the woods. He was sure they were going to stick to the field, moving along next to the trees.

The does stopped, heads popping high and ears alert, sniffing at the air. The lead doe snorted and stamped a delicate hoof, tail held high in a warning flag.

With a sudden panicked lunge, she jumped sideways and bolted, the other one following, darting back the way they came.

Stanley watched them, wondering what is up. He turned to stare at the woods, studying them, but cannot see anything that might have spooked the animals.

With the deer gone, he is alone with his thoughts again. But he does not feel alone. Stanley has the uneasy feeling he is being watched. It's not the first time either.

He looked across the field to the distant houses, trying to catch the movement of a curtain, someone standing in their yard, any sign of who is watching.

He senses the sensation of being watched was coming from the other direction, from the trees.

He turns and studies the woods but finds no movement.

"Something must have scared those deer," he muttered, thinking whoever is watching him must be hiding in the trees. That has to be what startled the two deer.

Curious, Stanley made his way across the field to the trees. They are silent except for the wind rustling the dying leaves that still cling to the branches and a few bony branches clacking against each other.

He looked down at the sound of leaves rustling. It is just the wind picking up some loose leaves and blowing them across the ground.

"You would think there would be something alive", he thought. "A bird or squirrel, but there's nothing."

"I must have scared them off," he decided.

Stanley cannot shake off the feeling of unease. Instead, although surrounded only by the trees, it grew.

The feeling of unease deepened, creeping through him and chilling him like frost spreading across a windowpane.

He feels a sudden urge to run, to get the hell out of there as fast as he can.

His legs did not move. His feet stayed planted firmly put. Stanley could not at first form the thought to wonder why he is still standing there.

Shadows seemed to creep in and the wind stilled, though he can still see the long grasses across the field dancing in the wind.

A loud bang somewhere in the distance broke the trance and he snapped out of it. He blinked, feeling disoriented and nauseous, his skin almost crawling with the tense feeling of being watched by someone malevolent.

"Bloody hell," Stanley muttered and returned to his truck, walking too quickly to look natural. He went home.

9 - Coffee Clutch Gals in Trouble

The very diminutive Libby Waterbourne opened her door with a curious expression. Before her stood the same young police officer who had visited old Mrs. Crampchet, Constable Timothy Birkham.

"Ma-am," he started, "we are canvassing the area. Can I ask you a few questions?"

"Certainly," she smiled up at him.

"May I come in?"

"Oh yes, yes, please do." Libby scurried out of the way, letting him into her home. Something about a man in uniform, with that bulky vest and gun, kind of thrilled and intimidated her at the same time. The fact that he is too young for her only somewhat diminished the thrill.

"Have you noticed anything unusual in the neighborhood?" he asked.

"Unusual?" Libby asked innocently.

"Yes, people hanging out where they usually wouldn't, strange cars or people you don't recognize; anything like that?"

"Well, there are a lot of strange cars and people with all those construction workers," she suggested helpfully. She knew it was completely unhelpful.

"No unusual activity; vandalism to you or your neighbors' private property, thefts from yards, anything like that?" he asked.

"No, nothing of the sort that I've noticed," she smiled up at him innocently.

"Have there been any thefts or vandalism to public property that you've seen or are aware of?" He paused. "Maybe around the new housing development?"

Libby frowned thoughtfully. "I have heard there have been a few pranks over at the new housing development. Kids probably, you know how they are when they're bored."

He finally came right out and said it.

"Ma-am, you were seen."

Libby tried to look innocently clueless, but they both know that she knows exactly what she was seen doing, and they both know that she knows he knows. It was mutually understood in the brief look they exchanged.

"You were seen vandalizing the tractors at the housing development."

It seemed almost ludicrous. This tiny slip of a woman sabotaging those great hulking tractors, acts of vandalism only someone with at least a small amount of mechanic's knowledge of the tractors could have done. And there was no way a woman of her tiny build would have the necessary upper body strength to do mechanical work on machines like this.

"Mrs. Waterbourne," Constable Timothy Birkham said, "you are under arrest."

While Libby was being led outside and put into the police car, Barb ran out of her house just a few doors up.

"Libby! What's going on?" she called as she raced over.

"I'm being arrested for vandalizing tractors in the housing development," Libby called back.

Barb rushed to her side, confronting the young officer.

"Vandalizing tractors?" She was incredulous. "Look at her. How could she possibly vandalize a tractor?"

Constable Birkham just shook his head, put the prisoner in the car, and drove away.

Barb stood there; hands on hips, watching the car drive off with her accomplice.

A few hours later, another officer arrived at Pamela's house.

Her heart fluttered when she looked up at him standing outside the threshold of her home the moment she opened the door to answer the summoning ding-dong of the bell.

The words "the jig is up" flashed through Pamela's mind.

"Ma-am, we're canvassing the area concerning some recent events. Can I come in and ask you a few questions?" the officer asked politely,

"Certainly officer," Pamela stepped back, "come on in."

She opened the door wider to let him in.

"Would you like some coffee?" she offered.

"No thank you, ma-am," he said.

With the formalities out of the way, he started on the questions.

"Have you seen any unusual activities around the Garden Grove Meadows construction site?"

"Unusual? Like what?"

"Anyone hanging around there after the workers go home, kids or teenagers playing around the site at night, strange cars or people you don't recognize or who shouldn't be there, that sort of thing."

"Oh no, nothing like that," Pamela said, playing innocent.

The officer noticed the faint lingering smell of paint and turpentine.

He looked around at what little he can see of the house's interior, not seeing any signs of renovations or redecorating.

"Have you been redecorating lately? Doing some home renovations?"

"No, no we haven't. Why?" Oops, Pamela realized her mistake as soon as the words were out of her mouth.

"Ma-am," the officer asked, "can I have a look around please?"

"Uh," she hesitated, "Why?"

He looked at her levelly.

"Ma-am, where do you keep the paint?"

"In the garage, but we haven't done any painting. There's just some old dried up cans in there." She feels like a little kid lying, knows she cannot lie her way out of it, but cannot help but try. She suddenly feels light headed. She is caught.

"Ma-am, maybe you should come down to the station with me to answer a few questions."

"Why? You already asked me questions. There's nothing I can't answer here."

"I'd like to take a look in your garage, if that's ok."

Pamela's heart sank. She doesn't know how she can get out of this. She can always say no, of course, but that would just make her look guiltier.

"Uh, it's right this way." She led the way to the garage.

The smell of paint and turpentine is noticeably stronger in the garage.

The young officer looked around the garage, poking around without really touching anything.

He came across the usual assorted pile of paint cans, turpentine, and used brushes that could be found in many homes.

He looked at Pamela knowingly.

"You have paint cans," he said.

"A lot of people have paint cans," she said, knowing it is hopeless.

He picked one up, giving it a shake. There is no telltale sloshing of paint. It is very light and pretty much empty. He turned the can. The dribble of paint running down one side looks dried and old.

It's the wrong color.

"I can never figure why people keep old empty paint cans," he thought.

"Really, there's no need," Pamela tried.

He picked up a large wide paint brush, tested the bristles between his fingers, and then brought it closer to his nose to sniff it.

The bristles still hold the slight dampness of being washed hours before. The smell of paint and turpentine still clings to the bristles, a difficult odor to rinse away.

He glanced at Pamela and then continued his inspection.

"Seriously, I-," Pamela broke off. It is useless trying to make excuses.

He picked up another paint can. This one was heavier, roughly half full by his estimate. He gave it a shake, the liquid sloshing heavily. Traces of paint smudges and the faded smears on the label look like someone had not only wiped paint slops from the outside of the can, but took the unusual extra effort of trying to remove them completely with turpentine.

"Ma-am," he looked up at her, "do you have anything like a screwdriver?"

She was done, defeated.

"Yes," she said quietly. Pamela retrieved a flat-blade screwdriver and handed it to him.

He popped the lid on the paint can. The color is a slightly lighter version of the ghastly color used to graffiti the billboard sign for the housing development. He is sure he has a match.

He looked at the woman standing before him looking guilty.

"How did you reach?" he asked her.

She pointed to a newer lightweight aluminum folding ladder. A paint dribble she missed matched the color of the offending paint.

"I have to arrest you, you know."

"I know."

The police car had barely started driving away with Pamela looking forlornly out its back window before Mrs. Henderson was on the phone to Barb.

"Hello," Barb answered the phone.

"Barb." Mrs. Henderson's voice is urgent, anxious. "Pamela was just taken away in a police car. I'm pretty sure she's being charged for painting the sign."

"Libby too," Barbara said. "She's been arrested for what she did to the tractors."

"Do you think they figured out about the other stuff too?"

"Well, I know they found the potty doors glued shut pretty quick." Barbara couldn't help but giggle, despite the seriousness. They could all be getting charged. A criminal record! She can't believe they'd all have a criminal record. She is scared and excited all at the same time and feels a little sick about it.

"They must have found out about the lock on that little trailer pretty fast too," Mrs. Henderson said. "I'm sure they've gotten in by now and found out what you did inside too." She hoped Barb didn't leave behind anything that would identify herself. It was pretty hard getting her in and out of that tiny window. Barb is sporting a few scrapes from trying to squeeze through there.

"Do you think they'll find the other signs?" Barb asked.

"Sooner or later, if they haven't already."

10 - Strange Gardening

The moon cast cold pale light against the dark shadows of the night. Clouds partially obscured the skies and the stars, moving with the winds up high in the atmosphere, passing slowly across the sky and bringing with them a wall of deeper shadows across the land below.

The big tractors at the Garden Grove site loom large and still in the darkness. They, along with the smaller tractors and equipment parked haphazardly around the site, look like strange exoskeleton creatures from another world slumbering motionlessly in the dark night.

Some unidentified night creature rustles in the darkness.

Something moves in the darker shadows of the small woods, shifting in the partial shelter of the twisted bare branches of the dead looking oak trees. Dry leaves crunched loudly.

It is getting colder out. Snow will start to fall soon.

The figure is impossible to make out as it skulks through the trees towards the jobsite. It is tall and stooped, like a bear walking on its hind legs. It is too scrawny to be a bear, of course.

Mrs. Crampchet stood at her window looking out, watching the figure creeping through the woods. The darkness and her aged eyes conspire to hide the creature's identity from her.

He broke from the woods into the cleared land beyond as she watched and the moonlight shone on his face, silhouetting his hat and profile. She can't make out the face from this distance but she knows who it was. That profile and hat are unmistakable.

"Why, it's that old codger Rusty Plowshare," she muttered.

"I see you!" she yelled at him even though he can't possibly hear her.

He skulked off across the construction site, a big burlap sack slung over his shoulder, stooping him forward with its weight.

"What is that old coot up to?"

Grabbing her shawl, the old woman shuffled to the back door and put on her worn coat and shoes as quickly as her palsied arthritis-knotted hands could. She wrapped the shawl around her shoulders as she shuffled out the door.

Rusty stopped, standing motionlessly and listening. He thought he had heard something. Looking hard through the scraggly twisted limbs of the bare trees, he tried to make out the shapes of anything that might not belong.

There was a crunch of dry leaves.

It is impossible to move without the sound of the leaves. Most of the leaves had fallen or been blown off the trees, covering the ground in a crisp blanket in shades of yellows, oranges and browns, the brittle leaves leaving the bare branches to their coming winter slumber.

"Just like me," Rusty thought. "These old oaks are almost at the end of their lives just like me. Their old limbs are just as brittle with age."

He heard another crunch.

He turned and looked, wincing at the pain the too quick movement caused in his old back with the weight of his cargo.

"Yup, old and brittle," he thought.

A face peered cautiously from the woods a little distance away. It sniffed and made another tentative step forward. At last, the deer walked slowly from the woods.

Rusty almost chuckled. The deer were overpopulated in the area, drawn by the safety of human habitation that kept their natural predators at bay.

Then he heard another sound of crackling dry leaves further back in the bush.

And another.

One more crackle came from the other side of him, coming from behind.

As the doe stepped from the woods, she turned to stare at Rusty. She turned away and walked cautiously along the edge of the woods, alert and watchful.

Moments later, a smaller doe followed. The spots on her coat had not quite faded yet.

"Probably this year's fawn," he thought.

A third doe, between them in size, followed in the rear, pausing to give Rusty a long stare before she hurried to catch up with the other two.

"Last year's fawn," he thought.

He watched them go for a moment. When no more deer followed, he continued on.

Some distance away now, the three deer froze, heads turning quickly and ears listening. They seem to be staring back towards the woods.

The matriarch flicked her ears and her nose twitched. She does not like something she senses. With a sudden startled bound, she bolted and the others followed, taking the path down along the river where the open ground will let them move faster and better see any coming danger.

Rusty moved on, keeping to the edge of the narrow strip of woods, walking along the grassy edge of the field where it was much easier going than through the trees. In most places, the trees and their undergrowth are just thick and wide enough to not be able to see through even with the limbs bare of leaves, stretching across half the yards along the street on one side. One area closer to the new Garden Grove site widens, arching out into the plowed fields and coming back in again to continue in the thinner strip of wild growth, creating a deeper pocket of trees. Where some houses backed on to the trees and the field beyond, the homeowners had cleared the ribbon of trees to a thin line that gave almost no protection or to open their view to the fields beyond. In summer, the trees and undergrowth are a sound muffling barrier between the backs of yards and the open fields of the world beyond.

Every now and then, Rusty heard the snap or crackle of nocturnal animals moving around in the bush.

At one point, a startled grey squirrel scampered across a branch, leapt from one tree to the next, and pausing to chitter angrily at him before scampering on up higher and leaping into yet another tree where it disappeared. He thought it is a strange hour for a squirrel to be about; when their night predators are most active.

"Something must have woke him up," he muttered.

"What are you up to?" he asked the squirrel with a crooked half-scowl on his face. "You should be sleeping at this hour, not off playing around in the woods. What has you so riled up at this hour?"

Shifting the sack on his back, Rusty continued on, setting out across the field.

He walked, stumbling a few times in the dark, until he reached the Garden Grove construction site.

He roamed the site, seemingly pointlessly, like he is drunk or confused and unsure of where he is going or where he is, or perhaps both. In reality, his mind is all too clear on his mission.

Mrs. Crampchet watched from the cover of the woods, shaking her head and muttering.

"Crazy old codger, always been nuts. Is he drunk or something?"

She tsked and tutted at the old man's odd behavior. Behavior that probably isn't all that odd considering where he came from, she considered. Even as a child, she'd heard stories and rumors about the Plowshare farm. Strange doings and bad deeds going back as far as the old people back then could remember. The stories went back for generations, to the time when these prairies were originally settled.

They were a strange family indeed.

At last, Rusty dropped his sack on the ground. Opening it up, he pulled out a short handled shovel with a blade that curved like a spoon. It is the kind of shovel you might use to turn over a few weeds in a garden, or maybe shoveling pig slop into a trough if you had pigs. With the shorter than normal handle, the shovel is too short to be useful doing an afternoon of real labor.

Jabbing the shovel blade at the ground hard, he put a booted foot on one side of the top edge of the shovel scoop, gripped the handle with both hands, and worked it as he pressed down with his weight, digging into the hard ground.

He dropped the scoop full of dirt next to the hole and jabbed hard at the ground again.

He continued on, jab, shove, scoop, toss; jab, shove, scoop, toss.

Finally satisfied, the old man jabbed the shovel blade into the ground so it stood up on its own when he let go, rubbed his hands on his pants, and dug around in his sack.

He dropped something into the hole, grabbed the shovel and started filling it in. When he finished, he stamped around on the spot, packing the earth down. Then he scraped it with the shovel blade, eliminating the menagerie of footprints stamped all over the packed-in hole.

The old man picked up his sack, grabbed the shovel, and shambled off to another spot some distance away on aged creaky knees.

He repeated the same process there and moved on to yet another spot.

It is obvious now to the observer in the woods that the old man's knees are taking more abuse than knees that old are meant to take. His shamble is becoming a limping shamble, his back looking more hunched and twisted. The old man stopped often to rub his arthritic hands together, flexing the fingers as if that will help the pain.

He will be nearly crippled in the morning with the pain in his ancient joints.

"What on earth is that that old coot burying?" Crampchet wondered.

Ducking behind a tree in the woods, she almost ran when Rusty Plowshare turned and started walking straight in her direction.

"He saw me!" Her heart pounded quickly in her chest. Not a good thing for a heart this old to do. She felt the pain lancing in her chest and down one arm. She grasped at her chest as if she could slow her racing pulse down by reaching through her flesh and bones to squeeze her heart into submission. The old woman's pain is mostly caused by her own conviction she is on the verge of a heart attack. She has no idea that women generally have different warning signs than the pain so often thought to inflict all heart attack victims because those signs more commonly affected men.

"The old bastard's going to kill me with a heart attack," she complained.

Instead of running, she froze, waiting for the confrontation that is to come.

It never came.

Rusty stopped before he got to the woods and started digging, oblivious to the old woman hiding in the bushes ahead of him.

He is still too far away for her old eyes to see clearly, but the color and shape of the object made it undeniable. She watched, incredulous, as Rusty buried an old yellowing bone. It is long, thinner in the middle, with thicker rounded ends.

"A bone? Is the old coot burying bones? Is that a leg bone? A human leg bone? Nah, it must be some kind of animal. But why is he doing it?" She barely uttered the words, trying to keep quiet and not be heard.

She watched in wonder.

"Crazy old farmer," she muttered. "Just what does he think will grow?"

She held her breath, almost panting with the effort, trying to steady her age weary limbs to hold still while she waited for the old man to finish. He is so close that if he turned he is sure to see her.

He hadn't seen her yet. Maybe he'll leave and not see her. She hoped so.

Finished his process of burying the bone, stomping down, and scraping away the mottled mess of footprints left behind on the tiny gravesite, Rusty picked up his empty sack, slung the muddy shovel over his shoulder, and began the long painful walk back up the field, through the woods, and to what is left of his old family farmstead.

The old woman waited until she is sure the old codger is out of hearing distance before she finally let out a big breath of air and moved in the loudly crunching leaves.

"He's nuts," she shook her head, muttering. "The old codger is flapping nuts. He's gone over the edge."

She didn't really seem all that surprised though, after all he does come from a family with a long history of odd behavior.

Everyone has always known the whole lot of those Plowshares are nuts.

Crampchet froze. She turned and listened. She thought she had heard something behind her in the woods. A chill coursed down her spine and she pulled her worn shawl tighter about her shoulders.

"Old codger's got me imagining things now," she muttered.

She started her own long and slow shuffle back to her little house.

At one point on the walk back home, Rusty Plowshare turned to look behind him. He kept thinking he saw movement behind and off to the side out of the corner of his eye, but each time he turned his head to look, he had not been able to see if it really was there.

This time he saw it. Rusty froze. Something is moving slowly through the dead bony fingers of twisted old oak trees.

He peered through the trees, trying to make it out, his eyes not so good anymore. It is nothing more than shadows behind shadows.

He shrugged.

"Must be more deer," he thought.

He continued on home.

11 - I See You, All of You

I see you.

I see you all.

Tramping, cutting, and ripping out the trees.

Digging and tearing up the land, making your roads and burying big lines of pipes like arteries beneath the ground.

Your big ugly tractors beeping and growling with the early dawn and turning into big sleeping piles of rubbish with the darkening dusk.

I see the others too.

Those silly women playing childish pranks.

The teenagers drinking their alcohol and messing around with the big trucks and tractors.

Chuckle.

I bet those workers wonder why their trucks and tractors all smell like piss.

And I see you too old man. Just what do you think planting those old bones is going to do? Is that supposed to entice me to come out?

We came here to this little community to get away from all of this, the never-ending noise and trouble-making neighbors. We came here before there was a community here, when it was nothing more than scrub, grassy hills, and old forests; some of us to escape our destiny, and our past. We came here to escape me.

There is no getting away, the petty gossips and the troublemakers, the hate and the fear, it's just human nature.

We never anticipated you though, old Rusty Plowshare, you and your crazy old family.

No, we never anticipated you.

I never anticipated you.

12 - Mrs. Crampchet Returns to Garden Grove

Work at the new Garden Grove Meadows residential development carried on like a normal jobsite for a few days. There were no new problems, no vandalism, and best of all no more poisoned gifts of dainties.

Things were looking better. There was a pause in work at another jobsite and the men were moved over to Garden Grove, doubling the work force. The site was buzzing with activity and the promise of making some valuable catch-up time.

Some of the poisoned men released from the hospital were at home recuperating and some had returned to work already. Dave McCormack was one of those men. The rest of the men still in the hospital were all steadily improving.

For the first time in what was starting to feel like a really long time, Stanley Rutthers was having a great day.

And just like that, it all came crashing down on top of him.

In celebration of things going so well, Stanley decided to treat the guys. He sent one of the inexperienced new guys off with enough money to buy coffees and donuts for the entire double-staffed work crew.

The fare was set up on a hastily crafted table consisting of some orange traffic control sawhorses and planks of wood.

Now, Stanley is in the little trailer office, still working on sorting out the mess of scattered and mixed up files caused earlier by a vandal in there, sipping at his cooling coffee. His donut sat with a bite out of it, jelly oozing and leaving a sticky mess behind.

He glanced up and saw something through the little dirt-smudged window that he really did not want to see.

A little old lady is hovering over the makeshift buffet like she is having trouble deciding what she'd like to have.

It is the very same old lady who had come shuffling painfully slowly up the road bearing the present of a large tray piled high with poisoned pastries.

"Shit!"

Stanley rushed out of the little trailer, the door banging a few times in its frame behind him. He jumped down the stairs to the ground, his feet missing the steps completely, and raced frantically for the old woman and the laid out coffees and donuts.

One of the workers is standing there, chatting with the old woman, a coffee in one hand and a donut in the other.

Another worker is looking over the donuts in anticipation, picking just the right one.

A third worker is just reaching out his hand to take a coffee.

Stanley crashed into the worker talking to the old woman, knocking him into the rickety temporary buffet table, causing him and the entire contraption and its contents to crash to the ground to the stunned looks of the other two surprised men. The man he slammed into cried out with the pain and shock of the hot coffee as it washed over him. Luckily, it had time to cool some on the drive over.

The men probably would have just brushed the dirt off and eaten the donuts if they were not also soggy with spilled coffee.

The man he crashed into is covered with spilled coffee and donut remnants. He'd lost his coffee cup, its contents the first to slosh over him as he fell, but still held up the other hand with the last remaining intact donut.

"Oops," Stanley muttered, recovering his balance. "Sorry man."

He held a hand out to help the other man to his feet.

The man looked up at him, mad. He hesitated, and then grudgingly took his foreman's hand.

He was even less impressed when the foreman accidentally knocked the donut out of his hand and stepped on it while trying to help him up.

"Uh, sorry," Stanley said to the worker again. He turned to the other two men who were standing there staring at him with stunned looks. "Sorry," he said to them.

It was no accident. Stanley is afraid the old woman might have done something, contaminated or poisoned the coffee or donuts in some way.

The official word was that the first poisoning of the crew had been purely accidental, and it made sense given her age. But he just couldn't help that feeling of doubt that hit him like a sledgehammer the moment he saw her hovering over the food; that and the memory of how ill his men had all been. Visions of the guys writhing in agony and vomiting weakly still haunt him.

The old woman seemed as though she hadn't noticed the planks, sawhorses, and coffee and donuts crashing to the ground with the man she'd been talking to.

She still prattled on, while leaning over the makeshift table that is no longer there as though trying to pick which delicacy to have.

Stanley turned to the old lady.

"Ma-am," he tried to get her attention. He felt like a little boy trying to talk to the scariest old school teacher in grade school. He had no idea why this old woman had this effect on him. No one else did. Even the scariest old school teacher in grade school had never made him this nervous.

"Ma-am," he tried again.

This time she paused in her dialogue with herself to look at him.

"You can't be here on a construction site. It's not safe."

"Oh posh," the old woman muttered at him with a dismissive wave of her wrinkled hand.

"Please escort this lady off the site," he said to one of the men still standing around looking dejected over the sudden tragic loss of the donuts and coffee.

Stanley walked away, leaving three confused men and one not so confused old woman behind.

Mrs. Crampchet thanked the man who escorted her from the jobsite when he got her past the roughed in entrance road, throwing in a little flirt for good measure.

He hurried away a little too quickly to be casual, while she smiled knowingly the moment he was gone.

She started shuffling her way down the street back to her little house.

Rusty Plowshare was hobbling along the sidewalk on his rickety legs. His face hardened when he spotted the young man escorting old Mrs. Crampchet from the construction site ahead. He had seen her go in and headed over there immediately. Unfortunately, he didn't move very fast these days.

He sped up his pace with grim determination.

"What are you doing?" Rusty demanded, catching up to Mrs. Crampchet as she shuffled alone up the sidewalk. His walk looked almost like a painful waddling, his arthritic old knees struggling to work and still recovering from their late night workout.

The old man's face is a cragged wrinkled mask of anger with rough white stubble bristling out from the chin and cheeks like miniature stubby porcupine quills.

His rheumy eyes, watery and red rimmed with the effects of age, flashed with fury.

"What in blazes were you doing there, old woman?" he demanded.

She looked at him innocently, not pausing in her slow shuffle home.

"Why I don't know what you are talking about Mr. Plowshare," she said.

"You know damned well what I'm talking about," he insisted.

She continued on, as if he were not worthy of her time.

"What were you doing there?" he demanded again.

"Why Mr. Plowshare," she said with a slow sly smile. "I didn't know you cared." She turned and looked at him. "You're not jealous of those young men are you?"

The look she gave him suggested that the very idea of him being jealous of or holding any notions towards her of any sort were about as appetizing and welcome as a rotting rat on a dinner plate.

This stopped him short for a second.

"Oh, stop that you old witch! What did you do to the food? What did you put on the donuts?" he demanded.

"Why, Mr. Plowshare," Mrs. Crampchet turned on him angrily. "Are you accusing me of something?"

"Darned right," he muttered angrily.

Mrs. Crampchet pursed her lips, properly outraged.

"I did nothing to their donuts," she hissed.

He glared at her.

"And what are you doing skulking around the construction site you old coot?" she spat.

Rusty clenched his knotted twisted fingers into a loose semblance of fists. They might have been fists ready to strike the old woman if not for the fact he had been reflexively clenching and straitening his painful fingers in an effort to ease their soreness ever since the night of digging. That and he couldn't tighten those arthritis knobbed fingers into a fist anymore.

"I wasn't," he started. "What do you know-?"

"Just now," she interrupted him. "What were you doing just now? Either you followed me or you were there already."

Vexed, the old man stalked off muttering to himself.

Mrs. Crampchet had never seen him so angry in all the years they both grew up and old in this small community, and she had seen Rusty Plowshare get very angry many times.

Mrs. Crampchet patted her purse with a bony hand, feeling the shape of the thing inside it that weighted it down. It is long and hard, it's curling tail almost poking out of her purse. It hadn't been easy to fit it in there.

She has no idea just how dangerous and unstable that very old stick of dynamite crammed in her purse with her lipstick, wallet, and a few tissues, is. She knows more than the average little old lady about dynamite and such things, but not quite as much as she should.

A bead of sweat slowly oozed out of the stick as she shuffled her way slowly home and is absorbed by the cloth fabric lining the inside of her purse.

"Crazy old coot," she muttered about the old man.

Stanley Rutther's world is not done crashing in on him yet that day.

13 - Forgeries

Bruce Copeland sat in his office brooding. He had spent hours poring over the different copies of the plans for the Garden Grove Meadows job and all the files of notes and communications for the project.

He is dumbfounded.

No job in his history as owner of Copeland and Howe Construction, or the years he spent working for others, has ever had the problems of this simple residential land development project.

It's a straightforward project; there shouldn't be all these problems.

There have been more errors by the construction crew and engineers on this one project than any other project. Even much larger and more complicated projects don't have half the problems.

Some of the problems involving that dishonest bribe-taking scoundrel Willie Williams at the municipal office were downright incompetence on Williams' part. Copeland isn't sure if Williams is involved in drawing many of the plans for work affecting municipal owned land. If he is, then the whole municipality is in trouble.

He can't see the other man in the municipal office making such obvious mistakes. Samuel Watkins is the main municipal engineer, doubling as a second inspector when things get too busy, the same as Williams fills in for him drawing up plans when needed. Sam Watkins has a reputation for honesty, professionalism, and quality work.

And the errors are only the beginning.

From his early days where all he was trusted with was digging ditches with a shovel, through his movement up the ranks on the various job sites, to the years he spent running his own company,

Copeland has never in his career in construction seen a job with so much seemingly senseless and random vandalism either.

Sure, other jobs have had their fair share of vandals, some more than others. It is an expected and unfortunate cost of doing business, like shoplifting is to the store manager. Every project has some random acts of vandalism, usually done by teens.

Like Garden Grove, the Waterford project, Riverbend, and Lilydale Acres were all victims of more than the ordinary vandalism, but they were all controversial.

That's what makes no sense. There is nothing controversial about the Garden Grove housing development.

Lilydale Acres. His stomach still soured at the thought of the high-risk mental institution that nearly caused a riot last year with the locals determined to not allow that project in their back yard. That project too had been plagued with vandalism.

The locals won that fight after a particularly volatile patient escaped from another high level institution and brutally killed a number of area pets, including a pet pot-bellied pig that was a local celebrity an mascot, and kidnapped three children. The children were found unharmed.

Apparently, the patient thought they were his lost friends from his youth growing up on the Old Mill Road. The children claimed he was convinced some kind of fairytale monster was after them and was only hiding them to protect them.

There never was any proof the patient was guilty of the gruesome animal deaths, but there was no doubt in anyone's minds. Well, except for the patient who swore it was the Old Mill Road monster, an urban legend of sorts in a small rural town.

Shortly after, the unfinished institution burned down by mysterious means. It was never rebuilt.

Maybe he was the Old Mill Road monster. The patient, that is.

As far as Copeland could remember, there were a number of grisly deaths and disappearances of pets and some children around the Old Mill Road area when he was a kid. He shuddered, remembering the fear it caused even here, miles away from Old Mill Road.

He wondered if his memory about what happened so long ago was right. On a whim, he decided to look it up.

Turning on his computer, Copeland did a search, found a link, and opened it.

The phone rang. He would have to read the article later.

After a brief conversation, Copeland hung up the phone, his stomach soured more.

There was more vandalism at the Garden Grove site.

"This is ridiculous," he muttered wearily.

There's been little proof of who's been behind any of it, but by his best guess he'd say there are probably more than one group or individuals responsible for the Garden Grove vandalism.

Lilydale had problems like this, but that was a controversial project.

This is just a straightforward residential neighborhood. It even has parks and other green spaces in the plans. There is nothing controversial about Garden Grove.

The door to his office burst open.

Doug Walton, the chief engineer for Copeland and Howe rushed in looking very excited.

"I've got it all figured out." He motioned with his arm for Copeland to follow.

In another room large scrolls of plans were laid out across large collapsible tables pushed together to make a larger table. Files and pages of notes were spread out across another table and around on the floor.

Copeland looked around at the mess.

"Have you figured out how the plans got changed and mixed up?" he asked.

Doug looked at him grimly.

"No, but I figured out what the correct plans should be."

What he is really thinking is, "Why would I do that? How would I even do that?"

"See," Doug pointed to a set of plans with notes penciled in all over it.

"Here, here, and here. Each plan had something different added that the others didn't."

He pointed to other markings on the plan.

"Here, here, and here. Each plan also had something different missing.

He pointed out a third set of markings.

"And each one had something different that was just changed."

Copeland studied the markings. There was something about them. A pattern? A familiarity? Just a hunch? It felt like that odd tingling of déjà vu, unexplainable but undeniable. He almost had a sense they were leading somewhere. Somewhere he might not want to go. An uneasy feeling settled in his already stress-soured stomach.

"Good. Let's get this straightened out and proper plans drawn up and distributed."

"Oh, but that's not even the best part." Doug seemed almost giddy all of a sudden.

Copeland looked at him.

"Here." Doug pointed. "This area here is the only one that has been changed or left out in every single copy of the plans."

"Okay," Copeland prompted unnecessarily, "so what's there?"

"Nothing!" The engineer almost giggled over the absurdity of it. "Just some trees that won't be knocked down until the first section is done and the first group of homes are being built. That section of the development won't even be started until maybe next year.

Copeland stared at the plans thoughtfully.

"Whoever was drawing up these plans was meticulous about the changes, but obviously knows that area doesn't matter yet. Or maybe they just got lazy and didn't bother to do it right."

"Maybe," Copeland said distractedly. "I want to know how these plans got so messed up, how so many mistakes were made by our engineers, and how different versions are getting sent to different offices. I want to know who is responsible for drawing up all these different versions."

"Oh, these weren't mistakes." Doug did not seem to notice the gravity of what he was saying; he is just stating a fact. "This was deliberate. They were forged, and it wasn't done by anyone in our office or anyone that we work with.

It's almost like whoever is doing this is specifically targeting that spot to leave it out of the plans. The rest is just kind of random."

He pointed to the incriminating corner of one of the blueprints.

"They are all missing the signature mark showing whose work it is. That's not something you just forget to do. It's as automatic as breathing."

"Forged!" Copeland's jaw would have dropped if he was the jaw dropping kind of man. But being the kind who was brought up to show very little emotion outside of anger, that's what he turned to instead.

Despite others' suspicions of this very thing, the possibility had never occurred to Bruce Copeland.

Copeland's face turned red. His eyes seemed to almost bulge out of their sockets.

Looking up at him, the engineer felt the urge to run.

"How the hell'd they get forged?" he roared.

People in the next business in the multi-tenant building heard his bellow through the walls.

Just then, the secretary poked her head in to announce an urgent telephone call for Copeland.

There was more trouble at the Garden Grove Meadows site.

14 - Sabotage

Bruce Copeland honked his horn impatiently, trying to ease his truck through the crowd gathered at the entrance to the Garden Grove jobsite. The entrance road into the site is the length of a city block and he is not about to park and walk in.

Some orange traffic control construction sawhorses manned by a couple of large ashen-faced workers from the site blocked off the entrance. Police could be seen milling around further in, likely guarding the scene. Beyond them two fire trucks and an ambulance sit idle. Men in firefighting gear are moving around just past the trucks.

The crowd moved grudgingly to let him pass as he slowly nudged the truck through the bodies, giving quick taps to the horn when they didn't move. They are the usual accident gawkers, mostly standing around with blank expressions, craning their necks and staring at anything that might give them a glimpse of something to make their dull day a little more interesting. Some seem downright giddy, as if a tragic event is just what they needed to make their day exciting.

Recognizing their boss, the two men pulled the center sawhorses out of the way when Copeland's truck came close enough to almost touch them, allowing barely enough space for the truck. They leaned forward aggressively with no-nonsense looks when some of the gathered crowd moved to go past the barrier too, stopping them in their tracks.

Copeland looked at the men as he drove past.

The beefy men guarding the entrance looked shaken.

They quickly replaced the sawhorses after his truck had passed the opening, blocking anyone else from entering.

Some of the gawkers were obviously itching to get closer so they could see more than the flashing lights and parked emergency vehicles ahead. But none of them are willing to take on the burly men whose duty it was to keep them out.

Copeland drove in towards the scene. He can see more vehicles now.

Large fire trucks loom over the single ambulance parked next to them, their lights flashing. Beyond them, more ambulances wait. Scattered police cars' lights flash an accompaniment to their beat.

Police tape fluttered where it is tied and stretched across to block off access to the area well in from where the men are blocking the road with sawhorses.

Workers milled around outside the police tape, looking lost. They look even more shaken up and pale than the men manning the entrance. It struck Copeland that he doesn't recognize any of the new faces working for him.

He parked quickly, got out, and hurried towards the center of the activity.

Ah, a face he recognizes, Dave McCormack. Dave is covered head to toe in dirt in stark contrast to the men around him.

"Dave," Copeland called to him as he approached him. "What happened?"

Then he noticed the blank look on a face that has never been without animated expression.

That's when he noticed that Dave isn't just covered with the usual jobsite grime.

Blood. Blood, dirt, and hydraulic fluid.

His clothes are full of it. His hair is matted with it. His face dripped with blood and fluid.

Dave stared back at him blankly. He raised his hands up, holding them out palm up before his chest, staring at his bloodied hands as if they held some dark sinister secret that he does not want the answers to, cannot know the answers to.

Bruce Copeland grabbed Dave.

"Dave! Dave! Are you all right?"

Bruce Copeland shook him by the shoulders, trying to make him focus on him.

Dave looked at him, his expression empty, his eyes haunted.

"Dave, what happened?"

"The hydraulics went." Dave's voice was dead, as empty of expression as his face.

"The hydraulics?" Bruce Copeland's mind raced, running through a list of equipment on site and what kind of condition each might be in. He doesn't know of any with hydraulics problems.

"Which one? Dave, which tractor?"

"All of them."

Now Bruce Copeland's face paled.

His arms dropped to his side. He stared at Dave in stunned disbelief.

All of them?

It isn't possible.

He ran past Dave, past the workers milling around with blank faces, finally noticing that Dave is not the only one who is bloodied. He ran past the ambulances, fire trucks, and squad cars, absently noting the sound of approaching sirens. He cannot tell how many are approaching.

Bruce Copeland stood there in shock taking in the scene before him, oblivious to the police officer trying to get him to move back.

Cat tractors are scattered around; large beasts of a tractor, smaller ones, and Bobcats, as well as other equipment. The long jointed arms of the tractors are bowed to the ground. Their clawed buckets seem to have been dug into the earth at unnatural angles.

This is not how they would dig or park the vehicles, Bruce noted.

Other machinery parked nearby looks normal, if perhaps hurriedly abandoned.

A road roller with fat knobs on the large roller on its front and heavy treads on its caterpillar track, the continuous band of treads encircling the wheels that drive them, looks like it had tried to flatten a Bobcat that was pushed up against a larger tractor.

It was partially successful in its attempt when the larger tractor's bucket came down on top of the Bobcat. Either the roller's driver was distracted or it was more than just hydraulics that had failed on equipment. The roller had managed to climb and straddle the small Bobcat, partially crushing it, before the frantic driver could stop it.

The roller now sits at an awkward angle with its tail on the ground and roller on top of the Bobcat, its treads partially off the ground.

Copeland stared at it in mute shock, unable to wrap his head around how it could have possibly managed to get on top of the Bobcat.

"How the hell did that happen?" he murmured. "It's not even possible."

A paramedic leaned into the cramped space, working to stabilize the Bobcat driver.

Bruce cannot tell if the Bobcat operator is injured or just trapped in the partially crushed machine.

Men in firefighter suits worked at the Bobcat with some sort of device. The sound of screeching metal filled the air and sparks flew as they attempted to cut the driver out.

"Jaws of Life," Bruce thought absently, his mind trying to take in the whole devastating scene around him.

Paramedic workers worked frantically on a couple of men lying on the ground, moving them to wheeled stretchers and loading them into the waiting ambulances to rush them away.

Construction workers were digging frantically with the help of fire crews at two piles of debris just in front of the two Cats parked in odd positions. They do not dare use the heavy equipment for fear of the injury it could cause if there is anyone alive beneath the dirt.

He finally realized a police officer is talking to him with annoyed patience. Bruce stared at the officer, but it took a moment for the words to register.

"Move back, you need to move back beyond the police tape," the officer was repeating.

Bruce blinked at him and nodded numbly, stepping back as ordered until he was behind the tape barrier. He had wandered past a section left open for emergency crews.

Bruce stood watching the scene. The sense of a presence crept into his subconscious, and then into his conscious mind. It's an unpleasant feeling. He glanced quickly and saw no one is near him, or even looking at him. He returned to watching the scene, his mind in numb turmoil as he tried to make sense of it, and suddenly feels a presence next to him with a startling almost physical feeling.

He turned in shock to find one of his men standing next to him. He feels only a small measure of relief at the familiar face, still feeling the uneasiness of that vague sense of an unwanted presence he felt just a moment before, but is now gone.

"What the hell happened here?" Bruce asked, his voice shaky.

The man turned to him, his eyes holding that hollow blank stare of someone who cannot believe what just happened is real.

"The hydraulics on the tractors just kind of gave out. Bang, one after another," he said. "When the hydraulics on the tractors gave, the buckets came down, dropping their loads, hydraulic fluid sprayed out like spurting blood.

We-we think two of them might have dropped their loads directly on top of some guys who were where they shouldn't have been. They didn't even see it coming. None of us did. It was so sudden.

Everyone was distracted, surprised when the hydraulic fluid suddenly started spurting and tractors breaking down."

They both stared at the men digging frantically.

"We know for sure a couple of guys got buried. Dave saw the dirt come down on one guy. He was standing right there in front of him, maybe two feet away. Dave got half buried too. We dug him and a couple others out. He said the other guy just kind of crumpled under the weight of the mud." He shook his head, feeling lost over what had happened. "But we don't know for sure if there are more. We just don't know if any others didn't get out of the way. Everyone was just running everywhere all of a sudden."

Bruce looked around again at the men covered in dirt and sprayed hydraulic fluid.

"That's a lot of blood," he said.

"It's hydraulic fluid," the worker said. "It was spraying all over."

"Why is the hydraulic fluid so dark red?" Bruce asked. "It looks like blood."

"I don't know," the worker said with a puzzled frown. He hadn't noticed before, but the color was off. It was too dark and too red.

Bruce stared at the men covered with red fluid and dirt, turning as he looked from man to man, stopping finally to stare at Dave, who is still ghostly pale and numb with shock. Dave stood motionlessly, staring vacantly ahead of him as everyone rushed around him, shivering from the shock, still holding his hands out as if afraid to touch them.

Dave, who is covered in dirt, blood, and hydraulic fluid.

If it even is hydraulic fluid.

"If that's hydraulic fluid, something has been mixed with it," Bruce said, talking out loud to himself. "Damned if it doesn't look like blood."

The thought of the tractors' hydraulic lines filled with blood sent a new chill through Bruce.

He wondered what had happened.

The whole scene had started with the road roller.

Seeming a little off when the driver got in and started driving, the braking system on the roller soon lost all ability to stop the heavy machine. When the brakes stopped, the driver tried to stop the roller, but was unable to budge the controls to take it out of drive. He fought the controls as he looked around in a panic. He tried to shut it down, but the engine would not turn off. He tried to turn it, to redirect it away, but it would not respond.

It was as though the machine was under the control of someone else and he was just along helplessly for the ride.

The out of control lumbering machine rolled into the Bobcat, trying to mount it. The fat knobs of its roller meant to pulverize ground clawed and caught at the Bobcat, its treads digging into the ground and its heavier weight giving it power over the smaller machine. It pushed it forward into a larger tractor while the Bobcat's driver screamed at the driver of the roller to stop. The driver of the larger tractor stared in mute surprise, snapping out of it moments later to yell at the roller driver too. The roller driver could only frantically fight the controls that would not respond.

The roller clawed and pushed at the Bobcat, pushing it ahead of it until it butted against the larger tractor. The roller continued pressing forward, crushing the small tractor against the larger machine. The roller kept pushing, the fat knobs of its roller gripping, the roller turning and clawing its way up. It impossibly climbed the Bobcat, causing a chain reaction of events resulting in the large tractor tipping to drop its bucket on the Bobcat as its own hydraulic fluid began to spurt through ruptured lines. Its weight against the smaller machine was more than the driver's cab could take.

Brakes had gone on other machines too, but their buckets dragging and digging into the mud proved to be an effective alternate braking system.

Men fought to control their machines, to turn them off, and finally clambering out of their engine compartments to disconnect their batteries, effectively killing them.

All of the machinery affected had been sabotaged.

For the rest of the day Bruce will keep picturing Dave staring at his bloodied hands like he didn't know where they'd come from.

Dave just stared ahead mutely, lost in a haze of shock that keeps going back to one thing, the moment all hell broke loose. He keeps glancing towards the small bit of woods that remain across the field.

He thought he heard the dry rustle of a very old voice coming from those woods, laughing softly. More strange than the sound that he is sure had come from there is the knowledge he could not possibly have heard it because the trees are too far.

But he cannot deny hearing it.

15 - Premeditated Attack on Garden Grove

The Garden Grove jobsite remained closed while investigators inspected the site and the equipment.

It took hours to question all the workers who were present when the accident happened, and some that were on the site and left before the accident.

After the accident closed down the site, many of the men scattered. Some stuck around because they knew everyone would be questioned, thinking that it was better to just get it out of the way quickly and be done with it. Some went home and some went about other activities, running errands or hitting the bar to drink away that chilled blank feeling, the numbness of shock from witnessing the crushing sudden collapse of heavy equipment on their fellow workers.

The loads of dirt dropped from the large tractors' buckets were carefully cleared. One man was discovered, crushed beneath the weight of the dirt that buried him, the trauma possibly killing him before the suffocation could.

Despite the authorities' best efforts to locate and question all the men, two workers were missing.

Other workers remembered seeing them at the site when the accidents occurred, but none could say for sure they were still there in the moments immediately after.

After getting a count of how many men were on the site and excavating the dropped bucket loads, the authorities were certain there were no more men buried beneath the mounds of dirt.

The disappearance of the two men was very curious and a little suspicious, although not surprising in this transient field of work where a lot of the workers were seasonally employed.

Residents in the area were also questioned. Surely, someone must have seen something.

No one seemed to have seen anything.

This was unusual in a small community where everyone always seems to know someone who saw something or have heard about what was seen.

Secrets do not live long in a small community.

Careful inspections of the damaged equipment made it apparent that they were intentionally sabotaged. It was done in such a way as to make the hydraulics on the tractors and brakes on the roller bleed empty or jam once they were put into use. The slow bleed wasn't enough to put the tractors out of business immediately. That would not happen until pressure was added through heavy construction use, forcing the fluids out more quickly. The altered fluids quickly overheated, stressing the lines until they burst, pumping out fluid like spurting blood vessels.

Tests revealed the hydraulic and other fluids had been tampered with, along with other vandalism involving the tractors' braking and steering systems. The hydraulic fluid that even the paramedics swore looked like blood proved not to contain any bodily fluids, leaving one large question. What exactly was it? Analysis of the fluid could not explain the dark red color or blood-like consistency that witnesses had reported. By the time the fluid was tested it looked like normal, albeit watered-down, hydraulic fluid. The conclusion: an unknown additive was added.

Investigators were also unable to explain some of the equipments' erratic behavior. They could not explain how the machine operators were unable to turn off the equipment. The most puzzling was how the road roller managed to climb the small Bobcat.

This act of vandalism was more sophisticated than the previous amateurish attacks.

This wasn't the act of a frustrated housewife like petite Libby Waterbourne, who had hacked away brutishly at the machines' parts earlier in comparison to the sophisticated thought-out damage done this time.

This was done by someone with the required mechanical expertise.

Copeland is sitting across from the police detective. It is his turn to be interviewed about the sabotaged tractors.

"Do you have any enemies Mr. Copeland?" Detective Hughes asked. "Anyone who would want to ruin your business perhaps?"

"No enemies," Copeland said. "I have a rival that sometimes makes trouble, Vern Lezkowitz, but he only does petty stuff."

"We're already looking into Mr. Lezkowitz," Detective Hughes said. "This attack was not aimed directly at you, but at your equipment. And I understand there have been other attacks of vandalism on this jobsite."

"All little stuff, kids and locals, until now," Copeland said.

"This was no casual act of vandalism. The level of knowledge required for the damage to the equipment suggests this was a premeditated and intentional act by someone who knew exactly what they were doing. There is more than just vandalism as a motive here.

Some of it even our best mechanical and lab investigators can't make any sense of.

Between this latest act and the others, it seems like an unusual amount of activity around this one jobsite," Detective Hughes said. He checked his notebook. "Multiple counts of vandalism to the site, trailer, and equipment. Skull bone intentionally planted, the discovery of which caused some groups to call for a permanent shutdown of the site, and we believe that was the motive behind that.

It's well known that Mr. Lezkowitz threatened you over your winning this job.

And there is the poisoning of your entire work crew at the Garden Grove site. Is there anything else?"

"No, that sounds about right," Copeland said, shifting in his seat.

Detective Hughes levelled his gaze at Copeland.

"The threats against you personally and against the Anc-Chor project; you haven't told anyone about those, have you?"

"No," Copeland said.

Detective Hughes nodded. "Good. Make sure you don't tell anyone. Not your wife, your mother, brother, or best friend. Some details have to be kept under wraps to help weed out false information from the truth."

Hughes looked down at his notebook and back up at Copeland.

"There are two of your workers we cannot locate. We got contact information from your office, but they've apparently cleaned out and are gone. Mr. Jim Keaner and Mr. Carlos Rodriquez.

You have no idea where those two workers might have gone?" Detective Hughes asked.

"None," Copeland said. "My best guess is they moved on. It's the nature of the business. It's a lot of seasonal work and the casual workers are often transient, moving from one place to the next to find work. Most likely they moved on to the next town or city since this job could be shut down for a long time."

"What can you tell me about these two men?" Hughes asked.

Copeland shrugged, "These boys aren't all boy scouts. Maybe they've brushed with the law before and didn't want to stick around to be questioned. Carlos Rodriquez was a pretty hard worker, seemed pretty straight up. The other guy not so much."

"How long have those two men worked for you?"

"A few weeks? I just hired them. I have a lot of workers off right now because of the poisoning. We had to bring in a whole new green crew. All these problems have also put us behind on the project, so I needed extra boots on the job."

"Did you hire them legally?" Hughes asked. "They aren't illegal aliens? If they are, you might as well just tell me. I'll find out sooner or later anyway."

"There's no illegals on my jobs," Copeland said, burning a bit with the accusation. "One of them was an immigrant but all his papers looked good. If he's illegal it's not on me."

This only confirmed Detective Hughes' suspicion. He has a feeling that there is something behind the acts committed against the Garden Grove project that have nothing to do with the housing development.

There were too many things happening and none of them seemed connected. Sometimes that was a good reason to dig deeper, to suspect a connection.

"Any chance they could be working for someone else?" Detective Hughes asked.

"Like I said, they probably skipped town to find work down the road. They could be working again by now."

Detective Hughes tilted his head, studying the construction boss. He leaned forward to drive his point home. This is a very serious question with far reaching implications.

"I mean, could they have been working for someone else when you hired them, secretly. Do you think they could have been set up to work for you so they could get on site without anyone being suspicious?"

"You think they did this? You think they sabotaged the tractors and caused that man to die, injured the others?" Copeland felt like this is unreal. He hadn't thought of the possibility, but now that it was laid out in front of him it is undeniable.

"What else do you think they might have done?" Copeland asked.

"That's what I want to find out," Detective Hughes said. "They weren't on your crew long enough to do much. But they could have come around before that. And who knows what they would have done if they had stuck around longer.

What do you know about the skull and other bones found?"

"Not much," Copeland said. "They're old."

"The skull was put there on purpose, recently," Detective Hughes said. "The archaeologist from the university confirmed it. Other bones were found. The soil was disturbed, not layered over the bones over time. They don't know because the ground was disturbed by the tractor that dug it up, but they suspect it's the same with the skull. They are not graves either. Each bone found was buried by itself."

"How long ago? Years?" Copeland asked.

"Some of the other bones are still being examined. So far, they are all animal bones. The question is whether any of them were planted like the skull."

This is a lie. Hughes is keeping this bit of information to himself. The other bones found are human as well, and very recently buried despite the bones themselves being old. Keeping key pieces of information secret is just part of safeguarding the investigation.

"I'm waiting for reports from the archeologist. The confirmed animal bones have been there for years, decades even. The skull was buried within the last week before it was found," Detective Hughes said.

Bruce Copeland's mind staggered at this bombshell. The petty vandalism he was used to. The poisoning was a shock, but proved to be the act of a crazy old woman. The recent vandalism to the tractors was disturbing and suggested there was something more behind it. But this?

"Who the hell would bury a skull on an active jobsite and why?" Copeland blurted out.

"That's just one of many questions I need to answer," Detective Hughes said. "Garden Grove is not a controversial job so the only reason for someone to be trying to shut it down that makes sense is a personal grudge, or their reasons have nothing to do with Garden Grove at all."

Copeland shook his head wearily.

"Now let's talk about these threats over the Anc-Chor project. I want to know more," Detective Hughes continued.

"You don't think that has anything to do with Garden Grove, do you?" Copeland asked.

"It's possible," Detective Hughes said, his expression showing his uncertainty. "I'll need a list of individuals and organizations you've received threats from concerning the Anc-Chor project and your copies of everything you've received."

"You guys already have everything," Copeland said.

"I know you kept copies," Hughes said. "Just give me the copies so I can check this stuff out for myself."

Copeland wondered why he couldn't just get the files from the other detectives. He had a sudden thought that the police are trying to eliminate his access to copies of the letters and emails.

"If he thinks I'm going to just hand over my copies and not just give him a copy of them, then he's mistaken," Copeland thought.

"Yeah sure," Copeland said. "I've got it locked away. Even my secretary doesn't have access to it. I'll get that stuff to you as soon as I get back to my office."

"Good," Detective Hughes said with a nod. Copeland picked up on the relief that showed in the man's expression and the change in his posture.

Detective Hughes's suspicions went beyond the left wing groups behind most of the threats. He suspected someone very powerful is involved and working against the Anc-Chor project; someone with a lot of people in their pocket. It is his job to find out who. He wants Copeland's copies of everything so he can control who has access to any evidence. The small jobsite trailer was already ransacked and Copeland's office could be next. Whoever was looking for something, Hughes needs to make sure they don't get the chance to find out what he already knows, or suspects.

"Just what is this Anc-Chor project about?" Detective Hughes asked. "What is this place you're building?"

"I don't really know," Copeland shrugged. "The man behind it, Mr. Chornelhus, is very secretive about the whole thing. I think it's some kind of lab or research facility."

"What kind? Medical? Drugs?"

"With all the secrecy I kind of think it might be something military or government. You know how secretive those agencies are. Even the crew building the facility doesn't know how anything they're building is supposed to fit together. Instead of building the place like we normally would, Chornelhus has us building pieces outside the building then a different crew trying to make it fit in place after. He hasn't even provided a full set of blueprints for the job. He doles them out piecemeal, having us build disconnected sections. The whole thing is going to be a mess by the times it's done. But Chornelhus is a pretty strange one. It might just be more of his strange behavior," Copeland said.

"I understand some of the groups against this project are environmental groups," Detective Hughes said.

"Mr. Chornelhus didn't exactly pick an ideal location for this project," Copeland said. "I don't know why he insisted on that piece of land. It would have made more sense to just switch locations and avoid all the trouble. There are a lot of other sites that would have been better. The usual local conservation groups have been lobbying against the project from the start. It's some protected grassland area or something. They're saying some protected bird or something might live there. They always seem to say that every time someone starts building on lots inside the city limits that sat vacant for as long as anyone can remember though.

But that isn't even all. Some of the native groups whose tribes have been here forever were protesting it too. Said that parcel has some kind of special significance to their people. It's supposed to have some kind of magic or curse or something. They wanted it to remain untouched."

"Those local groups don't usually resort to petty vandalism," Detective Hughes said.

"Yeah well, we've got more than just the locals getting on the protest bandwagon," Copeland said. "World Protection Order and Global Rescue and Planet Rehabilitation have jumped into the fight. Probably one of the local groups decided to bring in a few heavy hitters."

Detective Hughes had to take a breath and think about this.

"World Protection Order," he said thoughtfully, "heavy hitter for sure. They have a fringe group of members who can get out of hand. I wouldn't put it past them to be behind the petty vandalism, but the premeditation and calculated expertise used in this latest round of vandalism just doesn't fit their methods. Some of the things that happened with the tractors don't even seem possible. It's like they were moved by some outside force in ways they should not be able to, the roller climbing and crushing the bobcat for one.

That Global Rescue and Planet Rehabilitation group is another story. They've been known to get downright dirty and have committed some pretty sophisticated attacks. They've used guerrilla tactics in the past too. Most countries consider them terrorists. But I can't see them sneaking around vandalizing in the night. They don't hide their actions, they do it right in front of the cameras, look for as much media attention as they can get."

He seemed to dismiss this as only one possibility. There were more to consider.

"I remember the political furor over this project too," Detective Hughes said. "Some of the project's opposition thought Mr. Chornelhus bought his way into building on that parcel of land."

"Of course he did," Copeland said. "I have no doubt he did."

"This is well worth looking into," Hughes thought to himself. He's heard of other cases of politicians and very wealthy and powerful businessmen playing dirty behind the scenes. Some of them he suspected to have even had people killed just to win, although no one has ever been able to prove who was behind it.

Copeland kept his own thoughts on that to himself too. He knows more than he wants anyone to know about the politicians and business leaders on both sides of this deal.

"A controversial project like the Anc-Chor project brings a lot of questions and demands for answers from a lot of people," Copeland said.

"And when those answers don't come a lot of people get offended," Hughes finished for him.

Copeland nodded.

"A lot of false rumors too," Copeland said.

"You get me that list," Detective Hughes said. "Everyone you know of who's made any threats against you, your business, both projects, and Mr. Chornelhus. No matter how small the implied threat I want to know," Detective Hughes said. "And, your copies of the documents you have."

It is a dismissal. The interview is over.

"If I have any more questions I'll be in touch," Detective Hughes said. "And if you think of anything you think might be relevant I want to know."

Detective Hughes sat back after Bruce Copeland left, thinking he should probably go with the man to make sure he gives him the paperwork he asked for without making any more copies.

He is convinced this latest act of sabotage against the Garden Grove site was not what everyone thinks it is.

He knows who the secret money behind the project is, and that somehow Garden Grove is tied directly to the Anc-Chor project. He just doesn't know how yet.

16 - Coffee Clutch Meeting

Barbara rolled over in bed with a groan and looked at the clock.

It is just touching onto six-thirty a.m.

The light from the digital clock glowed brighter than the diffused early morning light glowing weakly behind the bedroom curtains.

The sun is still struggling to get up.

The sound of beeping and growling tractors that woke her up isn't that loud inside the room, it is more of a distant annoyance.

But it still woke her up.

"Are you kidding me? Really? Six-thirty a.m.?"

She looked at the window, noting the near darkness beyond.

"Can they even see? It's still dark out!"

Rubbing her sleep weary eyes and still half asleep, Barb got up and stumbled to the kitchen to make coffee.

Later, after seeing the kids up, fed, dressed, and off on the school bus, Barb abandoned her now cold half cup of coffee for a fresh cup, pouring the old coffee down the drain before refilling the cup.

She settled into the living room armchair with a sigh and a sip of her coffee, thinking that one of these days she'll actually be able to finish that first coffee while it's still warm.

She was running through a mental list of the things she needed to do today when the ringing telephone interrupted.

"Hello," she said, answering the phone.

"Barb. Coffee. My place. Quick!" Pam's voice sounded hurried. "We need to talk."

"I'll be there in a few."

A few was a few longer than a few. It was closer to an hour before Barb showed up at Pam's house.

Expecting it to be a typical school day of doing chores around the house, Barb hadn't even brushed her hair before seeing the kids off to the school bus.

In fact, she hadn't even really gotten dressed. A quick swap out of her pajama bottoms for sweat pants and an open sweater tossed over her pajama shirt was topped off with tying her messy hair in a quick ponytail for the walk to the bus stop.

While the housewives all know of this all too common housewife quirk, none of these women would admit to doing it.

Unfortunately, it took Barb a good hour to get herself together enough to be presentable; something many housewives dispense with entirely by year four.

When Barb finally arrived at Pam's house, she found that she was the last to arrive. The rest had already been there for some time.

There was an obvious giant gorilla in the room. You know the kind, one of those great big hairy ugly tensions that no one wants to admit to and risk popping its bubble and dirtying themselves with the inevitable fallout.

You could cut the tension in the air with a butter knife.

Libby was glowering.

Mrs. Henderson, who Barb wondered how she managed to become a regular member of their coffee group, was sitting stoically with her back straight and a regal air of superior haughtiness.

Pam looked almost panicked.

Barb looked to each in turn, wondering what is going on. Whatever it is, it has the girls all worked up.

She gave Pam a look and said, "Ok, spill the beans."

"We were just talking about some of our extra activities," Pam said.

"Extra activities is one way you can put it," Libby cut in.

"And a little more extra for some," Pam added cattily with a harsh look towards Libby.

Barb looked at her quizzically.

Mrs. Henderson, the eldest of the group, just sat silently above it all, as though she were above both the activities in question and the ongoing discussion about them.

"I didn't do it!" Libby snapped.

"Well you did it the other times," Pam argued.

"Yes, but it wasn't me this time."

"Oh really?"

"Really."

"Then who else would have vandalized the tractors?" Pam demanded. "I don't think it was the kids. They've done some drinking and left smashed bottles and some spray painting. They've never done any real damage. Only you did that."

"But I wouldn't do this," Libby sniffed. "I swear I didn't do it. I wouldn't even know how!"

"Do what?" Barb finally cut in.

"You didn't hear?" Pam was incredulous. Surely, Barb had heard about the vandalized tractors and the injuries caused by them. It was all over town. There couldn't be anyone who hasn't heard about it.

"Hear what?" Barb asked.

Pam gave Libby a warning look that said 'keep your mouth shut because I can't believe what you did.'

"Well," Pam started, her voice dripping with sarcasm. "Somebody messed around with the tractors again and a bunch of the workers got hurt."

"But,..." Libby tried to cut in.

Pam silenced her with a look as she cut her off.

"And the only someone that we know has been messing around with them is Libby!"

Barb looked first at Libby then at Pam.

"I heard about that, yes. But, are you sure?"

She turned to Libby.

"Libby, did you?"

"No I didn't"

"You did," Pam cut in. "Who else then?"

Libby looked like she is about to cry.

"I don't know, but it wasn't me."

Pam was about to say something, but Barb interrupted her.

"Pam, hang on. I want to hear what Libby has to say about it."

Pam glowered at her, crossed her arms over her chest defiantly, and retreated to get Barb a coffee and refills for the rest.

"Ok Libby," Barb said, encouraging her to speak.

"I didn't do it. Honest! When I did it the other times, I was careful. I only messed around with stuff that would make the tractor not start. I don't know what I'm doing much, not like a mechanic would. But I've been around enough of these machines. My dad was a contractor remember? I know a little bit about them. I kind of know what is mechanical and which affects the hydraulics and brakes."

"Ok."

"Whoever did this cut hydraulics lines or something, but not all the way. I would never do that because it could be dangerous if you didn't disable it completely."

"Like what happened," Barb said.

"Right!" Libby said.

Libby was relieved that someone is finally listening to her.

"Some men were hurt pretty bad," Barb said.

"One of them was even killed," Pam cut in.

"I didn't do it," Libby whispered.

Mrs. Henderson finally joined the exchange.

"I think she's telling the truth," Mrs. Henderson said.

"Then who?" Pam asked.

"Let's hope the police figure it out," Barb said.

"I hope so," Libby sniffed. The police had already been to her house to question her. It seems that once you get caught doing something you automatically become a prime suspect the next time someone does it or something like it.

So far, Libby has been caught for vandalizing the tractors, and Pamela was discovered to be the one who painted the billboard sign. Neither of their husbands were very happy about having to bail them out of jail and hire lawyers for the women. In fact, it would be fairly safe to say their men were pretty pissed off about it.

"None of us have been found out yet about the other stuff we did to the jobsite," Barb said. "But you can bet what we have been caught on has made us all the prime suspects for anything else that happens."

"We have to stop what we're doing right now," Libby said. "If we're lucky we won't get charged with the rest of the stuff we did that they haven't caught us for yet."

"You know," Barb said, looking around at the group, "I can't help but feel like this is somehow our fault. It was just a joke to us, just stupid petty stuff. And someone else got in on it, copying us, and took it too far."

The others nodded in agreement.

"We took it too far," Pam said, voicing what they are all thinking. "If they pin this on Libby they could charge her with murder or something."

The thought of one of their own being charged with such a serious crime is frightening. They also feel bad now about what they were doing, as though somehow their tricks caused someone else to get in on the act. They feel like it was somehow their fault that someone else took their minor sabotage and vandalism, acted out of frustration, too far and a man was killed and others were badly injured.

They never intended anyone to actually get hurt.

They were just bored and overtired and fed up with the constant noise from the tractors. They were just lashing out, mostly out of boredom and a warped sense of justice and fun.

Barb thought briefly about her missing necklace. She was wearing it that day when they snuck out in the dark of night to mess around with the construction site. She thought she was still wearing it when she crawled in through the little trailer window with the help of Mrs. Henderson.

She discovered later, after she got home, that the necklace was missing. All she could do then was hope that she had lost it somewhere that if found it would not be associated with the jobsite.

It was a gift from her husband, years ago when they were dating. It was a delicate thin gold chain with fancy scrollwork lettering.

The pendant was a single word.

Barb.

17 - Construction Trailer Mess

Stanley Rutthers and Dave McCormack spreading their work out together is more than the tiny trailer office can manage. But cleaning up the mess left behind by an intruder in the Garden Grove site trailer turned out to be a bigger job than Stanley thought and he had to get some help sorting it all out. This is going to take days to sift through all these papers.

"Wow, whoever did this sure took their time doing it," Dave said.

He has a disorganized mess of stacks of papers and files in front of him that he is in the process of sorting out.

It had not taken long for Stanley to discover that someone had methodically swapped around papers and files.

Lists of contacts were written over, changing telephone numbers and names so that the originals were unreadable. Some of them were even quite vulgar.

Whoever did this had a nasty streak.

When the vandalism was first discovered, it had looked like the tiny office was ransacked. Possibly, it was someone looking for money or someone trying to get information. But there wouldn't be much information that could help someone who wasn't actively working the jobsite, and this wasn't a high competition job either. It is a big project as a whole when all the future homes are factored in, but not something a little information stealing and sabotage could take away. The construction of the homes themselves would be spread across multiple contractors. Also, there was no cash kept in the little trailer office.

It did not make any sense.

The nature of the vandalism made even less sense. It was outright childish.

The police had given the little trailer a routine going over. But with the likelihood of actually catching the culprits and the value of anything inside both being so small, there was little they could do. They dusted for fingerprints; leaving black chalky dust behind on those surfaces they might have been able to lift a print from. Those surfaces where prints could be lifted were plastered with them from years of use by many people.

Stanley figured it would probably be some time before they heard back on whether anything came back from the prints, if at all.

He now has the time consuming job of sorting the mess out and trying to figure out what, if anything, was taken.

Dave flipped through a file to determine how messed up it looked on quick glances and plunked it down on one of the piles.

He bent over, digging in an open filing cabinet drawer by his feet. There are only a few small cabinets in this tiny office. He is amazed at just how much stuff there could be to go through. There were files from old jobs that should have been pulled and filed at the company office when the jobs were done that were still here in the little trailer.

"Sure is a lot of junk for a tiny office," he muttered.

Something caught his eye, a metallic glint.

There is something in the bottom of the drawer, caught beneath the bottom corner of a couple of files.

He pulled the files out.

It is a delicate gold chain.

Dave pulled it out and held it up to look at it. It hung limply from his fingers, the clasp still closed on the ring and the ends a clean break where a link had opened up and fallen away.

"Hey Stan, you wearing jewelry now?"

"Huh?" Stanley looked over, about to ask Dave what he had said.

He spotted the thin chain dangling from Dave's thick fingers.

"Where'd that come from?"

"Filed." He nodded his head toward the open drawer of the little cabinet.

"Humph, I'll have to ask the other foremen about that."

Before being brought to Garden Grove, the trailer had been at another jobsite with a different foreman.

Picturing any of the other foremen wearing the delicate gold chain made Stanley want to laugh. Well, except maybe Mark. He was kind of feminine in a way.

"Someone must have been messing around in here."

Both men smiled, lewd comments coming to mind that did not need to be said.

Wives do not mess around in dirty little construction trailers. Girlfriends did that, and usually only the paid ones. But those kinds of girlfriends were not the kind you would expect to own a gold necklace.

Dave dropped the chain on the corner of the little table that acted as a small desk.

He was just about to go back to sifting through the files when he noticed the edge of something poking out from beneath the files still in the drawer.

He pulled it out, turning it over in his hand, examining it.

"Found the rest of the necklace."

With a shrug, he dropped it on top of the chain.

Stanley glanced over at it. He didn't think much of it until that quick glance. Something about it piqued his interest.

He picked up the pendent and looked at it. It is in the shape of a name.

"Barb," he said. It doesn't really mean anything to him. But he is curious with that adolescent curiosity of knowing someone got some and some faceless woman named Barb was giving it out.

"Say, isn't that the name of the municipal engineer's wife?" Dave said, looking at the pendant in Stanley's hand with more interest now that the other man seemed interested in it. It just popped out without any thought. Neither man gave the comment any thought, at least not until later.

They both shrugged it off with a laugh and continued their task of sorting out the mess.

18 - Murdered Child

Old Rusty Plowshare stood at the edge of the woods not far from his property line.

His weather-lined face held the most incredible scowl. His age-faded eyes are squinted into tight puckered slits as angry looking as the tight line of his frowning mouth. His eyesight isn't so good these days and he has to squint to see most things.

Today he is trying to see clear across the field to where construction on the new housing development was once again put to a stop days ago.

"Serves 'em right", he muttered, thinking about the workers injured when the tractors' hydraulics gave out.

The old man doesn't know who was behind the sabotaged hydraulics. "If I did I'd shake his hand," he thought.

Unfortunately, it was only a temporary reprieve, again. The tractors had been repaired and the site is back in action.

Old man Plowshare is mad.

He is mad about the new houses.

He is mad about the outsiders moving into his town.

He is mad about the construction.

This is his land. This land had been in his family since the land was first settled generations ago. His family worked this land, hunted in the woods, and lived on this land.

Hunted. Yes, oh yes, they hunted. You don't hunt a small forest like this once was without learning every bit of it, every tree, every rabbit burrow, every stump and stick.

Kids made up stories about things that go bump in the nights, taking delight in scaring each other with stories of the woods. Stories of strange things happening in the woods were passed down through generations and laughed off as superstitious nonsense. Sometimes people get lost, even in a tiny woods like this once was, which never was much of a forest even before most of it was clear-cut for farming. And sometimes they're found. They are all trespassers; trespassing even without knowing what they're doing, that someone owns this land; or something does.

Then someone came in and bought out the land from under his feet and Rusty could have torn their guts out. The woods are not owned by a someone and no legal wrangling to steal claim to them can change that.

The rightful owner of those woods should not be disturbed.

He is mad too that the workers still haven't found his latest treasures he'd buried around the jobsite.

That first skull wasn't enough to shut down the site permanently, but he is sure these treasures will.

He might have laughed if he wasn't so angry right now.

Rusty turned to what is left of the old growth woods, searching them suspiciously.

He has that creepy feeling again, like he is being watched.

"Watch all you like," he muttered to the trees. "Watch all you like."

In the distance, the tractors came to a stop one by one.

Someone is shouting.

Rusty took note of where each of the distant fuzzy shapes of the tractors are.

A partially toothless smile cracked his age-lined face. It is a smile that would make small children cower behind their mothers.

He clapped his hands, squealing a croaked laugh.

Rusty Plowshare's walk is almost a jig as he turned away to start the shambling walk of an arthritically crippled old man home.

He had seen all he needed to see.

One of the workers leaned over in the cab of the Cat tractor he is operating, looking at the dirt he had just scraped up with the big bucket.

"Shit!"

He shut down the tractor, climbed out, and walked to the front to take a closer look.

It is the same young worker who had insisted the authorities be called when the skull was discovered.

There is no question in his mind this time as to what he should do.

The other workers had given him a pretty hard time about that first job shutdown after he insisted on doing what he thought was the right thing and reporting the skull discovery. And there has been one shutdown after another with the old lady's poisoned pastries and the vandalized equipment and accidents.

He himself had lost a lot of pay because of the shutdowns. You don't get paid for not working in this line of work. Another shutdown would probably get someone lynched, probably him this time.

But that isn't what is on his mind.

He reached out his hand, his fingers itching to touch what is there dirt covered and sitting partially buried in the clumps of mud like a rounded rock, to see if it is real.

He pulled his hand back quickly then reached out again and picked it up gingerly, not sure he wants to touch it. He turned it over, examining it.

It is another skull. This one is much smaller. It looks kind of human. Kind of human, but not completely. Deformed? He guessed it is the size that a small child's skull would be, a misshapen small child's skull, one who had suffered from some kind of head deformity. He thought it has to be human although doubt nagged at him.

It has a perfect little hole in the top of the skull, faint stress fractures crackling out from around the hole.

Unceremoniously dropping the skull back into the dirt-filled bucket, he turned and walked away, heading for the trailer where he knows the foreman, Stanley, is still busy sorting out the mess left behind by the vandals.

Dave is standing in the office too, making the small office feel smaller. He had come into the site office to see Stanley a few minutes before about something on the blueprints.

When the Cat operator got to the little office trailer, he opened the door without knocking.

Stanley looked up at the young man in the doorway and Dave turned towards him.

"I quit," the young man said abruptly.

Without another word, he stalked off, got into his truck, and drove away without looking back.

"What the-?" Stanley stared after the man in confusion. "What now?"

Dave just stared after him curiously.

Stanley and Dave left the little trailer together, watching the man's pickup drive off the jobsite.

"What was he doing before he came to the office?" Stanley asked.

"Working the Cat," Dave said, pointing at the now motionless tractor.

Stanley headed for the tractor, Dave following.

It didn't take long to discover why the man had suddenly quit.

Stanley stared at the rounded object dropped carelessly back on top of the dirt in the Cat's bucket.

The small skull stared back at him with its empty sockets, expressionless. He can see the perfect little hole and knows this baby was murdered. A chill sliced through him and he turned to look at the still untouched trees across the field.

He has no idea what prompted him to look that way.

He shrugged it off and looked at Dave.

Dave has a peculiar look on his face. He too is staring across the field at the trees.

Feeling Stanley's stare, Dave turned and looked at him, trying to act casual but feeling like he just got caught in something, although he has no idea what. He turned back to staring at the small skull.

Stanley turned away and walked through the jobsite yelling to the men.

"Shut it down!" he called. "Shut it down! Works done for today!"

One by one, the tractors ground to a stop, standing silent sentry over the ill-fated jobsite.

Stanley is heading back to the little trailer office when he spotted Willie Williams getting out of his truck in front of the trailer office.

"Damn," he muttered.

"To what do we owe the pleasure of this visit?" he asked, approaching the inspector.

Williams smiled a serpentine grin. "Just seeing how things are going," he said.

Stanley felt sick suddenly. Dealing with this man right now is the last thing he wants to do.

"Come inside," he said, letting Williams go into the trailer first.

He looked back, found Dave, and signaled to him to make the call. With a sinking feeling, Stanley joined the inspector inside the trailer. He wants to keep the inspector contained and away from the discovery on the jobsite. Williams will find out about it sooner or later, but Stanley would prefer it to be later.

An odd feeling filled the stomachs of the men gathered to look at the little skull. It is a bad feeling, a sickness of trying not to think about what might have happened to the owner of that skull and what that baby might have looked like with that misshapen skull.

Within moments, the call is made. The jobsite is shut down once again and the authorities are on their way.

News spread quickly about the murdered infant's skull.

One of the men turned red in the face, thinking about the bone he had just crushed and buried with his tractor so it would not be found and risk a shutdown if it too turned out to not be animal.

19 - Observer

I see you old man, watching the workers again.

What kind of trouble are you up to now?

I know you hate me and my kind. You hate them too, the newcomers who have not been here for generations.

What is going through your mind old man?

You look like you are waiting for something.

Ah, it looks like they found something. You look happy, downright giddy about it even.

Oh, what have you done? Just what are those old bones you planted?

Ah, yes, the child.

I know the child.

I know the child well.

What is your trick old man?

What are you trying to do, planting those old bones? The child?

20 - Negotiating the Bribe

Bruce Copeland sat across from the building inspector, watching the man study the page of handwritten notes on the table before him. The scrawl could have belonged to a doctor or lawyer, illegible to anyone else.

Willie Williams' face is skinny in a weasel way despite the wide girth of the rest of him. It matches his personality.

Copeland isn't a fool. He came to this meeting fully expecting to leave considerably lighter in the pocket.

Not all inspectors are on the take of course, but this one leaves no doubts that the wheels can be well greased where he is involved; and these wheels need a lot of greasing.

There is a problem with the plans for the Garden Grove job again.

This job is losing Copeland money with all the vandalism, accidents and other problems that have caused repeated shut downs of the jobsite. It just doesn't make any sense that such a straightforward job would have so many problems.

Copeland's problems are about to get a whole lot bigger.

The inspector's chair creaked as he shifted his weight. He is dragging this out, torturing the man sitting across from him who has so much riding on his decisions. He had just finished inspecting three of Copeland's jobs - Mansfield Manor, Riverbend, and Waterford. They all had the usual run of the mill problems, nothing an average amount of palm greasing couldn't fix.

Williams is about to break the news to Copeland about the Garden Grove project being shut down yet again and he is practically salivating with the reaction he knows he will get. The foreman, Stanley Rutthers, had tried to contact Copeland and couldn't reach him to tell him about the new discovery of human remains.

Williams knows this because he had just shown up to check things out at the Garden Grove site when the discovery was made.

He was there when the foreman was calling around trying to track down his boss.

Unfortunately Copeland's phone had fallen out of his pocket and down behind the seat of his truck without his knowledge. The lonely phone had sung its song and vibrated away all alone in the truck with no one to hear.

Williams is gloating to himself about the news he is about to share, knowing that it will mean a big supplementary payday for him to not keep the job shut down indefinitely this time after all the other problems. It doesn't matter that the discovery of a murdered infant's skull meant that decision might not be his to make. After he has his money Williams will just shrug it off and call it unforeseen circumstances. There are no returns on bribes.

And it isn't just the human remains that are at issue at this meeting. He had discovered more errors in the plans.

Serious errors.

The skull is just the icing on the cake.

But he will soften the builder up with the other jobs first, catch him off guard with the Garden Grove news. It will make the shock have a bigger impact.

They went over the list of problems on the other job sites, Williams making more out of them than reality, ceding on some points and pushing others. It is the usual game of cat and mouse negotiating how much of a bribe Copeland will need to give him.

When that list was resolved, Williams dug into the real meat of the meeting.

"I went down to the Garden Grove site to check things out," Williams said casually. He left it hanging, giving Copeland time to think and weigh out the possibilities with the unusually troublesome jobsite.

A chill went through Copeland the moment he heard the name Garden Grove. He waited. He knows Williams is playing games.

"Have you heard from your boys over at the jobsite?" Williams asked.

Judging by Copeland's relatively calm demeanor, Williams is pretty sure Copeland hadn't heard anything about the bones in the time it took him to drive from Garden Grove back to his office for their meeting. And under the circumstances, he decided not to say anything to the foreman about the errors he had discovered on the plans when he had stopped in at the jobsite. He saved that for the boss who is now sitting across from him.

"No, I haven't." Copeland immediately got an uneasy feeling. Something is up, something more than this weasel of a man fishing for a little extra palm greasing even though he was not supposed to be inspecting the Garden Grove project today. That wasn't supposed to happen for weeks, if they keep pushing the guys at the rate they have been to get caught up.

"Why?" Copeland asked

"Oh, well," Williams paused gleefully, trying not to show how pleased he is, "as I said, I stopped by the site to take a look around."

"And?"

"And the jobsite is shut down again."

It took a moment for it to register in Copeland's mind. His mind balked at the information. He really does not want to hear this. He wished he had something to settle his roiling gut. His stomach had suddenly soured.

Then his thoughts turned to the man who had just delivered this punch to his gut.

"That son of a bitch weasel," he thought.

He is mad.

He is sure the inspector is toying with him. If it is a joke, he thinks he might just kill the man. If it is not a joke that leaves two possibilities. One, something else has happened at that cursed job and some heads are going to roll. Or two, the inspector is squeezing him for more money using the fact the job has been such a mess of problems. In that case, he is pretty sure he will kill the man.

Copeland has had enough drama with Garden Grove.

"What did you shut it down for this time?"

A flash of fear suddenly crept through Williams at the hard expression on Copeland's face and his dangerously calm tone.

"It wasn't me." Williams put up placating hands, "I didn't shut it down."

Copeland just sat there, breathing, trying to control himself.

"They found some bones at the site."

"That's old news."

"No, these are new bones. They're old too I think, but, I mean they found more."

"There are lots of cow bones in the area."

"This wasn't a cow."

Copeland raised an eyebrow, waiting for the weasel of a man to spit out the rest.

"It was another human skull," Williams said with a tinge of fear. He is afraid Copeland is going to blow. For the first time since the thrill of seeing the site close down earlier that day, Williams is regretting his plan to use it against Copeland. Copeland calmly sitting across from him, eyes hard with barely controlled anger, is scaring the crap out of him.

Copeland groaned. This will shut them down for a few days, maybe more. He has a sinking feeling there is more to it.

"It was a child's skull," Williams dropped, even as he tried to tell himself to stop there. He can't. It is like a train wreck that you just can't stop. He almost blurted out the rest of what he had planned to say, but self-preservation won and he managed to cut the other words off before they escaped. He is itching to say more.

"Probably another settler," Copeland said, dismissing it.

"Let's hope so." Williams tone has an undercurrent of warning. He is trying to placate the man now, talking as if he is on Copeland's side and only telling him this in an effort to help him.

With that out of the way, and being something of a letdown for Williams who was hoping for more of a reaction from Copeland, but not the cold deadly anger he got, it is time to get down to the meat and potatoes of the meeting.

"I found some more problems with the Garden Grove plans," Williams said flatly. He feels deflated and on edge, afraid of Copeland. He kept eying him.

"Yours or ours?" Copeland asked.

Williams is instantly defensive over this. He is not a man to ever acknowledge his own mistakes and is quickly offended if anyone else ever suggests he could be fallible.

"They're your plans, not mine," he snapped out then cringed inwardly. Copeland is still burning mad across from him and he imagined he could feel the heat of that anger.

"So what is it this time? Drainage ditch not deep enough?" Copeland asked, his voice cold with the attempt to keep it under control.

The thinly veiled barb did not sit well with Williams. It is his job to plan out things like drainage on municipal owned land.

"Natural gas line in the way?" Copeland dug at him again.

Both men know there are no natural gas lines in this rural area; at least not the kind running underground servicing a residential area. The only natural gas lines that might run nearby are transport lines designed to move large volumes for consumption in larger communities somewhere else. Those would not typically run through a regularly ploughed farm field on the edge of a small but growing community.

It is more obvious sarcasm.

"Look," Williams eyed Copeland flatly, getting ruffled with his own anger. Angering him could cost Copeland more to get him to overlook anything. "This is serious. You have some serious problems here and I can't let the jobsite open again until they're fixed. Even then I might not open it again."

Copeland looked at him sourly.

"First of all, your surveys around the woods are all wrong," Williams started.

"Probably some locals moving the survey markers; wouldn't be the first time that happened." Copeland isn't fazed.

"All of them? And by this much? Usually they'd just yank them out if they weren't just messing around by a few feet."

Copeland just shrugged. It is taking everything he has to put on a calm front. Beneath it, he is fuming. His whole planning department is going to get fired when he gets back to the office.

"Your lot measurements are all wrong. Property frontage on the cul-de-sac isn't even wide enough for a narrow driveway on three of the lots. You don't allow the minimum required distance between the houses and the edge of the properties on most of your lots."

This isn't good. If this is true, that could mean the whole development has to go back to the drawing board. It isn't a simple matter of adding a few A's and B's to some lot numbers, a quick fix when you build a street from both ends only to find when they come together you ran out of lot numbers in the middle. The whole development might have to be re-planned from scratch. That could also mean having to tear out and redo all the work that has been done so far. His planning department isn't just going to get fired, they are going to get drawn and quartered.

"And your Northeastern properties are on land that isn't even included in the project. That's private land that wasn't bought up with the rest."

"This is getting old," Copeland thought. Before firing and possibly murdering his planning department, he is going to demand answers.

Just then, there is a knock at the door.

"Sir," a woman poked her head in apologetically. She is the municipal office clerk. "There's someone on the phone looking for Mr. Copeland, says it's urgent."

21 - Anc-Chor Project

Copeland found his phone when it started ringing the moment he got into his truck. Surprised it was not in his pocket, he first patted his jacket pockets as if he had to confirm it was not there. Digging behind his seat for the phone, he glanced at the number on the screen quickly without answering it.

It can wait.

He tore out of the parking spot and rushed down the road.

This is bad. This is very bad.

There has been an explosion at the Anc-Chor project.

Copeland drove recklessly in his urgency to get to the Anc-Chor site, his mind contemplating the job, putting off dealing with the emergency until he gets there.

The Anc-Chor project is controversial on a number of levels.

First, the facility is being built on one of the few diminishing natural grasslands remaining in the area. A unique mix, actually, of natural grassland and wetland that is being continuously pushed closer to extinction with the move over the last decades to make every square mile of land usable and put to economically beneficial use.

It was home to more than one species of flora and fauna on the endangered list, a fact that was overlooked in the reports as the result of some generous acts of bribery in the right places on the part of the investor.

Conservationists and wildlife groups were in an uproar over this from the start and some of them can get quite nasty. Just ask anyone who has come up against the guerrilla tactics of the planet saving organization Global Rescue and Planet Rehabilitation when some of their less restrained members are pushed to their limits and go rogue.

Then there were the groups of indigenous people fighting the development, claiming it had special significance to their people, held a special power, and demanding the land must remain untouched.

There was also some political fallout over the project with accusations of political pandering, improper campaign donations, and illegal backroom deals.

Heads rolled, a few powerful politicians toppled, and when all the finger wagging was done and the project was assured a swift death, it just went on as though nothing had happened.

At a loss for how they lost the fight, the conservationists and wildlife groups went back to their respective corners to lick their wounds and plot their next courses of action.

Copeland was one of the very few who knew that both the politicians and the businessman who secretly were really behind pushing the project through were the ones who triumphed while their relatively innocent rivals were framed and took the fall, losing political face. This also put him in an awkward spot.

One of these powerful men could decide at any time that he is too much of a risk to keep around. The construction world has been paved with its share of bodies throughout its history, as is the case in anything where massive amounts of money are tossed around.

The project itself brought with it its own controversies, all born of the very secrecy of the project and the Chornel Corporation.

The simple truth is that no one actually knows what the Chornel Corporation actually does or what the Anc-Chor project it is building is. The only thing anyone knows is that the Chornel Corporation and its CEO and apparent only member of the board and sole stockholder, Mr. Chornelhus, are very wealthy and powerful.

As with any time the unknown is faced by a group of people, rumors spread like wildfire.

Those rumors ranged from a secret military weapons facility creating superbugs being released into hospitals to test their potency before turning them on enemy countries, to a genetic think-tank experimenting on human babies and cloning powerful politicians and multi-billionaire corporate heads. There were even a few joke polls going around spamming email inboxes and social networking sites as to just how many copies of a few particular extremely wealthy or politically powerful individuals are really walking around.

Conspiracy theorists embraced the possibilities. It is the new Area 51 with labs for both alien autopsies and studying captured aircraft. That the building would be used for creating vaccines that would implant unsuspecting victims with trackers so the government would know their every move. Or the facility would use the new technologies in smart televisions and phones to spy on people in their own homes. It all depended on which conspiracy theorist faction they belonged to.

The reality may be much more mundane than anyone would want to believe, or more terrible.

Only Mr. Chornelhus could say for sure. Mr. Chornelhus, a multi-billionaire eccentric recluse, has been the center of many of the odd stories and rumors himself and the sole man behind the Chornel Corporation.

Only three people are allowed access to Mr. Chornelhus in person outside of his personal security team. One of those is his maid, and the others his secretary and personal assistant.

Grainy photos of faces reported to be Mr. Chornelhus would show up now and then in the gossip magazines, along with wild stories about alien visitors from another planet and strange impregnated creatures giving birth to his offspring.

Legitimate newspapers and magazines only offered the occasional suggestion of more plausible things he's rumored to be involved in.

For all of these reasons the Anc-Chor project was a hotbed of rallies, picketing, sabotage, and threats. Security on the project is heavy and present around the clock. Mr. Chornelhus not only has his own personal security team, but as with many large and powerful corporations, Chornel Corporation has its own paid for police unit for additional security.

Everyone involved in the Anc-Chor project is sworn to secrecy, kept from knowing anything about what anyone else is doing, and even occasionally forced to build blind without knowing how what they were building is supposed to fit into the building or work with other parts. All of these are the result of Mr.

Chornelhus's quirks and cause regular costly fixes when things do not work with the plans or fit together.

Workers also regularly quit the project over frustrations with the old man's strange demands or threats from opponents to the project against their safety and their families.

The sound of a siren caught Copeland's attention, snapping his thoughts away from the project.

He glanced into his rear-view mirror to see a police car with flashing lights reflected back at him.

"Damn!"

Getting pulled over isn't unusual for him. It happens a lot when he has a project that people aren't happy about, and he has two controversial projects on his plate, plus the strangely troublesome Garden Grove Meadows.

He snapped on his right turn signal to indicate his willingness to cooperate and started to brake.

A part of Bruce Copeland hoped the police cruiser would just blast by him, off to more important business. He doubted it though. He'd been pulled over too many times lately, and he knows darned well he was speeding in his rush to get back to the city.

The gravel on the shoulder of the road crunched as the two vehicles came to a stop at the side of the road.

Copeland waited impatiently while the officer just sat in his car behind him, probably running his plate.

The officer isn't. He knows exactly who he is pulling over and he does not like him. Bruce Copeland does not seem to care about traffic laws, racking up tickets and not paying them. It is not the tickets that annoy him; it is the attitude behind them. His dislike for the man makes him feel aggressive towards him. He is just making Copeland wait because he hates this detail and resents being put on it. He is biding his time until his transfer out and back into doing real police work.

Finally, the squad car door opened and he got out.

Copeland studied the cop in his side mirror.

The officer approached his car with the bullish gait of a bully with a badge.

Copeland groaned when he recognized the officer in his side mirror. This man had pulled him over more times than the rest of the cops combined. His glove box is bursting with tickets, most of them earned.

He rolled down his window and began reaching for his registration.

Copeland is surprised when the man got to his window, looked in at him with an odd look, and spoke words he was not expecting.

"Mr. Copeland, you need to follow me, sir."

22 - Superstitions and Suspicions

Professor Richard Mackin's office door burst open. He looked up from his laptop in surprise at the sudden intrusion to find his young assistant, one of his students, standing breathlessly in the doorway.

"Professor Mackin, you have to come see this!" she said breathlessly, her chest moving with her quick breaths. She had run all the way from the lab to the professor's office.

"What is it?" Professor Mackin asked.

"A skull," she said, her breath still coming fast from both her run and her excitement.

"Must be a pretty exciting skull," Mackin joked.

She nodded eagerly. "It is."

Mackin got up from his desk, walking around it to meet her at the door. She is young and easily excited, but this level of excitement is contagious and he could not help the curiosity it stirred in him.

"Let's go look at this skull."

He watched her lead the way, amused by her excitement.

"When was the last time you felt that excited over a find, old man?" he mused silently to himself.

Moments later Professor Richard Mackin found himself standing before the table in the lab where the small homo sapien-like skull rests on a softly padded platform.

The skull of an infant stared back at him with its empty sockets. The un-fused skull bones and holes where the fontanelles would have been, the soft spots that allow the skull to grow with the baby, gave evidence to the infant's young age. The perfectly round small hole in the skull gives a clear indication of how this baby had probably died.

Mackin is just as giddy now with excitement as his young assistant who is watching on, raptly waiting for his reaction.

He can't move at first, is afraid to breathe.

"This is just so incredible," he thought.

"Where did it come from?" he asked.

"It was found at some construction site."

He stepped closer, studying the skull.

"The coloration, it is old. It is remarkably preserved. Looks human, but not quite. The shape is all wrong. Pre-homo sapien? No, that is not right. The coloration, it is not that old."

"It's not some kind of monkey? Ape? Is it even human?" the assistant asked.

Mackin walked around it, studying it from each side.

"No, it's definitely human. Modern." He paused. "He, or she, was born deformed. I have never seen anything like it. What disease could cause deformity like this?"

"You've seen other skulls deformed from disease?"

"I've studied hereditary diseases through history, particularly those that cause curious deformities. The sufferers of these diseases have been thought through the ages to be anything from cursed or servants of demons to being blessed, having magical powers, or even a god. Many old myths are probably based on ordinary people deformed by disease.

I have never seen a disease that causes deformities like this."

He turned to her, excited.

"We have to date it. Find out how old it is. How many generations. A hundred years?"

"How old was the baby?" the assistant said quietly, staring sympathetically at the small skull, it's small round hole glaring back in evidence to the infant's murder.

"Is there more?" Mackin asked. "So young, the bones are softer, would degrade fast. We are lucky the skull is this well preserved. But if it is, maybe there is more of the skeleton to be found."

"This is all that was brought in."

Mackin looked at her, his eyes gleaming with excitement.

"We have to go to where it was found, look for more remains. If the skull is this deformed, imagine what the rest of the body might look like."

This sent a chill down her spine, just thinking of the horrible deformity this poor baby may have suffered.

"What are you going to do?" she asked.

"I'm going to talk to Director McPhearson about getting us on that job site to look for more remains."

"He's the head of paleontology and archeology, how is he going to get you on a job site?"

"It's old bones, who better?"

Samuel Watkins drove up the roughed in road of the Garden Grove jobsite and stopped just outside the trailer that serves as a jobsite office. He is the municipality's main engineer, who also sometimes fills in as inspector, and is consistently honest to the disappointment of many a contractor trying to pass off improperly done work.

He is here to discuss some of the problems with the Garden Grove plans with the foreman.

It would have been easier to meet in his own office where they could have laid out the plans spread across large tables, but the foreman is stuck here answering questions and keeping an eye on the jobsite while a team from the university carefully excavates the spot where the baby's skull was discovered. The skull had already been whisked away to be examined.

Samuel can see the workers from the university hunched over their little excavation area. It is a tedious painstaking job he would never want to do.

He got out of his truck, pulling out his always-present briefcase and rolled up blueprints to take with him.

Some of the archaeological people are wandering around the large construction site, taking notes and doing measurements. This piqued his interest and he stops halfway to the trailer to watch. He suspects that they are deciding where else they should start digging to look for more remains.

He spotted three other locations that they are staking out to excavate too. They look to be placed randomly to him.

He turned back to the trailer, mounted the few steps, and went in without knocking.

Stanley is sitting inside. He looked up to see who is coming in. He looks very tired and badly used.

"Hey."

"Hey."

The formalities of greeting out of the way, Samuel got to the point.

"OK, let's see what we can do to get some of these problems with the plans straightened out so when we're done here we can get your jobsite up and going again," Samuel said.

"The sooner they get done and we get back to work the better," Stanley muttered, indicating the people excavating outside. "They're kind of creeping me out."

Something about people choosing to spend their days digging around in the hopes of finding dead people bothered him.

"Why so many dig sites?" Samuel asked.

"Seems after finding a second skull they decided they have to do a more thorough search of the area for any more."

"Heard anything yet about the child's skull?"

"Yeah, but not much. It's old too, like the first one. Murdered obviously, probably because it was deformed." Stanley pointed at his own head. "Hole in the head."

"Native or settler this time?" Samuel asked.

"They're not sure yet. Seems the skull is shaped all wrong and it's got them confused. Sounds like they don't think it's native, but they just won't say for certain. Actually, it sounds like they're not even sure it's human, but say it's not primate either.

They suggested that if it is human it's likely that the family may have been massacred because of the child's deformity.

Sounds like a bunch of superstitious nonsense to me. The professor over there said either the child is native and they blamed the settlers for bringing a curse on them and murdered the family, or the family was killed for having a deformed child, the natives thinking the child was cursed or a monster. Apparently, there have been stories handed down about natives in the area murdering settlers over deformed children they believed to be bad spirits.

Of course, it's all speculation. They think there's a good chance they'll find more remains." The explanation seemed to tire Stanley even more.

"Or the settlers killed their own, if the kid was that deformed?" Samuel suggested. "If it is native, it looks like you'll be out of work. They'll have to shut it down for good. Out of respect, if it's a burial site or something."

"Not me, but more than likely a lot of the guys on the crew will be out of work. This job will be done, probably shut down permanently," Stanley said.

"Either way, it sounds like it could be one hell of an old murder scene," Samuel said.

Samuel noticed the gold necklace sitting where it was left next to a coffee cup that looked like it had been sitting there for a very long time, its cold contents pale, the cream separating from the coffee, and very uninviting.

He stared at it, recognizing the scrolled word pendant.

Barb.

The necklace he gave his wife as a gift years ago.

Stanley noticed Samuel staring at the necklace.

"Found it in the trailer," Stanley said. "Figure someone was using the trailer to mess around."

He looked at Samuel.

"Say, Barb, isn't that your wife's name?"

He didn't really mean anything by it. He is just pointing out what they both are thinking, and that it is a funny coincidence.

Samuel didn't smile.

"Actually," Samuel said slowly, "can I see it?"

Stanley reached for the necklace and handed it over.

Samuel looked it over although it really isn't necessary. He knew the moment he'd seen it beside the cup that it is his wife's necklace.

"That is my wife's necklace, he said."

The possibilities hung in the air between them. Stanley wished he hadn't made that crack about someone messing around.

Samuel would not have been using the trailer for a secret meeting with his wife, or with any other woman.

"It must have caught on me and then fallen off when I was here the other day," Samuel said, looking troubled despite trying not to show that finding the necklace there bothered him.

"Must have," Stanley agreed, helping him save face.

It is an easy out for an awkward moment for both men.

Stanley didn't think Samuel's wife would have been in the office for a clandestine affair with one of the guys from the job, but it wouldn't be the first time something like that had happened. He cannot deny the possibility. Of course, it is also possible that what Sam said is true.

Samuel isn't thinking about the possibility of his wife's infidelity. He is thinking about how he remembers feeling the necklace snag on him when he was saying goodbye to his wife before leaving the house. It hadn't even occurred to him at that time that it could have broken and stuck to him. Now he is thinking about the possibility it could have been there, trapped in his clothes, and fallen off him during his late night clandestine visit to the little trailer. He wasn't there messing around in the capacity Stanley had implied.

As Samuel was pocketing the gold necklace, Stanley's thoughts turned to the two housewives charged with doing some of the vandalism to the jobsite.

He thought about the strange meticulousness of the mess done to the inside of the trailer and glanced at the small window. You would have to be smaller to fit through there. Not the size of the average man.

Samuel's wife is skinny.

The same thing occurred to Samuel but he put it out of his mind. Surely, his wife wouldn't be involved in something so immature. He pushed the thought away, deciding it is certain the necklace had fallen from him.

Then the thought occurred to Stanley. "How'd the necklace get in the filing drawer? Had it been caught on Samuel and fallen off like he said? It would not have gotten in the drawer, unless... What would he have been doing in the filing drawer? He has had no reason to be in there. Nah, it's probably nothing." But his mind isn't going to dismiss the thoughts so easily.

Neither man shared their thoughts on how the necklace got there as they worked together on the messed up plans.

23 - Strange Meeting

Copeland is surprised the police officer didn't give him a ticket, and even more surprised to be told to follow the cruiser. That's the sort of thing that only happened in movies.

When the police officer who pulled him over instructed Copeland to follow him, he thought it must have been a pretty serious explosion at the Anc-Chor project if they sent a police escort to bring him there.

His whole body numbed and his stomach filled like a pit of cold dread. He was on the precipice of breaking out in a cold sweat.

He put the car into gear woodenly as the officer got into his car. It feels like the world is racing past, staring at him as he followed the cruiser.

The next thought came only fleetingly.

"Wonder why he isn't using the flashing lights or anything." Copeland dismissed it as quickly as it came. It doesn't seem important compared to the gravity of the situation they are headed towards.

Copeland is right about the severity of the explosion, but he is wrong about the escort.

It does not take him long to figure out that they are not going to the location of the Anc-Chor project. In fact, they are not heading towards the city at all.

When the squad car turned and headed out away from town in the wrong direction for the city or anything else of consequence, Copeland had an urge to flee. Instead, he grudgingly continued to follow.

"Where the hell is he taking me?"

He wished he had some way to contact the officer and tell him they are going the wrong way, to ask him where they are going. Copeland tried flashing his headlights at the car to get the officer's attention.

Either he didn't notice or he is ignoring Copeland's attempt to signal him.

Copeland tried the horn, but got the same lack of response.

"Damn! Where are you taking me?" he muttered.

He wondered what would happen if he stopped following, if he just turned around and headed back the other way. He doesn't have time for games. He has to get to the Anc-Chor site.

The urge to run grew stronger when the cruiser turned down a dirt road.

It is the old abandoned Stone Farm. This place doesn't have a bad mojo, it is bad mojo. It is something of an urban legend, or better described in this case as a rural legend. No one ever comes here. The old Stone place would likely sit forever on the books as a property without an owner. No one in his or her right mind would buy it.

The cruiser ground to a stop followed by Copeland's truck in front of the dilapidated buildings that were once the Stone Farm.

Both men got out of their vehicles and slowly approached each other.

Copeland half expected the cop to pull his gun out and execute him on the spot, a hired hit, probably hired by someone against the Anc-Chor project.

"This way." The officer motioned Copeland to follow him. He hates this detail, playing security to a wealthy corporate CEO, and resents not being able to do real police work. The officers are being regularly cycled in and out of this special security unit at the insistence of the corporation paying for them, the Chornel Corporation. It seems they want to avoid any familiarity with the people providing arms-length security.

Their shoes kicked up a cloud of dry dust that followed them as they walked to the decrepit old barn.

Looking up at it, Copeland is amazed it is still standing. It has a decidedly strong lean to the lee of the wind. He is a little afraid to go inside, and not just because he is expecting a bullet in the head the moment he steps through that wobbly doorframe into the darkness within.

"Jeez, is this thing going to come down on top of us?" he wants to ask.

The police officer walked into the building without hesitation, confident.

Copeland ducked involuntarily as he entered the structure, not even realizing at first that he is ducking.

It took a moment for his eyes to adjust to the shadowy interior.

"Mr. Chornelhus!" he exclaimed in wide-eyed shock. This is the last thing Copeland expected.

"Hello Mr. Copeland." Chornelhus did not offer his hand to shake hands. He has an aversion to being touched.

Copeland just gawked. For once, he is at a loss for words. The man is dressed as always in an impeccable and obviously very expensive tailored suit. His face is as clean-shaven as if he had just done it, and his more white than grey hair is trimmed and combed perfectly. His face shows his age despite his meticulous grooming and well-maintained healthy lifestyle verging on obsession. Although Copeland doesn't know how old Mr. Chornelhus is, he would guess he is easily in his seventies, possibly even in his early eighties.

"You look surprised Mr. Copeland. But of course you are."

"But, the explosion-."

"Yes, yes, Mr. Copeland. That's why I had you brought here. I need to talk to you, but under the circumstances I couldn't possibly risk showing up anywhere I might be expected to show up at. Now could I?"

Copeland glanced at the officer, now wondering if he is tasked in an official capacity with protecting the man behind the project. It seems strange that Chornelhus is there without his always present private bodyguards.

"Um, yes, I mean no, Mr. Chornelhus," Copeland stumbled out the words.

"The explosion was very unfortunate," Chornelhus said.

"Yes it was."

"But do you understand what this means? Do you have any idea why someone blew up my property or who?"

"Uh, no Mr. Chornelhus sir," Copeland said.

His mind feels like it is running at breakneck speed. "Is he asking me because he thinks I might know, or because he plans to tell me?" he wondered. His dealings with the reclusive businessman since this project started had shown Copeland that there was always more to the man and his intentions than he let on.

Copeland glanced at the officer who stood passively by as though completely unaware of the presence of the two other men or the conversation.

"Well, the way I see it there has to be one of two things happening here," Chornelhus continued.

Chornelhus is surprisingly calm for a man who just had a very large investment blow up.

Copeland just waited. It doesn't do anyone any good to interrupt a man like Chornelhus.

"There's a lot of people who don't like our little project; a lot of people who don't like me too. But judging on some of the other jobs you've done in the past, some of your competitors, and the problems you've had on the Garden Grove job, I'd say there's probably a lot of people that don't like you either Mr. Copeland."

"I-uh," Bruce started.

Chornelhus didn't give Copeland a chance to talk.

"Yes, Mr. Copeland, I know all about the Garden Grove job, and for that matter about every job you've ever done."

Copeland stared at him, digesting this.

"It wouldn't do for a man like me to do business without fully investigating the background, and foreground for that matter, of everyone I do business with. There's just too much conspiracy in the world if you ask me."

Chornelhus waited now for Copeland to speak.

"Ok, so what's your theory on the explosion?" Bruce asked after a moment's hesitation to realize the other man was letting him speak now.

It is clear to Copeland that Chornelhus knows more about it than the investigators would ever learn no matter how deep they dig.

"Well, one possibility front and center in my mind is that someone is trying to make trouble for you Mr. Copeland. Considering your past, the threats over my project, and the strange problems you have been having on such a common project as the Garden Grove one; that seems the most likely. Doesn't it?"

Copeland thought about this. He doesn't have to think hard. He had already considered that possibility himself concerning the problems at the Garden Grove site before the explosion at the Anc-Chor project happened.

"It's a possibility," Copeland said. "It seems even more likely that someone is following through on their threats against your project, assuming the Anc-Chor explosion wasn't an accident."

Copeland was not being defensive or deflecting the blame when he said this. It was simply stating facts they both know, weighing the possibilities.

He looked at Chornelhus, curious.

"Why do you think it's more likely someone targeting me than the project?"

"It's no accident I can assure you," Mr. Chornelhus said with a wry smile. He dropped the smile and continued.

"Mr. Lezkowitz is your biggest competitor isn't he? In fact, I'd say it's pretty safe to say that he's your arch rival, your enemy even."

"Well, I wouldn't go so far as to call him my enemy," Bruce said.

Actually, Bruce Copeland would go so far as to call Lezkowitz exactly that. But it is bad business to start throwing the "e" word around.

"Well Mr. Lezkowitz certainly made his thoughts on the subject clear when you won my project. In fact, he was quite frighteningly volatile about it from what I understand," Chornelhus said.

"I heard he didn't take it too well," Bruce admitted.

That is actually an understatement. Lezkowitz had screamed and thrown a chair at the wall, embedding three of the legs into the drywall. He immediately fired any employee unfortunate enough to step within his sights, and then telephoned Copeland to spew an unintelligible barrage of loud angry sounds that gave the impression of vulgar insults and violent threats. While Copeland only had the personal experience of the disturbing phone call, he had heard all about the rest not long after when a few of the fired employees came to him looking for a job.

Nobody seemed to know what happened after that, before Lezkowitz had enough time to calm down.

It would not surprise Copeland at all if he were to learn that Lezkowitz was behind all the vandalism at the Garden Grove job. In fact, he is strongly suspicious of it, but he cannot find any proof he was behind either the tractor damage or the altered blueprints. Although, for the life of him he cannot figure out how the man could have managed to swap out the blueprints. Only his own staff and the inspectors had access to those. And for Lezkowitz to get one of his guys to forge the blueprints, well that would be career suicide for the engineer involved. He could not wrap his head around anyone being willing.

What could possibly be worth risking your career and jail for?

He had even set up security cameras at the Garden Grove site after the last act of vandalism that caused so many injuries when the tractors' brakes and hydraulics failed. It was done without anyone knowing about them. Even his foreman Stanley Rutthers does not know about the cameras.

Copeland was convinced he would find either Lezkowitz himself caught on video or one of his employees.

Strange, not a single camera has so far been able to catch any of the mysterious vandals.

Some of the cameras caught nothing but the workers going about their jobs, and an inordinate amount of time spent scratching various body parts he really did not want to watch being scratched. He caught a glimpse of an old man walking around the jobsite one night, but that was it.

One camera filmed a deer that seemed to notice the equipment and grew curious about it. Apparently, the animal did not like being filmed because it snorted snot on the lens and then backed up a step and broke the camera with its antlers.

Two cameras quit working. Copeland could not figure out why, and has not been able to get them working again.

Apparently, the vandals have taken a step back for a while after the workers were injured in the last attack.

"You might be interested to know;" Chornelhus said. He seems almost amused. "That Mr. Lezkowitz was seen at my property shortly before the explosion. No one seemed to know what business he had there."

"Did you tell the police?" Bruce asked.

"No need."

Chornelhus seems too confident. It makes Copeland's stomach edge towards turning sour.

"If they don't figure it out for themselves the man will be taken care of," Chornelhus said.

Copeland does not want to hear that. He hates Lezkowitz, but he does not want this. Besides that, not only does it make him an accessory to anything that might happen to the man, it makes him someone that might one day need to be taken care of.

Is this man a businessman or a mobster? Copeland wondered. He dismissed the question as irrelevant. When you have the money Chornelhus does, the lines between the two blur.

"Of course another possibility that is very likely is that one of our many mutual enemies of my project decided to take action into their own hands," Chornelhus said.

Copeland had to think about this for a minute, to figure out just what it was that Chornelhus is saying.

"You mean..."

"Yes Mr. Copeland," Chornelhus elaborated, "as I said, the explosion was no accident. Someone against our little project very possibly has decided to make good on their threats."

Copeland considered this. A moment ago Chornelhus seemed to be trying to shift his suspicions onto Lezkowitz, intentionally ignoring his suggestion the attack was directed against the Anc-Chor project because the attacker was against it. If it wasn't for Lezkowitz's enmity and all the vandalism on the other site, he wouldn't have thought anything other than this possibility.

So, they had two strong cases to consider. Which is right? Who was behind the explosion at the Anc-Chor project, and could it be linked to Garden Grove?

"Of course," Chornelhus added, interrupting Copeland's thoughts. "It could also just be that someone is trying to kill me."

He seemed too casual about the suggestion.

Copeland does not know what to say about this. He does not believe this suggestion for even a second. But it does not really surprise him that someone might want the man dead. After all, Chornelhus is a very wealthy man, and great wealth comes with great power, risks and the possibility of powerful enemies.

Blowing up the project to do it makes no sense at all.

For that to be the case, they would have to have reason to believe Chornelhus would be on site during the explosion. Unless they planned to take him down when he showed up afterwards to survey the damage as most men would.

"They underestimated him," Copeland thought, "Chornelhus is not like most men."

From what he knows of the recluse, Chornelhus would not have been found at the jobsite on any day, not during construction or even to witness the aftermath of the explosion. He is still finding it hard to believe the man had left the sanctuary of his life enclosed behind expensive walls, luxury, and security guards to come to an old abandoned farm to meet with him. The wealthy man has people to do these things for him.

"Well, off you go," Chornelhus dismissed him. "You should be getting along to see just what happened at my property."

And with dismissing him, Chornelhus promptly ignored Copeland.

A little confused and hesitant because he thinks he should say something but doesn't know what and knows he has been summarily dismissed, Copeland turned and left the barn.

The police officer watched from the doorway as Copeland got in his truck and drove away.

"Hopefully I'll make it to the Anc-Chor job without any more strange meetings," Copeland said to himself.

24 - Assessing the Damage

Bruce Copeland arrived at the Anc-Chor jobsite to find a sea of probing flashing lights.

He could see the heavy smoke billowing into the air long before he got there.

The place is full of fire trucks and police cruisers. Most of the ambulances had long gone, rushing victims off to the hospital. A few remained, waiting on standby.

Sawhorse construction barricades had been moved and strung with police tape, cordoning off the area. Police officers and fire crews mill about, either waiting to be needed or securing the scene and watching for anyone suspicious looking.

Copeland wondered what they are waiting for. The fire still raged furiously in the buildings under construction.

Other crews of firemen are battling the fire with powerful high-pressure hoses, adding white billowing steam to the black smoke, the two mixing into a roiling grey cloud rising over the intense heat.

There is a lot of rubble littering the ground.

The explosion was a serious one. The blast had caused extensive damage to the site and the partially built buildings. It is easy to tell where the explosion originated, that building had been torn apart, shredded. Its remains boil with the raging fire. Smoke and steam billowing, the starving flames battle against the powerful driving force of the firemen's water hoses.

There were a lot of serious injuries in this powerful blast, men were killed immediately and some were taken away writhing in pain to die later from their injuries. Still more would survive their injuries. Some, perhaps, permanently disfigured or crippled.

Copeland wavered on his feet, looking at the destruction. He estimates the damage runs into the millions, how many depending on how much damage the structures surrounding the main focal point of the blast had suffered.

He looks unusually haggard, like a man who had just been to Hell and back again.

Copeland feels sick at the carnage around him, knowing that the worst of it, the injured men, some charred beyond recognition, had been cleared away before he arrived.

He is not the best boss to work for. In fact, many of the men who work for him despised him. He is gruff and abrupt with most people. Copeland is not a people person.

But despite his shortcomings as a person and a boss, Copeland feels responsible for the injuries on his jobs. The worse the injuries, the more responsible he feels.

It does not matter that this was clearly not a workplace accident.

Bruce Copeland barely arrived on the scene when the detectives that were there looking for witnesses found him.

It will be a long night at the police station for Copeland, giving statements and going over endless lists of who might have something against him personally, his company, the Anc-Chor project, and to the best of his knowledge Mr. Chornelhus.

That same night three children sneak out of the house. The oldest, a boy named Kevin, leads his sister and her friend who were having a sleepover on this daring adventure.

The girls giggle nervously as they follow him to the door. Their dog starts barking, dancing with excitement; sure they were taking him on a walk.

"Shhh Hatley," Kevin hissed at the dog.

Hatley is the name his sister came up with for the dog and he hates it. Dumbest name ever in his book, just like his sister. He still resents that their parents let her name the dog instead of him.

Kevin has a great prank to play on her. He is going to leave his sister and her friend alone in the woods.

He knows how scared of the woods she is. It is not like it is big or far away. It is really just some trees and bushes between the houses and fields that everyone calls 'the woods'. They would find their way out in minutes and be back home so it never occurred to him there could be any danger in it.

The dog's tongue lolled out dumbly and he wagged his tail expectantly.

"Fine," Kevin grumbled, "come on but be quiet." He opened the door.

Hatley charged out the door ahead of them on cue, happily running around sniffing the ground.

"Where are we going?" his sister whispered.

Kevin turned to the girls with a superior look. "The woods."

The girls exchanged nervous looks.

"I don't like the woods at night," his sister's friend said. "Maybe we shouldn't."

"Come on chicken," Kevin teased and the girls followed him reluctantly.

The dog raced back and forth, sniffing at everything and lifting his leg to piddle on half of what he sniffed, ensuring every dog who comes after will know he was there.

When they reached the woods, the dog crowded close to them, almost tripping the kids. He looked at the woods with a worried look, head down and tail tucked low, and whimpered.

"What, are you chicken too?" Kevin asked the dog with a mischievous grin. "Come on, it's just a bunch of trees and squirrels. You afraid zombie squirrels will eat your brains?" He sneered at the dog.

Kevin swallowed and eyed the woods warily as they approached them. He walked into the woods a little too quickly, trying to hide his own fear behind false bravado. He cannot be the one to chicken out now after daring the girls to do it.

The girls followed reluctantly.

"I feel like someone is watching us," his sister whispered to her friend.

"Someone or something," the other girl whispered. "It gives me a cold shiver." She hugged herself nervously.

They reached a thinning of the trees that opened into a small clearing and the dog stopped. He turned and looked at them all with worried eyes, tail between his legs, and the hair on his shoulders and spine rising. He whimpered then let out a low warning growl and backed up a few paces. With a frightened yelp, he turned and bolted, leaving the kids behind.

The girls clung to each other, looking around the dark woods with fear-filled eyes.

The dog cried out from somewhere.

"There's something in the woods!" one of the girls screamed. They turned and ran, tripping over fallen branches and scraping knees in their panic. They did not look back.

The girls ran back to the safety of the girl's house, sobbing, and they charged in the door and slammed it behind them.

Woken by the noise, her parents stumbled groggily from their room.

"What's going on?" her dad asked.

"There's something in the woods," she sobbed, "something really bad and I think it ate Hatley."

Staring at the dirty disheveled girls, they realized pretty quickly what happened.

"What on earth were you doing out there?" her mother asked, rushing forward half chastising and half in need to comfort the frightened girls.

"Kevin, he said he had something really cool to show us," she sobbed.

"Where's your brother" her dad asked, his voice rising in anger. Whatever that boy was up to, and he knew it was probably to pull some mean prank on his sister; he is going to be in a lot of trouble.

The girls turned and pointed at the door they had just come in.

"In the woods," they said together, still shaking and their eyes big with fear.

While her mother took the girls and wrapped them in blankets and gave them hot chocolate to still their frightened shivers, her dad put on his jacket and shoes and went out to find her brother.

Morning dawned before her father finally returned exhausted from the search. Kevin stumbled behind, pale faced and shaken, his eyes empty with shock. The girls woke up groggily and rubbed their tired eyes, watching him with worried looks.

Exhausted from sitting up waiting most of the night, the kids' mother paled when she saw her son.

Kevin looked more than tired and in shock, with deep bruised looking circles under his eyes. He looked somehow less than he was before, thinner, almost a little shriveled even.

"What happened? What's wrong with him?"

"I don't know," her husband said, "he won't talk."

They never did find out what happened to Kevin in the woods.

25 - Samuel Watkins Under Suspicion

Stanley and Dave are both at the Garden Grove jobsite checking out how the search and excavation for human remains is going.

As the foreman, Stanley is there mostly to keep an eye on the jobsite and the people staking out selected areas to excavate in their search for more possible human remains.

Dave is there because he has nothing better to do. He was bored sitting at home.

Prior to the Anc-Chor explosion, with the Garden Grove site closed, and the Anc-Chor project running behind schedule because of the problems caused by Chornelhus's patchwork of information given to the builder, all the men off work at Garden Grove had been moved to the Anc-Chor job.

This was an unfortunate turn of events for the men who went happily to the new site, relieved to not be out of work and without pay for the next while.

Many of those men were there working at the Anc-Chor site when the explosion went off with a booming roar that could be heard miles away and shook the very foundations of the buildings for blocks around. Dave was one of the men who was supposed to go too, but he had opted out for now. He wanted nothing to do with that jobsite with all the threats that had been targeting it.

The survivors are wishing now that they had simply been sent home to wait and see if their jobsite would reopen soon or not.

At the Garden Grove site, Stanley and Dave are standing around watching the meticulous excavation of a single square foot of ground marked off with twine. It is only one of many similar sections in a larger square block of area that is marked off.

"Sam Watkins was in the trailer the other day helping me go over the plans that have been messed up again," Stanley said.

Dave nodded, expecting his foreman and friend to continue with news about what was wrong with the blueprints.

"He saw the necklace we found," Stanley said instead, "turns out it belongs to his wife."

"His wife? I bet that'll raise a few eyebrows," Dave said with a smirk.

"We both figured it fell off him when he was there before," Stanley said, "but you're right, it could get a few tongues wagging if anyone found out."

"So, we better keep quiet," Dave said. "Don't want to make the man who can get this jobsite back up and running again angry."

He looked at Stanley with an amused expression.

"Hey, I found some video cameras around the site. Looks like Copeland set up some surveillance," Dave said.

His face turned a little red with the memory of the mixed anger and embarrassment he had felt when he found them.

"The first one I found was already damaged and I decided to look around and see if there was any more. I was a little pissed about the boss spying on us and disconnected them." He looked a little sheepish.

Stanley looked at him, shaking his head.

"Hope you weren't caught on tape," he said. "Copeland will have your ass if he knows you disconnected them." He was surprised by the news of the cameras' existence. He is the foreman and should know about anything like site surveillance on his site. The fact Copeland did not even tell him tells him that Copeland does not trust anyone, including him.

"It's too bad I disconnected the cameras," Dave said. "I don't know how long they've been there, but Copeland will never give us access to the recordings now. If I hadn't, maybe we could have seen who the inspector's wife was there to mess around with."

He said it as a joke, neither man really believing the inspector's wife would be messing around in their trailer with anyone, her husband included. They both laughed.

Neither man really thought anything of it.

But then something clicked for Stanley.

He turned back to Dave, giving him a serious look.

"That necklace," he said, "we found it inside the filing cabinet drawer."

"Yeah, ok," Dave said. He still didn't think much of it.

"It was underneath the files," Stanley said, "after someone broke in and messed with them."

"Oh," Dave said, the word drawn out, as the revelation hit.

"He wouldn't have," Dave was incredulous.

"I wouldn't have thought it, but someone broke into the office and that necklace is the only clue." Stanley's expression is grim. "There's no way it could have gotten under those files in the drawer unless the person messing in there dropped it while digging in the drawer.

"Altering files like that doesn't sound like something Sam Watkins would do," Dave said.

"No, you're right. It doesn't sound like him. There's nothing he could possibly gain from it either." Then Stanley had another thought.

Dave spoke before he could fully put that thought together.

"Those housewives that did some vandalism; what if one of them was Sam's wife? What if she was the one who broke in and messed up the files? She could have lost the necklace herself," Dave said.

Stanley thought this over.

"I'm not so sure," he said. "I just can't see his wife being involved in something like that. I've met her and she just isn't the sort.

It had to be him that broke in and dropped the necklace. Either that or he snuck in when we were busy and it wasn't locked. He said he remembered feeling a tug and the necklace catching on his button or something. He said himself he was sure it fell off him.

It had to have fallen off him while he was digging through the filing drawer. He had to have been in there looking for something. I just can't see him messing with vandalizing the files the way they were. He had to have been in there too, maybe before the vandals broke in. But I can't figure why. What would he be looking for?"

Dave just stared at him for a moment while it sunk in.

"We should go to the police with this," he said at last.

"Not yet," Stanley said. "We should go talk to him first, confront him with this and see what he says. He's always been honest, not like Williams. I don't want to ruin his reputation if it turns out to be nothing. We'll see how he reacts then decide if we should go to the police with this."

"You're right," Dave said. "Let's go."

They went to their separate vehicles and drove away, headed for a showdown with Samuel Watkins.

Moments after they drove away an excited cry rang out across the construction site.

Another old bone had been discovered and it clearly was not animal.

26 - Confrontation

Stanley and Dave pulled up in front of Samuel Watkins house, parking their trucks on the street. They both sat in their vehicles for a moment, putting off the inevitable confrontation. Either way, right or wrong, this will cause trouble for them.

Stanley got out first, looking back at Dave where he sat in his truck behind him and waiting for him to follow.

Dave sighed and then got out; trying to take some comfort in the fact there are two of them against one man.

The street light pole by his truck has a missing dog poster. "Please help find Hatley," it said with a picture of a girl hugging a dog.

They went to the door, both feeling jittery with nerves, and listened to the melodic ring of the doorbell chime when Stanley pressed the button.

After what felt like an eternity, they finally heard footsteps approaching from within.

Samuel opened the door, surprised to see them.

"Stan, Dave," he said in greeting. Samuel sensed trouble from the men's grave expressions and the tension coming off them.

"What's up? Did something else happen at the jobsite?"

"No, nothing new," Stanley said, "but we do have to talk to you."

"Come on in," Samuel said, stepping back to let them in. He turned away briefly as he did so.

With a guarded look exchanged behind Samuel's back, Stanley and Dave entered his house, feeling like they are entering the dragon's cave.

"Beer?" Samuel asked, being sociable.

"No thanks," Stanley said. He would have liked one, but under the circumstances, it didn't feel right taking the man's hospitality.

"So what's up?"

"The necklace we found in the trailer," Stanley started, skirting around getting right to the point, "you're sure that's your wife's necklace?"

"No doubt about it," Samuel said. "I recognized it immediately. So did she when I showed it to her."

Samuel is wondering what he is getting at. They have already been over this. He has a bad feeling he knows what this is about.

"Well Sam," Stanley said, "it occurred to me that it's a little odd where we found the necklace."

"How's that?" Sam asked, immediately not liking the way this is going.

"We found it underneath files inside a filing drawer," Stanley said.

"So?" Sam is on the defensive now and he cannot stop the hot flush he feels burning his neck and face. There is no explanation he can give for the necklace being in a drawer in the construction office.

"It also happened to be right after someone broke in and messed around with the files."

The accusation hangs heavy in the air between them.

"Just what are you getting at?" Sam asked defensively, shifting his stance.

"I'll come to the point," Stanley said. "Your wife or you broke in and messed around with the files, or maybe was searching through them for something before someone else broke in and messed with them and vandalized the trailer; and I doubt it was your wife. You did it, didn't you? Were you looking for something? And did you mess around with the files too? What was that about?"

Samuel just stared at him in mute shock, his expression showing confusion, surprise, and anger. He had been in the little trailer office, but not to rifle through their files. His mind reeled at the question, how did the necklace get in the filing drawer?

"What are you talking about?" he demanded.

"I know it was you," Stanley said. "The necklace, there's no other explanation for it being inside the drawer and under the files. You said yourself you were sure it caught on you and fell off you."

Both men are staring each other down, their hearts beating faster with the tension of the moment.

"What were you doing Samuel?" Stanley asked. "What were you after?"

"I never messed with your files," Samuel said angrily. "Now get out of my house! Get out!"

Dave and Stanley backed towards the door, Dave more than happy to open it and give them an escape route the moment he was within reach.

"How many times have I been in that trailer?" Samuel asked. "How many times have I worked with you, always honest? How many times have I helped you over the years? I was there helping you, we were going over the blueprints, sorting out the problems with them, why they weren't matching."

"There has to be some reason for it being there," Stanley said. "Yeah, you've helped us out a lot and you've always been honest, and we've always been good. But I can't help how this looks for you. I just thought you should hear it from me first, you know, before we have to go to the police."

Stanley and Dave made their hasty retreat outside, heading for their vehicles, listening to the accusations thrown back at them from the open door; accusations of stabbing the man in the back with their accusation.

Stanley paused to look back, regretting coming here to confront Samuel. What if he is wrong? The guilt weighed heavily on him.

"I was only trying to help you Stanley!" Samuel called out the door after them before he slammed it closed, shutting out Stanley's shamed look.

Dave turned to Stanley as they walked back to their trucks.

"Do you still have the necklace?" he asked.

"I gave it back to him," Stanley said.

"So we don't have any proof it was him in the files," Dave said.

"No, we don't," Stanley said. He regrets now letting Samuel take that necklace. He messed up. It was the only proof that might have pointed to whoever had been into those files.

Barbara heard Samuel yelling downstairs and the door slamming. She paused in putting laundry away in their drawers to listen. What was he yelling? Would there be more?

She could hear him muttering down there, moving around, moving things too roughly, and decided to go downstairs to see what is going on.

She felt tense as she went down the stairs, wondering where he is down there and what is wrong.

She found Samuel in the kitchen. His face is a twisted mask of anger, but his eyes hold hurt and confusion.

He turned and stared at her when he heard her, not saying a word.

"Is he angry at me?" She wondered.

"What's wrong Sam?" she asked.

"What did you do?" he asked, his voice filled with cold anger.

"What do you mean?" She is taken aback. "Who were you yelling at? What's wrong?"

He took a menacing step towards her and she wanted to retreat, but she held her ground. Barb is afraid she knows what this is about.

"Stanley Rutthers was just here accusing me, ME, of breaking into the site trailer at the construction site here and messing around with the files!" They both know he is talking about the Garden Grove development.

He is breathing heavily with anger, staring her down, waiting for her to flinch.

"He found your necklace underneath files that had been messed up, inside a filing drawer."

Barb's eyes shifted as she thought.

"So that's where I lost it," she thought, carefully keeping that thought to herself. Her heart is beating fast. She feels panicky. She cannot lie to her husband.

"Y-you didn't tell me where you found it," she said, delaying the inevitable.

Sam just stared her down, the silence between them huge and serious.

"I know all about the vandalism the other women did," he said heavily. "I'd hoped you weren't involved. I didn't believe you would be, but now..." He let that thought hang open in the air, its meaning clear. How can he trust her now?

Barbara feels deflated. She can see it in his eyes. It is as if she had betrayed him and not some faceless construction company.

"I'm sorry. It just kind of happened. We were all doing stuff, and then we thought-," she trailed off.

"Thought what?" Samuel demanded.

"We thought it would be funny. We didn't take anything, I just messed around with the files a little and scattered some stuff around," Barbara said. Her voice is small. She feels small.

"Do you know what this looks like?" Samuel asked. "Do you know who they think did it? Me, that's who! Nobody thinks a couple of women could have gotten in there. They accused me of breaking in and messing with the files! Do you know what this means?"

Barbara cringed, knowing exactly what it means.

"DO you?"

She nodded, tears burning at her eyes.

"I'm going to lose my job!" Samuel started pacing angrily, his fists clenched and grinding his teeth. "My career!" He whirled on her. "I'll probably go to jail! All for some stupid childish prank!"

Barbara is sobbing now, covering her face with her hands.

"I'm sorry, I'm so sorry," she sobbed.

"You're sorry!" Samuel spat.

Samuel turned away and stormed out of the house, slamming the door so hard behind him that dishes rattled in the cupboards and decorations on the walls shook. He jumped in his truck, the engine roaring to life as he cranked the key too hard in the ignition, foot already pressing the gas and nearly flooding the engine, and screeched out of the driveway, tearing off down the road.

He has never been so angry.

Of all the stupid things she could have done, couldn't she have just left the trailer well enough alone?

His mind reeled and his eyes blurred with tears.

Her childish prank left behind proof implicating him in the break in.

He had broken into the trailer before the women went on their little vandalism spree, but he had been careful not to leave anything that might implicate him and no sign anyone had been there.

Now that they suspect him of messing around with the files, they might discover his real purpose for breaking in. They might discover what he has been doing.

He is going to jail. He is going to lose his job and his career that he had worked so hard for so many years for.

All for one stupid childish prank.

Samuel is so filled with blind rage he feels like he could kill Barbara.

He is so focused on his anger and the trouble she had caused that he almost missed the turn.

He is going too fast to make it anyway.

Samuel braked and turned the wheel, recklessly trying to take the turn even though he knows he is going too fast.

The truck rocked and the rear fishtailed. The truck overshot the turn and headed for the deep ditch.

Sam's eyes widened in fear, his muscles tensing, refusing to listen to his desperate command to react. Almost too late, he reacted, stomping on the brake and spinning the steering wheel, overcorrecting and losing control of the hurtling truck. It veered, the tires squealing as they tried to grip the pavement until they hit the loose gravel shoulder, crunching on the gravel and kicking up a cloud of dust with the stones and sandy fill. The tires lost traction on the gravel and the truck spun wildly out of control.

Samuel gripped the steering wheel, watching the world spin by, helpless to do anything about it.

27 - Copeland vs. Lezkowitz

Bruce Copeland feels more exhausted than he ever had. After a long grueling night of answering questions, he was finally allowed to go home. When he got there, he went straight to his bedroom and fell onto the bed, falling asleep still dressed.

His wife turned over, giving him an annoyed look, and rolled back away from him, shutting out his snores and going back to sleep. She has no idea where he has been or what he was doing and is angry with him for not coming home or even having the decency to phone. She does not suspect him of anything adulterous. She cannot picture any other woman wanting the gruff lout. But she does worry that he is going to work himself to death one of these days.

In the stress of the aftermath of the explosion, phoning home was the last thing on his mind.

When he finally woke up she was already up and gone out.

His eyes are red and sore from exhaustion. He rubbed them and stumbled to the bathroom where he tried splashing water in his eyes before stumbling to the kitchen for coffee.

He found a partial pot of now cold coffee. Grabbing a cup, he poured some in, noting the oily swirl of the coffee bean oil on top and put it in the microwave to warm. The coffee looked extra strong. It will taste dreadful, but hopefully will give him the extra kick he needs this morning.

He winced at the first sip of the too hot drink. It tastes as bad as he expected it to. The coffee maker had automatically shut off some time ago, long enough for the coffee in the pot be cold, but it still tasted burnt after a few hours sitting on the element.

He drank it anyway before showering and changing.

Grabbing another foul serving of coffee to go, he jumped in his truck and rushed down the street. He has a man to see.

Copeland raced through traffic, running a red light on the way and ignoring the screeching tires and blaring horn of the angry driver who narrowly avoided t-boning him.

Tearing into the parking lot of a single-story multi-tenant commercial building that stretched long down the block, he ground the truck to a stop in the gravel lot, stopping at an odd angle to the door and jumping out before the dust had even cleared.

The sign on the building said Lezkowitz & Sons Construction in heavy bold lettering. Other signs included an electrical contractor and custom shop that would build items you could not readily buy in all sizes like fireplace glass doors.

There are no sons in the business except for Vern Lezkowitz himself, being the only one of his father's three sons who was willing to come into his father's business. His father had desperately wanted all three to come into the business with him when he rebranded the company with the "& Sons" added to the name. Lezkowitz senior had passed on some years earlier from a heart attack, leaving Vern to take over the business than none of his brothers wanted to run.

Copeland grabbed the door handle in a fierce grip, yanking it open violently and storming inside.

He has a bone to pick.

The secretary jumped at the suddenness of the door being torn open, looking up in stunned surprise at the angry man barging in.

She recognized Bruce Copeland immediately and reached for the phone after the initial paralysis wore off. She doesn't get the chance to call her boss.

Copeland looked around the moment he entered the building then bellowed.

"LEZKOWITZ!"

Frightened, the secretary backed away into a corner as if it might offer some protection from the violent anger of the intruder.

"LEZKOWITZ!!!"

Vern Lezkowitz came out of his office with an annoyed look, ready to tear into whoever is yelling in his office.

He looked flustered the moment he saw Bruce Copeland's rage filled face. His first reaction is to duck back into his office and hide, but Copeland spotted him only seconds after he saw Copeland.

"Lezkowitz!" Copeland barked, following after the retreating man. "What were you doing skulking around the Anc-Chor site?"

He advanced threateningly on Lezkowitz.

Lezkowitz, a tall and wiry thin man, looked small before the shorter Copeland. He seemed to shrink into himself as Copeland advanced, making him look even smaller.

"I don't-," he began but Copeland cut him off.

"You know damn well what I'm talking about! You were seen! What were you doing there? What did you do?"

With nowhere to run, Lezkowitz has no choice but to go on the defensive.

He does that by lashing out in anger right back with the only thing he has to use against Copeland. He started on a rant about being on the verge of losing his business and blaming Copeland for it.

"I needed that Anc-Chor project and you stole it out from under my nose!" Lezkowitz shot back. "I'm on the verge of going under and that project alone could have saved my business, in just one job!" He railed on at Copeland.

He is getting himself worked up. Copeland isn't listening to the rest of his rant though; he is occupied with his thoughts.

"So, Lezkowitz is going under," Copeland thought. He had not known things were that bad for Lezkowitz. "Does he really think he can save his business in just one job? If he does, he's a bigger fool than I thought. It'll take more than one job to dig a business out of bankruptcy. It does give him a motive for sabotaging the Garden Grove site though. This explains why Lezkowitz might be desperate enough to do these things. But would he actually have gone so far as to blow up a site with workers on site?"

Copeland turned his attention back to Lezkowitz, who is still ranting on about Copeland stealing jobs and putting his business under. It is obvious he is cracking under the strain and has pretty much lost it. It is a cutthroat business of companies trying to under-bid each other to win contracts and not always easy to come in with the lowest bid without taking a loss on the job.

"You took the Lilydale job from me, the Waterford, Mansfield Manor, and Garden Grove too!" Lezkowitz ranted. I'm struggling to keep this business going and job after job you've scooped up from under my nose! You are a crooked man and can get business only by stealing it from others! You're putting me out of business on purpose!"

Copeland gave Lezkowitz a look filled with such a commanding 'I've had enough' tone that Lezkowitz almost simpered like a dog groveling to the alpha, visibly deflating as his words trailed off.

"I earned those jobs fair and square, just like any of the jobs you won and you know it," Copeland said in a low threatening voice.

"Now you are going to tell me what you were doing at the Anc-Chor site, and if you did cause that explosion I'll be coming after you! I've had it with your nonsense! You are also going to stop vandalizing the Garden Grove site, and stay out of my business altogether! In fact, it might be in your best interest right now to just close up shop and pack your bags!"

Lezkowitz paled. He had not heard about the Anc-Chor explosion. He had been hanging around the jobsite, but had left before the explosion.

"Explosion? I don't know anything about any explosion!"

"Bull! You were there, and moments later the whole damned place blows up! A lot of men were killed or seriously hurt! You murdered them!" Copeland is shaking with fury.

Lezkowitz shook his head in confusion and self-defense.

"Whole place? Murder? No, I had nothing to do with any explosion!"

"Then why were you there?"

Off guard, Lezkowitz just blurted it all out.

"I-I knew you are in trouble; the Garden Grove site getting shut down and trying to keep up on the other sites, and the Anc-Chor project being behind schedule. I just thought if I could hire a bunch of your guys away from you, cause a few more problems, you would lose the Anc-Chor project and I could take it over. A-at least, with all the problems at Garden Grove you might have to abandon it to concentrate on Anc-Chor and I could take over Garden Grove.

I went there to offer your guys jobs. I was going to maybe mess with the equipment a bit, but nothing to cause an explosion. I couldn't even do that because there were security guards. I couldn't even get close enough to talk to any of the guys."

Lezkowitz already regrets the words that had spilled out of his mouth. His face turned crimson. He does not know why he blurted all that out. He feels shaken and cornered.

Copeland stared at him hard. The underhanded sneakiness of what he said he was planning does make sense for the man, but causing a deadly explosion is going too far even for a man like Lezkowitz.

He jabbed a finger hard in Lezkowitz's chest, painful and threatening, punctuating his words with repeated jabs.

"You killed those men at Garden Grove." Copeland's voice is quiet and deadly.

Lezkowitz paled. He wanted to take a step back, but is frozen in place.

"You will stay away from my men and my jobsites! You'll stay the hell away from Chornelhus, and you'll stop vandalizing Garden Grove! Understand?"

Lezkowitz swallowed the lump in his throat with an audible noise, nodding. Confusion mixed with his fear.

"Garden Grove? I haven't had anything to do with any of that," he said. "I-I heard that was a bunch of women."

Lezkowitz's heart pounded in his chest. He was there at the Garden Grove site, planned to sabotage the tractors, but he did not. He had been interrupted and fled into the trees.

Then … then … he does not know. His mind is a blank in the moments after that. Did he go back and mess with the tractors? No, he does not think so. He was in the woods, confused, and then left. He went home.

"The petty stuff yeah, but not the latest." Copeland snarled. "Only a man who knows the tractors could have sabotaged them, and swapping out the blueprints. I don't know how you did it, but when I figure it out, when I can prove it, you'll be hearing from me."

"B-but I didn't do any of that, I swear," Lezkowitz simpered. He had heard rumors about the blueprints and now he knows it is true.

Copeland turned to go, stopping at the door and turning back to give one last warning shot.

"If I find out you did have anything to do with the Anc-Chor explosion..." the pause hangs heavily in the air between them, "I'll be coming for you."

He turned and left.

Lezkowitz is pale and trembling as he listened to the roar of the other man's truck starting and tearing out of the parking lot with a spray of gravel that pelted the front of his building, a large stone chipping the building's large front window with a loud thock as it struck the glass.

"Are you all right Mr. Lezkowitz?" his secretary asked anxiously, stepping forward timidly, afraid he might not be.

"No, I'm not alright," he said and stumbled into his office on stiff legs, closing the door behind him.

28 - Spying on Old Rusty Plowshare

Old Mrs. Crampchet is bent over in her garden picking out weeds and collecting the odd late ripening tomatoes and cucumbers when she looks up and sees the hunched figure of the old man in the distance. He is standing at the edge of the narrow strip of woods.

"Now what is that old coot up to?" she muttered as she straitened up, putting a hand up to shield her eyes from the sun so she can see him better.

Just watching Rusty Plowshare in the distance is agitating her.

He looks like he is just shuffling around watching the archeology students from the university searching for more old bones around the Garden Grove development across the field.

"Why are you so interested old man? I know you're up to no good; always have been."

After long moments of watching them, the old man finally turned and began to walk with some difficulty along the edge of the woods, heading back towards his home.

"You are the devil Rusty Plowshare," Crampchet muttered, following his movement, "and I'm going to find out what you are up to."

Keeping him in sight through the trees, Crampchet follows old man Plowshare, keeping up easily with her arthritic legs because of his slow elderly gait, both of them moving at more of a limping shuffle than a walk.

She ducked behind a tree a few times when the old man turned to look behind him suspiciously after thinking he heard a noise. She resumed following when he turned back and continued on.

When they reached his yard, Crampchet hid behind an old derelict truck rotting at the edge of Rusty's backyard, watching.

Rusty went into the old wooden shed. She can hear the clattering of stuff being moved around as he rummages for something. An old rusting metal bucket came flying out the open door, bouncing off the ground with a dull clang then rolled and finally came to rest.

She can hear him muttering, the voice irritated, although she cannot make out the words. She leaned forward, trying harder to listen. It doesn't help. She still cannot make out what he is saying.

He emerged from the shed and limp-walked to the old barn, a long out of productive use building that should have been torn down decades earlier. Now it is little more than an oversized shed that no longer fits with the building codes for the types of structures allowed on the rezoned land it sits on, outliving both its purpose and its lifespan.

"What are you looking for old coot?" she muttered as Rusty vanished into the dim interior.

There are more sounds of him rummaging through stuff, tossing it about and muttering. A few cats flee the disturbance inside.

Crampchet cannot help but look around at the yard, appalled at the mess and clutter all over the unkempt property. A rusted and bent-bladed push-powered grass cutter leans against an old rain barrel with half its boards missing, grass growing through the cutter's dull blades in defiance. An old tractor tire competes with a bottomless boat for space, the boat's wood bottom long ago crumbled in rot. A group of rusting wheel barrels huddle in conversation, their flat front tires fused together by the tall grass and weeds growing around them. And this is only a few of the things littering the yard. There are broken flowerpots and discarded boots, garden tools missing their blades and old wood crates like the ones glass soda pop bottles once were delivered in. Much of the litter strewn about is unrecognizable pieces of something larger. An old dresser sits in the middle of the yard, the front of one drawer hanging precariously from one corner, a long abandoned bird's nest spilling out from the drawer. The grass is long and dry, patched with bald spots, and probably hasn't been cut in years. Even the truck she is hiding behind is an eyesore, a small tree having forced its way up through the rotting floor, worming its way through the decomposing material and rusting springs of the seats, and is growing up through the driver's seat as if it is about to take the old truck for a joy ride at any moment.

Other old vehicles, engine parts, tires, and rotting seats are piled close by. She is pretty sure she heard the squeal of a rat coming from one of the piles, answered by another nearby.

There are also cats everywhere, of every color and description, as scraggly and unkempt as the yard; all feral and scrawny, jumping at every sound and motion.

Crampchet puckered her lips in disgust. She knew it is bad; it had been for some time, growing worse over the years after crazy old Rusty Plowshare had gone over the edge and become a hoarder. But she hadn't guessed it had gotten quite this bad.

She turned her attention back to the doorway of the barn and there is the old man standing frozen in the doorframe, glaring at her, his eyes beady and squinty, making the creases around them deeper.

Rusty Plowshare searched the old wooden shed, moving stuff around carelessly and even tossing an old bucket over his shoulder. Irritated at not finding what he is looking for, he moved on to the old barn where the search continued. He is getting more agitated at not finding it.

"Now where did I put it?" he muttered angrily, shoeing cats out of his way as he tossed things aside. Startled cats scattered and scurried about, scrabbling for purchase, one scrambling up the wall using its sharp nails to climb the rough wood planks to just hang there halfway up where it clung staring at him with a spiteful look.

Giving up on the barn, Rusty stepped into the doorway to move on to searching one of the other sheds and froze the moment he saw her.

Crampchet!

She is leaning out from where she is obviously hiding to spy on him behind the old Ford truck. Her age-lined face is twisted in a look of disgust, staring at his yard.

He narrowed his eyes, squinting to see her better, glaring angrily.

She turned to look at him as if feeling his glare, their eyes locked from across the yard.

"What the Sam hell is she doing here spying on me?" Rusty hissed.

He started forward, hobbling across the yard to confront the old woman.

Crampchet's eyes are locked with his, keeping her frozen in place until he moved and broke the connection. He is hobbling towards her. She looked around quickly, thinking she should get out of there fast and dismissing it. At her age, you do not move fast.

Instead, she waited.

"Let him come to me," she muttered. "He doesn't scare me."

"Old woman!" Rusty yelled as he approached. "What are you doing skulking around my property? Are you spying on me?"

"Oh just mind your own business you old coot," she countered.

He clapped his jaws at her, flabbergasted.

"Mind my own business? Mind my own business? You're the one on my property spying on me!"

She waved him off as if he were speaking nonsense.

"Oh just leave me alone old man," she snapped. "I'm weeding my garden!" She stooped down and grabbed at some long weeds growing in the long dry grass, yanking them harshly out of the ground.

Rusty stomped his foot in frustration.

"Your old tricks won't work on me," he said. "I know you're still sharp as a tack even if you can fool everyone else into thinking you've gone senile."

Crampchet dropped the pretense and gave him a sly look.

"And I know you're up to no good Rusty Plowshare. You were up to no good when you were a boy, and you were up to no good when you were a young man, and you are up to no good now."

"And you're no lady either," he growled. "Do you think I don't know you poisoned those men on purpose? Just what are you up to old woman?"

"Well I don't know what you're talking about Rusty Plowshare," she sniffed, giving him a disdainful look.

He stepped closer, leaning in too close. She can smell his breath and his old man smell.

"I know all about you Mrs. Crampchet," he whispered.

"Get off me old man!" she snapped, pushing him away.

"Get off my property and stop spying on me!" he spat back.

She gave him a suspicious look.

"Just what are you doing with those old bones you're burying over at the construction site? What are you up to Rusty Plowshare?"

"It's none of your business old woman!" He grabbed her, turning her around against her will and pushing her ahead as he walked, walking her away from his yard back towards her own.

"I know what you did then and I'll find out what you are up to now old man!" she yelled at him over her shoulder as she struggled to break free from his grasp.

He leaned in close, putting his mouth right to her ear.

"And I know what you did," he hissed before moving her along again.

He gave her a final shove.

"Go home and mind your own business woman," he muttered, turning around and doing his old man shuffle back, muttering and mumbling to himself.

She stared after him a moment then turned and started on her slow way back home.

"I'll find out what you're up to Rusty Plowshare," she muttered.

29 - Secrets and Evidence

After an exhaustive search of the Garden Grove Meadows housing development, with some more scattered bones found and no other artefacts to suggest it might be either an old village or burial location, it is decided the jobsite can open again.

The bones that have been found are in the process of being analyzed, having been packed carefully and taken back to Professor Mackin's lab in the archeology department of the university for tests. It is clear the human remains are very old and the disturbed ground proves that they had been buried only recently. Others were scattered animal bones that naturally occur and are covered up over time.

In the university lab, Professor Mackin, a man in his fifties wearing a lab coat and round wire-rimmed glasses, is studying bone shavings under a microscope, making thoughtful noises to himself.

He pulled that slide out and grabbed another, sliding it in place and studying it. Turning away, he jotted down notes and checked another slide, growing more excited. He took more samples from the bones, running them through various tests over the many hours that followed, setting some aside for his young assistant.

Mackin has lost all track of time and has no idea night has already passed into morning.

"Professor Mackin, have you been here all night?" his assistant asked, surprised when she walked in the door to find him already hard at work and looking disheveled and exhausted. She noted immediately he is moving with the nervous energy of someone running on too much caffeine, no sleep, and driven by an urgent excitement. She has seen him like this before.

He waved the question off.

"I've found some interesting things," he said. "We need to run more tests to confirm. Here, take these." He shoved a tray into her hands, indicating a machine. The tray has compartments with carefully labelled bone shavings. He doesn't need to explain. She knows what tests to run on the bones.

They both work late into that night running and rerunning tests on the bone samples until he is satisfied. Mackin sleeps for four hours in that time, snoring loudly with exhaustion, when his assistant insists he take a break and nap.

The next morning he is waiting outside the director of archaeology's office when he arrived at work.

"Professor Mackin, you look like hell," Director McPhearson said. "Did you even go home last night?"

"I have to talk to you," Mackin said urgently, "about the bones from that housing development."

McPhearson nodded, waving him into his office as he unlocked and opened the door. Following the professor in, he put his briefcase down and sat in his chair behind his desk.

"Okay, talk."

Makin was too excited to sit and paced the floor in front of his desk.

"After sorting out the cow bones and a few deer the rest are all human," Mackin said, "Caucasian, male and female, and different ages from infant to elderly."

"Okay," Director McPhearson said. "So what are we looking at? There's no record of any cemetery ever being there. Was it an old massacre site? That was the best theory being handed around."

Mackin shook his head.

"No, I don't think so. There were no artefacts, no arrowheads or anything else. The bones seemed to be left at random and just a few bones from any one body. No two bones from the same body were found close enough together to be natural either. I don't have any proof, but in the circumstances and the damage to one infant skull, I think they were all murdered," he said.

"And the ground was disturbed. The bones have all been planted there very recently. They also had other similarities. They were all related, although mostly distant relatives, and they all had a similar gene that probably caused the same deformation in them. The remains also shared certain markers that suggest a culture of inbreeding. Not as close as siblings or parent-child; more likely second and third cousins like many close-knit communities used to do when there was little movement of persons moving in or out of their community. There are some more isolated communities where it's still common."

Makin stopped pacing to stare at his boss.

"I think we have a very old series of murders on our hands."

McPhearson considered it then shrugged. "That's not unusual. I understand the area has a sordid past. A lot of settler families were butchered back in the day. There are even old stories of some native tribes believing certain deformities were a sign of evil spirits and they would murder entire settlements believing the white men brought the evil spirits on them. It didn't matter who had the deformity, white or native. Although, I have no doubt the white settlers killed their fair share of people, some the natives were likely blamed for."

"But these bones are unusual," Mackin said, his superior's lack of interest doing nothing to dampen his excitement.

"The soil layers were not untouched strata. The soil was disturbed. These bones were not there before construction in the area began. They were planted there very recently, maybe only days ago by my guess. This is not just a bunch of old murders; it's a mystery that is still in play today. Someone wanted those bones found."

"Whoever is behind planting the remains must be trying to shut down the project, though I couldn't guess why," McPhearson said. "I cannot see any other reason for choosing that particular area for the remains.

"I'm not sure there isn't more to it than that," Mackin said with a doubtful frown. "I've been researching the history of the area and I'm convinced that burying the remains at Garden Grove has nothing to do with objections to the housing development. I think something else is going on."

When the dust cleared Samuel Watkins just sat there for a while breathing heavily and taking in the fact that he is still alive.

The whole world seems to be tilted at an impossible angle, but it is really the truck that is tilted. It came to rest on the steep slope of ground leading to a sheer drop off.

He leaned forward cautiously, peering over the edge with a strained look. A small river tributary, more like an overgrown creek, meandered by below. Centuries of water erosion had cut it deep into the ground.

Sam had been so angry that he had not taken the time to put on his seatbelt when he left.

When the truck hit gravel and begun its uncontrolled spin, leaving Sam helpless to do anything but go along for the ride, the truck had tipped precariously, at one point on the verge of going into a full roll. At the speed he had been going it would not have rolled just once, or even twice. It would have been tossed across the ground like a child having a tantrum on a tiny toy truck, only with a much more devastating outcome. The truck could have been completely destroyed and him with it.

The near roll was the second time Sam was sure he was about to die in that short ride after losing control on the loose gravel.

Right before that, as he fought for control, the truck skidding, the strangled hold of the brakes doing nothing to slow it on the loose gravel as the tires lost all purchase; he was hurtling directly at a pole that would have connected with the truck in a bone jarring jolt that would have sent him flying through the windshield where he surely would be broken by the impact.

That was the first time Sam thought he was going to die.

Approaching that drop off with no way to stop was the third time. Apparently, luck was on his side in that brief moment when he thought he would die three times. The out of control truck finally came to a rest on the steep slope on the verge of slipping over the edge.

Sam ran a trembling hand through his hair, tears burning his eyes.

He rubbed them away.

Men don't cry and neither will he.

When he thought about Barbara this time his anger was deflated.

Stupid foolish Barb, her and her friends playing childish pranks, they don't know what they've done.

They did not know how they might be risking his career, and maybe even his freedom.

"If they find out it's me who altered and switched the blueprints," he moaned, "I'll be going to jail. We'll lose everything. My job, my career, our retirement, our savings, our house. Everything.

They won't understand I'm only doing this to help them."

Still shaking and unsure if the stalled truck would start, Samuel tried turning the key. The truck choked a little, but roared to life.

He fastened his seatbelt with shaking hands, put the truck in reverse, and began working his way out of the mess he is in. With luck the loose gravel will not send him sliding back down and beyond to the water below.

He has someone he has to go see.

Stanley Rutthers and Dave McCormack stopped for a few beers to calm their nerves. They both feel agitated after the confrontation with the municipal planner.

With time to think, their suspicions found new conviction.

"I just can't get my head around the idea Sam Watkins could be the one messing with the blueprints. I don't want to think Sam would do something like this," Stanley said. "Why would he? I can't even see what he could gain from it!"

Dave shook his head in confusion, agreeing.

"It doesn't seem like him," Dave said.

"But who else could have done it?" Stanley asked. "Who else could have had the access to all the offices the blueprints were switched at? Who else has the skills to redraw them? He has both. Anyone else would have to be working with more than one partner to do this. Samuel Watkins is the only one with both the ability and the access to make up the forged blueprints and switch them."

"It just doesn't make any sense. Why would he? What could he possibly get out of it? What if he's innocent?" Dave just could not get past his doubts. "We could ruin his career with this if we accuse him. Even after he's proven innocent, this will destroy him."

Stanley shook his head unhappily.

"I like Sam too. I don't want to see his career or his life ruined. Take away what a great guy he is and he is the only one that fits."

"We have to find out before we confront him again or go to the authorities," Stanley said. "We have to find evidence and figure out if Sam is guilty of altering the plans or not."

He swallowed the rest of his beer purposely as he got up.

"We'll start at the office. Copeland must have any files that managed to record from his surveillance system in his office. We will dig up letters and notes maybe that we can compare his handwriting to the printed lettering on the blueprints, anything connected to him that might suggest a reason he would do this.

Then we'll check the Garden Grove site again and other sites Sam was involved in."

"Let's go," he said, not waiting for Dave to gulp the last of his beer before walking away.

30 - Rumors and Confessions Over Coffee

The atmosphere in the room is uneasy despite the soothing aroma of freshly brewed coffee steaming up from the cups on the table.

The housewives of the coffee clutch are huddled around a table in a back corner of a mostly empty coffee shop. It is the odd day out when they meet there, during the business lull, for a chance to get out of their houses to someplace public that does not involve grocery shopping.

Their idle banter has toned down to a conspiratorial whisper as they all leaned in to hear their shared secrets.

"I was walking the dog," Pamela continued, "and I saw old Mrs. Crampchet and old Mr. Plowshare fighting at the back of his property." Her urgent tone expressed the strangeness of the event. "And it wasn't just some argument like usual, they were wrestling! They were actually locked in a physical fight!"

The other women smirked and giggled at the image of the two frail elderly people wrestling.

Mrs. Henderson levelled a knowing look at them all.

"Those two have a past that goes way back," she said. "My mother once told me she thought the two would have gotten married if Crampchet's father had not been so much against the then young Rusty Plowshare."

The women all gasped appropriately at this world shattering news. Mrs. Henderson leaned back importantly, enjoying being the center of their clique for a change.

"Plowshare and his family have always been a strange lot, surrounded by all kinds of unpleasant rumors and old wives' tales. Some, even, that his great great grandfather murdered another man, maybe even his wife too.

The story is that this man had tried to woo old Plowshare's great great grandmother before her family made her marry the Plowshare man. Plowshare thought his wife still had feelings for her beau. He was a very jealous man. There were rumors that he remained her lover after she married and was even the father of some her children. Plowshare believed the rumors about his wife and murdered her lover in a jealous rage. Some believe he murdered some of their children too, thinking they were the illegitimate children of his wife's lover, and later murdered her too after keeping her locked away a prisoner in her home for years bearing him more children.

It was believed the man's insanity was inherited by his surviving children and passed down through the generations.

Strange things had always seemed to follow that family.

When her father grew angry over her dating the young Rusty Plowshare, Crampchet instead ended up marrying Krandall Crampchet, who her parents thought was a more acceptable match. The pair never had children and, years later, he died in his sleep from unknown causes.

Some suggested Crampchet herself had poisoned her husband; others suspected Rusty Plowshare of foul play, while the authorities dismissed it as natural causes despite the thrill of the rumors."

She leaned back with a satisfied look, drinking in their shocked reactions.

Barbara Watkins looked around at the ladies at the table. They are already getting into sharing shocking stories and she really needs to get hers off her chest, so she decided to dive in.

"Two men came to my house and accused Sam of breaking into the Garden Grove trailer and messing with the files. They were pretty angry."

They turned to her with the usual murmurs of surprise and sympathy.

"Sam had my necklace. He said the men found it in the trailer and that he told them it must have fallen off of him; that he thought it snagged on his button. That's why they thought it was him."

"Are they charging him?" Libby asked, full of concern.

"But that was us, you!" Pamela gasped, leaning in close so no one beyond the table can overhear.

"He knows you did it, doesn't he?" Mrs. Henderson asked.

Barbara nodded, tears springing to her eyes.

"He was so mad," she said. "I've never seen him so mad. He left and he hasn't come back."

"Oh poor thing," Libby said.

"Don't poor thing her," Mrs. Henderson said, not unkindly. "It was her idea."

"But he left and didn't come back!" Pamela said in Barbara's defense.

"Of course he's mad," Mrs. Henderson said. "If they really think he did this he'll lose his job. He is the municipal planner. This could ruin his whole career."

Barbara looks even more haunted. She paled and feels sick suddenly.

"What's wrong?" Pamela asked, concerned.

"There's more," Barbara said. "Someone's messed around with the blueprints for the housing development. They made up new blueprints, changing them, and snuck in and switched them with the real ones at all the offices that had a copy. I heard him talking about it on the phone the other day. I didn't think anything of it at the time. I didn't know it was the plans for Garden Grove he was talking about.

If they think he broke in and messed with the files, they'll also think he's the one who changed the blueprints and planted them in the different offices. He won't just lose his job, he'll go to jail! But he's innocent, I know he is. Sam wouldn't do something like that."

Libby nodded.

"It definitely does make him look guilty since he does have the skills, knowledge, and access to all the offices because of his job," Pamela said.

Barbara has to think about this although she does not want to. Could he have done it? Is that why he was so angry, because he did swap the blueprints and might be caught because of her? It's not like him, but he has been acting odd lately. Something is going on with him. He's been more distant, preoccupied, and something has been obviously bothering him. Maybe he's innocent and just worried they'll think he did it. And he is the only one she knows of who could have done it.

"Do they suspect him yet?" Pamela asked.

"I don't know," Barbara said. "I think so. It didn't sound like they were going to the police yet and they only accused him of messing with the files. I think they're giving him a chance to show he didn't do it, but how will he? And what if they decide he swapped the blueprints too?"

"It definitely sounds like he'll be their first suspect. We will just have to find out for ourselves then who was switching the blueprints so Sam doesn't lose his job or go to jail," Pamela said.

They all looked at her. This is wrong. They are just a bunch of housewives. It is also exciting, an adventure.

"Do you know who besides your husband would have both the ability to draw a blueprint and access to all the offices with copies?" Mrs. Henderson asked.

Barbara shook her head tearfully. "No one that I know of. The inspector in his office, Willie Williams maybe, but nobody likes or trusts him and I don't think he has the skills to draw up whole new fake blueprints. Only someone they trust could have had the access to switch the plans without anyone noticing."

Mrs. Henderson nodded her head thoughtfully.

"We will start with making a list. We will make lists of everyone that might have been able to access each office, everyone who might be able to access the Garden Grove blueprints, everyone who might be able to make a blueprint, who we think might do something like that, and reasons someone might want to do that. Whoever is doing it may not be working alone. Someone could have made the blueprints and then someone else switched them."

This does not really make Barbara feel any better. What would have made things better would be if she could push away that nagging question. Could her husband have possibly had a part in the altered plans? She has a feeling she is missing something she should know. Maybe something she saw or heard but cannot remember. She wants to believe he is innocent, but something in her gut keeps nagging at her, making her wonder. Just how well do I really know Sam? Could he have done it? Would he? But why would he do something like that?

Barbara needs to find out, one way or the other.

31 - The Trouble with Samuel Watkins

Samuel Watkins sat at a table of questionable cleanliness in a booth in a dimly lit hole in the wall coffee shop. He has chosen one of the back booths towards the rear of the restaurant away from the windows and where the poor lighting seems to struggle even more to reach.

A steaming cup of coffee sits on the table in front of him, the oil of the coffee bean creating a mini oil slick on top of the dark liquid.

The waitress's buttocks wobble like gelatin beneath the skirt of her uniform as she waddles away after pouring his coffee.

He poured sugar into the too strong brew; it spilled into the cup from the open hole in the lid of the sugar jar like white sand, vanishing beneath the surface.

Samuel has his back to the rear of the restaurant, facing forward towards the door as if to watch for a companion to arrive and join him. From the back of the restaurant, high-backed booths lined the wall halfway to the door where they become small wooden tables placed too close together all the way to the other end beyond the door. He can see everyone in the small place, the stools attached to the floor along the counter, the old coffee maker sitting mutely on the counter with pots on the warmers. In the middle old pies have congealed on plates beneath glass, a cash register that is probably from the eighties waits to ring up people's orders, and the typical bell hangs over the door to jangle its annoying non-tune every time someone comes in or leaves. An opening like a large glassless window to the kitchen behind the long counter with bar stools allows the cook to pass orders across to the waitress.

"They probably feed more cockroaches and rats than diners," he thought.

He added creamer, sniffing the cream first, unsure it is safe to use. The liquid swirls as it hits the oil slick, the two swirling together as he pours. He stirred it with the spoon, half expecting the spoon to come out with the end dissolved off, and lay the utensil carefully on his napkin.

He took a sip doubtfully and grimaced. It tastes as bad as he expected it to.

Someone sits sipping their beverage in the booth behind Samuel, his or her back to him, hidden by the high backed booth. Only the occasional movement of the person's elbow as the cup is raised to sip, seen when one looks down the aisle, gives away their presence. The stiff fabric covering the elbow suggests a coat.

Samuel is talking to the unseen person at the table behind him without turning or otherwise giving any indication he is addressing them.

Noticing, the waitress gives him a look from across the restaurant, thinking he is entirely nuts sitting there talking to himself.

He tells the unseen person about the men from the Garden Grove site who visited his home, that they suspect him of sabotaging the site office files and his fear they might also suspect him of swapping the Garden Grove blueprints.

"My wife can take responsibility for her own mischief with the files, but if they go to the police with their suspicions that I'm the one who forged and switched the Garden Grove blueprints, I'll look guilty. I'm the only good suspect; maybe even the only one who has both the skills and access to all the offices. They won't have any reason to look anywhere else for a suspect," he said, his voice heavy with strain. "I could go to jail!"

Samuel sighed heavily, shaking his head dispiritedly.

"I can't continue like this. I just can't do it anymore. I can't risk it. I'll lose everything, my job, my career, my family, my home." It is more than a confession of guilt. It is a desperate plea for understanding, for absolution, like talking to the faceless man on the other side of a church confessional.

The person behind him just continues silently sipping their steaming beverage.

"I know why we're doing this, why it has to be done, but I just can't do it anymore. I'm out."

He paused as if he might get a reply, maybe even some justification for what he is doing. Samuel took another sip of his vile coffee and grimaced, wondering why he is even drinking it and wondering how they managed to ruin coffee.

He hung his head and let another sigh escape.

"I know it's important. I know that no one else can help them, help us all. God help those fools, Copeland and his men. They don't know what they're doing."

He pushed his coffee away.

"All right, I'll stick around, but just for now. I just wish I knew what I'm doing will help."

He got up with the weight of all the stress and fear weighing down his shoulders, tossed some money on the table to cover his coffee and a tip, and left.

The unseen person in the booth behind him never said a word; they just went on silently sipping their beverage.

Lezkowitz sat in his old beat up truck across from the Anc-Chor site, staring at the still smoking ruins. There are still hot spots beneath the ruined buildings that would continue to smolder until they either ran out of fuel to burn or are uncovered and extinguished. With luck, they would not flare up again into bright flames.

He watched the large equipment digging in with its teeth, growling and tearing at the rubble, scooping up debris and depositing it in the back of waiting dump trucks.

On the ground, men in safety suits and hard hats are conducting a more careful excavation under the direction and watchful eyes of the arson investigator, mindful of the possibility they might find the buried remains of some of the victims still beneath the rubble. Fire crews poke and search for those hot spots that could flare up again into a fire.

Lezkowitz smokes a cigarette as he watches, the orange glow flaring as he sucks on the cigarette and the smoke pooling in a cloud inside the truck cab as he exhales.

His expression is unreadable as he sits, just watching.

It is late evening when Stanley Rutthers and Dave McCormack let themselves into the Copeland and Howe Construction company office. One being a foreman and the other a long time trusted employee, they both have keys to the office and the alarm code.

They have already searched the Garden Grove jobsite, Dave showing Stanley the surveillance cameras he found and sabotaged. They had inspected the cameras to discover where they feed to, but turned up nothing. They are each wired to a battery pack and have a wireless feed. They found nothing but the cameras, no recording device on site anywhere inside or outside of the trailer office. The feed has to be going back to Bruce Copeland's office.

After they find the surveillance videos and watch them, they plan to search their engineer's office for any evidence that might point to or away from Samuel Watkins. There has to be some kind of evidence concerning the forged blueprints.

Stanley was supposed to have destroyed the earlier forgeries but he did not. He had stashed them in the back of the cupboard with old blueprints for past jobs instead. He did not know why he was doing it at the time, and had no reason to believe they were anything but errors. He is glad now that he had kept them. Tonight they are going to sit down and compare them all, marking the errors and changes from each copy on one blueprint to see the big picture once and for all.

Stanley has a feeling it might just reveal something, some clue perhaps that might tell them why Samuel is messing around with forging the blueprints.

"Let's start in Copeland's office," Dave whispered. "The video has to be there somewhere."

Stanley nodded, moving in that direction.

"Why are you whispering? There's no one here."

"Good question."

They started searching Copeland's office, going through every filing cabinet drawer, cupboard, and desk drawer that is not locked and turned up nothing. How is he receiving the signals from the cameras? They hoped it would be as easy as finding a device with a drive they could view without having to get access to Copeland's password protected files.

"We'll have to jimmy the locks," Stanley said, pointing at the one locked desk drawer. They had come up with a few locked obstacles; a cupboard, one drawer in the desk, and a filing cabinet.

"You take the cupboard," he said, bending down to study the desk drawer and rummaging in the other one for anything that might work to pick the desk lock.

Dave started working on the cupboard.

They do not hear the front door open.

Bruce Copeland is out of sorts. Things have been going very badly lately. Between all the problems at the Garden Grove site, the petty vandalism, accidents, tractors sabotaged, and the forged blueprints, he is at the end of his rope on this project and feels like he is being torn in too many different directions.

Then there was the explosion at the Anc-Chor site and the unusual meeting with Mr. Chornelhus.

Bruce does not know what to think about anything anymore.

As Mr. Chornelhus suggested, Lezkowitz makes a good suspect in all of it, the vandalism and sabotage at Garden Grove and the explosion at the Anc-Chor site.

But it does not feel right. Lezkowitz is a hack and a desperate man with a very bad temper, but this is not his style. The petty vandalism maybe, but not the rest.

And why was Chornelhus pointing the finger at Lezkowitz instead of just letting the police sort it out? Something feels fishy there too.

Besides, Lezkowitz would not have had access to forge the blueprints and switch them in all the offices, especially not at the Copeland & Howe office. He also doesn't think Lezkowitz would have had the patience or foresight to pull off something like that.

Something else is nagging at Bruce. He wishes now that he did not have all the copies of the forged blueprints destroyed.

"There is one thing I can do right now." Bruce thought. "I'm going back to the office where I can have a glass of whiskey without the wife nagging me and watch the video surveillance from Garden Grove again."

A short time later, Bruce pulled into the lot at Copeland & Howe, noting Stanley's truck sitting in the lot and thinking nothing of it. It is not unusual for the foreman to leave his truck; sometimes to go for drinks with the boys or sometimes his wife picked him up. His old truck also broke down a lot, so more than likely it was dead again.

He got out and went to the door. The place is quiet and dark as usual.

He put his key in the lock and opened the door, letting it close behind him as he pocketed his keys and turned off the alarm.

Bruce got halfway to his office before it registered on him that the place was not completely silent, and that the armed light may not have been lit on the alarm panel.

He froze, listening, his heart pounding.

Burglar?

The sound is coming from his office.

He stepped forward, leaning forward a little, one cautious step and then another until he can see the partially open office door. The light in his office is on.

The sounds are definitely coming from there.

Anger took over where common sense should have and he barged into his office to confront the burglar.

Bruce froze in the doorway staring in surprise at the two men who froze, staring back at him.

"Stan, Dave, what the hell are you doing?" Copeland's voice is stilted with the shock of this discovery.

It is immediately obvious to him what they are doing. They are ransacking his office searching for something. The question just kind of popped out in his surprise.

"We found the surveillance cameras at the Garden Grove site," Stanley said quickly. "Where's the videos? We need to see them. Copies of any letters and forms filed with Samuel Watkins too."

"Why?" Copeland is immediately suspicious. "Site security is my business."

"We found a woman's necklace in the trailer," Dave said.

"So you want to find out who's getting it on in the trailer? Who cares?" Copeland complained, annoyed and assuming they are on a childish mission.

Dave shook his head. "It belongs to Samuel Watkins's wife. A bunch of housewives got busted for some of the vandalism at the site. She was probably one of them. The police are still trying to figure out who all was in on it. I bet she's the one that messed around with the files."

"We think he was in there too," Stanley said. "Sam said he thinks the necklace caught on him, that it fell off him. That puts him in the trailer. But he was nervous. He had to think then said it quickly, like he was making an excuse. He wouldn't have to make excuses if he wasn't hiding anything. He was definitely hiding something."

"He's in there lots, this office too," Copeland said doubtfully.

"We found it in the filing drawer beneath the files," Dave said. "We think he's been in there digging around in the files," Stanley said.

"Unlikely," Copeland said, brushing it off immediately. "Sam wouldn't have wasted his time with the childish vandalism done to those files. It's ridiculous. He wouldn't risk throwing away his career to do something like that."

"That was our first thought too," Stanley said. "We dismissed it just as fast. He wouldn't do something like that. We were sure he didn't alter the files and toss them around. But Sam said himself that it had to have fallen off of him. Either his wife was the one who vandalized the office and he's protecting her at the risk of losing his job and career, or he really was there digging in the files before they were vandalized. Since that group of housewives was already caught for the other stuff, it doesn't make sense for him to risk everything to protect her over the files. He has to be covering for her for a reason, or covering for himself. We're sure it's to cover himself for something else."

Copeland could not believe it.

"This is a pretty heavy allegation you're making against a man we all know to be honest and above reproach; a man whose life could be destroyed by an allegation like this," Copeland said gravely. This is not the sort of allegation you make lightly.

"So you think he broke in and searched the files. For what?" Copeland asked.

"We don't know, but we think he's behind the forged blueprints," Stanley said.

Copeland is stunned. He stared at them in disbelief.

"There is no doubt, the blueprint errors were not errors. There's too many, too consistently. Someone is doing this to mess with this project on purpose, but we have no idea why.

Bruce, they've been forged and he's the only one who has the skills, access to the necessary information, and access to all the offices where forged blueprints were swapped for the originals. Hell, he could have even swapped them right under our noses with us watching. He always seems to have extra blueprints with him. He could have done it at any time without having to break in."

Copeland has to think about this.

"It's possible," he said, "but I still can't see Sam doing something like that. Why? What could he gain from it? He'd have everything to lose if he gets caught and nothing to gain from doing it."

"That's what we need to find out," Dave said.

"First, we need to see those surveillance videos and see if we can place him sneaking in or out of the trailer, then we have to find any evidence to suggest who might be guilty, anything to tell us why he would do it."

Copeland looked at them suspiciously.

"You found the cameras," he said. He is sure now his own men were the ones who tampered with the hidden surveillance cameras.

"Did one of you mess with those cameras?"

Stanley and Dave both denied it, but the look of guilt Dave could not hide revealed the truth.

Copeland decided to let it slide for now. He has bigger problems.

"It's all here," Copeland said, turning on the computer, "what little video I got." They waited for it to boot up.

He keyed in his password to access the computer, located the video files, and they went through the video files one at a time. There isn't much.

"I couldn't get some of them to work at all," Copeland muttered. "The ones that did work took me days to get the feed to work and didn't get a good picture. It's like something is interfering with the signal. It doesn't make sense, it should have worked fine there. I never could figure out what is interfering, there's no radio tower or anything close enough. And then they got disabled." He gave Dave a sidelong glance.

They watched machines and men move at high speed, the sun cross the sky, slowing it down when they spotted questionable movement. They watched as a curious deer approached a camera, sniffing at it and blowing snot on it and finally hit it with its antlers, breaking it. The feed cracked and fizzed, the deer fracturing with the broken lens. It continued for some time, the image distorted by the cracked and snot covered lens, making it seem grotesque.

Night deepened and in the fast forward the distant woods seemed almost to move, as if it were creeping forward towards the camera. It gives them all a creepy feeling. A dark shape like a black veil of fog seems to move apart from the trees, a shadow rushing towards the lens, trails of fog like grasping fingers. They half imagine they might hear a strange cackle if there had been sound.

Then dawn crept quickly over the scene and the daylight proved the fog and moving trees were nothing more than a trick of the night shadows and then the feed finally cut out.

They were running through another file when Dave stopped them.

"Wait, what's that?"

Copeland went back and played it back at normal speed, going back again and playing it slower and then slower.

A shadow moved just at the edge of the picture, unidentifiable, but it looks stooped over and seems to move slowly. But it is no use. They watch it over and over, but it doesn't help. They cannot make out who it is or what they were doing, assuming it is a person.

"We won't find anything. I set the cameras up too late to catch any of the vandalism," Copeland said, "and they were disabled too soon to catch anything after the site was shut down."

"Let's move on," Stanley said. "We'll search the whole office for any other clues to prove Samuel Watkins' guilt or innocence. Check the files, phone messages, notes, anything and everything."

"By the way," Copeland said as he started searching his own office, "I got a call today. Garden Grove is cleared to reopen. We are back in business. I already called some of the men to be there in the morning. I've been trying to contact the two of you, but you didn't answer."

Stanley and Dave look at each other sheepishly. They have their phones turned off because of the sneaky nature of their coming into the offices to search for the video and clues.

32 - Startling Discovery

The coffee clutch pulled up in front of Barbara Watkin's house in their cars. Barb ran inside and into her husband's home office, hurriedly searching through his desk until she found what she is looking for. She pocketed the spare set of keys. The rest waited in their cars outside.

Being a conscientious man, Samuel played it safe on most things, always buying the extra insurance, paying for the extended warranty on purchases, keeping extra copies of important documents, and even making sure they have a backup for the backup on the smoke detectors and checking them frequently to make sure they work. Smoke detectors weren't even enough. Barb teased him about this when he installed multiple units in different parts of the house, each detecting fire, smoke, or carbon monoxide. If they ever did have a fire, it would be a cacophony of blaring alarms.

He also kept spare keys to everything, just in case. This particular set has the keys for everything Samuel has a key for in the municipal office, including the front door. The building itself has no security alarm, so needing a pass code is not an issue.

Keys in hand, she raced back outside.

While Barb was inside searching for the keys, the other women were swapping cars. They are going to go to the municipal office in one car.

The women are excited by their adventure and a little frightened as they drive to the municipal office. The parking lot is empty and a lone light post lights the small paved lot. The building itself is in darkness, a single dim light burning somewhere inside casting a weak glow inside the front window.

Barbara almost backed out when they got to the municipal office door and she had to fish the pilfered keys out and unlock the door as they all huddled in the darkness, looking around furtively to make sure no one saw.

Samuel was already so angry with her over their breaking in and messing around in the Garden Grove construction trailer. He still has not come home after storming off. She is very worried both for him and for their marriage. Would he really leave her over this? Or did he just need time to cool down? She had tried calling his cell phone, but he did not answer, each droning ring in her ear adding another taut string of stress to her rattled nerves.

The lock clicked softly as the tumbler moved and turned with a dull thud and they are in.

"What are we looking for?" Libby asked as Barb swung the door open.

"I don't know," Pamela said.

They all filed inside and looked around the office as if they had not each been there many times before. The place feels very different in the dark and in the act of illegally breaking in.

"Just watch for anything that seems out of place, looks suspicious, or has to do with the Garden Grove development," Mrs. Henderson said. "Notes, phone messages, anything. Which is his office?"

"This one," Barbara said, showing the way to his office.

The municipal office is small with a small main office area holding one desk and two small offices, one each for Samuel and Willie Williams. There is a separate room they jokingly call the war room. It holds a large drafting table and chair and two other large tables pushed together where blueprints can be laid out and studied or drawn up.

"So, this is Williams' office?" Pamela asked.

Barb nodded.

"I'll start searching here," Pamela said, going into William's office. "If anyone is doing anything illegal, I'll bet it's him."

Mrs. Henderson went into Samuel's office and turned on the computer, searching through his desk while she waited for it to boot up. She waved Barbara over with the keys when she found most of the drawers locked.

Barbara unlocked the desk for her and then unlocked the filing cabinet, searching the files there.

With the computer on, Mrs. Henderson started searching files on it.

"How did you get in past the password?" Barbara asked, looking over at her in surprise.

"I know a thing or two about computers," Mrs. Henderson said with a wink, not elaborating.

"It seems there is a lot we don't know about our quiet Mrs. Henderson," Barb whispered.

Mrs. Henderson only grinned, continuing her search.

Libby is searching the main office area, going through the secretary's desk, filing, and a stack of phone messages.

Their search of the municipal office proves fruitless. As each exhausted searching her area they gathered together by the exit.

"Ok ladies," Pamela announced, "it's time to move this operation to Barb's house."

"Make sure you leave everything exactly the way it was," Barbara said nervously. "We don't want anyone suspecting we were here."

Minutes later the lights are off, door locked, and they are piling back into the car.

When they arrive for work the next time, the secretary will suspect her boss Willie Williams of snooping through her desk, Samuel Watkins will look at his cupboard door with a frown thinking that he'd thought he remembered locking it, and Williams will yell out to their secretary, asking if she had been in his office.

When the women arrived at Barbara's house, she went to the kitchen to make coffee, changed her mind, and instead uncorked a couple of bottles of wine, filling glasses for everyone.

They start the search in Samuel's home office; Barb looking at each of them anxiously and reminding them to make sure nothing is disturbed or left out of place. Sam is a meticulous man and sure to notice the slightest thing out of place. She carefully put the spare keys back exactly as she found them, reaching back into the drawer to shift the smallest key to the top, just as she is sure it had been.

They are sure they would be more likely to find any evidence here if Samuel has been up to anything.

Mrs. Henderson turned the computer on and they all watched in awe as she quickly bypassed Samuel's clumsy passwords and started searching his computer files.

"How'd you do that?" Barbara asked.

"Easy, he used your name and birthday," Mrs. Henderson shook her head disapprovingly, "the same as at the municipal office. Not very imaginative, is he?"

"No, not really," Barbara admitted.

They each picked something to search.

Barbara is searching a low filing cabinet drawer when she came across a piece of paper. Her eyes widened with surprise as she scanned it. She glanced quickly at the others to make sure no one is watching and shoved the paper inside her shirt before going back to going through the motions of flipping through the papers in the files. She cannot concentrate on anything but that piece of paper after that.

She is stunned. She cannot believe it. This just cannot be true.

At the Copeland & Howe office, Bruce Copeland spread out a set of blueprints for the Garden Grove site on one of the large tables. Dave spread out another and the three started comparing them.

"I wish now we had kept all the other copies," Copeland complained as they bent over the two sets of blueprints. He is jotting notes on a piece of paper. They cannot mark up the blueprints that are needed for the job.

"Wait," Stanley said. He went to the cupboard where old blueprints are stored, rummaged around, and brought back an armload of rolled blueprints. He looked at his boss sheepishly.

"I didn't destroy them."

Copeland looked at him in surprise.

"Good man," he said, yanking the blueprint off the table. "We can mark on those ones."

He grabbed one of the blueprints that should not exist and spread it on the table.

They started going through each blueprint, carefully marking every error and discrepancy they can find on the one copy.

A picture slowly began to emerge.

33 - The Next Phase

Mr. Chornelhus is sitting at the large desk in his office reviewing the insurance paperwork from the Anc-Chor project explosion. The office is richly opulent as only an extremely wealthy man's office would be. The large space also has a fully stocked elegant bar and a sitting area with couches and chairs and tables, and windows that take up an entire wall of the penthouse office.

Despite the evidence of the fully stocked bar, Mr. Chornelhus does not drink. The idea of poisoning his body with any substance he considers impure or tainted with chemicals is entirely distasteful to him.

Gentle classical music plays softly; almost undetectable to the ear. Hidden somewhere in the room a small atomizer silently puffs its perfectly timed scent into the air. Like the music, the scent is very subtle and delicate, unnoticeable if you are not looking for it.

Mr. Chornelhus is convinced the music and fragrance present on a subconscious level heled to calm the nerves and stimulate the mind. Similarly, he believes other stimuli have other affects. He believes people are more in tune with the five senses than they even realize, the stimulus doing everything from making you healthier and smarter, extending your lifespan even, to an outright attack against your senses. Unpleasant sounds and smells like the crush of traffic, he is certain, suck years from your life in a single trip.

Mr. Chornelhus makes a point of avoiding such things as much as possible; bringing to him what he would otherwise be forced to expose himself to negative stimuli to achieve. He once had an entire ballet company come to him, including the backdrops, symphony and everything, to perform a particularly popular show so he would not have to endure the noise and smell of traffic to go to the theatre. Mr. Chornelhus does not actually like ballet, but watching it is what he believes people of his class are supposed to do.

The papers Mr. Chornelhus is going through are a seemingly endless roll of red tape. He has to make sure the insurance papers are perfect.

Mr. Chornelhus is not just a perfectionist; he also stands to gain significantly from the insurance for the damage. The project will be a little delayed but that is a price he has to pay and, as a side benefit, he will be a wealthier man for it. He never does anything he is not certain to come out ahead in.

He looked up at the sound of a light knock at the door and one of his security men came in.

This is his own personal security man, paid well enough to guarantee his absolute loyalty, and one of very few people allowed access to Mr. Chornelhus.

"Sir," the man said deferentially, "Mr. Lezkowitz has been seen hanging around the site again. He's just sitting in his truck smoking and watching."

Mr. Chornelhus nodded. This is playing right into his plans. With his every move, Lezkowitz is walking deeper into playing scapegoat if the politicians find public outcry demands one. And if not, no investigation like the one currently underway to determine who blew up the Anc-Chor site is ever considered complete until someone goes to jail.

"How is the work clearing the ruined site coming along?" Chornelhus asked.

"It's right on track," the security man said. "We're good to move ahead."

"It's time for phase two then," Chornelhus said. "Send in my assistant."

The security man nodded and left his office, closing the door behind him.

Mr. Chornelhus closed the insurance file on his desk and went around to the bar. Taking a glass, he added ice and poured himself a scotch.

He put the drink down.

He will not actually drink it, but making a celebratory drink at a time like this was what you are supposed to do.

He had witnessed his own father and his business associates do it on many occasions, and his grandfather and his group of wrinkled white-haired business associates too.

He grew up well tutored in the back room dealings behind the scenes, how business decisions are really made when vast amounts of money are involved, while made-up over-perfumed wives pretend to be enraptured by the arts at ballets and symphonies, each trying to outdo the other in their pretense of the importance they put on such things. The wealthy all-male corporate heads corner each other while holding tumblers of expensive scotch and other similar drinks, discuss who is sleeping with whose daughter or decades younger paid for with a lavish lifestyle wife. After a few drinks, they barter businesses, projects, and people like the other boys from the large non-wealthy world outside his much smaller opulently wealthy world bartered trading cards on street corners as he watched from the safety of his family limousine as it drove by.

This is the world Chornelhus grew up in. Only he is superior to his father and grandfather and their associates, just as he is superior to those he himself has business dealings with. He does not poison his body with alcohol, and has such power that he does not have to meet them. They come to him. Always.

He grinned at his own reflection staring back at him in the outwardly tinted windows that take up the entire wall, looking out from the office high in the top of a steel and glass tower to the city spreading out below him.

There is a knock at his door and his assistant came in.

His assistant is a young man, an unpaid intern, and almost too eager to please. Mr. Chornelhus's security people had done a very thorough background check on the young man, as well as having him sign an intimidating large contract when he hired him.

He always chooses a young intern instead of hiring someone more qualified for a few reasons. Interns are cheap, often working for nothing but the experience they gain. They are young, naive, and innocently unaware of things. And he can shape and mold them into what he wants, discarding them like rubbish if it does not work out.

Unfortunately for the interns, Mr. Chornelhus is a very private man and his assistants have access to very sensitive information. That is why he only hires interns with no family to come looking for them.

"Mr. Chornelhus?" the young man asked.

"We're ready for phase two," Chornelhus said. "We'll start phase three simultaneously. No point waiting unnecessarily."

"Yes sir."

Phase two is the implementation of a publicity campaign. Marketing makes the business world go around. The entire purpose is to tell people that he, Mr. Chornelhus, is not the enemy the opponents of his project publicly claim him to be. Poor Mr. Chornelhus is the victim, his property blown up in an attack committed most likely by a fanatical environmental group or other opponent to the project, and one that has killed a number of workers, family men. They will play him as the victim, grieving for the dead and injured workers and their families' losses.

People generally do and think whatever the media tells them to.

The intern left to do his bidding.

Chornelhus smiled. Yes, the publicity campaign will not win over the masses, but it will allow them to save face. Public opinion can too easily be swayed by simply offering a less uncomfortable path to take. Give them a bigger enemy to turn on. And the patsy the environmental group will turn over will be an easier target than the man all the news agencies suddenly turn from monster to victim.

And if that fails, he still has the unfortunate Mr. Vern Lezkowitz he has set up and who is unknowingly waiting to take the blame. He will not be as tasty in the mouths of the media hounds, but he will do. Chornelhus always has a secondary plan in case the first sees an inopportune outcome.

"It is a shame we have had to be put behind schedule," Chornelhus said, talking to himself since there is no one else in the room. "But I had it all wrong. The plans were all wrong. I had to blow it up and start all over.

Grandmother will be pleased. She will just have to be patient and wait a little longer until it is built. I have to be able to look after her properly."

His eyes shine with madness.

"They cannot keep you from me forever," he said.

"And now for phase three. I'm almost there, almost there."

"I know where you are now grandmother," he called out to the woman who must be long deceased. "I am almost ready for you. I will just have to look after you myself, keep you close until we finish rebuilding. And when it is finished, The Anc-Chor Project will be grand! The things we will do will be amazing!"

34 - The Boys Will be Hungry

The orange glow of dawn had not faded away to clear blue skies for long before the peacefulness of the small community was interrupted once again by the incessant growling and beeping of heavy construction machinery.

Work has resumed with a vengeance at the Garden Grove development. The project is well behind schedule with the accidents, vandalism, discovery of old human remains, blueprint errors, poisoning of the workers, and the frequent site shutdowns.

This is on the verge of costing Copeland & Howe a lot of money. The investors behind the project who hired Copeland & Howe had wisely inserted a clause in the contract allowing them the option to penalize Copeland & Howe if the company failed to complete the various phases on time.

The men are going to be working long hours, pushing the boundaries on the limits for the mornings and evenings to put in as many man-hours as possible to play catch up.

Bruce Copeland is on site himself today to supervise and coordinate the work. They have to get enough done on phase one to begin phase two in very little time. Hopefully, whoever the real money is that is behind the Garden Grove development will believe phase one is on track or forgive the delay with the promise of keeping phase two on target. Copeland himself does not know who the private backers of this project are. He only knows they are wealthy and powerful, too much so for such a small project, he thought.

Large tractors are attacking the ground, scraping away the precious topsoil and depositing it in dump trucks to be hauled away and re-sold to the homeowners at additional profit for the company.

Others work diligently on getting the roads down, digging out the drainage, and laying the sewer and water lines.

Men are marking out lot boundaries and pounding in the temporary markers, their orange tape waving in the wind like the flags of conquering explorers.

The moment he sees men loitering around, Copeland is on them, hounding them to find something else to do if they are waiting for something.

Libby Waterbourne is putting on coffee, still half asleep and hasn't yet noticed the growling and beeping noises when the loud banging of a large tractor banging its scoop on the side of a dump truck startled her, making her drop the coffee pot. The glass carafe exploded in an eruption of glass and a wave of spraying water when it hit the floor, soaking her feet and legs.

She swore as she looked around for the source of the noise. Her first thought is someone is beating on the door, but almost immediately she realizes what it is.

The coffee clutch is supposed to be meeting at her house for coffee today.

Stepping carefully, Libby went around the mess to the broom closet, grabbing the broom and dustpan. She swept up the mess, water and glass together, using the broom to push it all into the dustpan to dump in the trash. It makes a mess of the trash bin, but she can hardly mop up the water with all that broken glass.

Hastily cleaned up, Libby has to move fast. The ladies will be coming soon and she has no coffee pot! Either they will have to switch houses or someone will have to bring a coffee maker.

Pamela is getting ready to leave and she is in a foul mood. The nonstop beeping of the construction machinery is driving her up the wall. She cannot stand it! It is like listening to an alarm clock you cannot shut off.

She is just heading to the door to leave when the phone rang. Pam debated ignoring it and decided to answer it.

"Hello."

"Pam, its Libby."

"I'm on my way."

"No, wait," Libby's voice is anxious.

"What's wrong?"

"I broke my coffee pot."

"Did you call the others?" Pam asked, thinking fast.

"I tried Barb first, but there was no answer."

"Ok," Pam said, "I'll grab mine and bring it."

"Thanks Pam." The relief in Libby's voice practically poured out of the phone.

When Pamela arrived at Libby's house with her coffee maker and intact carafe, Mrs. Henderson was already there.

Pamela and Libby immediately went to put the coffee on.

"Where's Barb?" Pam asked. "I thought she must have already left if you couldn't reach her."

"I don't know. I thought so too. She hasn't come yet," Libby said.

The three women sat to wait for the coffee to brew, the nutty aroma filling the house with its tantalizing smell.

"They started construction again," Libby said. "That banging made me jump, that's why I broke the coffee pot."

"That constant beeping is driving me nuts," Pam sympathized. "Why do they have to beep like that too? And the dog! He won't stop barking with all that noise!"

Mrs. Henderson shook her head.

"They're going to drive this whole town crazy with that noise before they're done," she muttered.

As they went on complaining about the noise and the garbage the workers leave behind, pouring coffee and revisiting old grudges, they worked themselves up an ever-increasing slope of anger, feeding off each other's frustrations over the construction.

"Where is Barbara?" Mrs. Henderson asked after a while. "She couldn't come?"

"I don't know," Libby said. "I talked to her last night and she said she would be here."

Pamela nodded. "I talked to her too. She said she had something she wants to talk to us about and that she would be here."

Libby looked at the others with concern.

"What if something happened? What if she got caught for breaking into the municipal office or Samuel noticed we were snooping in his office?"

Old Rusty Plowshare is in a foul mood.

He slammed and banged things angrily as he went about making his morning coffee and breakfast.

He banged the old tin coffee pot down on the old stovetop, the water inside sloshing so that the pot edged sideways on the element when he let go of its handle, threatening to tip it right off the edge.

He knocked debris from the counter onto the floor, carelessly shoving it out of the way to make room for the egg carton.

Rusty cracked his eggs harshly, breaking the yolks and having to scoop out the pieces of eggshell with his fingers.

He plunged down the toaster button so viciously that it refused to stay down, popping right back up to fuel his fury.

Finally sitting down with burnt toast and undercooked eggs, Rusty Plowshare attacked the newspaper, tearing it open as if it were the reason for his anger, tearing the page.

Too angry to read it, he crumpled it and shoved it aside.

He can hear the distant noise of the construction machines.

With a growl, Rusty got up and shuffled to the back door. Going down the steps with some difficulty, he reached the ground where he is swarmed by hungry stray cats, the more feral ones darting about like panicked rabbits. He snarled at them, swinging his fist as if he might actually reach them and kicking at them although they quickly leapt beyond the reach of his foot.

Rusty made his way towards the back of his lot where he has a view of the distant machines lumbering around the Garden Grove development. Some of the cats follow, meowing after him.

He is furious that the work has begun again on the housing development, land that had been in his family for generations and which they are violating. They have no business being there as far as he is concerned.

He raised his arms into the air, shaking his fists angrily at the distant machines.

"I'll stop you yet!" he shouted, though the sound would not carry far enough away for the workers to hear.

"I'll stop you once and for all!" he vowed.

Rusty turned and went to the old leaning barn. Pairs of eyes stare at him from many places, following his movements, cats hiding amid the piles of rubble, useless junk hoarded by an old man.

He began searching for something.

"You don't know what you are doing," he muttered as he rummaged around.

Shifting a pile of boxes, he unburied a pile of molding carpet scraps. Moving these aside, he revealed a pile of old hunting rifles and shotguns, some black as coal and others rusting. He dug through the pile of long guns, moving weapons that may or may not be in working condition.

He dropped one. It clattered to the ground, its rusted sliding bolt popping out to reveal an unspent round still in the chamber. Without a thought, he picked it up, tossing it carelessly on the pile of guns.

The distant growling of tractors and banging can be heard even inside the small house. Old Mrs. Crampchet took the whistling teapot off the stove and placed it carefully on a fancy crocheted tea cozy before shuffling to her kitchen window. She looked out at the source of the noise, seeing the workers back to work at the Garden Grove development. From her window, she can make out just one small piece of the new housing development. She can just see the one tractor come into view and move behind the other houses again. Some men stand around within her view, seemingly watching the tractor.

With a small smile and a nod, she moved away from the window.

"Tea can wait," she said.

Humming, Mrs. Crampchet pulled down an old cookbook from a shelf, its binding splintered and cracked and dust from the old glue of the binding powdering her housedress sleeve.

She went about the kitchen collecting ingredients, putting them next to a mixing bowl, humming all the while. Many of the containers are old tins that the baking supplies were placed into from their original packing.

She knows the recipe by heart, but opened the book anyway, flipping immediately to the page she wants. The edges of the pages are all yellowed with age. It is an old habit of hers to check the recipe book.

Putting her finger on the page as if to read, her old eyes no longer able to focus very well on the small print, she begins putting the ingredients in the bowl, sometimes measuring and sometimes not, slowly mixing whatever it is she is baking.

"The boys will be hungry," she smiled as she worked.

35 - Talking About Garden Grove

Lezkowitz pulled up in the small parking lot of the municipal office, his truck door creaking loudly as he opened it. His lack of sleep shows on his face.

He went into the office and looked around to see who is in. The secretary clerk is not at her desk. She must be on a break, he guessed.

Willie Williams is the only one in. Lezkowitz almost smiled. This is to his advantage.

He went to Williams' office and knocked on the open door.

Williams looked up.

"Morning Vern," Williams said.

"Good morning Willie," Lezkowitz said, entering the office without waiting for an invitation. "I've come to talk to you about the Garden Grove project. I understand it's pretty far behind, keeps getting shut down, a lot of problems and all. I'm thinking maybe Copeland has bitten off more than he can chew. You know, if he gets shut down off that project for good I could take it over and get it on track pretty quick. I could get it done much sooner and without all the problems Copeland has had. I don't know why you haven't pulled his permit altogether yet."

Williams gave him a knowing look. If he did not already suspect Lezkowitz of being behind at least some of the vandalism at Garden Grove before, he does now.

"Garden Grove is already back on," he said. "Copeland got the go ahead and they're back at it today. The workers are there right now."

"You could still shut them down," Lezkowitz said. "Pull his permit. I know there has to be some grounds with all the trouble they've had. It would be worth your while to see me take over the job."

Williams raised his hands, palms up, shrugging.

"It's out of my hands for now. I can't just pull the permit after they got the go ahead to go back to work. I have to have a reason."

Lezkowitz's eyes burned with anger. He turned and stormed out of the office, leaving the building. He would have slammed the door if not for the air-compressed door closer that prevented it.

Williams chuckled over Lezkowitz's little tantrum after he left.

Professor Richard Mackin is surrounded by a pile of books and letters and notes. He is pouring over them. There is something about those old bones dug up at the Garden Grove development that just does not sit right with him. He does not know why, it is just a gut feeling.

He is sure the answer lay in the history of the area.

The fact there was no record of there ever being any sort of cemetery on the spot does not mean much. In the days of the settlers, it was not unusual for family members to be buried on the family farm if there was no church or cemetery. They were even sometimes buried along the side of the trail when they lost someone while travelling across the plains, as an alternative to having to carry the decomposing body with them for days until they reached their destination by horse drawn wagons. That the owners of the bones were all related suggested it was likely they came from an old farmstead burial plot.

The lack of artefacts also meant little; few survived this long.

The shared deformity evident in the bones on the cellular level is what first caught Professor Richard Mackin's attention, keeping the questions rolling over and over in his head. It was coded in their DNA. That, combined with the old stories about the local natives butchering entire families of homesteaders when a child of either race was discovered with a deformity, believing the invading white men had brought evil spirits with them, and the indications on the remains that at least one was murdered, tells him this was no ordinary family burial plot they were dug up from.

Then again, the infant may be the only actual murder victim. That skull was the only bone with irrefutable evidence of murder. He or she could have been murdered after being born deformed.

That was not unusual for the day either when trying to look after one sickly child could mean the neglect of a healthier one.

Whether the infant was the only murder victim or not does not matter to Richard. There is a long buried secret here and someone is trying to make sure it is found by burying these family bones where they will be found.

Richard shook his head in regret at the piles of books and notes. He cannot shake the sense that he is just so close to finding the secret behind the mysterious bones.

The possible murder of the long ago family was not unusual for the times. But he feels compelled to do further testing on the bones, including aging them in his usual thoroughness when it comes to running tests.

With a last regretful look at the piles of printed clutter that refuses to give up its secret, he left to return to his lab.

The university is eerily quiet at this late hour. It is a relief to Richard that he does not have to go through the deserted underground tunnels with the fat pipes running along the ceilings and maze-like twists and turns.

When he started at the university, his office was in another building and he had to brave the tunnels. It was the only place they had room for him. Since then, a number of aged professors with tenure had retired or passed away; the only way the university could get rid of a tenured professor.

Richard has always felt anxious in those tunnels. If anything happened, there is no place to go except to run uselessly through them. It is too much like the rat mazes he had spent years working with previously. The rats endlessly ran their maze, memorizing the treats, tricks, and torments, only to have the maze taken apart and changed to frustrate them more.

It is that sense of being a rat trapped in an ever-changing maze with no escape that Richard dislikes the most about the tunnels. It does not matter that steel and brick could not be so easily manipulated.

He shuddered at the thought and hurried through the too quiet hall to his lab.

The quiet of the university at night always makes Richard think he hears noises that are not there, leaving him on edge before he even heard anything.

He slipped into his lab, closing the door behind him. He had a brief temptation to lock the door, but pushed it away. He is not going to be one of those paranoid guys who thinks a bogeyman hides in every shadow. He had heard too many of those stories from other professors who were a little more than half crazy.

Richard went immediately to the case where the bones from Garden Grove are stored. He looked at them through the glass, his eyes drawn to the small child's skull. A baby. The parts of the skull had not yet fused of course, allowing the bones to be pulled apart as the brain beneath would have grown with the infant's body. The posterior and anterior fontanels, the soft spots on the back and front of a baby's head, had begun closing, which put the baby's age at more than nine months. It would take up to around eighteen months for the ossification of the bones of the front spot to close it completely, so he knows the baby was younger than that.

If he had to guess, Richard would say the infant was murdered at around his or her first birthday, but that is not his area of expertise.

Opening the case, Richard delicately took the small skull out and carried it across the room where he set it down on a metal table. He turned on the lamp over the table and positioned it to better shine on the skull.

He began to work, re-running tests he had already run more than once. He does not expect any of the tests to reveal anything they had not already. So far, the results have been consistent. Proof in science is getting the same results from the same tests over and over and over again.

After re-running tests on the skull he moved on to do the same on the other human bones discovered at Garden Grove.

When Richard finally finished running the tests one more time on all the bone samples, he sat down wearily. It is time to give up on the tests and accept that the results will not change. As exhausted as he is, it cannot slow the excitement burning through him.

The bones do not come from a single family murdered in an attack as he had first suspected, but rather they come from multiple generations of the same family. And this is not a simple grandparent to grandchild generational group either. The ages of the bones themselves span more than two hundred years, with no two bones belonging to the same victim.

The implications are overwhelming.

Whoever they were, someone had been killing them for generations and carefully storing their remains. These bones do not appear to have been left buried in a cemetery, or even rotting away in the dampness that would permeate a mausoleum here.

The most disturbing find of all is the simple fact the bones have been deliberately planted at the construction site very recently, possibly only days before their discovery. He cannot help but wonder how many more there might be that have not yet been discovered, and where they have been kept all these years until they were buried at Garden Grove.

Professor Richard Mackin returned to his research over the next days, expanding it with each possibility that came to him. He poured over every old record of the area that he could find, books, old newspapers, and birth and death records. The records from the church were harder to get, marriages, burials and baptisms. But with a lot of begging and promising that he is only seeking to discover the heritage of the deceased so he could make sure they are given proper burials as required by their faiths, he finally had some success. He looked into any group that might have vital statistics on the population both current and going back a few hundred years, census lists, and voter registrations.

As he followed the data, he had found himself compelled to continue right up to the current generation. It got harder to get the information with the newer generations, privacy concerns shutting down some sources completely and making the limited information from others too vague to be useful.

He wrote to historical societies and sent letters to retirement homes, begging for any anecdotal information anyone could give him.

Richard is beginning to put together a story that left him feeling quite startled and a little queasy. It is also exhilarating.

He carefully drew a series of charts, family trees that sometimes intersected with each other and at other places branched off to nowhere with a notation whether the branch ended or its fate is unknown. Scores of notes are piled around that he checked or added to as he worked. On a blue sheet, he jotted down questions to be resolved. He chose blue because to him it represents what he thinks of as the great big blue unknown. Blue like the endless sky above, the color assigned to the vast unexplored oceans even though it was an inaccurate color. Blue like the shadowy snow painted in depictions of the immense stretches of mostly uninhabitable and unexplored Arctic and Antarctic at the top and bottom of the world. Blue is the color assigned to all the big unknowns of the world.

He sat back with a heavy sigh, rubbing his tired eyes.

"And just what am I going to do with this?" he asked the empty room.

On a large sheet of paper before him is a sprawling family tree that is larger and more interconnected than any he had ever seen before. It is not unheard of for small communities to have second or third cousins marry, though usually the relationships in the general population are more distant than that. A few small communities would even have second and first cousins marrying, particularly in the earlier days of settlement when whole extended families might settle in an area with little prospects outside the extended family for marriage.

Some religious communities are also knows for keeping their marriages closely related by blood.

Even in old civilizations it was not unheard of, even for siblings to marry, to keep the family power intact.

None were quite like this.

This is the first he has ever seen such a wholly interconnected familial group outside of a closed community religious cult in his studies and research. In the families these bones come from, there are very few marriages as far back as he could trace, and going right up to the present day surviving relatives, where a non-blood related person was married into the family.

He looked at his watch. He has to run. He is meeting with Mrs. Bainswood, a resident of one of the nursing homes in the city who he was told is especially interested in telling him some stories about the area. She had wanted him to visit and be gone before her daughter, a Mrs. Henderson, came to see her. At over ninety years old, he hopes she is of sound mind.

Stanley Rutthers is just turning into the parking lot of the municipal office when Lezkowitz came tearing out in his truck. He stopped to wait for the other contractor, wondering at the look of rage twisting the man's features and why he is driving like that.

He parked and went in, finding the clerk just sitting down at her desk as cheerfully as ever. That is, she glowered at him when he walked in and did not bother asking if she could help him, pointedly ignoring him and returning to whatever it is she does there. The woman is never cheerful.

Looking around, Stanley is relieved to see Samuel's office empty and Willie in his.

He knocked on Willie's open door, letting the man invite him in instead of just walking in. Williams gets annoyed if you do not knock first.

"You got a few minutes?" Stanley asked.

He is hoping he might get a few answers from the man without coming right out and asking what he wants to know.

Willie is not a man to be trusted. He would use any dirt he can against anyone to earn a few extra bucks.

Asking him questions that could ruin another man's career has to be done very tactfully, but they have to find out if Samuel could be behind the altered plans, or even behind some of the vandalism.

Unfortunately, Stanley would leave no wiser, only learning what his boss Bruce Copeland already suspects, that Lezkowitz is very likely behind some of the vandalism at Garden Grove. He also left a bit lighter in the pocket for that useless information.

Willie Williams knows nothing about Samuel Watkins that Stanley could not get from him without outright asking and telling him about their suspicions against him.

Dave has a blueprint spread out overflowing over the small desk in the little Garden Grove office trailer. He is going over the sabotaged plans again while he is tasked with sitting here to babysit the jobsite and deal with any problems while the foreman is off somewhere else. So far, they are coming up with nothing, but he is determined to find something.

Then a thought occurred to him. They had marked all the oddities and errors from each of the copies of the plans onto one, going over all the ones that were supposed to be destroyed and were not. What they have not thought of is adding in the human bones found on the jobsite. They were only recently planted there, so why had they not thought to add them too? Could they have something to do with the rest?

Copeland must have thought so, he decided.

When Bruce Copeland learned the bones had been intentionally planted, he had told the two guys on the crew he thought he could trust, Stanley and Dave. They were to watch for anything unusual and anyone behaving oddly, on and off the crew.

Dave started making a list, plotting the locations where each bone he knows of had been discovered at the Garden Grove site.

Finished, Dave looked over his list. He has them all.

Another thought struck him. What if there are more bones that have not been found yet?

Dave went out and started wandering around the site, moving over the ground that had not yet been touched by tractors or marked off by the university for excavation, searching for any signs the earth was disturbed. Some of the crew paused to watch his odd behavior.

When Dave found the first spot that looked like it may have been dug at and smoothed over to cover up signs someone was there, he ran and grabbed a handful of orange tipped wooden stakes and a mallet.

It took him a bit of searching to find the spot again.

Whoever dug it up did a good job of covering it up. He pounded a stake in the middle of the spot.

Dave continued his search, looking for more spots where the ground may have been dug up.

"What are you doing, Dave?" one of the workers called out to him.

Dave looked up. He cannot tell any of the guys about his suspicion, especially when they do not know who is behind it all. He will return after hours with Stanley and Copeland to dig up the spots.

"Just marking off some stuff for the next phase," he called back. "Got to get a jump on things; being so behind on the project."

The guy just shrugged his shoulders, not believing his story, but not really caring either. It is not his problem, whatever Dave is up to.

The coffee clutch wives have a plan. They are going to separate and try to run into a few key people who might be able to give them some answers on pretense of it being accidental. They each have a person assigned to them. They are going to find, purposely run into, and chat up the wives of the men working in the offices where copies of the blueprints are filed.

You never know what the wives might know that nobody thought of. They overhear phone conversations and husbands tend to vent and tell their wives things.

The next time they meet for coffee they will share what they learned.

And if any of them heard from Barbara, they are to immediately let the others know. All attempts to contact her so far had failed.

They are all getting concerned. Where is Barbara?

The explosion at the Anc-Chor project keeps nagging at Bruce Copeland.

He is on his way to talk to the fire chief to find out if the explosion was an accident or not. The chief had promised the preliminary investigation would be done by today. The full investigation will take much longer and is hampered by the unusually swift reopening of the site. Normally it would have remained closed until the full investigation is complete, but orders have come down from the top to release the property so the damaged buildings could be cleared away and construction could begin again.

The first thing Copeland did when he heard the site is open was to contact the fire chief. The fire chief had been furious. It is this anger that spurred him to be willing to give Copeland his unofficial opinion early in the investigation. Copeland and the fire chief also go way back, so the chief knows his unofficial word will stay confidential.

Copeland has no doubt Chornelhus had well greased the hands that hold the keys to opening the jobsite.

If the explosion was intentional, the most likely culprits behind it would be one of the more volatile environmental groups fighting against the project.

Lezkowitz is a good suspect too, especially since he has been hanging around the jobsite. But it just does not sit right with Copeland. He cannot stand the man, but he also cannot believe Lezkowitz would murder those workers like that. And there is no way he has the guts or ability to sneak into a place like that under heavy security and plant a bomb.

Whoever did set that explosion had to have known they would be murdering a large number of people setting it off during peak hours like that.

Copeland continued thinking it through as he drove on.

Who would benefit? Chornelhus has insurance, of course. It is a requirement for any project. Would he be profiting from the insurance claim?

Copeland has to admit it is possible, probable even, for a man like Chornelhus.

But it also put the project behind. Who would benefit from that? The insurance company would be out for the damages, but they would not pay out losses for the construction delay. The workers lost the most, many losing their lives. Some lost limbs and would be unable to return to this kind of work.

It is possible this could put the needed pressure on the politicians to put a stop to the project if the environmental groups against it make enough noise, but there has been no sign of anyone even suggesting that. Outside of the initial shocking headlines of the explosion and deaths, the newspapers have been strangely quiet on the attention-getting shock headlines that would have normally continued for days or weeks until something better came along to sell papers. Instead, pieces began running that are low key, sympathizing with the Anc-Chor project and its founder Mr. Chornelhus, as if they were victimized more than the men torn violently to pieces and burned alive were.

So far, all of the usual groups that jump to claim responsibility for something like this are keeping silent. There were too many innocent people hurt. Even the more hard-core groups do not want their name attached to this.

Copeland arrived at the fire hall and parked his truck, going inside.

The fire chief is waiting for him. They made their greetings, shaking hands, and Copeland followed the chief to his office.

They are long time acquaintances and are meeting to discuss the Anc-Chor explosion off the record.

"Well, we're certain it wasn't an accident," the chief said. "The question is who is behind the explosion. Do you have any suspicions?"

Copeland shook his head. "Nobody you wouldn't already be looking at."

The fire chief nodded.

"We already have investigators looking at Lezkowitz. There is evidence pointing to him, but it doesn't feel right for him. We're not sure yet, but I have a gut feeling the evidence might have been planted to implicate him."

This makes Copeland pause. Lezkowitz is being framed? By who? His secret meeting with Mr. Chornelhus comes instantly to mind, the meeting where the wealthy businessman had sent a police officer to pull him over and escort him to the meeting. He suspected the officer would have put him down on the ground and handcuffed him if necessary to get him there. When they actually arrived at the old abandoned farm, he had thought it possible he was about to be executed until he was led into the dilapidated barn to find Chornelhus waiting for him.

"What are you thinking?" the fire chief asked, studying Copeland's face.

Copeland brushed him off. He cannot point fingers on just a suspicious feeling, even though he suspects the chief has the same suspicions.

"It's nothing," he said quickly. "I'm just surprised. Lezkowitz seems too obvious, and blowing up a site like this doesn't seem like him, even if he could get past the security and pull it off. He's more of a petty vandalism kind of guy."

"We're also looking into the various groups that have made threats against Mr. Chornelhus and this project. That could take a while."

Confirmation someone else has the same suspicions makes Copeland feel certain his suspicions are right. But, he still has a few doubts that are not yet confirmed. The environmental protest groups would not have tried to frame his rival, a nobody running a failing construction company, with something like this. It would have no political value.

"I have to run. I have other things I need to do before I get back to the office. If you find anything I need to know or have any questions, you know where to find me."

The men shook hands and Copeland is off.

In his truck again, he is driving without paying attention, focused instead on his thoughts.

Could Chornelhus have blown up his own building? Why? What could he possibly gain from it?

Screeching tires and a blaring horn snap him out of it and he slammed on the brakes and cranked the wheel hard, looking up, startled, into the terrified eyes of a woman behind the wheel of a car. Both vehicles sit next to each other at odd angles in the road

He had narrowly missed smashing into the woman's car, braking and swerving at the last moment.

She looks shaken but he took his foot off the brake and kept going.

He has some things he has to find out.

Copeland decided to start with the library.

The library is not a place he ever imagined he would go. He is just not a book reading kind of guy.

Something about the place makes him feel uncomfortable too. He is not sure if it is the hushed quiet, the rows on rows of endless books, or the ancient feel of the place. The library feels like a place for ancient scholars, not a man who never reads for pleasure and is more comfortable digging a hole in the mud than walking into a stuffy mausoleum for dusty books.

When he got inside the library, Copeland just stood there looking as lost as he feels. He has no idea where to start. Finally, a young man came and asked if he could help him.

"You look a little lost, sir," he said, looking at Copeland with an obliging smile. "Do you need help?"

"I need to look some stuff up," Copeland said lamely, trying to think of what he needs. He is not sure what he needs and even less idea where to start.

"What do you need to find?" the young man asked.

"History on a company, a big one and the guy who runs it, and on some environmental groups.

The young man nodded. "I think I can help. Come with me."

The search proved much more difficult than Copeland could have possibly imagined. He would not have had a chance without the eager young man who took charge and thrilled in the challenge.

The environmental groups are the easy part. Digging up information on Chornelhus on the other hand proved nearly impossible. The deeper they tried to dig the more it seemed almost as if Chornelhus does not even exist. Perplexed by the lack of information, the young man took him on an impossible to follow maze of searching improbable online sites, old news microfiches, and dark web online communities. Copeland is sure not all the searches are legal.

As he watched, dumbfounded by the sheer speed the young man flipped through web pages, Copeland is pretty sure he had even tried to hack into Mr. Chornelhus's and the Anc-Chor Corporations computers.

All he could do the whole time is watch in silent awe as the young man flew through search after search, feeling completely deflated and useless.

With each successful information hit, Copeland felt more on edge, but for reasons that have nothing to do with his lack of knowledge in digging for information someone might not want found.

Hours later, Copeland left the library with a dazed look on his face and a stack of papers in his hand. Included in that stack is a list of other places to dig up more information at and what he should look for in each.

The young man had helped him pour through books and find what they could online, printing and photocopying pages. He seemed eager to please, finally having something more interesting to do than finding a book on a shelf.

Most of the information his young helper dug up is pretty ordinary. Some of it is not.

Getting into his truck, Copeland put the stack of papers on the passenger seat beside him. He looked at it as if it is a monster.

"If this is true," he mumbled as he started the truck. He shook his head, not finishing.

Copeland is disturbed by what he had just learned and the implications.

36 - Old Mrs. Crampchet Is At It Again

Mrs. Crampchet hummed to herself as she first put her coat on and carefully buttoned it up with fingers that shook from age, her wrinkled skin looking thin and papery, and then wrapped her shawl around her shoulders.

Picking up the tray of delicate little carefully decorated cakes with both hands, she struggled with the door, finally making it outside.

She shuffled along the sidewalk, purse swinging from its straps hooked over one arm, carrying the tray in both hands.

It takes her a long time to get to the Garden Grove development, but she is not in any hurry. At her age, until that moment when Death comes knocking on your door, you have all the time in the world.

Many of the workers on the crew are not the original crew and are unaware of the old woman's previous visit with poisoned treats. After an investigation, it had been deemed an accidental poisoning, the unintentional act of an addled mind and poor eyesight conspiring to make the old woman grab the wrong ingredients.

Most of the workers are busy, being pushed hard to play catch-up, and do not notice the old woman shuffling up the road into the construction site.

Two men are standing around talking outside the trailer office.

They pause and looked up at the approaching old woman, watching her curiously.

She held up the tray proudly when she finally reached them.

"You young men are working so hard," she said in her crackly old woman's voice, "you must be working up quite an appetite. I brought you some little cakes."

The men eyed the treats like little boys starving for cake.

One of them took the tray from the old woman.

"Here let me take that." He looked around for somewhere to put it down.

"Thank you," he said to her retreating back. She had already turned and started making her way back up the road.

She waved a hand without turning around, continuing her slow shuffle.

The men went back to their conversation, each picking a little cake off the tray as they talked.

A stray dog that had been hanging around all morning whined at their feet.

The man who took the tray looked down at the dog.

The dog sat in front of him, staring up at him, tail wagging eagerly and licking its lips while staring hungrily at the cake in his hand.

He shrugged and tossed the little cake to the dog, taking another cake off the tray for himself.

The dog caught it in the air, happily gulping it down in one swallow and sniffing the ground for more.

They continued talking, holding their cakes in their hands.

He lifted the cake to his mouth to take a bite, glancing down at the dog.

He pulled the cake away from his mouth in horror, staring at the dog convulsing on the ground, bloody foam at its mouth.

Turning to the other man in shock, he leapt forward, smacking the cake out of his hands as he raised it to his own mouth.

The startled man stared at him and he pointed down at the poisoned dog dying on the ground.

"What the hell?" the other man asked.

Old Rusty Plowshare watched the old woman shuffle up the road toward the housing development with the tray in her hands.

"What is she up to now?" he muttered.

His anger grew when his suspicion was realized and she turned up the road into the construction site.

"That old woman is going to ruin everything!" he growled.

37 - Samuel's Secret Revealed

Barbara Watkins's initial reaction to what she found in her husband's filing drawer in his home office was numbing shock.

It had been all she could do to stuff the paper in her shirt without the others seeing it. After that, Barbara continued with the search and cleanup with the other women, working mechanically and feeling dazed.

When she finally found herself sitting alone in her house after the others all left, Barbara just sat there staring at nothing. After a long time, she pulled the paper out again to look at it.

She has to confirm if she had only imagined it or if it is true. Her hands tremble as they hold the paper, her eyes memorizing every last detail, her mind refusing to let it sink in.

"H-he never told me," she stammered.

Barbara finds it hard to believe. Samuel was adopted! The paper proves it. He also knows or he would not have this paper.

It is a letter from an adoption agency answering his request to find out who his birth parents are. The agency confirmed he was adopted but refused to give him any more information than that.

She read it over and over again and finally decided to snoop some more in his files. Now that she knows exactly what she is looking for, she has a focus. She spends long hours meticulously going through his files, late into the night, and is back at it the next day.

Barbara missed the next meeting with the girls for coffee and did not stop to answer the phone when it rang. She is obsessed with finding out more.

At last, armed with the letter and his birth certificate and nothing else, Barbara headed out. She soon found out that playing private detective is harder than she imagined. She visited the library and the newspaper office, the hospital and finally phoned the adoption agency since they are too far away to go there in person. She needs to confirm somehow what the birth certificate says.

Barbara found the agency reluctant to reveal any information at all, quoting privacy concerns. They would not even consider checking their records for her.

Old newspapers revealed nothing of significance. Samuel did not even grow up in this town. But if one or more of his birth parents lived here, it explains why he was so insistent on moving here when they bought their house. She had not wanted to leave the city. He had been so insistent on finding a house in this particular town. Not just any community just outside the city, but this particular one, and could not give her any reason why at the time. Now she knows.

When Barbara returned home, she is relieved to see Samuel's truck in the driveway. He came home at last. She has not heard from him since he left so angry with her over her necklace in the little construction trailer. She was starting to worry he had left for good.

Barbara pulled into the driveway and turned off the car and just sat there for a moment, staring at the house. She wants to race in there and grab Sam and hug him.

But another thought stopped her.

"What if he's in there packing to leave me?"

Finally, she cannot take it anymore. She has to find out.

"Sam?" she called anxiously as she entered the house, "Sam?"

He came from his office, looking shaken.

Barbara looked at him levelly, mentally preparing to defend herself. She knows immediately from his look that he noticed someone had been rifling through his files and that he would be thinking they had been robbed.

"Someone's been in my office searching it," Samuel said. "I haven't checked the rest of the house yet to see if anything's been taken."

He is shaken by the discovery that someone had been in his office. He knows it was not a burglar because they would not have been so methodical. And they would not have bothered to try to put things back the way they were. Could it be someone suspicious of him? Could it be someone involved in the vandalism at Garden Grove, or one of the environmental groups opposing the Anc-Chor project? But why would they try to hide their tracks? What would be the point?

Barbara does not know that it is not a robbery he is worried about. He is worried someone broke in to search his office for other reasons, to get proof against him. He is certain someone has already searched his office at work.

"It wasn't a burglar," she said.

Samuel looked shocked, trying to decide what she means.

"I know," she said simply.

"Know? Know what?" Samuel asked, confused.

Barbara's face started burning with the coming confrontation, bitterness over his secrecy seeping into her.

"Why didn't you tell me? Why would you keep something like that a secret from me?"

Samuel started sweating, his pulse quickening and his mind racing. What does she know? Does she know about the blueprints? How?

He can only stare at his wife mutely.

"Why didn't you tell me you were adopted?" Barbara demanded. "That's not the sort of thing you keep secret from your wife! Why would you even think you couldn't tell me that?"

Samuel feels dizzy suddenly. He's adopted! So that's what this is about! Relief washes through him at the same time as that feeling a little boy gets when he did something really bad and knows he's in trouble with his mother. She doesn't know about the plans after all! He had also kept his being adopted secret for a reason. He did not want anyone to know, including his wife.

Anger flushed through him, replacing the anxiety. The only reason she would know this is if she had rifled through his files and found the letter from the adoption agency. He felt the burn of betrayal; that his own wife would snoop through his stuff.

Is she the one who searched his office? No one else? Did she somehow get in and search his office at work too? But, why? No, she couldn't have. She has the access here, but not at the office. That had to be someone else. Someone else could still have broken in to search his home office too. He felt dizzy with it all. Someone is snooping on him, trying to catch him, and he suspects it is the guys from Garden Grove. They are the only ones who suspected him of anything. He feels bad for thinking Barbara could have broken into his office at work; that she is trying to find evidence against him for some reason.

So why was she searching his files at home? And the adoption, that secret is out now and she is furious that he kept such a big secret from her. That is a marriage ruining secret.

Samuel hung his head. Embarrassment joined the other emotions pulling him in different directions. He did not want his wife to find out he was adopted. He himself had learned by accident some years ago and decided to find his birth parents.

Some things are better not known.

Barbara looked at him, the hurt edging past her initial anger.

"Why didn't you tell me?" she asked more softly, a tremor of pain in her voice.

"I-I didn't want you to know," Samuel said.

"But, why?"

"My parents," he said, "I mean my real parents," he broke off.

"Your mother is old Mrs. Crampchet," Barbara said apologetically, as if apologizing for the truth. It was on the photocopy of an old faded birth certificate she had found when she returned to search his files more thoroughly; the document from his files that Sam had taken a few years to dig up, but she had not wanted to believe it.

Initially Barbara had been sure it had to be another Crampchet, not that nutty old woman. But then she had to admit the truth to herself. And she almost did, but the idea was too absurd. It had to be a mistake.

Samuel nodded. "Crazy old Mrs. Crampchet is my mother."

"But how?" Barbara asked. Who his mother is was even more shocking for her to learn than that he was adopted. As far as anyone knew, the crazy old woman had never had a single child! Her investigation supported this.

She pulled out the photocopy she had made of the old woman's husband's obituary, holding it out as if somehow it proves he is lying to her.

"It says in Mr. Crampchet's obituary that he was survived by his parents, siblings, and wife. There is no mention of children," she accused. "I went and talked to some of the old people around town too. It was well known that Mrs. Crampchet had never married again after Mr. Crampchet's sudden death. If the woman had an illegitimate child after that it would have been well known town gossip."

"She had no kids," Barbara pressed, expressing her confusion.

"I did all the research," Samuel said in a low voice, "dates, her age, my age. She got pregnant after her husband died."

"Why that old tramp," Barbara said with a sly smirk. "How did she keep it secret?"

"Not funny," Samuel said. "She obviously had as much reason to keep it secret as I did. It was a different time then and the stigma of having a child out of wedlock, even for a widow, would have been difficult to live down. Especially if she is old fashioned."

"Somehow I doubt crazy old Mrs. Crampchet would be too concerned with that," Barbara said.

She considered this, and then asked, "Who's the father?"

"I don't know," Samuel said.

"Maybe that's why she wanted it kept secret, because of who the father is. The birth certificate only says unknown."

"Could be, or if she really doesn't know who the father is."

"I don't believe for a second she doesn't know. We should go ask her," Barbara said excitedly. She is so relieved that the answer is so simple. He is just embarrassed that his real mother is crazy old Mrs. Crampchet.

It took some convincing, but at last Samuel agreed to go visit his birth mother with Barbara. He did not tell Barbara that he had already tried that. Mrs. Crampchet had refused to tell him who his father is. A part of him hopes his wife will convince the old woman to give up his real father's identity.

The same young officer who had visited Mrs. Crampchet following the first poisoning of the Garden Grove construction workers is back to visit her again.

This time the poisoning was averted. Well, nearly averted. The only victim was a dog who did not survive the poison.

Constable Timothy Berkham remembers his first visit all too well. The old woman's confused state as she mixed up the sugar and flower while trying to make tea. And then not knowing who he was, mistaking him for someone else.

That first poisoning was found to be accidental, the results of a senile old woman who perhaps could not tell her baking soda from the poison she puts out for rats and mice. He suspects she has some fat well-fed rodents living in the house.

It looks like the seemingly well-intentioned old woman is at it again. Once was an accident, but twice he has more trouble with believing it was not intentional. Was it really an accident? Everyone knows old Mrs. Crampchet is nuts, senile. Is it really that far out there to think she might have poisoned those men on purpose? But why would she?

No, he decided. Most likely, she is just a doddering old fool that blind luck has stopped from accidentally poisoning herself yet. He will be careful about not ingesting anything in this woman's home. He is sure the woman is suffering dementia and is a danger to herself.

Constable Berkham had done some asking around about the old woman before coming this time. Some of the other elderly people in town think she had poisoned her husband decades ago and seemed to relish telling him about it in more detail than they could possibly know, even if it had been true. The single page report on her husband's death decades ago ruled it natural causes.

Nobody knew who this Johnny is that she had confused him with. It sounded like a son when he was here last time, but apparently, the old woman had never had any children.

He checked around the perimeter of the house before knocking on the door.

"Hello, Mrs. Crampchet?" he called out loudly through the door as he knocked. When the old woman did not answer, he moved around the house, looking in a few windows.

Berkham thought he saw movement inside.

He went back to the door, pounding harder.

"Mrs. Crampchet! Police! Are you all right in there?" He waited, listening for movement or a response. He thought he heard movement, but the woman did not answer.

He pounded on the door again. He tried the knob and like before found it unlocked.

"These trusting old people," he muttered, "they never lock their doors."

"Mrs. Crampchet? Mrs. Crampchet! Police! I am here to check that you are okay. I'm coming in!"

He opened the door cautiously, looking around before entering. He is instantly assailed by the delicious aroma of baking. The officer walked slowly deeper into the house towards the kitchen.

"Mrs. Crampchet? Police! Are you okay?"

He nearly jumped when the old woman suddenly appeared in a doorway, shuffling along and seemingly oblivious to his presence.

"Mrs. Crampchet?"

The old woman turned, looking startled, clutching at her chest with a pair of sharp knitting needles attached to unfinished knitting and a roll of yarn in her hands.

"Goodness!" she gasped. "You startled me!"

Her frightened look changed to annoyance.

"What are you doing sneaking around scaring old women, young man?"

"I just came to check on you Mrs. Crampchet," he said. "Just to make sure you are all right."

"Of course I'm all right, young man," she waved him off, moving towards the kitchen, seeming completely unconcerned that a stranger was in her house or that he was a cop.

"Uh, Mrs. Crampchet, there's been an incident over at the Garden Grove jobsite," he said, following her. "Do you remember going there?"

"Of course I remember," she said indignantly. "I brought those boys some little cakes."

"Yes ma-am," he said, "that's what I'm here about. "There was a problem with the cakes."

"Oh dear," the old woman said, turning around. "Was there not enough? Do they need some more?"

"No ma-am, I don't think they want more." He hesitated, thinking how to put this delicately. "Did you put anything, uh, unusual in those cakes?"

"Certainly not," she said. "I used the same recipe I've used for years."

She moved towards the stove.

"Tea?"

"No thanks ma-am."

The old lady put on a kettle for tea then moved to the cupboard where tins of baking ingredients are still laid out and half a dozen delicious smelling mini loaves of dense bread sit. They look and smell like banana bread.

The table is set with two places with small plates and matching delicate flowered tea cups on saucers, a bowl of sugar and a jug of nearly empty milk. It is the kind of set up you would expect to see for tea at your grandmother's house.

Berkham walked over to the table, picked the lid off the sugar bowl and looked inside. It looks like sugar.

He picked up the milk jug, watching the old woman cut one of the dense loaves with a bread knife. Taking the lid off, he sniffed at the milk and made a disgusted face at the smell that assaulted him. The milk is sour. He put the cap back on and put it back on the table.

"You're not, uh, going to use that milk for your tea are you?" he asked.

The old woman gave him a chiding look.

"Of course not dear, that milk is spoiled." She continued slicing the bread, humming, and set the slices on a plate.

She brought it over to the table, holding the plate out to him.

"Fresh banana bread? I just baked it."

It smells temptingly good but he shook his head, politely declining.

"No thank you ma-am," he said. "Now are you sure you didn't put anything unusual in those cakes? Maybe changed an ingredient? Added something? Maybe something that didn't quite look or smell right?"

"Nonsense young man, I've been baking since before you were born."

The old woman took a piece of banana bread off the plate, set the plate down, and brought the piece to her mouth.

Berkham looked around the kitchen, his gaze settling on the banana bread ingredients laid out on the counter behind her.

Flour, baking soda, salt, eggs, butter, brown sugar, blackening banana peels, and a box of powdered cleanser. The warning labels on the box were discretely put in a bottom corner warning the product is corrosive and poisonous. Next to the box is a measuring cup, powder dusting its side and the counter, blue specks in that powder.

He turned quickly back to the old woman who is just biting into the slice of banana bread, staring in horror as she bit a large piece off and began to chew it.

"NO!" He tried to stop her but it is already too late.

The old woman swallowed and stared at him with a curious look.

"There's plenty more if you really want some," she chastised.

"No," he said urgently, pointing to the counter, "the powder! You put that in the bread!"

"I certainly did not, young man," she said. The old woman turned and opened the oven, carefully taking a tray out with her apron folded to act as an oven mitt.

"I used the last of the other flour on the banana bread. I used that new box on these."

He looked to the garbage and saw the crumpled remains of an empty flour bag.

The cookies in the tray smell delicious.

"Johnny will be here any time now, you know," she said as she turned away and set the tray down on the stovetop to cool.

Berkham is shaken. He had been certain the old woman had just poisoned herself, and if she eats those cookies she will have.

"Mrs. Crampchet, you can't eat those cookies."

The old woman turned to him, looking confused. Then her face brightened.

"Johnny!" She threw her hands up, shuffling towards him faster than he imagined possible and throws her arms around him.

"Johnny! You're here!"

She tried to pull him towards the table. Not knowing what to do, the young officer let her.

"Sit Johnny, sit. Your father will be home soon." She hummed as she took the now whistling kettle off the stove; spooned tea leaves that he suspects might be crushed dried parsley into the cups and poured water in.

Timothy Berkham feels bad watching the old woman. She is obviously too far gone and a danger both to herself and others. It is sad to see someone finishing their life this way. She kind of reminds him of his grandmother too, and that makes the situation sadder.

She will have to be committed for her own good, and to keep her from accidentally poisoning herself or anyone else.

"Mrs. Crampchet," he started, "someone is going to come and see you; to help you."

"Why Johnny, you are already here. What other help could I need?"

He shook his head.

"No Mrs. Crampchet, I mean someone will be coming to talk to you, maybe to take you where you can be looked after. I'll just make a call and they'll be here soon. I'll wait with you until they come, if that's all right with you."

"Whatever you need dear," Crampchet said. "When your friends get here they can have some banana bread too, Johnny."

She hummed as she prepared for tea. Her eyes narrowed as she turned away from the young officer.

Mrs. Crampchet knows exactly what he means and it just will not do. She will not be taken from her home!

Barbara's heart is fluttering worse than it had on her very first date. She feels jittery with nerves, weak with anxiety, and frozen in a sweat of fear.

She is sitting in Samuel's truck outside of Mrs. Crampchet's house, the two of them about to go in.

Barbara cannot decide if her excited nerves are a good thing or bad.

She feels like she is on her first date again.

Her very first date had proved to be as exhilarating a night as she had expected. It also had not been with Samuel, and while the evening had been wonderful, the relationship turned out to be a very short lived disaster.

She steeled herself for what is to come, nodded at Samuel, and said, "Ok, let's go."

She followed him almost reluctantly up the walk to the front door.

Samuel knocked.

"Mrs. Crampchet," he called, "its Samuel." He still feels odd calling the old woman by any of the familiar terms reserved for mothers.

There is a brief sound inside and a long pause before the door finally opens.

The old woman peeked out the crack before opening the door further to let them in.

"Oh good," Mrs. Crampchet said. "You're just in time for tea."

"Uh, Mrs. Crampchet," Barbara said hesitantly, feeling she should introduce herself too. "I'm Barbara Watkins."

The old woman waved her words off.

"I know who you are, this is a small town."

She shuffled along through the small living room, stopping at the kitchen door.

"You two have a seat here." She indicated the worn living room furniture. "I'll be right out with the tea."

Barbara sat, feeling completely awkward.

"I should go help her," Samuel said. "You sit and try to calm your nerves. I can see how nervous you are." He patted her hand reassuringly and followed the old woman to the kitchen.

Mrs. Crampchet put the kettle on the stove to heat for tea again. A now cold tea sits on the table, crumbled green leaves, some sunken to the bottom and some floating in the clear water. A second cup sits ready, empty. Apparently, she had a tea date planned. He hopes their unannounced visit will not be a problem.

Samuel looked at the cup of ruined tea, thinking it odd. He picked up the small can marked Tea and looked inside it, sniffing at the contents.

"You don't want to use that," the old woman said without turning around, putting banana bread slices on a plate. "That's parsley." She opened the cupboard and took down another canister marked Tea.

"Here's the tea."

Samuel looked around the kitchen.

"Where are the cups and plates?"

She pointed and he headed for the cupboard. Samuel noticed the tray of now cool cookies on the stovetop and went over, sniffing at them. They smell delicious.

He reached out to take one off the tray, surprised to find his hand suddenly smacked sharply without warning.

He turned to find Crampchet standing next to him with a warning look. How did she get across the kitchen so fast? He stared at her in mute surprise, resisting the urge to rub his smarting hand.

"Those are not for you," she chastised, turning back to the kettle on the stove that is beginning to whistle.

Samuel saw the baking ingredients still on the cupboard by the loaves of banana bread.

She spotted him eying the powdered cleanser.

"I like to clean the counters thoroughly after baking," she said. "Nothing works better than the good old rough powder cleanser."

They heard a noise from somewhere in the house and Samuel's head turned to look, but there is nothing to see.

"What was that?" he asked.

"Just the cat," Crampchet said.

He looked at her curiously. "I didn't know you own a cat."

The old woman noisily clattered the cups and spoons, making the tea.

Shoving little teacup saucers and teacups at him, she changed the subject, quickly following with the plate of sliced banana bread. "Here, take these to the other room, dear, the tea is ready."

Between the two, they brought out the teacups, teapot and banana bread, little plates to eat off, and cream, sugar, and honey to sweeten the tea.

"So, to what do I owe the pleasure of this visit?" Crampchet asked as she sat down with some difficulty. Picking up her teacup, she stared at Barbara.

Her stare made Barbara want to squirm.

Mustering her courage, Barbara decided to jump right into the purpose of their visit.

"I found Samuel's adoption papers," Barbara said. "I did some research too, just to make sure."

She paused, hoping one of them would jump in to fill the awkward silence.

"Samuel was adopted," she finished, realizing how dumb it sounds the moment the words were out of her mouth.

"That's lovely dear," Mrs. Crampchet said, sipping her tea.

Barbara looked to Samuel for help, but he did not offer any. He is busy looking around the room. She wondered what he is looking for.

Samuel has a sense that something is off, almost like a déjà vu, and one that feels wrong.

"The papers show that you're his mother," she confronted the old woman with the knowledge, expecting her to wince or deny it or otherwise respond in shock that her secret is out.

"Of course I am dear," the old woman responded, silently stirring her tea with a little spoon as if Barbara had said nothing more important than that it might rain later in the week.

The silence ticked by while Barbara stared from the old woman to her husband and back again in shock.

"You're not denying it?" Barbara asked at last. She looked at Samuel again, noting his guilty look.

"Now why should I deny it?" Crampchet said, not looking up from stirring her tea. The woman is irritating her, but she does not show it. At last, she looked up, looking Barbara squarely in the eye, almost defiantly.

"Samuel is my son," she said.

Barbara reflected on this, her mind swirling. So she admits it. He is her son. But, their ages? She met the old woman's stare.

"But your age, his age," she managed, "How? Everyone knows you never had children. Or, at least that's what everyone thinks."

She looked to Samuel for help, but he just sat there looking awkward. She turned back to the old woman, the mother-in-law she never knew she had.

"You- you must have had him after your husband passed away."

The old woman nodded confirmation, not saying a word as she sipped her tea.

Barbara looked from the old woman to her husband again, realization dawning on her. But of course, she should have known this immediately.

"You already knew," she accused him. "And she already knew that you knew. You came here before to confront Mrs. Crampchet about being your mother! Why didn't you tell me you already talked to her?"

Samuel looked at her guiltily.

"Yes, I came here before. She didn't want to admit it at first, but then she did. We talked about it and decided to keep it a secret. We've kept that secret ever since until you went snooping and found the adoption papers. We've met regularly too to talk. Sometimes here, sometimes we meet in a coffee shop in the city."

"Y-you've been picking her up and taking her to coffee in the city and I never knew?"

He shook his head. "We meet there."

"But, how does she get there then?"

Samuel shrugged. He does not know. He never asked.

"Rusty drives me," Mrs. Crampchet said around a mouthful of banana bread.

They both turned and stared at her, stunned.

"Rusty?" Barbara exclaimed. "But that old man can't drive!"

"He does just fine," Crampchet said a little testily.

Noises came from somewhere in the house, muffled. Samuel and Barbara both looked around, wondering at the source, and the old woman muttered something unintelligible about the cat and started noisily stirring her tea.

Samuel and Barbara both have the same thought. They both cannot remember the old woman ever owning a cat. In fact, they thought she did not even like cats.

More, Samuel is confused because he does not remember her ever having or saying anything about a cat during any of his visits to her home. He feels edgy, like something is wrong. It is something indefinable, a gut feeling.

Half getting out of his chair he said, "Maybe I should go check it out, just to see what it is."

"It's nothing dear," the old woman said, waving him back down. "It's just the cat. He's too shy to come out for company."

Samuel sat back down reluctantly, looking in the direction of the sound uncertainly. He is too polite to just go snooping through the woman's house without her permission.

The sounds continued but Crampchet ignored them, clattering her teacup loudly on its little plate and clinking her spoon stirring the tea that did not need stirring.

She turned back to Barbara, changing the subject back, "As you were saying dear?"

Samuel had trouble bringing his attention back to the conversation. The sounds are a distraction, especially when he cannot wrap his head around her having a cat.

Barbara pulled her attention back to the old woman.

"Who is Samuel's father?" she asked.

"You really should have some of this banana bread, dear," Crampchet said, pushing the plate towards her. "It's really good."

The subject change is just too obvious.

"You don't want to tell me, do you?"

"Your tea is getting cold," Crampchet said a little sternly.

Barbara studied her more closely, thinking. Who could it be? Then it hit her. She remembered what Mrs. Henderson had said at one of their coffee clutch meetings about Mrs. Crampchet. The old woman and old Rusty Plowshare had been an item once a very long time ago. People even thought they would get married until her disapproving father put an end to the relationship. She had ended up marrying someone else instead, someone her family approved of and chose for her.

She stared in shock at Samuel and back at the old woman.

"You hooked up again with Rusty Plowshare, didn't you?"

"Nonsense, that old codger..." Crampchet started angrily, as if the idea is ridiculous, her cheeks turning pink with a high flush and her eyes shining.

Samuel stared at her in shock.

"You did!" he said, incredulous. "Rusty Plowshare is my father!"

"Certainly not!" she said, indignant. "Now I have things to do and you should run along and come visit another day."

With her defensive response, Crampchet's refusal to answer the question of who his father is, and Samuel had asked her that many times before, makes it all too clear.

Samuel Watkins is the illegitimate son of Rusty Plowshare and Mrs. Crampchet, the two craziest old birds the town ever had!

Samuel and Barbara are too shocked to put up a fight when the old woman hurriedly ushered them out the door, barely giving Barbara a chance to grab her purse.

They stumbled out on wooden legs, mechanically making their way to the truck. Samuel blindly put the key in the ignition and turned it, put the truck in gear and drove halfway down the block before he even realized he is in the truck and driving.

Something else occurred to him and Samuel pulled over and put the truck in park, turning to his wife.

"Why were you searching through my files?"

Barbara's heart fluttered. It is an extremely awkward moment. She is put on the spot with no choice but to tell the truth. But how can she? He will be furious, hurt, and it might just mean the end of their marriage! She had hoped he would not think to ask this question.

"Samuel, I..." She broke off.

He stared levelly at her.

"Why?" he asked again.

38 - The Last Stand of Old Growth Woods

Bruce Copeland returned to his office armed with the disturbing information he had learned about the Anc-Chor project. Most of it is confusing. It just makes no sense to him. He is at a complete loss. What does it mean? He has no idea what to do with the information.

He pulled up in front of Copeland & Howe. The two vehicles in the lot belong to Stanley and Dave. They are the only ones there.

He looked at his watch. The place should be empty. Darkness is creeping in across the sky.

Bruce Copeland cannot help but shiver with a chill that does not quite reach from the cool evening air to his back.

Getting out of his truck with a heavy sigh, he went inside the building.

In the back room, Stanley Rutthers and Dave McCormack have blueprint copies laid out and are going over the compiled blueprint that they had previously marked all the errors on, adding more things to it.

"What are you adding now?" Copeland asked as he stepped into the open doorway.

The two men jumped, startled, looking up with that trapped deer in the headlights look. They are both feeling edgy, like they are doing something wrong, although they know they would not be in trouble for being there. They did not hear Copeland come in.

"Dave found more spots at the Garden Grove site that look like they've been disturbed and then someone tried to hide it," Stanley said.

Dave nodded. "I think there might be more bones buried."

Bruce looked from one to the other, turning his attention back to Dave.

"Did you dig any of them up?"

"No," Dave said. "The crew was still there and I thought I should leave it. Maybe go back after hours when no one is around just in case there are more human bones. I don't want to get the site shut down again. I just marked them off with stakes and made a list."

"Good thinking," Bruce said.

"We're adding those spots to the combined blueprint," Stanley said.

Bruce walked over, studying the blueprint while Stanley went back to work adding the marks to the paper. Dave watched, pointing out spots he thinks Stanley missed.

A voice called out from the main office area.

"Hello?"

All three men looked up, exchanging glances.

"You expecting anyone?" Stanley asked his boss.

"No," Bruce said, "either of you?"

They both shook their heads no.

They were about to step out when the visitor poked his head around the corner, looking into the back room. When he heard voices, he had decided to come investigate.

"Is one of you Bruce Copeland?" the man asked.

"I am," Bruce said, "and you are?"

The man stepped into the room, fumbling with the mess of paper rolls and file folders in his arms; along with a well-worn leather bag that is stuffed too full to close, loose papers spilling out of it.

He tried to extend a hand to shake hands, nearly dropping some of his load in the process.

"I'm Professor Richard Mackin," the man said. "I have some questions for you about the Garden Grove development site."

Bruce made an attempt to shake the man's hand without making him drop any of the stuff precariously held in his arms.

"This is Dave McCormack and Stanley Rutthers," he said, indicating the men behind him. "They both probably know more about the site than I do. Stanley's the job foreman."

The professor nodded greeting to the two men.

"What do you need?" Bruce asked.

"Well, for a start, would it be possible for me to see the Garden Grove site blueprints?"

Bruce pursed his lips. This is an unexpected request and one that normally would be refused without question. He is about to say no when Dave spoke up.

"Hey, I know who you are!" Dave said. "You're the professor digging up the site looking for more bones. You studied the ones that were found."

This makes Bruce and Stanley both pause, wondering if this man can help solve that one problem. It is only one of many problems they are facing, but it is a big one.

They are also wary of telling this man anything that might lead to another site shut down and cause a more intense hunt for more human remains.

Professor Richard Mackin nodded, grinning, happy to be recognized. He spotted the blueprints laying spread out and darted eagerly towards the one Stanley and Dave are standing over.

"Is this it?" he asked, already studying it without giving the men a chance to answer or to object.

The three men exchanged uneasy glances, unsure what to do since he is already looking at it, their indecision giving him extra seconds. They cannot deny it when the larger bold letters clearly label it so.

Professor Mackin started jabbing his finger at spots on the blueprints, asking what they are. Stanley and Dave answered in one word responses. The man seems to have taken over the office with an excited air of a man used to commanding his students' obedience.

He pulled out his own map, unrolling it, matching landmarks and confirming, nodding his head and saying yup or ok each time.

He nodded to himself in satisfaction then turned to the men watching him in confusion.

"This is exactly what I thought," Professor Richard Mackin said.

"What is?" Bruce asked, still considering whether he should throw the man out or not.

"All of this land the town is built on was owned by one family once, the Plowshares, and they go way back," the professor said.

"I've studied the bones and done a lot of research on the area, old stories and myths, and the families that were around then. I've dug up some pretty interesting stuff. There are secrets the Plowshare family would not want revealed and I believe there is a really big one buried somewhere on that land. A big enough secret that it could re-write the local history." He jabbed his finger at the blueprints for emphasis, looking around at his audience expectantly.

"What kind of secrets?" Bruce asked. He has a bad feeling about this. One more shutdown of the site will seriously hurt his business. He is already losing money on Garden Grove.

This sounds like the kind of thing that could shut down a jobsite permanently.

"Do you know the history of the land?" Richard asked.

He got a mix of responses.

"There are a lot of old stories about the area, passed down by word of mouth," the professor began, "some from the settlers and some from the native inhabitants' side. One of the most common is the old stories of the native inhabitants murdering entire families both of the settlers and their own people. The aboriginals believed the settlers had somehow angered their ancestors, who were like gods to them, and brought down a curse on them all. The attacks were driven by fear and superstition over the birth of deformed children. Some stories say it was the settlers whose children were deformed and some that it was the natives. Some of the stories say that the settlers brought an ancient evil with them from another world, one older even than the aboriginals' ancestors. They say that this evil, whatever form of devil it was, made the aboriginals' ancestors angry and afraid. They, both the people of the tribes and the settlers, were believed to be cursed by this ancient evil."

He looked at the men meaningfully, playing the role of the professor giving the class lecture.

"My belief is that it was probably both sides that had families butchered. Unlike many other superstitious old stories, I believe this one is true, at its root anyway.

Most myths and old wives tales do have a foundation in fact, however small, but they get twisted so much over the generations that the truth is often completely lost.

I believe children were in fact born deformed, or at least with a condition that caused the deformity to develop as they grew and aged. The bones from the Garden Grove site confirm it. It's no curse, of course. Not knowing any better, people of the time thought anything they could not explain was the result of supernatural forces of some sort.

Most likely, it is a gene being passed down from a family of settlers, spread across both cultures through interbreeding between the settlers and the aboriginals.

The deformity was either visibly carried and the union involving aboriginals was most likely a forcible attack on the woman, or it lay dormant, the father a carrier of the gene and unaffected, passing it on in the consummation that resulted in pregnancy, passing it both through his own wife and the native girls he impregnated.

Whether it was known or not, the carrier fathered children who carried the gene and produced more children with the gene and so on, some of which would have been visibly affected by the gene, while others were just carriers, carrying it on down the line without anyone knowing they had it.

When babies started being born with the defective gene, and as they grew, their features and limbs became twisted, giving them horrific appearances and even crippling them, the aboriginal people would not have known what to make of it. They would have never known a disease like this before.

The aboriginals would have reacted in fear. They would have done everything they could to appease their ancestors and their gods, begging for their forgiveness, making the most serious of sacrifices even.

When all else failed, they resorted to the only thing they had left. They did butcher some families, mostly their own people, in fear of the curse."

"How do you know it was passed down by a man?" Stanley asked.

"I don't," Richard said. "It just seems more likely. A deformed woman may have birthed children from her own husband, but probably not. Let's face it guys, given the choice between a visibly disfigured wife and healthy young women, odds are the husband would have found his, um, release, elsewhere. And a man can father many more children than a woman can birth, and for longer periods. Given the child mortality rates of the times and the likely numbers of affected offspring, I'm almost certain it had to be a man who carried the gene here."

"But what about the settlers' families?" Dave asked. "Weren't they butchered too?"

Richard shook his head.

"Apparently not. That part I can't figure out. There are no real records and no graves to exhume from that time. Maybe they spared the settlers' families out of fear, but the history of human nature would suggest that fear would have led to a full-scale massacre.

But it didn't end there. The story of the bones speaks for itself.

There have been murders committed over the generations, but not the massacre of whole families the old stories suggest. They're spread out, one or two deaths per generation for hundreds of years.

The ages of the bones suggest some of them were even brought overseas with the family when they immigrated here, stored and kept for generations. While others buried the bones of their deceased, these people kept them with them like some kind of family treasure."

The professor looked at the other men, hoping the strangeness of it all is not lost on them. He continued.

"It's almost as if a token sacrifice were being made, perhaps to some pagan god in a religious ritual. The murders began long before the settlers even came to this continent. Some of the bones buried at your site predate this continent being settled. They had to have brought the remains with them for some reason. The victims were all twisted forms, suffering from the affliction of deformities caused by the gene, and they range from infants to elderly, both male and female."

"So, they weren't all killed soon after birth? Some lived with it for years until they were killed?" Stanley was stunned. "Did they start killing them as babies only after they moved here?"

The professor shook his head.

"The aboriginals massacred the whole family when an infant or child began to show the signs of the deformity in their own village. And I don't think it was always apparent at birth, but rather some would have grown into the deformities over years. But there are no markers to indicate any of the Garden Grove bones have aboriginal DNA.

All of the bones that were recovered at Garden Grove were from the same family line, the Plowshares. And they were killed at different ages. Some of the women may have even given birth to children before they were killed. But it stops a few generations back. That's the most recent of the bones found at your jobsite. Either that's when they stopped killing their own, or the line with the gene died out. Of course, it could just be coincidence, too, that whoever buried the bones did not use anything more recent. Or it could be that it has become harder to avoid burying their dead in a cemetery in the last few generations. But, I'm thinking it is more likely the line carrying the gene either died out or became so watered down that the deformities stopped. I searched, but could find no mention of people suffering deformities in the area that would match.

What I have not been able to figure out is whether these Plowshares actually worshipped some demon god, maybe putting these deformed people in a position of religious icon or acolytes, or if they were living in fear of their beliefs that their family was cursed, that a demon hunted them and twisted the bones and features of their children. Were they making heartfelt offerings to their gods or trying to appease a merciless demon?"

The three men just stared, shocked. This was both improbable and impossible, but the possibility had to be there. People have done horrible things over the history of mankind in the name of their religions and beliefs.

"Of course this is all theory," the professor said. "I need to investigate more, find more remains and other evidence to confirm what I think. But, I don't think I'll find it here. I have to find out who is planting the bones and where they kept them. I expect they have more, possibly even the entire skeletons."

"This gene, the disease that mutated them, what is it?" Dave asked.

The professor's eyes gleamed with the thrill of a career-altering discovery.

"That's the best part," he said. "I don't know. It is something we have never encountered before, a complete unknown, a new disease or gene mutation. Or a very old one no one has discovered before."

Dave is the most gullible of the three, and is more than half convinced now that there really was some supernatural link, and that it maybe was not only in the minds of the Plowshare's ancestors.

He stepped closer to the professor, his eyes urgent.

"Do the placements of the bones have meaning? I was thinking that the locations where the bones were buried are relevant. There has to be some purpose behind them. Maybe some religious meaning, you know, with your belief this is all based on some old religious cult?" He indicated the combined plan spread across the large table.

He stared at the professor eagerly, waiting for confirmation.

Richard turned to the plans, looking them over while shaking his head.

"It's not likely," he said. "What are these markings here?

Stanley looked sheepish and felt foolish.

"Those are where the bones were found and where we think there might be more buried," Stanley admitted.

Richard looked at him in surprise.

"This isn't something you would normally mark on the blueprints, is it?" He asked.

"No," Dave admitted.

Stanley stepped in to explain.

"There's so much weird stuff happening, the blueprints tampered with, vandalism, men poisoned, old bones planted, that we've started trying to see how it all pieces together.

Someone has been tampering with the blueprints for the site, making new copies, each with something different changed and swapping them with the originals filed in different places."

He shrugged.

"We're trying to find out who did it. We took all those forged copies, filed and switched repeatedly in various offices, and put them together, marking all the errors onto one plan. The last thing we did was add the spots bones were found and where Dave thinks the ground was disturbed and more might be buried."

Richard studied the map in rapt curiosity.

"These things all just look random and meaningless to me," he said, pulling out more maps and documents from his case and pouring over them in search for something.

It is not the bone sites or the discrepancies between the plans that interested him.

"There is no pattern in your markings that suggest they were deliberately set out to form some religious symbol or anything," Richard said distractedly as he searched.

He pulled himself away from the diagrams, turning to the men.

"I would say they are meant only as a distraction, an attempt to permanently shut down the jobsite."

"But why?" Bruce asked. "There's nothing special about the Garden Grove site."

"Oh, but there is," Richard said, his eyes gleaming with the intrigue. "Maybe not where you are working right now, but very close. There is a very old secret here, probably an old cult history that the families involved are embarrassed enough about to do anything they can to shut down your project to keep the secret hidden."

"But there hasn't been anything like that here!" Bruce exclaimed. "I've never heard of any kind of cult activities. I mean, you hear of them, but it is always someplace else."

He looked at the other two men for confirmation.

"None of us has ever heard any talk about cults or strange stuff," Dave agreed.

"The closest is the activist nuts chasing down the Anc-Chor project," Bruce muttered, but that's nothing to do with this. And that's politics and money, not cults."

"If there was some old dark secret here people would talk about it," Stanley added. "Kids on the playgrounds would jump rope to chants about it or turn before a mirror in the dark to see the witch or monster or whatever. With the social media technology today, nothing like that could be kept secret if it did exist. It has to be so long ago that any of the families that were involved are gone and buried, moved away, are so old they couldn't possibly do anything about it, or it's been forgotten after parents have kept the secret from their children and then died."

"You would be surprised what dark secrets a family can hold onto for generation after generation," the Professor said. "I've even uncovered rumors of whole families involved together in serial killing and burying bodies for generations in secret graves. It is likely all in the name of their cult beliefs, is my thought."

Richard turned back to the plans, drawn to them. He studied them, so focused that the other men in the room were sure he'd forgotten they were even there.

Richard straightened suddenly with a cry, loudly clapping his hands and making the men jump. He just made an exciting discovery.

He whirled on the three men, laughing in his excitement.

"There it is! I found it! I'm sure of it!" His finger stabbed at the blueprints.

"That's just trees," Bruce said, looking at the blueprint.

"Exactly!" Richard exclaimed. "How long have those trees been there? How many decades, centuries even?"

Bruce shrugged. "I think that's what's left of the woods that used to be here. They were carved up bit-by-bit and chopped down for farms and homes before this place became a town. More was cut down as those three or four buildings grew into a real town."

"YES!" Richard almost shrieked the word.

"The answer behind everything lies beneath the ground in the woods. I'm sure of it!"

"It has to be," he said breathlessly. "Based on the old stories, old maps, and my research of the area's past, I am convinced something is hidden there. And I believe it was brought over from overseas by a family that migrated here generations ago."

Richard turned to them urgently.

"We have to go there and look, dig it up. I know there is something there that someone does not want found! That's why they're messing with your jobsite, trying to shut it down!"

Bruce Copeland thought that is the most ridiculous thing he has ever heard. He shook his head in disbelief at the nonsense this man is spouting. Those woods have never been touched or dug up as far as he knows.

More, he is surprised by the rapt look of belief on Dave's face. "Dave? Really? I thought you had more sense than that," he thought.

Stanley at least looks skeptical. But what is going through his mind is the possibility. Could it be true? Could a family really think something someone did generations ago is worth this much trouble to keep secret?

"What could possibly be there after so long?" Bruce asked.

"I don't know," Richard said, "but the possibilities could change what we believe about the history of this whole area."

"Why would they bury those old bones if they kept them all these years?" Stanley asked. "Why now? Why not some other bones? There must be some reason."

"That I don't know," Richard said with a frown. "Burying those particular bones are sure to arouse curiosity. Maybe they are desperate to stop all development here. Any other un-extraordinary bones would have only put a temporary stop to the construction. Either they wanted it shut down permanently, or they did not think anyone would look as closely at the bones as I did. But even that doesn't make sense. These bones were carefully preserved for a very long time. Why would someone turn their back on that to just bury them in the ground now?"

Bruce stepped closer to the combined plans, looking at the blueprints and some of the maps and papers the professor has spread out, wondering how a university graduate could be so gullible to believe this superstitious nonsense, when something jogged in his mind.

He moved swiftly across the room, startling the others, and grabbed the Anc-Chor project blueprints. He spread them out on the table, covering the Garden Grove one, stabbing a finger at the paper.

His expression grim, he flipped through the professor's papers and grabbed one, putting it on the Anc-Chor project blueprint.

"Look!" he exclaimed, urging them all to look.

The three men came forward and leaned in, looking at the plans but seeing nothing interesting. The blueprint is a technical drawing, all clean lines and angles, while the professor's paper is a rough sketch of the fields the Garden Grove development is being built in. The sketch includes the woods off to one edge, a few of the old trees drawn in darker and more detailed, with the clearing that is more a space devoid of tall trees than a clearing. It includes rough landscape details of the nearby area that may have been visible and in around the same location. There is a large rock, dips and hills in the softly rolling earth, the meandering narrow river and its off-shooting creeks.

Richard is the first to understand. His expression turned to shock over the realization.

A portion of the Anc-Chor blueprint has a resemblance to his sketch of the woods and the trees he had unintentionally sketched in more detail, including the large rock and a thin line of nearly dried up creek running along one side of the woods.

"One more thing," Bruce said and he rushed back to his office, returning with a stack of papers that had been hurriedly put together. He shuffled through them quickly and pulled out a wrinkled page, a poor quality picture. The darker areas melded together into an indecipherable dark mass, and the faded spots were too faded so that part of the sketch is missing. It is clearly a bad photocopy of a bad photocopy.

He put it down and pointed at it. The picture is mostly hard to make out, but enough so that they can tell it resembles the professor's sketch of the area.

He looked up at them.

"Chornelhus believes in demons."

Stanley and Dave looked at him in disbelief. Chornelhus is a very wealthy and very powerful businessman. He has to be well educated, too well educated for believing in stuff like that.

Richard caught their look. "It's not that farfetched," he said. "It's well documented through history that even the wealthy and educated are just as susceptible to believing in the spiritual without proof. Despite the lack of physical proof of the existence of gods, angels, and demons, there are a great deal of people throughout history through to today who believe in the existence of them from the most powerful and well educated to the least. You cannot claim to believe in Heaven and Hell without acknowledging the belief in the devil and his minions, or in God and his angels.

Stanley and Dave nodded, they hadn't thought of it that way.

Bruce shook his head. "No, I don't mean he believes in the idea of all that. I mean he believes in demons as actual creatures that live and walk the earth, and that have nothing to do with God or Christian religions.

Fishing a page out of his case, Richard slapped it down on the Anc-Chor project blueprint. The letter-sized sheet of paper does not come even close to covering the large blueprint. He pointed first to the blueprint then to Bruce's picture and his own sketch, and back to this new picture, showing the others what he now realizes is so obvious.

This is not one of Richard's own sketches drawn as he tried to sort through the piles of information he researched for the bones discovered at Garden Grove. It is print out of a much older drawing, and better drawn, of what appears to be creatures that resemble trees or trees that resemble creatures, or perhaps were meant to be some kind of mutation of the two combined together. The twisted shapes almost appear to dance in the moonlight that is cast like a spotlight on them, bony bark covered skeletal fingers reaching for the sky like the bare branches of the trees in his sketch. The world surrounding them is devolved into a dark smudge. Vague shapes of landmarks in the close area surrounding them stand out in the darkness.

It looks like the creatures or trees or whatever they are had been caught and frozen forever in the midst of some ancient ritual.

Their placements within the drawing match the similarities between the Anc-Chor blueprints and Richard's sketch of the Garden Grove area. It is, in fact, a good quality version of Bruce's poorly photocopied picture.

Stanley and Dave see the resemblance between the drawing, sketch, and the plans but they don't understand.

Richard turned to Bruce, indicating the plans for the Anc-Chor project. "What is this?" The urgency in his voice sent a chill down all their backs.

"The Anc-Chor project," Bruce said gravely. His mind is in turmoil. The strange things he had learned about Chornelhus, the suggested implications of what it means for the project, it is unbelievable.

Mr. Chornelhus isn't just some eccentric billionaire. There are implications his strangeness goes well beyond that into ancient pagan beliefs and even stranger beliefs from what may be even older religions and superstitions. The man is possibly a cult all on his own.

He looked up at the others, his expression becoming grimmer.

"Chornelhus is insane. I think he blew up his own project."

Dave and Stanley turned to him in shock.

"But why?" Stanley asked. It just made no sense to him. And how could the Anc-Chor project in the city possibly have any connections to a small bit of ground that can't be more than a couple of acres on the edge of a small bedroom community outside the city that is all that remains of an old untouched growth of woods?

"He's into all kinds of old cult beliefs," Copeland said. He pointed at the evidence before them, the blueprints for the two sites and the sketches.

"It looks like he's made some crazy connection between the two places, the Anc-Chor project location and these woods. He's recreating these points, the woods and these landmarks inside the main building of the Anc-Chor project."

The whole thing just seemed too strange to be true. There is just no point to it, at least no sane one.

"Blood sacrifice," Dave whispered as if saying it out loud would somehow make it true, picturing the torn and bloodied bodies of the men that were caught in the explosion.

It seems ridiculous even as he thought it, more when he realized he actually said it out loud, but all this talk about curses and ancient beliefs had given everything a strange and surreal feeling.

"No," Richard said, lost deep in thought as he tried to work it out in his mind. "It's something deeper than that. The land the Anc-Chor project is being built on is sacred land to the aboriginals. They believe that there is magic locked into the earth there. That is why they are so opposed to the project being built there."

Outside night is falling. It's getting dark out.

39 - No Good News

Old Rusty Plowshare is in a state like he has never been in before.

As he read the newspaper article, his hands trembled, making the newspaper rustle, his fingers tightening to crumple the edges.

He exhaled a breath that is half groan and half growl.

Rusty folded the paper carelessly, more crunching than folding it, and tossed it on the coffee table.

His eyes hold a faraway look that would raze distant forests if they got in the path of his furious glare.

The newspaper article boasts that the recent spate of attacks at the Garden Grove construction site had taken on a whole new level with the intentional planting of old human remains. It went on further to say that authorities are investigating to determine who had put them there and why, as well as where the bones may have come from. The writer suggested that some teenagers may have vandalized graves in a cemetery to steal the bones.

Rusty humphed in irritation.

"Grave robbing!" he spat. "Vandalism!"

He burned with the fury. His attempts to shut down the Garden Grove site have failed! He thought that their finding those old bones would have shut down the site permanently, like what had happened at other sites before where old remains of the people native to the land were found. They were declared places of historical significance and became untouchable. Those were not like this. They were places where the bones were just left there naturally, or were the locations of long ago settlements, not like Garden Grove where he had placed the bones to make them think they were there naturally.

Unfortunately for Rusty, he is not up with the times and current technology. He had not even imagined the possibility they would be able to determine the bones were planted and had not been there all along as he wanted them to think. He also did not have bones from native inhabitants. The bones he has were all saved by his family over hundreds of years from generations of deceased relatives.

"Vandalism taken to a whole new level," he muttered, repeating the words from the article. "I'll show them a whole new level all right. I'll have to take this to a whole new level."

He got up stiffly and shuffled to the door. He had not bothered taking his shoes off and he left a trail of dried mud to the door. He usually did not bother with the shoes except for once a day anymore. It is just too hard to get them on and off. He regularly cursed the effects of aging, when your joints get stiff and sore and you can hardly bend over anymore even to take your own damned shoes off.

He shuffled off towards the old leaning barn, cats watching him warily from their hiding places in the yard, some scampering and scattering and others following at a safe distance.

There are a lot more cats in the barn. There are very few mice in there, even though the floor is mostly dirt, the doors do not close anymore, sagging as they do on their rusted hinges, and the walls themselves were rotting away and full of holes. There are also ample places for mice to nest and hide.

He moved around the barn, shifting things and digging through piles of debris, looking for something and muttering the whole time.

In his rage-fuelled focus on his task, Rusty Plowshare does not notice the police car parked in the barn on the other end that had not been there before, covered with old blankets, empty flowerpots, wood boxes of knick-knacks, wood pallets leaning against its side, and other rubbish.

Rusty Plowshare has an idea. He is not sure it will work, or if he can pull it off. He has more scheming to do.

Mr. Chornelhus is standing at the large window of his penthouse office, staring out at the world below; his world. The city sprawls out before him, other buildings trying to mimic the grandiose of his and all failing. No one will stand above him and so Mr. Chornelhus has his people pay tribute to whatever palms are necessary to keep his building taller than the rest. He rules these people below. They bow and scrape to him, crawling over each other to please him, praying to the one thing that has power, their god the almighty dollar. Money buys power and power buys more money, and Mr. Chornelhus has both in spades.

"Enter," he said at the sound of a tentative knock at the door.

His personal assistant came in, ducking his head nervously. The young man makes an effort to pull himself together, stand tall, and sound strong before Chornelhus could turn around and see his moment of fear. Mr. Chornelhus does not like any sign of weakness in the people closest to him.

He is terrified of his boss.

It is too late. Chornelhus had seen the young man's reflection in the window and is already contemplating replacing him.

"Sir," the assistant began, "our man at the environmental group World Protection Order has agreed. They are going to issue a formal statement taking blame for the explosion at the Anc-Chor project. They are already working on setting up a scapegoat, one of their more radical marginalized members. They will announce that he acted on his own without their authorization."

Mr. Chornelhus nodded, not bothering to turn around. He already knows they will do what they are asked. You do not say no to Mr. Chornelhus.

The assistant cleared his throat before continuing.

"We got more information on what Bruce Copeland was doing. He was doing research on the Anc-Chor project, and on you."

The assistant ducked forward quickly, handing Chornelhus a folder.

Chornelhus turned to take it, paused, and looked at his assistant before taking the nondescript manila folder.

"Everything is here?" Chornelhus asked.

"Yes sir," the assistant said. "Everything Mr. Copeland searched on and read is there. The first few pages are an outline in point form of what he looked for and what he found." He swallowed hard.

Chornelhus nodded and took the folder, opening its cover and glancing at the first page, his eyes roving down the list, his lips tightening in anger. Most of the information is unimportant; some of it is much too revealing of the man behind the name Chornelhus.

"How did Copeland find out some of this?" Chornelhus's voice is low and dangerous. "This is not public record anywhere."

"He got the help of a very resourceful college student working part time at the library," the assistant said.

Chornelhus is not happy. People should not be poking around in certain things. He investigates them. They do not investigate him. "The next time Mr. Copeland finds himself pulled over by a police officer it likely won't be for an impromptu meeting, or to issue him a ticket either," he thought.

He looked up, meeting his assistant's eyes.

"Is there any progress on the Garden Grove site?" Chornelhus asked.

The assistant paled and started sweating more. Bringing Mr. Chornelhus bad news is never a good thing.

"The site is getting back on track sir, but there is something else. The professor who is looking at the old bones, Professor Mackin, his assistant told me he discovered something big about them and went on a frenzy of researching. He researched everything from the history of the people and families, the history of the area, old wives tales and legends of the area, witchcraft and religious myths, and even diseases, deformities, and how things are carried and passed down through genes.

It looks like he's found links to you, sir."

The assistant stared at his boss nervously, waiting for a response, but none came. At last, he spoke again.

"Sir?" And again, more fearfully after a pause where still no response came, "Sir?"

Mr. Chornelhus finally broke his silence after what felt like an eternity to the young assistant.

"And where is Professor Mackin right now?" he asked. "I might just have to send someone to talk to him."

The assistant feels like he is about to faint. An icy sweat gripped him, his stomach lurched, and the world suddenly seems to be spinning.

"H-he's at the Copeland and Howe office."

Mr. Chornelhus's face turned to marble. He turned slowly and walked to the fully stocked bar where he calmly made a drink.

He never drinks alcohol.

This time he did. The foul stuff burned in his mouth and throat.

Without warning he spun, sending the tumbler across the room, its rich amber contents spilling across the floor, droplets flying, as it somersaulted in the air, bursting as it connected with the stunned assistant's head.

The assistant flinched and blinked at Chornelhus in shock, frozen in terror and surprise, alcohol dripping down his head and glass shards caught in his hair and fallen to the floor around him.

The surreal shriek that came from Chornelhus broke the spell and the assistant fled for his life, closing the office door behind him to put a barrier between him and a cacophony of breaking glass, loud thuds, and enraged screams.

Mr. Chornelhus has completely lost it.

Trembling, the assistant barely made it to the stunned secretary's desk, stumbling on weak legs. He fell against her desk, gripping it for support like a lifesaver.

"C-c-call h-his s-security guy," he chattered, his teeth rattling with shock and his hands trembling uncontrollably.

She blinked at him in surprise until he pushed himself off her desk and bolted for the door and the elevator in the hallway beyond.

The secretary finally picked up the phone receiver, dialed, and talked for a few moments, then replaced it. She sat staring fearfully at the closed door with the sounds of a madman destroying the world on the other side.

Moments before the security man arrived, it went silent on the other side of the closed office door.

When Mr. Chornelhus's top security man showed up, he looked at the secretary and she silently waved him to go in. She still looks shaken despite the quiet now coming from the inner office.

He opened the door cautiously and peered inside.

It looks like the top floor of the building had exploded, except the large windows are still intact. Debris and broken pieces of furniture, glass, and shredded chunks of paper are strewn about.

Mr. Chornelhus is sitting calmly in his desk chair sipping from the one unbroken glass in the room.

"I have a few things for you to do for me," Chornelhus said calmly. "Oh, and send housekeeping up too."

The coffee clutch girls are more than worried now about Barbara Watkins. She has not been answering her phone or returning any calls for days now. She also missed all their coffee meetings. With all of the things going on this is very troubling.

Pamela is out walking her dog when she spotted Samuel Watkins' truck drive by with Barbara in the passenger seat. She nearly dropped the leash and squealed with relief at the sight of her friend.

Picking up on his master's sudden excitement, the dog turned to her. Not seeing a stick or ball in her hand, he decided there must be something wrong somewhere and started barking while looking around, unsure what he is barking at.

"Shush!" Pamela hissed at the dog. He kept barking until she pulled the leash, dragging the dog home. She cannot get the dog home fast enough. On the way, she sees Samuel's truck stop in front of the Watkins house and Barbara get out. She watches the truck as it drives away before turning to walk up the driveway and into her house.

Pamela sped up, hurrying to get rid of the dog.

As soon as she is in the house, Pamela is on the phone, calling the girls to let them know Barbara is home.

In minutes, they meet in the road in front of Barbara's house.

"You go up and ring the bell," Libby said to Pamela, "you're her closest friend and you saw her get dropped off."

Pamela hesitated, not wanting to be the one to do it. They are all feeling awkward, certain that something must be wrong.

Finally, Mrs. Henderson took charge and marched them up to the door as a group, ringing the bell herself. She gave a warning look to anyone who looked like they are ready to bolt. That is Libby.

A shocked looking Barbara answered the door.

The women immediately swarmed her, gushing over her and asking what is wrong.

Shaking her head, Barbara let them in. The women ushered her to the couch, sitting around her as if to protect her from threat or fleeing, while Pamela retreated to the kitchen to make coffee. She has been in Barbara's kitchen enough times to know it like her own.

"What happened?"

"Where have you been?"

"We were so worried!"

They are all speaking at once, faster than Barbara can react, and she only sits staring at them, still stunned by what she had learned at Mrs. Crampchet's and from her confrontation with her husband in the truck after.

They move on to excitedly telling about who they saw and talked to and what they learned. They have learned nothing.

Pamela waved them to silence, staring at Barbara, reading something in her expression.

"You learned something!" she exclaimed. "It's something big!"

Barbara looked at each of them in turn, licked her dry lips, and hesitated.

"Samuel is adopted," she finally said.

The women look at her in surprise.

"You never told us that," Pamela said, her voice a little accusing. She feels put out that her friend would have kept something like that a secret all these years.

"I only just found out," Barbara said, explaining. That makes the revelation even more shocking, that she had not even known that her own husband was adopted.

"Who are his parents?" Libby exhaled, just realizing as she spoke that she has been holding her breath.

"Old Mrs. Crampchet," Barbara said, looking at them, still in her own state of stunned disbelief.

"Who's the father?" Pamela asked.

"We don't know," Barbara said. "She won't say, but we think we have an idea who it is."

"Well? Who?" Pamela and Libby leaned in closer, eager for the dirt.

"That crazy old man, Rusty Plowshare," Barbara said, feeling her face flush with embarrassment at the idea of being related in any way to the old man. The crazy old woman is bad enough. To have her husband related to both of the town crazies is too much.

Pamela and Libby gaped at her with identical expressions, their jaws dropped open and eyes wide with shock.

Mrs. Henderson leaned back in her chair, looking thoughtful, lost in her own thoughts as she took the information in. "That explains a lot of what I learned from my mother," she thought.

Barbara's eyes sting with tears that threaten to come.

"There's more," she said, her voice cracking with the sudden constriction tightening in her throat. "I'm sure now he's the one who planted the altered blueprints."

All three women froze in shock.

"Are you sure?" Pamela asked.

Barbara nodded unhappily. "I don't have the proof, but I know it. I just don't know why. It was him."

Mrs. Henderson nodded as if she has just come to a decision.

"Well then I guess we'll just have to find the proof, won't we," she said.

40 - Searching the Woods

Bruce Copeland is in the yard at Copeland & Howe loading the last of the equipment into the back of his truck. A small Bobcat tractor sits on a flatbed trailer hitched to the truck.

He is preparing for that night's adventure.

"This is nuts," Bruce muttered under his breath. "I can't believe I'm actually doing this."

Stanley Rutthers and Professor Richard Mackin are going to meet him at dusk at the small piece of woods that is all that is left of the forest that once covered the Garden Grove site and most of the land the town now sits on before it was cleared away generations ago for farms and homes. They are going to search the trees for whatever it is the professor thinks is hidden there.

There will be little light that night with the heavy cloud cover and the moon just a slit in the sky above that.

Dave McCormack is at the Garden Grove site today filling in for Stanley as foreman. Bruce is working the crew there as late as possible as a cover for their activity in the woods, hoping anyone hearing the growling of the small bobcat tractor will think it is the workers at the site.

Loaded and ready, Bruce got in the truck with a rough sigh and headed on his way. When he gets there, he will take a back way in, turning off and driving across the grass against the back of the properties to park where the truck will be out of sight to anyone close enough to wonder why it is there. Vehicles on the highway will see it, but it will be no more than a passing curiosity in the distance, if they noticed it at all.

Bruce arrived at the spot and parked, cutting around at an angle so the trailer is bent at a 30-degree angle from the truck, its back end pointing towards the woods.

Professor Richard Mackin is already there. He sprung forward eagerly to meet Bruce before he could even get out of his truck.

Stanley came wandering out of the woods where he had been visually staking it out in his mind based on the crude map the professor had drawn. He had asked the professor where he got the information and was quickly lost in the man's long rambling answer.

"How long have you been here?" Bruce asked, pulling tools from the back of the truck.

"About twenty minutes," Stanley said. "He was already here." He thumbed towards the professor who is excitedly looking around.

The growl of the tractors at the jobsite across the field is a constant low rumble.

Stanley walked to the truck, pausing to look at his boss. He wants to tell him that the place feels wrong. But how do you tell someone something that sounds completely crazy and you do not even know how it feels wrong?

He cannot shake that creepy déjà vu feeling of being watched by something or someone who really does not want them there. It is a sense of danger tingling down his spine. A sick feeling in the pit of his stomach. He feels like he should be afraid, although there is nothing here to be afraid of.

Stanley shrugged, trying to shake off the feeling. They are the same feelings he gets at the Garden Grove jobsite every time he is there since the first day they brought in the equipment and started staking it out and breaking ground. Only now, the feelings of dread and danger are stronger.

The anxiety still clings to him, unshakeable.

"What the Hell is wrong with me?" he thought.

Stanley climbed up onto the trailer while Bruce set the ramps in place and Stanley backed the tractor down to the ground.

Turning the machine around, Stanley drove it slowly ahead towards the area where the professor wants to start. He climbed down, grabbed one of the shovels from Bruce, and they began poking around at the ground, searching without really knowing what they are looking for.

Richard poked around, checking lists and diagrams, asking questions about locations, and finally picked a spot.

"Right here I think!" he exclaimed. He wants to start at just the right place.

Armed with shovels, they start digging where the professor said. When that spot proved to be unlikely based on some vague thing only the professor seemed to know they moved to another and tried digging there.

Stanley stopped digging and looked around the trees.

"You notice there are no birds or squirrels?" he asked. "Don't you think that's a bit odd?"

Bruce looked around and shrugged.

"Guess they don't like the company," he said and went back to digging.

They would try a number of spots over the next while, some only exploratory searches with the shovels and others with the deeper bite of the tractor. Each time Richard had them move to a new spot it seemed more likely to the two construction men that this is a big waste of their time.

"The chill in my bones is more than just the chill night air. I can feel you out there, traipsing across my grave in your nighttime dance. What do you think you will find in the woods?

I see you, poking your noses in dark mossy places, turning over decades of rotting leaves that have been untouched by any but squirrels and the probing hooves of deer looking for acorns."

The figure pulls a weathered shawl closer about bony shoulders with age knotted hands, as if it might help to ward off the chill of the soul.

"You do not know what you do.

Secrets are best left sleeping."

Evening is drawing deeper towards night and the last of the dull grey daylight is failing as the setting sun dips beyond the edge of the horizon. The clouds prevent the sun from casting its brilliant orange and red display as it says goodnight.

The fading light casts deep shadows across the world as equipment continues to growl and crawl across the ground at Garden Grove, headlights shining bright and rude against the growing darkness as the men try to get that last heartbeat of sunlight in. Some of the men are working overtime at the Garden Grove site, trying to catch up on a job that is seriously behind schedule. They will work until that very last shred of sunlight vanishes.

Dave McCormack is driving one of the Cat tractors just on the edge of a ribbon of trees bordering the new development and extending off across the field behind the houses. It is not as small as a Bobcat, its long bony arm coming up and bending down at its elbow like an insect's appendage. On the end of that arm, a bucket with ragged teeth is poised above the earth, ready to bite deep. The tractor looms darkly against the background of pale grey sky, the trees behind it tall naked scraggly black skeletal limbs twisting towards the sky.

He is between the trailer office and the trees across the field where his boss, foreman, and the professor are meeting. He saw the professor's car, and then Stanley's truck, when they arrived. More recently, the headlights bobbing across the field told him Bruce had finally arrived.

Dave looks up at the fading light. He will not be able to keep the workers on the site much longer. It is getting late for the men to be working, even for a job as far behind as this one.

He pushed and pulled at the levers, turning the tractor body on its track and bringing the bucket down, its teeth sinking into the earth with a groan of the straining hydraulics, the engine growling. He leans, craning to look up at a dead tree that is leaning precariously against another, its barren trunk shifting as the tractor tears out its rotting roots. He has to be careful that he does not cause the dead tree to fall on the tractor.

Dave did not hear the sharp crack that echoed against the sky, or the plink of the treated safety glass of the windshield, over the loud growling of the machine.

He looks down in surprise at feeling something small bounce off his wrist, just catching sight of the tiny projectile of displaced glass as it vanishes somewhere inside the tractor. He pauses in moving the controls, looking around in confusion and trying to figure out what that was, and then freezes.

Dave stared at the windshield, the tiny hole glaring at him, web traces of cracks radiating out like a child's drawing of the sun, the edges of cracked glass glinting brighter than the rest of the windshield in the fading light. His eyes narrowed, focusing on that small hole, leaning forward to study it.

It was not there before.

He pales and looks sick suddenly.

Dave turned and looked around the cab, spotting the hole in the seat back. He fingered the hole.

If he did not lean over and stare up at the dead tree at that moment, the hole would be in him instead.

He looked around quickly at the darkening world. Everything at ground level is dark shadows against darker shapes, a sharp contrast to the lighter sky above.

There is no sign of where the shot could have come from.

Dave killed the engine with a trembling hand and opened the door, ducking low as he climbed out. Keeping the tractor between him and the direction the shot seemed to have come from; Dave slunk back towards the jobsite.

The first man he saw stared at him in confusion, wondering why he has an odd look on his face.

"What's the matter?" he asked.

"Nothing, just hit a line," Dave lied. The assumption would be a power line, which could be dangerous. "We're shutting it down for the night. Call everybody in and send them home, quickly."

The urgency in his voice and his shaken demeanor worried the other man and he ran to do as he was told.

Dave's mind both reeled and froze. He moved without understanding, reacting without the ability to think.

One thought is playing in his mind.

"Someone tried to kill me!"

The bobcat growled as Stanley worked the controls, digging where the professor is sure they will find something. Bruce studied the hand drawn maps doubtfully. Richard watched eagerly, now and then darting off to the side to double-check some imagined landmark.

Taking a shovel, Bruce started poking around near where the bobcat is digging.

The darkness is growing within the trees, the world fading to black despite the weak light still clinging to the sky above.

Stanley stopped when he spotted a dark movement on the edge of the trees. Leaving the tractor to idle, he climbed down and moved away from the tractor's glaring headlight to see better.

The movement soon revealed itself to be a figure walking swiftly towards them.

"Dave," Stanley greeted the figure when he finally could make out who it was.

Bruce and Richard turned to Dave, their expressions becoming concerned when they see the shaken look on his face.

"What happened?" Bruce asked. Scenarios played through his mind. More vandalism, an accident, something else found to shut the jobsite down again.

"Someone shot at me," Dave said, looking at them with the blank-faced shock of a crash survivor.

The three stared, the words not registering at first.

"Someone shot you?" Bruce finally choked out.

"Tried, missed," Dave said. He still feels weak and shaky. "I think we should get out of here."

They stared at him, not knowing what to say.

Finally, Richard broke the silence.

"I think this proves I'm right," he said.

The professor begins telling them more of what he learned.

"Only one of the families living here now was here when the settlers first came. The rest seem to have come along a few generations after, and of course since then more new families moved in and out of the area."

They looked at him; waiting for the answer they know will come. The man likes to talk.

"The Plowshare family; although they didn't always call themselves that. The name had been changed at some point, which was not uncommon, and the records are sketchy, but I have every reason to believe they are the only one left of the original families to settle the area."

"Ok, so what does that matter?" It was not asked to be rude. Bruce is genuinely interested. This sneaking around at night looking for hidden things, getting his hands dirty, and solving this big puzzle is filling him with a sense of adventurous excitement he hasn't felt since he was a boy fighting imaginary pirates and stealing their gold.

He also is shaken by Dave's revelation that someone had just taken a shot at him. He wants answers, whether or not they will answer the question who is behind the shooting.

The professor rubbed his hands together eagerly. He always gets a thrill when he has a pupil tuned into his lectures instead of just staring at the endless sea of bored expressions that usually fill the lecture hall. He seems to be oblivious to the gravity of the situation, that there is someone out there in the darkness armed with a gun, who had just shot at one of them.

"It's the only family that makes sense to have any secrets. They owned most of this land too at one point."

"But the only Plowshare left is that old coot Rusty Plowshare," Stanley said. He looks around nervously before continuing. He wants to get out of there, but is not sure which direction is safe to go, if there is one.

"That old bird's crazy as a loon. He's a hoarder too. Any secrets he has are probably buried in that old barn that's about to fall over on his property. There's no way that old man could be doing all this vandalism at Garden Grove. He's so old he can hardly walk. And there is no way he could have had anything to do with the blueprints."

Stanley looked around anxiously again. He looked at Dave, wavering on his feet, pale and shaken, and looking like he is about to faint.

"Hey guys, I really think we should get out of here."

Richard's eyes fairly sparkled with eagerness to tell them more.

"I did more digging on the family, once I knew which one it is," Richard said.

Mrs. Crampchet looked out her kitchen window and saw something she does not want to see. She leaned in to get a better look, squinting to see through the growing darkness and the distance.

"What the hell?" she muttered.

There are figures moving around in the woods. Lights moving in the dark. She is just able to make out that it as a Bobcat tractor. Someone is digging in the woods!

"Damn it!" she swore, pushing away from the window, distressed.

Her family has lived here for enough generations to know that this little community has harbored a lot of dark secrets over the generations, that there are skeletons buried in places other than the cemetery. Most people have one or two of the proverbial skeletons in their closets, and some families have more than others.

She shuffled to the back door, her movements urgent, rushed.

Her hands shaking, she grabbed her coat and struggled to get it on, her fingers fumbling with the buttons. She has trouble with buttons these days, even when she isn't in a hurry. Now she is in a hurry like she hasn't been in since she was a teen trying to sneak out to see a boy, terrified of getting caught before she could slip out. Coat finally on, she pulled her boots on with less difficulty than the buttons had given her.

The old woman straightened and turned to the door, reaching for the knob.

She turned the knob and pushed the door.

Nothing happened.

"What?" she muttered, pushing on the door again and staring at it in confusion.

Crampchet moved to the window in the back door, pressing her face against the glass to see.

Someone had barricaded the door so she can't get out!

She grasped the knob in frustration, rattling the door in its frame with all of her feeble strength, causing sharp pains of arthritis to tear at her hands.

"No, no, no," she muttered in desperation. "What have you done?"

She shuffle-ran to the front door and found the same thing there. She turned the knob and pushed but the door would not open. Going to the living room window, the old woman pressed her face to it, straining to see the outside of the door.

She cannot see, but she knows, it is barricaded too. She is trapped inside! If she were younger she could try climbing out a window, but at her age she simply isn't mobile enough. She would be certain to break a hip or another bone in the fall too.

Not for the first time in her considerably long life, Crampchet cursed her late husband's relatives for their nonsense in building the house with doors that open outward. Normally they swing in to open, but not this house.

The house is over a hundred years old. Like many houses built in its era, the house was built by family and neighbors before building codes were enforced. Before most of the building codes existed.

The patriarch of the Crampchet family at the time was paranoid of intruders breaking in. At his insistence, the family had built all their houses like this to make it more difficult for an intruder to kick the doors in. There were other oddities built into the Crampchet family homes for the patriarch's often thought to be misguided security concerns, but most of those have been lost in the decades of decay and repair the houses have endured, until all but one has been demolished to make way for newer homes.

Mrs. Crampchet has always known of their fear of that and still thought the extra precaution unnecessary.

"Bloody backwards Crampchets," she muttered in her frustration.

The old woman wailed in desperation, frustration, and fear.

"What have you done?" she muttered over and over again, trying the door again. In mindless desperation, she went back to the back door and tried it again as if it might have somehow come unstuck.

Muffled sounds come from the root cellar beneath the house. They are unintelligible.

Mrs. Crampchet turns in the direction of the narrow door tucked discretely in a corner of the room. It is the only access to the root cellar beneath the old farm-style house. The door is almost invisible behind the stuff piled in front of it.

"Shut up down there!" she yells.

Shaking her head and muttering, she goes to the phone on a little table in the living room. It is an old landline phone, likely at least forty years old. Pulling out a little worn out address book that looks as old as the rickety table, she struggles with her weak eyes to see, flipping the pages to find what she wants.

She dials the phone and listens to the rings until it is answered.

"Hello," a male voice said, "Samuel Watkins."

"Sammy," the old woman croaked into the phone, the stress in her voice clear. "I'm trapped in my house! Someone blocked the doors so I can't get out. There are people digging in the woods! I have to get out there!"

"That's terrible," he sympathized. "You're okay? You aren't hurt or anything?" His sympathy does not sound sincere.

"I'm fine," she said. "But I need you to come right away and get me out. I have to get out there!"

"I'll be there when I can," he said, although his tone sounds like it is a lie. "Why don't you just make yourself some tea and relax for now. Actually, it's probably the safest place for you at the moment with people digging around in the woods doing who knows what."

She pulled the phone away from her ear and stared at it, annoyed.

"I'll be there later some time, maybe in the morning," she heard his voice coming from the phone receiver still held at a distance. His voice is small and far away. He sounds preoccupied.

She cannot believe he said that to her. Probably the safest place for her right now? Her eyes narrow with suspicion and she hangs up the phone.

"Samuel," she muttered, her voice dry and raspy, "was it you that trapped me inside?" She now suspects he is the one who did it. Why else will he not come help her? And he did not sound surprised or concerned at all by her predicament. She shook her head, muttering to herself.

She turns her focus back to the woods. Was Samuel out there with those people digging? She has to get out there and stop them.

She knows if he is out there, Samuel will be trying to stop them. He will also be in a lot of danger. All of them in the woods are.

The old woman is starting to panic. She clutched at her chest, her irregularly beating heart sending a pain impulse that makes her feel like she must be having a heart attack. She feels her chest constrict and thinks that she cannot breathe. It is only a panic attack, though, and her breaths continue to come quick and shallow. The signal is not even coming from her heart, which is only beating faster, its irregularity happening only in her imagination.

"Ok you old woman," she muttered, "you can do this." She tried to think past the image of the barricaded doors and someone finding her mummified remains months or even years from now, laying on the floor in soiled clothes with a thick layer of dust and cobwebs blanketing her like they showed on that television show about mummies in Egypt.

Struggling to read the little phone book again, she dialed another number. This time she is calling Sam's house number instead of his cell, hoping that he will not be the one to answer.

Crampchet nearly cried in relief when a woman's voice answered.

"Barbara," she croaked urgently, "you have to come over right away! I'm stuck!"

"Stuck?" Barbara is confused. The woman doesn't seem to be talking sense.

"In my house, I'm stuck!"

"Where?" Barbara thought quickly, where could an old woman get stuck? "Did you fall? Should I call an ambulance?"

"No, no, no," Crampchet is getting impatient. "I'm stuck! Some prankster barricaded the doors! I can't get out of my house! I need you to come and get me out."

"That's awful," Barbara gasped. She cannot imagine who would do something so unimaginably cruel, and to an old lady yet. "I'll call Samuel; he'll be there right away."

Crampchet growled under her breath at the woman, composing herself before talking again. It would not help to yell and offend her so she refuses to help.

"There's no time for that," the old woman moaned piteously into the phone, invoking Barbara's sympathy with her tone of utter helplessness and desperation. "I already tried that. He's too busy. Sammy said to call you. You have to get over here immediately!"

"Uh, okay," Barbara said, her voice shaky, feeling the woman's panic over the phone. "I'll be right there."

Crampchet hung up with a self-satisfied smile.

Barbara's mind is reeling. How bad is it? Who would do such a thing? She started trembling, frightened for the old woman's safety and that she might not be able to free her.

She decides to call in the cavalry to help her. Picking up the phone, she begins making calls to the coffee clutch.

A few minutes later, they all descend on the old woman's house.

41 - It Has Awakened

Barbara Watkins and the coffee clutch all arrive at Mrs. Crampchet's house at about the same time.

Libby rushes over to Barbara, hugging her arms and making sounds of sympathy and worry.

Pam and Mrs. Henderson go to the front door, inspecting the handiwork that is trapping the old woman inside. It does not look like it will be easy to move. There is a large old chest freezer that is padlocked closed and chained to the railings on both sides of the steps with another padlock securing the heavy chains.

"Someone go around back and check that door out too," Mrs. Henderson called.

A curtain flutters inside the house and they spot the old woman peeking out at them.

"Don't worry Mrs. Crampchet, we'll get you out!" Mrs. Henderson called out to the old woman inside.

Barbara and Libby go around to the back. An old large refrigerator is leaning against the back door. It looks like it probably weighs about the same as a small elephant. A long towrope is wrapped around it and around the back railing, and around and around and around. Barbara feels dizzy just thinking about how many times it must be wrapped around. A mountain of debris is dumped in front of the fridge.

"Why on earth does the old woman even have railings on the back door?" she wondered out loud. "There aren't even steps here, just one step down."

Libby shrugged. "She's old. Maybe it gets slippery?"

They go back to the front.

"The back is even worse."

"Okay then," Pamela nodded, "let's get to work."

The chains at the front hang with some slack, drooping in a wide shallow U. Pamela pulls on one of them. If they can pull the freezer ahead, they might be able to open the door enough for the old woman to squeeze through.

Pamela and Mrs. Henderson try pulling on the freezer, but it is impossible to budge. Pamela fingered the padlock on the lid.

"It must be packed with something making it too heavy to move. Just a sec, I have some tools." Pamela runs back down to her car and opens the trunk. She had quickly tossed some random tools in there before rushing over, not knowing what they might need. Luckily, one of them happens to be lock cutters.

She runs back with the lock cutters and cuts the chain tethering the freezer to the railings. It clinks and jangles dully as it falls away, banging loudly against the metal railing. The noise makes them all flinch and look around guiltily as if they are the ones up to no good instead of rescuing an old woman.

She put the loop of the padlock between the cutter's blades and squeezed as hard as she can. She is not quite strong enough to squeeze the unwieldy cutter arms together, the tensile metal of the padlock much stronger than the chain. Mrs. Henderson stepped in and they both grab the arms and squeezed together, finally making the cutters slice through the hardened metal.

They open the lid to find it filled with bricks.

"Start hauling the bricks out!"

When they got enough bricks out to make the freezer moveable, they each take a corner and the four women struggle with the heavy freezer. It teeters at the edge of the first step and Mrs. Henderson cries, "LOOK OUT!"

Libby and Barbara jump out of the way just in time as the freezer tilts and goes over the edge, banging down the steps with enough force to dent the sides and chip slices of concrete off the steps.

They let out a cheer and scramble for the door, old Mrs. Crampchet meeting them at the door. She is trying to get out, but the four women are pushing their way in, forcing the old women back in.

"Are you okay?"

"Are you hurt?"

"Do you need anything?"

"Is there anything we can do?"

They are all talking at once and Mrs. Crampchet tries to look past them to that exit that is calling to her. She needs to get out there and stop those men in the woods!

The women go further into the house, looking around as if they expect to find an intruder waiting to attack the old woman.

"Thank you ladies," Mrs. Crampchet said, "now I really need to go."

She is heading for the door when muffled sounds come again from the basement.

"What's that?" Libby asked.

"Nothing, the cat," Mrs. Crampchet said quickly, looking at the women anxiously and wanting them out of her house.

"What's this door?" Mrs. Henderson asked, inspecting the hidden door where the muffled sounds are coming from.

"That's nothing," Mrs. Crampchet said, distressed. She moved toward the woman to try to move her, decides to change tact, and instead looks around with a confused look.

"Johnny? Where's Johnny?"

"Who's Johnny?" Barbara asked, going to the woman's side, worried by the look of blank confusion on her face and wondering if this Johnny could be the person who blocked the doors.

Mrs. Crampchet turned to Barbara. "Oh Sarah, stop being silly, now come help me with the tea." She took her arm, leading her towards the kitchen.

Barbara looked to the others for help.

"Sarah? Who's Sarah?" she asked. "I'm Barbara," she said to the old woman who seems to be confused now about who she is.

Mrs. Henderson stopped inspecting the door, watching them and thinking the old woman must be senile.

"Sarah, call your friends to come. I have fresh cookies to have with tea," Crampchet said, still pulling Barbara to the kitchen.

Libby and Pamela hesitate, finally following to help Barbara with the crazy old woman. They are worried too about her strange behavior and confusion. She needs help.

Mrs. Henderson starts to follow, but is drawn back by the muffled noises to that narrow door almost hidden in the corner of the living room.

Inspecting it, she finds the latch and opens the door. The muffled sounds come louder. It is dark below. She can just make out the first few steps going down. They are very steep and made of old rough wood planks, probably when the house was first built and never intended to be used much. This house is more than a hundred years old, and below is probably where coal was stored from the days when people used coal to heat their homes. Or, it could be a cold cellar for storing food before there were refrigerators and electricity.

She turns backwards to go down like a ship's ladder. The stairs creak precariously under her weight as she climbs down.

Barbara, Pamela, and Libby are startled by the cry that comes from the other room. They rush to investigate, leaving the old woman alone in the kitchen.

"What is it?"

"What's going on?"

"Mrs. Henderson, are you all right?"

They look around, getting more worried when they don't see her. They hear muffled sounds and scuffles.

Pamela spots the open door first and rushes towards it, looking down into the darkness with a worried frown.

"Mrs. Henderson? Are you down there? Did you fall? Are you all right?" she called down anxiously; sure the woman must have tumbled down into the opening to the blackness below.

Moments later, a shaken looking Mrs. Henderson crawls up the steep stairs behind a disheveled young man in a police officer's uniform.

Constable Timothy Berkham looks around warily at the women. His uniform is rumpled, his hat and utility belt with his weapons are missing, and he looks shaky and pale. He still has ropes around him that were used to tie him up, some hanging off and frayed at the ends where Mrs. Henderson had used a pair of rusty gardening sheers she found in the cellar to cut him free. The gag is pulled down and he still wears it around his neck. His hair is mussed and he looks dazed. He touches a hand to the back of his head, wincing with the pain the light touch causes.

The women stare at him in disbelief.

"What?"

"Who?"

"How?"

"I-I found him tied up downstairs," Mrs. Henderson said, her voice as shaky as she looks.

"Where's the old woman?" the officer asked, his voice shrill with stress. "She's dangerous!"

He advances cautiously, looking around.

"The old woman took my gun, she's armed." The gravity he feels over the situation is lost on the women who cannot see this old woman as being dangerous. They are only focused on him, staring in confusion, and not thinking at all about the old woman.

"Who are you?" Pamela asked, blocking him in her shock as he tries to take control of the situation.

"Constable Berkham," he said shakily, sounding almost as if he is unsure of the answer.

"How on earth did you get down there?" Libby asked.

"The old lady tricked me into going down there. The next thing I knew everything went black. She knocked me out from behind," he paused, looking back towards the narrow doorway in some disbelief. "Down there, she tied me up."

"How did a little old lady manage to knock out a man?" Pamela asked.

"What I can't get is how did she get up and down those stairs?" Mrs. Henderson said. "I could barely do it, and Mrs. Crampchet can barely even walk!"

Berkham moved past the women, checking the house.

"I need you all to vacate the house," he said, pushing past them. "She might still be in here and she's armed. But don't go anywhere; I'll need to get your statements."

"Where is she? Where's the old woman?" the officer called out from another room.

"She's in the kitchen I think," Barbara said.

"No, she isn't," Berkham said, coming back from that direction.

Surprised, the women look around; realizing none of them has seen the old woman since Mrs. Henderson cried out when she found the trapped officer.

A search of the house recovers the officer's hat, but nothing else. His utility belt with his gun and handcuffs, his radio, and his keys are all missing.

So is Mrs. Crampchet.

The old woman has slipped out. She is gone!

He looks even more distraught, lost. He sits down, groaning unhappily. He needs to take a minute to think. This does not look good. He thinks he may have been down there for a few days, although it feels longer, trapped by an old woman nearly crippled with age and arthritis, and he had lost his gun and everything.

Berkham jumped up and rushed to the front window, waves of dizziness washing over him from the movement. He is definitely concussed.

He looks out the window anxiously and staggers back, looking paler. He sits on the sofa, his head dropping to his hands.

"What's the matter?" Libby asked, staring at him with concern.

"You didn't see a police car out there, did you?" he said, not raising his head.

The women all look at each other in confusion, shaking their heads and muttering no's.

He groaned again, a pathetic sound.

"Young man," Mrs. Henderson started gently, "sir, what is it?"

He looked up at them with a look of utter despair.

"She took my car too." Things have gone from bad to worse for him. He is only a rookie, still pretty new to the force, and young. He worked hard to be accepted on the force and is at the beginning of a career that has just been dealt a lethal blow. This is a career killer.

"Where's the phone?" he groaned at last.

Barb showed him the phone, an old landline that is older than he is.

He called in to the police station, looking very unhappy while he talked, turning to face away from the women as he tells his duty sergeant his story, and then hung up.

"So, what happened?" The women are all clustering around, eager for the gossip.

"Well, they are relieved that I'm safe and they can call off the search," he said, still red faced with the memory of the hysterical laughing he had heard in the background as the sergeant relayed the story to those who could hear.

"We have to all stay here and wait. They're sending a couple of units to come and debrief all of us and to take me to the hospital to be medically cleared.

Mrs. Crampchet took advantage of the women's distraction when Mrs. Henderson came up from the root cellar with her guest.

"It's too bad," she said as she slipped out the door with a regretful look back, "it was kind of nice having the young man around."

She shuffled down the sidewalk as quickly as her old legs would let her, cutting across darkened yards to the back, heading for the woods.

She has to stop those fools digging around out there.

They don't know what they are doing.

The weight of her purse is almost too much, the officer's handgun rests on top of the sweating stick of dynamite inside. She shifted the purse, relieving the pressure on her arm. She had left the handcuffs and everything else with the car in Rusty's barn.

Barbara Watkins cannot believe everything that has been going on. It feels like her world just keeps getting turned upside down on her.

Shakily, she pulls out her cell phone and calls her husband.

"Samuel Watkins," he answered.

"Sam, it's me."

"What do you want?" He sounds impatient, annoyed by the interruption. She can tell something is bothering him. Probably a problem at work, she decides. He is working late tonight, but she is not so sure he is doing legitimate work. His stress is most likely to do with his altering the blueprints, she suspects.

"I know you're busy, but I have to tell you about your mother, Mrs. Crampchet."

"I really don't have time for this right now. Can't it wait?"

"No. She's missing."

"Missing?" Now he sounds alarmed. "But, I-she's," he broke off. He cannot tell his wife he knows the old woman is trapped safely inside her house. That would give away too much and he does not have time to explain now why it is best she stay there.

But, alarm bells are ringing in his head. Why is his wife saying she is missing?

"She called me," Barbara said, the feeling of urgency increasing as she talked. "She was trapped in her house. Someone barricaded her doors!"

"So she's still there then," he said, relief in his voice. "I'll be there to deal with it later. Unless she's having a heart attack, she'll be fine there for now."

"No," Barbara insisted, trying to get him to listen, "she's gone! We got her door open and we got inside and found a police officer she had tied up in the basement, and now she's gone! We lost her!"

The part about the police officer does not register with Samuel. He only heard the rest and that was all he can focus on at the moment.

"You-you got her out?" Samuel is not happy about this. Things are about to happen and he had trapped the old woman in her house to keep her safe. He knew she would go to the woods as soon as she noticed people out there.

Barbara is taken aback by his reaction. Why does he sound so upset they rescued his mother? His response worries her. What is going on?

"Samuel, what's wrong?"

"You let her out?" he repeated. "You lost her?"

"Sam," Barbara tried to get through to him, to get him to answer her. "Why are you so upset that we let her out? You're scaring me!"

The strain of finding the old woman deliberately trapped in her house, and then the police officer she had imprisoned in the basement, and now her husband's reaction, is all too much. Barbara started shaking. Something bad is going on here and she does not know what it is.

Suddenly the rest of her words hit him like a stone.

"What did you say?" Samuel asked, his voice shaky. "What's in the basement?"

"A young man, a police officer," Barbara repeated. "Mrs. Crampchet had him tied up down there. I never thought she could have done something like that; she's so old and can barely walk. But he said it was her, that she did it."

Samuel has to force himself to listen, to take it all in and let the words register. It makes no sense.

"That was the noise we heard, when we were at her house. It was him trying to get our attention, to call for help," Barbara said.

Samuel does not hear this last part; his mind is too focused on other things. Everything is falling apart, and right now when it is all about to come together.

"Stay there, I'm on my way," he said urgently and hung up.

Barbara stared at the phone for a moment before hanging it up. She doesn't have much choice since she has to wait for the police to come and take all their statements.

The Bobcat growls and chugs as its bucket scrapes at the ground, digging in to scoop out a mound of earth.

Still shaken by the attempt on his life, Dave is standing back watching while Stanley works the machine, and Bruce and Richard are arguing over the hand drawn map. He had wanted them to leave, to abandon this. Whoever took a shot at him is still out there. But the professor is determined and talked the others into staying.

Dave keeps glancing around, nervously looking for any movement, the glint of a gun, or the reflection of eyes; anything to give away someone sneaking up on them in the growing darkness to kill them.

Stanley is driving the Bobcat, reversing the machine and turning it to dump the bucket of mud, when he spotted movement through the trees. He stopped, staring through the growing darkness, trying to make it out.

A deer? No, he thinks, not with all this noise. A nosey neighbor maybe. He shut the machine down, expecting a confrontation with someone angry about the noise, and climbed down from the tractor.

Bruce and Richard look up, wondering why he stopped. Dave spots the movement against the darker trees and tense, wondering if it is the shooter. He has to force himself to stand still and not make a run for it.

Stanley points to the woods in answer to Bruce's and Richard's questioning looks and they turn to look, trying to see what he is pointing at.

Then they spot it too, movement, and visibly tense. They are not supposed to be here and they have all had that nagging thought in their minds that Dave's shooter is still out there somewhere in the darkness.

The four men watch, sighing a collective breath of relief when they spy the slow shuffling gait of someone who is either very old or otherwise has difficulty walking.

It cannot possibly be the shooter, they each are thinking.

The figure is approaching them and before long Stanley and Dave recognize the old woman coming through the trees.

Mrs. Crampchet.

"What the hell is she doing here?" Stanley muttered.

Bruce and Richard look at him in confusion.

"Do you know the old woman?" Richard asked.

"Yeah, we know her all right," Dave muttered, not happy to see her.

Bruce turned to look at him. He has a suspicion and Stanley is about to prove it true.

"That's the old woman who poisoned the work crew," Stanley said, "and came back and tried it again."

"Three times," Dave said.

"Well, we don't actually know if she tried to slip anything into the coffee and donuts that day," Stanley said, looking at Bruce, his expression serious. "But we do know she brought poisoned baking twice."

Bruce nodded. Now he knows exactly who the woman is. It seems incredible that this nearly crippled old creature shuffling slowly towards them is capable of trying to kill an entire work crew. It is impossible to believe an old woman would have a reason. She has to be either totally nuts to do it, or completely senile and did not know what she put in the baking.

Richard looked from man to man in astonishment.

The old woman is scolding them for being there, telling them to go home and shaking her purse at them before she even got close enough for them to hear her. Then she remembers the gun and sweating dynamite in her purse and thinks better of it. She switches hands to shake her fist at them, purse free.

"Stop it!" she yelled at them. "Just stop it! Get out of there! You have no business digging around in there!" Her age-crackled voice is hoarse and hard to understand at a distance. She repeats herself as she keeps coming towards the men.

When she reached them she slapped Stanley in the arm, his bad luck for being the closest, yelling at them.

"You boys just get out of here! You don't know what you're doing! You have no business here!"

Bruce is chuckling at the old woman's assault on his employee. Stanley does not think it is very funny, although it does not actually hurt.

"You shouldn't be out here ma-am," Stanley said, trying to redirect the old woman away.

She pushes past him angrily, turning her wrath on the professor. She eyes him up. The rest of these men are construction brutes, but this one looks like he might have the intelligence to listen to her.

"Get out! All of you! You can't dig here!"

Richard stares at the old woman in rapt fascination as if he has just made the archaeological discovery of a lifetime.

Finally, he breaks free of his speechless state and is able to address her. He blinks off the shock of seeing the old woman and the implications, noting her age, anger, and the intelligence in her rheumy eyes. He cannot stop himself from grinning and it seems to aggravate the old woman even more. He steps forward.

"You're Mrs. Crampchet, aren't you? The Mrs. Crampchet?" He is eager to hear what he is sure the answer will be.

"You know I am. Now you boys go home! Go on, get out of here!" She shook her fist at him, advancing on him, threatening.

Richard seems intent now only on his discovery of the old woman and what her presence proves to him in his own mind.

He looks at her in awe.

"Crampchet; descendants of one of the original families out here. I thought they were all gone long ago. Your family must have all kinds of stories passed down, right from the first settlers to come to this area. They did pass them down, didn't they? Oh, I'll just bet you know all kinds of old secrets about this place."

This shut the old woman up and she stared at him suspiciously.

"How old are you Mrs. Crampchet?" Richard asked, studying her like an old mummified corpse. "I'd bet you're a lot older than you let on."

He is oblivious to the insult his statement implies, seeing only his own awe and wonder at her existence and what he believes it means.

She pursed her lips at him. "I'm no older than anybody else my age," she snapped.

Richard laughed as if she had cracked a joke, but it is no joke to the old woman.

She advanced on him, grabbing him and trying to push him away from the woods.

"You all just get out of here! Go home!" she persisted.

Richard turned and looked back to where they had been digging, and turned back to the old woman. His large grin widened more.

"You know what's buried in these woods, don't you?" Richard said. "You know where it is!"

"Nonsense, there's nothing here!" Crampchet snapped.

"You get out of these woods," another age-weary voice crackled at them from behind, this one deeper.

They turn to see an old man with an old rusty shotgun, its recoil likely to knock the frail old man off his feet if it is even capable of firing.

"He's got a gun!" Dave exclaimed, half-choking on the words in alarm. His mind reels back to the tiny hole in the tractor's windshield back at the Garden Grove site, and the perfect little hole in the seat where the bullet had just missed him. It does not connect for him that the shotgun is the wrong type of weapon for that finely aimed shot.

Dave stepped back, looking around at the others, confused because no one is moving. "Why aren't we all running?" he thought, half sure the old man is guilty of trying to kill him, but held in place by a nagging doubt and everyone else's lack of motion.

Richard blinked in surprise, staring at the old man.

"Could that be?" Richard exclaimed. "Is that Mr. Plowshare?"

He turned to the others, incredulous and bursting with excitement.

Stanley nodded. "That's Mr. Plowshare, another thorn in our side on this project."

Looking past them, Crampchet yelled at the old man.

"Rusty, you just mind your own business! Go on, get!"

Rusty Plowshare turned on the old woman, his gun muzzle turning with him and making everyone except the old woman duck and dodge.

"Go home old woman," he yelled at her, then turned his attention back on the men along with the business end of the shotgun.

Richard seems oblivious to the danger, staring at the two old people in awe. He seems unaware that they are more than just objects for observation and turned to the other men.

"Do you know who they are?" he asked eagerly. "They're what are left of the original families to settle here. They're the key to all of this. Those original families intermingled some, but kept the marriages mostly within the small group of families that originally settled the area, cousins marrying cousins. Why, I bet they both come from the Plowshare family line that carries the gene that caused the deformities."

He is thrilled. He has the opportunity to get samples he cannot get from the old bones, if these two elders would be willing to give them. He will make history. He, Professor Richard Mackin, will go down in the pages of history as the pioneer of a newly discovered, and now not entirely gone, ancient disease.

Richard opened his mouth, burning to ask, and paused. He thought about it a moment and then seemed to change his mind, staring at the old man curiously. He has so many questions that he does not know what to ask first. Finally, Richard settles on one.

He turned to Rusty Plowshare.

"You only carry the Plowshare name, don't you? You are Rusty Plowshare, but you aren't a true Plowshare are you? You are the other secret the family has kept hidden."

"Is it true?" Richard asked eagerly. "About, is it your great great great grandmother? No, it is only two 'greats', isn't it?"

Rusty Plowshare stiffened at this man's bringing out the old family dirty laundry to air. He clenched his jaw and his hands tightened on the shotgun, his eyes narrowing angrily and pointing the gun at Richard.

Richard turned back to the others again as if forgetting the old man is there; or at least that Plowshare is no more than an archaeological find.

"Old Mr. Plowshare here isn't even a real Plowshare. Did you know that? He is the descendant of his great great great grandmother's lover and is not a Plowshare at all.

There are old stories that Mrs. Plowshare had a lover, or at least it was rumored she did. She was one of the few outsiders who married into the family and had no Plowshare blood. She had a baby from that lover and her husband murdered the other man in a jealous rage. He kept his wife locked up, a virtual prisoner in her own home, and she had more children. Plowshare could not have doubted the others were his, there was no way for them to be fathered by anyone else, but he still refused to believe they were his and eventually murdered her too along with some of the children.

The bodies were never found, so he was never charged. It was only rumor and heresy over their disappearances. Perhaps a few may have believed they had simply run away, but the news of the day points the finger of guilt at Mr. Plowshare being guilty of murder and getting away with it.

I think that generation of Plowshares were all carriers of the gene. They would pass it on, but not necessarily be physically affected by it. Not one of his children showed the signs of deformity, so he was convinced none of them were his. Every generation at least one child grew the deformities, didn't they? Except that one generation? Of course there was no guarantee any of them would have the active disease, it's a roll of the genetics dice, but the gene was stronger in the family before relocating here through generations of inbreeding. After that the gene had been weakened as Plowshares increasingly married outside the family."

He turned to Rusty, looking for confirmation. The old man only glared at him.

"Plowshare tried to keep his children's suspected illegitimacy a secret because of the shame it brought on him, even the children were not allowed to know. But it was through the town gossip that he learned about the lover and it was impossible to stop its spread. When the lover mysteriously disappeared and his wife stopped leaving the house, the gossips had a party with it.

Mrs. Plowshare instilled the need to keep his true paternity secret in her son, Mr. Plowshare's great great grandfather, and it was passed down through his children and grandchildren. So was the secret of the murders of his real father and his mother, and the desire for vengeance against the real Plowshare family."

Rusty turned to the old woman.

"See, I told you I wasn't crazy! All these years I told you!" His voice rose with the declaration and his vindication.

"Just crazy with revenge," a voice said.

They all turned in surprise to see Samuel Watkins. Even more surprising is who is with him. It is Mr. Chornelhus who had spoken. Behind them Mr. Chornelhus's personal security men stand ready to move on his signal.

"Mr. Chornelhus!" Bruce said, incredulous. He looked from one to the other, suddenly putting it together.

Chornelhus turned to Bruce.

"You should not have been so nosy Mr. Copeland. I investigate others, they do not investigate me. Did you think I would not know?"

Bruce blanched, trying to hide the sudden rush of fear. He is a dead man.

"Why are you digging here in the woods?" Chornelhus asked. "Why are you disturbing ground that you are not being paid to dig?" His eyes flashed with anger.

Bruce's mind worked. What is buried here in the woods that Chornelhus is so interested in? And the professor too, whatever it is he is very interested in it.

Samuel stepped forward. "You just wouldn't give up, would you?" he said to Bruce. He is carrying a rifle suitable for deer hunting and Dave eyed both him and the rifle suspiciously.

"You!" Bruce advanced angrily towards Samuel, stopping when he saw the armed men in the darkness behind Chornelhus.

He stared at Samuel, accusing.

"You're responsible for the blueprints! You changed them, forged new copies and switched them! But why?"

"To stop the construction. I had to stop the development from going in."

The pieces seemed to be clicking into place but they are still making no sense.

"You were behind the sabotage to the equipment too, weren't you?" Bruce said.

Samuel nodded. There is no point denying any of it now.

"Why Sam?" Stanley asked, feeling betrayed. "We worked together on how many projects? Why this one? Why now?"

Dave doesn't know who to suspect of shooting him. He doesn't want to think Sam Watkins could do something like that, but he is here in the dark with a deer rifle. The old man's shotgun does not look like it would even work. He stared at Samuel, the hurt of betrayal in his eyes.

Mr. Chornelhus eyed Samuel, but spoke to Bruce. "I needed the Garden Grove development slowed down. I made a mistake with the Anc-Chor project. Garden Grove was moving on target and you are digging too close to the woods. I am not ready yet for what is buried here. I could not let you disturb the ground here too soon."

There are still too many loose pieces that make no sense, too many questions and too many people. The three construction men and the professor just cannot wrap their heads around it.

It is clear to them now that Mr. Chornelhus and Samuel Watkins were working together to sabotage the Garden Grove development project, to slow down the work there while the Anc-Chor project is redesigned and re-built after the explosion there. There is no question now in Bruce Copeland's mind that Chornelhus had blown up his own multi-million dollar project. But why? Because he made a mistake? So he can rebuild at the expense of the insurance company? And what could that possibly have to do with Garden Grove and whatever is buried here in the woods?

And what does the old man Rusty Plowshare have to do with any of this?

And the old woman Mrs. Crampchet, why is she here? Why was she poisoning the work crew?

Richard's mind kept working through all the possibilities, the answer is right in front of him. It clicked.

"You planted the bones," Richard said, pointing to Rusty Plowshare. You had those old bones, kept hidden somewhere through generations of the Plowshare family. You're the only Plowshare left that would have known where the bones were, the one non-Plowshare descendant who happens to come from the line of an illegitimate son."

"Were you two working together?" He looked between the old man and Samuel. "No, Mr. Watkins is obviously working with Mr. Chornelhus. So who is working with you Mr. Plowshare?"

"I work with no one!" the old man spat.

"But why does the old woman keep trying to poison the work crew?" Stanley asked.

"To stop you imbeciles from digging where you shouldn't," Mrs. Crampchet muttered, angrily brandishing her fist at them. "You have no idea what's buried out here, what you're disturbing."

"So you two are working together?" Stanley asked the elderly man and woman.

The two looked at each other and almost laughed; only there was nothing funny about this and their expressions were almost maniacal.

"So you're not working together then? You are all three trying to stop the housing development for different reasons? The same reason?" It just seems to be getting stranger.

"You don't know what's in these woods," Mrs. Crampchet hissed, looking around as if afraid someone is eavesdropping.

Rusty Plowshare puffed up his scrawny chest and balled up his withered fist, glaring at the construction men and holding his weapon with only one hand.

"You took this land from my family!" He thumped his chest for emphasis.

"You took it and sold it off in pieces, and let him get his paws on it!" He jabbed an angry finger towards Mr. Chornelhus.

"We held on to this land, the Plowshare land, for generations, for one reason only – to keep him and his kind off it! You ruined everything!" The pitch of his voice grew louder and shriller as he spoke, his breath coming heavy by the time he finished.

Mr. Chornelhus chuckled, stepping closer to the scattered group.

"They didn't take your land old man, I did," he said, his wicked grin showing the amusement in his voice for what it really is, disdain. "I own the companies that invested in this land, I pulled the strings to have the land seized and auctioned off, and I carved it up into pieces to sell off, keeping only what I need."

Rusty turned towards the dark looming shapes of the barren trees, his expression making it clear what Chornelhus's goal had been. The woods.

"Over my dead body," Rusty growled at Chornelhus.

"Oh, I plan on that," Chornelhus said.

His security men stepped forward threateningly and he waved them off. "Not that way," he snapped at them, annoyed by their ignorance.

Everyone except Rusty is staring at Chornelhus in confusion.

The look he gave them in return is mocking.

"Mr. Watkins is working for me," Chornelhus confirmed.

"You just don't get it yet, do you professor?" he asked, turning to Richard.

Richard's confusion only deepened.

Chornelhus jabbed a finger at his own chest proudly.

"I'm the last Plowshare, the last real Plowshare. This land belongs to my family, not this illegitimate offspring." He jabbed an accusing finger towards Rusty and the old man bristled at it. "And so does what's on it, or should I say under it."

Richard gaped at him.

"You're the last Plowshare?" he gasped.

He stepped forward eagerly, excited and nearly exploding with the questions he is dying to ask.

Bruce spoke first.

"You're behind all this? The plans? The sabotage?"

He turned to Samuel.

"You're working for him? Swapping out the plans for him?"

Mrs. Crampchet gave Samuel a chiding look and he nodded, looking guilty. She knows Sam was sabotaging the blueprints and vandalizing the site to try to get the site shut down, and had thought it was only towards their own goal. She did not know he was also working for the enemy, Chornelhus.

"Why?" Bruce asked.

Samuel shrugged, giving the old woman a wary look.

Samuel moved to stand beside the old woman, an act that revealed they are working together.

Chornelhus gave him a guarded look, revealing his surprise at realizing Samuel was working against him even while he worked for him.

None of this makes sense to the three construction men.

"We're Plowshares," Samuel said, indicating Mrs. Crampchet and himself. He turned to her.

"I know that's why you never had children, except for me. I was an accident that came later, after you murdered your husband."

He turned to the shocked faces staring at them.

"She hated her husband. She married him only because her father made her. Mr. Crampchet was a Plowshare descendant too and pairing them off would strengthen the curse they both carried in their blood. The curse had weakened over the generations of mixing with the blood of others from outside the family line and almost none of the babies were born with the deformities anymore."

He turned now to Rusty. The old man's face is grim.

"Rusty Plowshare and my mother were in love back when they were teenagers. Neither of them knew then that she had Plowshare blood, but her parents did. And only Rusty and his mother knew that he had no Plowshare blood. She was a descendant of that first illegitimate Plowshare baby, a clean line of illegitimate children carefully kept and concealed for generation after generation while the family continued inbreeding in an effort to keep the curse strong.

Even when the Plowshares married others infected with the curse through all those generations, cousins marrying cousins, that one child every generation was born without the curse, conceived outside the marriage to carry down the clean line and its revenge against the Plowshare family and its curse.

My mother's parents knew she was of the Plowshare line and knew only that Rusty didn't show any signs of carrying the gene. But her husband Krandall Crampchet did. He was the first in a long time to have developed the visible deformities, although they were only slight. So they pushed her into marrying him to strengthen the line.

When my mother learned the truth about her husband, that he was related to her by blood, she made sure she would not have children. She had heard the whispers of the Plowshare family background, and the inbreeding in the area, but had not yet connected the two.

When her father started pressuring her to marry Krandall Crampchet, who was also more than ten years her senior, she became determined to learn more about her own background and the secrets her family kept hidden.

After the wedding, she unhappily tolerated her life for a while. When her husband consummated the marriage, she learned of his deformity and became suspicious. The idea that she may have married a decedent of the Plowshares sickened her. There were rumors of terrible things they had done throughout the generations. It was well known in the area that the Plowshares were thought to be insane.

My mother hated the Plowshare line and everything it was. To her they were monsters, just like they were generations ago to the people native to the area when the family settled here.

But that was only part of her misery. She did not know it yet, but Krandall, Rusty, and her, all share the same family line. Like their shared great great grandmother, my mother too loved a man her family did not approve of. She resented her husband and her marriage. After a while, she started poisoning Krandall, keeping him ill, until she had enough and put an end to it all with a higher dose of poison.

She and Rusty became secret lovers after that and when she found out she was pregnant she still did not know about her own Plowshare blood."

Dave interrupted, looking confused.

"But, if she hated the Plowshare family so much, why was she in love with Rusty Plowshare?"

"That's easy," Richard said. "She knew Rusty was a Plowshare, obviously since it's his name, but when she was a teenager she had no idea that she and her family were Plowshares too.

Love does not care about history. It just hits when it hits. And she was in love with Rusty Plowshare before she learned any of her family's background. Probably before she learned anything more than the old wives' tales told about the Plowshare family too.

The Plowshare family name had no significance for her outside of the rumors spread around town about their history. They were just another family in town and she never believed the rumors until she had to face marrying a man she was horrified at the idea of marrying. Her family tried to scare her away from Rusty Plowshare with his twisted family history and the curse and deformities they carried. A history she learned soon after that she shared."

Samuel nodded. He continued.

"But now she had an illegitimate child coming, and one she didn't want despite the father being her long-time love. In those days, it was a big deal to have a child out of wedlock, especially for the woman.

When she broke the news to Rusty, he went wild. He knew all about the Plowshare family history. It was passed down in his family from mother to child, keeping the special secret of his line between only those that did not carry the Plowshare gene, and who carried with them the promise to get their revenge on the Plowshares for that long ago torment and murder of Mr. Plowshare's wife.

As sick as it was, each generation that one child who carried the revenge instead of the cursed gene made sure their own child born out of the family would marry someone with the Plowshare blood. It was all part of some twisted plan to weaken the line and eventually destroy them once and for all.

Rusty told her everything, except that which he was sworn to secrecy about, that he himself is not a Plowshare and about the plan for revenge.

She knew only that he is a Plowshare and all the terrible things said about the family are true. She was terrified the child would carry the curse and develop deformities. And, she still clung to the old way of thinking that having a baby out of marriage was a big disgrace and had me in secrecy, giving me up for adoption."

"How do you know all this?" Richard asked in surprise.

"When I found out I was adopted I started trying to learn who my real parents are. I learned who my mother is, and some of her background. But then I discovered that Mr. Chornelhus is related to us too and I contacted him. He filled in a lot of information about the Plowshare line and my mother. He knew about her, one of the last of a dying blood line."

Samuel turned to Mrs. Crampchet, who is staring at Chornelhus with surprised suspicion.

"He knew about you already, Mother. He knew about me too and was just waiting for me to come looking for him. He told me everything except the identity of who my real father is. I'd assumed my father had probably passed away years ago."

Mrs. Crampchet glowered at Samuel.

"How could you work with that man? After you knew who, what, he is?" she demanded, spitting out the word 'man' like it is dirty.

Samuel feels hurt by her anger even though he understands the reason for it.

"Yes, I worked with Mr. Chornelhus, but only as a means to an end," he said, his tone pleading for his mother to understand. "I didn't believe any of this until I talked to Mr. Chornelhus. He convinced me, showed me the proof.

Together you and I were going to destroy whatever is hiding somewhere on these acres of land. After finding Mr. Chornelhus and talking to him, I knew we couldn't do it alone. We needed

Chornelhus to find it so we could release it and try to destroy it." Samuel had not told his mother about any of this before.

"You would destroy it after what I told you?" Chornelhus hissed. "After learning what it is? After I trusted you with something which only one of our blood line is worthy of?"

"I used you, yes," Samuel said to Mr. Chornelhus.

Chornelhus seemed to visibly age as he glared at him. He suddenly does not look so powerful now. He is just another crazy angry old man like Rusty Plowshare and Mrs. Crampchet.

Samuel turned to the others. "It didn't take me long to see how insane Mr. Chornelhus is; dangerous and crazy, but our only chance. The more he told me what this thing is the more I knew it isn't enough to keep its secret hidden, to keep it trapped from the world. It has to be destroyed."

Samuel went on, "I knew we could not allow the housing project to continue. Eventually they would have dug in the wrong place and broken the seal that traps the creature in its tomb.

My mother had thought it was hidden in the last bit of woods still standing and kept saying she felt its presence there, but I was not convinced. The woods had spread much further once. It could have been anywhere on acres of land. I had searched the woods thoroughly, but found nothing. I was sure it had to be somewhere else. But I did not know where."

"Chornelhus seemed to somehow know. He was so full of confidence he knew exactly where to look," Samuel finished.

Mr. Chornelhus is growing impatient now.

"Yeah, alright," he cut in, "so I'm not quite the last Plowshare. Now that everybody knows who everyone is let's get this business finished."

He pulled a diagram out of his pocket and turned to Samuel.

"I need you to dig right here," he indicated a spot on the diagram.

Samuel nodded towards Bruce's crew. "Show them. They'll dig and I'll make sure they're in the right spot."

Mr. Chornelhus held the paper out to one of his security men who took it and brought it to the construction men. Bruce glowered at him as he took it. They all looked it over, Richard with the most interest.

It is more than just a diagram of the area; it is a copy of an old picture that must have been drawn at least a few hundred years earlier. The picture depicts a clearing in the woods with twisted creatures dancing around a fire, their grotesque deformities accentuated by the glow of the firelight in the darkness. The shadows of the barren skeletal limbs of the trees overhead seem to loom over the creatures as though the trees themselves are about to scoop them up and devour them. Central to the activity is a tomb partially buried in the ground with strange markings carved on it. The dancing creatures appear to be burying the tomb with rocks and dead branches and handfuls of mud.

Samuel pointed to the trees around them as reference points to find the right spot that matches the picture map. They are remarkably identical to the trees in the picture.

Samuel brought the rifle up threateningly.

"Get in the tractor and start digging or I start shooting."

Bruce nodded and Dave climbed up inside, driving the tractor to the spot and working the levers, the bucket digging into the hard ground that had not been touched for generations. The bobcat growled as it strained; the blade of its bucket cutting through the mesh of roots and hard soil.

"I can't believe you believe any of this nonsense," Bruce snarled at Samuel under his breath.

Samuel ignored the jab.

Mrs. Crampchet is obviously very distressed about the digging, growing more so with every passing breath. She fidgeted and clutched her purse tightly, on the verge of crying out to them to stop.

Rusty Plowshare looks ready to tear Chornelhus apart with his bare hands. He is focused on the other old man, glowering at him, his fists clenching against the rusted weapon in his hands.

"What's buried here?" Richard asked at last, desperately wanting confirmation of his suspicions.

"The Plowshare family history," Mr. Chornelhus said, watching the excavation eagerly.

Bruce is studying the picture and the similarities begin to stand out for him. He turned to Chornelhus.

"The Anc-Chor project," he said, it matches the picture too."

Chornelhus smiled at his revelation as though sharing a secret joke.

Richard looked at them both in confusion.

"What do you mean? What matches?" Richard asked.

Bruce pointed to points on the diagram, showing him what matched. The locations of the trees in relation to the tomb at their center.

"The Anc-Chor project, these are an exact match," Bruce said.

Richard's expression changed from confusion to curiosity to amazement. It is an old pagan religious symbol predating Christianity and used for trapping spirits, malevolent ones.

He turned to Mr. Chornelhus, his mouth gaping open. It took a moment before Richard could speak.

"You think something alive is buried here! You actually think this demon or evil spirit the native inhabitants and the first Plowshares believed in is real!"

Richard looked in turn at Mrs. Crampchet, Rusty Plowshare, and Samuel Watkins, and then turned back to Mr. Chornelhus as he continued.

"You all think whatever is buried here is alive!" It is inconceivable to him that people today could believe something so incredible. Buried and alive for generations, possibly hundreds of years!

"Oh, but it is," Chornelhus sneered. "It's here and it belongs to me, to the real Plowshare family."

He turned to Bruce who is still staring at him with a look of sickened understanding and shock over what he now knows.

"The Anc-Chor project, the laboratory, it's for this – this thing you think is buried here," Bruce said. "You think you're going to take it there and study it, control it."

"That's what I thought at first," Chornelhus admitted. "But then I realized I had it all wrong. So I blew up the Anc-Chor project so the insurance money would pay to do it again the right way."

He looked smug. "Why use my own money for what someone else will pay for?"

Except for Plowshare and Crampchet, the others stare at him in horror. He had killed and maimed all those men just so he could change his construction plans and have the insurance company pay for it.

Chornelhus turned to watch the bobcat eagerly, oblivious to their stares.

"Yes, I had it all wrong. You cannot contain her that way, not with cement and rebar. No, they had the answer right here in the picture," he said.

He turned back to the others.

"You cannot control her at all, you have to honor her, make sacrifices to her. You have to feed her the twisted bodies of her own deformed children.

I am not ready yet to awaken her, to bring her out of the tomb that imprisons her beneath the ground. But you people just couldn't wait. You had to dig."

His eyes are manic, filled with insanity.

"She's hungry," he whispered.

Suddenly the trees around them begin to creak and groan; the sound coming from the very core of the ancient lumber.

Branches crackle and snap, breaking off where they had died and gone brittle over the seasons.

Mrs. Crampchet let out an anguished wail.

She looked around fearfully.

"You woke it up," she hissed.

Dave's digging with the bobcat had broken the seal. Startled by a large branch falling with a loud thump on the tractor's arms right in front of the windshield, he stopped digging and the tractor's growling immediately quieted to idling. He looked around in shock at the cracking and breaking trees around him and scrambled from the cab just as the old woman cried out her anguished wail.

He rushed over to the others. "What's going on?"

Rusty Plowshare moved to Mrs. Crampchet's side protectively, looking up at the trees fearfully.

"My great great grandmother vowed we would put an end to this," he coughed, fear gripping his throat and constricting it so he had trouble getting the words out.

Chornelhus's rapt stare brought their attention to something in the woods.

"Oh she has already awakened," he said, his eyes eager. "The construction at the Garden Grove site woke her. She's just been waiting to be freed."

They turned to see a hunched figure approaching slowly. The thin frame wrapped in a tattered shawl that, combined with the darkness in the woods, hid its face. It looks emaciated and its limbs twisted and deformed.

The figure shuffles forward in the arthritic walk of the very old, struggling over the debris of long fallen deadwood.

Richard stared in confusion. Where did this person come from?

Bruce is apprehensive. His upbringing cries out that he should go help, that you are supposed to help the elderly when you see them struggling, but the woods have enveloped them all in a sick feeling of dread.

Something about the figure struggling towards them feels very wrong.

Chornelhus stared in rapt excitement.

Stanley and Dave listen to their urges. They move to help, driven by an ingrained response to help someone very old and having difficulty.

"Stay away from it!" Rusty hissed.

"Don't touch it!" Mrs. Crampchet wailed.

"No, let her come on her own," Chornelhus said excitedly. "It is like birth, rebirth, she has to do it on her own. Let the effort strengthen her."

Stanley and Dave pause, looking at them and then back to the approaching figure.

The figure comes on with excruciating slowness, struggling and crawling over the fallen trees as if climbing from a deep hole.

It turns to look at each of them when it finally arrives on the edge of the group and pulls back the shawl to reveal its face with trembling hands.

The old woman's face is a twisted mess of deformity lined with a web of wrinkles in her ancient age-withered skin. Age spots mottle her flesh and her hair hangs in thin white wisps from a nearly bald scalp.

She is older than old, looking as you would imagine the elderly would look if one were to escape death, surviving for years which can be counted in the hundreds.

The old woman clapped her jaws as if to speak but no words came out. She seems very frail, weakened perhaps from hunger.

Chornelhus rushed forward. He seems to have forgotten the rest of them are there.

Richard stared in disbelief.

Bruce, Stanley, and Dave look confused.

Mrs. Crampchet clutched her purse tighter and Rusty Plowshare's hands tightened on his shotgun.

"Come Grandmother," Chornelhus said, offering her his hand. "I am making a new home for you."

The ancient woman stopped before him and raised her face to stare into his. She reached up to him with her hands, touching his face. She picked at a short hair there that had not been there a moment before, growing from where no moustache grew on his cleanly shaven face.

They all stared, wondering what she is doing.

"I must have missed a hair," Chornelhus thought, thinking of when he had shaved last and letting her do what she will. He does not wonder too much about it even though he is very dedicated to his appearance being perfection. It is not important right now. At this very moment, the only thing that matters is her, Grandmother. A small smile plays about his lips, like a little boy enjoying his grandmother's attention.

His security men are amazed to see this. Their boss avoids all human contact, finding physical touch especially distasteful.

Grandmother pinched the hair between the aged fingers of one hand and pulled. She pulled and pulled, using the fingers of both hands, first with one then the other as the hair came from his face, the strand growing longer as she keeps pulling it, moving up and across his upper lip. It leaves a red line behind, the skin unbroken from this thread which must have cut through the flesh to be pulled out so. It is as if she is pulling some invisible thread from beneath the skin surrounding his lips, the thread growing by more than the distance it stretched across his mouth as she pulls it out. Only, as she pulls it out, it is not quite invisible, but only nearly so.

The spectacle is grotesque, surreal. It churns their stomachs sickeningly as they watch. And yet as much as each of them wants to look away, they are drawn to stare in rapt fascination, like watching an unavoidable accident slowly unwinding.

Grandmother does not stop pulling until she has gone all the way across the upper lip, down, and across much of the lower lip, leaving an angry red line behind that is fading already. The near invisible growing thread moves as if alive, sinuously.

"What is that?" Chornelhus asked, looking confused now, as though somehow his memory is becoming lost.

"Only one of your sins," the old woman's voice came out dry and brittle like the rustle of ancient paper.

Finished, she looks at the thread squirming sinuously between her fingers as if it were some delectably tasty long worm, balled it up with both hands, and popped it in her mouth, chewing, her eyes eager with hunger and saliva dripping down her chin.

Behind her, Mr. Chornelhus seems somehow less, sagging, older, thinner, and more tired. His face has lost some of its color and his eyes are hazy with confusion.

The old woman turns then to the others, measuring them up, her look hungry.

"We have to put it back in the ground," Rusty rasped, looking around in a panic.

Richard took a step towards the old woman, drawn by the tidal wave of questions swirling in his head.

How old are you? Where did you come from? Were you buried all this time? For how long? What are you? It is all improbable, impossible, yet happening right now before him. This thing, whatever it is, it is somehow alive, real, and in the very real flesh and blood form of a very old woman.

He does not know where to start and can only stare in rapt awe.

The old woman looks from one to another, as if sniffing out some invisible sign, and finally turns her attention to Mrs. Crampchet and Samuel, ignoring the rest. Her stare is fixated on them as she stumbles towards them, not breaking the stare even to look down at the uneven ground that trips her up. Her eyes zero in on them and her body follows as if dragged along for the ride and given no choice but to go through the motions of walking.

Mrs. Crampchet holds her ground, staring back at the other old woman defiantly.

Samuel shrank back, taking a few steps back, not knowing why the old woman makes him feel so afraid. He does know one thing, though. He is here to destroy her, it, whatever it is.

He was not expecting it to be a frail looking old woman.

The two old women stare each other down, defiance against hunger, shriveled face to even more shriveled face.

"She seems drawn to them," Richard gasped. "Like she somehow knows they're descendants of the original Plowshare family."

"You don't know what you've done in waking this monster," Mrs. Crampchet hissed, keeping her attention on the ancient creature.

"Your old stories about the natives believing in curses and evil spirits are true!" Rusty snarled, watching the women as if he is expecting them to fly at each other at any moment in a battle to the death. "The curse is true!"

He turned to the others who are staring in disbelief.

"The Plowshares were cursed before they came to this land generations ago. Cursed for their own evil deeds, their children and their children's children cursed to have their limbs twisted and misshapen as punishment and to forever have their sins and the sins of their descendants feed the curse."

"But it's only a disease, a genetic disorder," Richard insisted. "There is no such thing as a curse."

Rusty continued, ignoring his interruption.

"The Plowshare children's deformities are the twisted lies their ancestors used to hide their shameful acts, making others suffer for their pleasure. They took their evil out on the wrong victim, and were cursed by a witch of the old world."

He pointed at the old woman who came from the woods.

"That thing is the curse they carry with them. It feeds off the evil in their souls, eats the sins of their twisted black hearts, their insanity. They brought the demon with them when they came here. They thought they could escape the curse, fleeing across the seas.

But it followed them and their children were still born twisted and deformed and the creature fed off them until they were nothing but empty husks, like a corn husk eaten hollow by insects. The curse carried down through the bloodline for generation after generation, their souls black and twisted inside."

Mrs. Crampchet took up the story where the old man left off. He sagged with exhaustion, the strain from these last few days catching up with him.

"Generations ago they figured a way to trap the creature. At first, the natives just drummed their drums and danced around fires chanting to their spirits, fearfully massacring entire families of their own people when the twisted deformities showed up in their children.

But then the Plowshares told the native elders about the curse and together they tried the natives' old rituals, combining them with the old world tales and ceremonies even more ancient than the natives' until together, with the natives' old knowledge of spirits and demons, they found one that worked to trap the creature.

But to keep it contained they have to keep feeding it. The more twisted and deformed the body of the soul they give it, the stronger the tainted blood is and the longer it keeps the creature satiated. They feed it only enough to keep it from breaking free in hunger, desperate to live, allowing it to slowly wither and starve to keep it weak, and to keep anyone from noticing. With records kept for everything today it's hard to have a child disappear and have nobody notice."

"They feed their own children to it, to her?" Dave is shocked at the idea.

Samuel nodded. "That's why we have to destroy it."

Chornelhus laughed. "You can't destroy her! She's a GOD!"

He signaled to his men.

"Enough of this," Mr. Chornelhus said.

His men stepped forward, training their guns on the group.

Chornelhus stepped forward, taking the ancient woman's hand.

"Come Grandmother, I'm taking you home."

She looked at him hungrily and he nodded.

"There is a lot there for you to eat. I have been preparing for you for a long time."

Mrs. Crampchet and Rusty Plowshare stared open mouthed.

Richard turned to them in confusion.

"What will he feed her?"

"Children," Bruce said, feeling the icy chill of the shock seeping through him. "The Anc-Chor project, the equipment, it's not just to contain this thing. He's also cloning, extracting DNA to make children to feed her."

"But, who's?" Richard was dumbfounded. "If all this is true, they would have to carry the gene, have the visible deformities."

"His own," Samuel said.

Chornelhus smiled smugly.

"I'm surprised at you Mr. Copeland. I really did not think you were this smart, but you figured it out.

My people have isolated the gene that causes the deformities, duplicating it and making it stronger in the cloned specimens. We have created purer children."

He turned to the ancient creature.

"You, Grandmother, will be very well fed."

"You're mad!" Richard cried. "You can't do this! Those children!"

"I can and I am," Chornelhus said.

With a wry smirk back at them, Chornelhus turned, leading the ancient woman away, the rest staring dumbfounded as his security men prepared for what is next. They move slowly, her elderly legs moving with the slow deliberateness of a woman more than a hundred years old.

And so she should. Her age can be counted in the centuries, an ageless creature created by man's own blind evil.

"Take care of them," Chornelhus said, giving his men their cue.

There will be no witnesses left behind.

As they turned to watch Chornelhus and the ancient woman walk away, Mrs. Crampchet dug in her purse, her hands trembling, easing out the stick of sweating dynamite.

The ensuing explosion will wake half the town, and the discovery of the ruined charred bodies will shock the world for days until the next gruesome tragedy hits the news.

Crampchet moved with a speed no one would have given the old woman credit for.

Chornelhus's men stared in stunned disbelief.

She lit and threw the unstable dynamite at Chornelhus and Grandmother. Her throw is off and the stick hits a branch, bouncing the wrong way. It spun with the deflection, the long wick curling and touching the side of the stick, igniting the beads of nitroglycerin sweat, blowing it up prematurely.

The booming crack echoed against the sky, sending sleeping birds to the air in panic, old oak trees twisting and groaning, their hard wood snapping in an explosion of fractured limbs.

Oblivious to the dynamite, Mr. Chornelhus and the ancient woman are hit with the force of the air exploding and are thrown forward.

Chornelhus groaned, barely moving, debris pattering his body as it rained back down. He mewled and moved shakily like a newborn kitten, his mind numb with shock. The world seems to have been suddenly thrust behind an impenetrable barrier that muffles all feeling, sight, and sound. The roaring in his ears is like putting a seashell to your ear to hear that dull rushing sound that is supposed to be the sound of the distant ocean.

It migrated to a dull ringing sound in his ears as he started getting his senses back. Feeling sluggish and fuzzy, Chornelhus's first thought is to wonder why he is on the ground.

Next is disgust at being on the ground. Dirt! Filth!

He pawed at the ground beneath him, trying weakly to push himself up.

Then he remembered the old woman.

"G-grandmother," he rasped, filling with panic.

The panic gave him resolve, which gave him strength enough to sit up.

The world is spinning and his eyes have trouble focusing.

When he spotted the withered body, the world fell out from beneath him.

"Grandmother!" He crawled to the prone figure, tugging weakly like a child pulling at his mother. "Grandmother," he groaned.

He brushed the debris off the motionless form, sure she is dead. His whole purpose is gone.

He struggled to roll the ancient woman over, brushing off the dirt. He sobbed, an emotion he and everyone who knows him had long thought him incapable of.

Her eyes opened. It is not the fluttering open or slow droopiness of one who is returning to consciousness; it is the sudden snapping open of the eyes of one who is entirely alert.

"You cannot kill me like that," her voice hissed through age-cracked lips.

She started laughing, her laughter dry and brittle, and it is the most terrible sound.

Chornelhus nearly choked on his relief she is still alive. He got clumsily to his feet, still dazed, and wobbled over to her, bending to help the ancient woman to her feet.

Taking his hand, she lets him pull her up, her movements shaky with great age and the weakness of hunger, just as they were before.

Chornelhus struggles, too weak and dazed to pull her up.

Chornelhus looks around for his security men. The woods are blasted and blackened, dry leaves and grass burning where the force of the blast was unable to blow the sheltered kindling out, the old trees beginning to catch fire too as the flames greedily lick at them. He sees charred ruined bodies lying around and cannot say how many there are or who. Some are just scattered pieces of scorched limbs. Smoke is filling the air and he thinks he can see movement, but is not sure.

Mr. Chornelhus and his ancestor had escaped the explosion. They were thrown clear of the devastation of the premature detonation.

Standing leaning against the car, Mr. Chornelhus's driver started and cried out with shock at the sudden booming blast. He looked around in confusion, wondering where it came from before he realized. He raced for the woods, looking around frantically. He wants to call out, but knows his boss would be furious. Mr.

Chornelhus always insisted on the strictest confidentiality and secrecy to all his movements, no matter what.

It took him only a few moments to spot Mr. Chornelhus struggling to pull up the old woman sprawled on the ground. He rushed over to help.

"Help," Chornelhus said weakly, motioning towards the old woman.

The driver rushed to their sides, taking one with each arm.

Under the cover of darkness, he got them to the car without them being seen. The black vehicle slipped away into the night.

The wail of distant sirens come as they are driving away.

Detective Hughes is about to go to bed when his phone rang.

He almost does not answer it.

"Hello," he said into the receiver. He listened, his face turning into a scowl. It is the office.

"There's been an explosion at the Garden Grove site," the voice on the phone said. "Looks like Chornelhus made his move."

"Are you sure it was him?" Hughes asked.

"Has to be," the voice said. "We put his private security men in the area."

"Where in the area?" Hughes asked.

"All over," the voice said, sounding a little shaky.

Hughes expression turned to bafflement as he listened to the voice explain what happened.

"We're never going to catch him now," he thought unhappily "unless we can get him on blowing up his Anc-Chor project and filing a fraudulent insurance claim on it.

When asked the next day about his security men who were blown apart with the others, Mr. Chornelhus shook his head sadly and wondered aloud what they could have been doing there.

In the mess of bodies and shredded remains, it will not be easy to piece together who and how many people had been there. The authorities will spend long hours collecting evidence and trying to piece the bodies back together.

END

Old Mill Road

(Short Story)

By L.V. Gaudet

This story is a work of fiction. Names, characters, places, and events are products of the author's imagination or are used fictitiously. Any resemblance to actual events, locales, or persons, living or dead, is entirely coincidental.

1 - Kids' Discovery

The four kids are standing around looking down at it. Darkness is already creeping across the sky, chasing the late afternoon sun away and made even darker by the shade of the tall trees surrounding them. Glimpses of open grass can be seen through the trees ahead where they entered the woods.

"I don't think we should tell anyone," David says. He is the oldest of the group, a virtual adult at ten.

"We have to," his younger brother Ian insists.

"They'll think we did it," Ian warns. "We could go to jail."

The third boy, Nick, youngest of the children, whimpers.

"I don't want to go to jail," Nick thinks, fear surging through him despite the numb shock. "That's where they put bad people like Uncle Harvey. Uncle Harvey scares me; a lot."

Nick looks at his sister Felicia for help, but she is oblivious to the terrifying thoughts in his head. He looks at David and Ian. They seem to have forgotten he's even there.

"I don't want to go live in jail with Uncle Harvey," Nick thinks, looking back at the gruesome spectacle on the ground before them. He starts to cry.

Felicia just stands there next to her little brother Nick, her face ashen, shivering although it is still quite warm and sticky with the humidity left behind by the waning hot day.

She knows they would not put them in jail like adults. They are only kids, after all. And how could anyone possibly think they did this? But, she does not say that.

She does not say anything at all and just keeps staring down at it with a sick feeling.

Felicia puts one arm around Nick to comfort him. He leans into her gratefully and huffs as he tries to get himself under control.

The breeze picks up, the gust of wind invading the woods to rustle the leaves, picking up and swirling any loose leaves it finds and letting them fall as they will. It teases at Felicia's hair, making it dance for a moment, and then the gust of wind is gone.

Felicia shivers harder under the onslaught of the wind, despite the lack of chill on it. "Someone walked over my grave," she thinks the old saying idly. It makes her shudder.

"Come on Nick," David says, looking down at him seriously, "you have to stop crying or they'll know something is wrong. We can't leave here until you stop."

Nick coughs and blubbers, trying to make the tears stop.

A crow stares down at them from its perch on a branch, their only witness, and then takes flight to vanish over the trees.

The sky grows darker, the sun lowering on the horizon, as they stand there mutely staring like worshipers at a grisly shrine.

Finally, with Nick's tears under control, they nod their wordless agreement, turn, and melt into the fast darkening woods, looking more like specters than living children.

This will be their secret.

2 - Vanished

Home from school, the screen door loudly bangs closed behind David. He drops his school bag, kicks off his shoes, and runs for the television in the living room.

"Don't slam the door," his mother's voice calls from somewhere in the house.

Ian comes in after him, closing the door more carefully than his older brother, and joins David lying on the floor watching cartoons.

"Psst."

David looks around for the source of the sound.

"Psst."

He gets up and walks to the kitchen doorway. Felicia is on the other side of the screen door, waving at him with a finger at her lips. He walks over.

"What?" he whispers, a little annoyed. His irritation quickly vanishes when he sees her face is discolored and her eyes are red and swollen from crying.

He slips out the door, careful not to let it bang on its spring-loaded hinges, and pulls her aside out of sight of anyone inside, full of concern for both her and their secret.

"What's wrong?" David asks.

"I don't know." Felicia looks at him with eyes filled with sorrow and fear, her voice choking on the words.

"What do you mean you don't know?" David squints his eyes at her in an expression that suggests he doesn't believe her.

"Of course you know what's wrong, otherwise you wouldn't be crying," he thinks. He says nothing, knowing she will speak if he keeps silent.

"Everybody's gone crazy," Felicia whispers. "Mom just keeps crying. Dad is stomping around yelling at everybody, strange people keep coming and going from the house. They whisper and stare at us with weird looks. No one will tell Nick and me what's going on."

David arches an eyebrow at her, his question unvoiced. He doesn't dare ask.

"Did you tell?" His mind screams it. He tightens his lips to keep from voicing those three terrible little words.

Felicia whimpers. "Dad was yelling at someone on the phone, at Mom, and at us. The police came to the house. Dad rushed out to meet them outside before they could come to the door. He yelled at them too."

Felicia's face is pale, her skin waxy, and she looks like she is almost too weak to stand.

"Like she's sick," David thinks.

David shakes his head slowly. This is serious. You do not yell at cops, everybody knows that.

"Do they know about what we found?" he asks, almost unable to, afraid of the answer.

"I-I don't know," she sobs. "I-I'm scared. So is Nick."

Felicia's mother's voice carries to them on the wind, calling her to come home.

"I have to go," she whispers.

David watches her run across from the back yard to the front street and away down the road toward home. She runs with that awkward gait of a girl whose growth needs to catch up to her long lanky legs.

The next day, David bangs the kitchen door open just as he always does when he comes home from school. This time he doesn't let it bang closed. His mother is about to yell out of habit to not slam the door, but he beats her to it. Dropping his school books on the floor by the door, David calls out.

"I'm going to Felicia's."

"Be back before supper," his mother's voice calls back.

Ian gives him a curious look as David passes him as he approaches the door, always arriving that moment after David.

Catching the door as David lets it go to slam closed, Ian closes it quietly, leaves his stuff by the door, and retreats to the living room to plop on the floor and watch cartoons.

David hurries across from the back yard to the front street and away down the road, following Felicia's path home from yesterday.

As is customary, David goes straight to the back of the house. The doors to Felicia's house are closed today. There is no whispering through the open screen door like at his house.

David frowns at the house.

"Odd. Felicia's mom usually has only the screen doors closed on a hot day like today to let the breeze cool the house."

He steps up to the back door and knocks, waiting.

When no one answers, he knocks again.

Nobody is here. The place has an empty feel to it, like it is deserted.

David walks around to the front. The front window curtains are drawn tight. He tries knocking on the front door.

"There should be someone here."

Still, there is no answer.

He walks around the house inspecting it, standing on tiptoes and trying to look in the windows, and finally pulls an old small wooden crate that had been left sitting by the back gate to a spot beneath a window. Standing on his tiptoes on the crate and pulling himself up by the window ledge, he can just see inside.

What he can see doesn't look right.

The house is not as tidy as usual. Felicia's mother is well known around town for being too neat.

It's nothing major that is wrong with the house, just little things that he can never remember ever being out of place when he was in the house. The large vase that always sat beside the living room end table with decorative sticks of some kind is tipped on its side; its sticks spilled half out. A shirt or something, he can't tell what, lies discarded on the floor. Past the kitchen doorframe, he can just make out one end of the dining table. Two flies buzz around an unfinished dinner there. The chair is pushed back as if someone had gotten up and left in a hurry.

That was the last he saw of Felicia and Nick and their family.

3 - Waiting at the Old Train Station

Years Later

The train rattles past the old train station without slowing down. Trains don't stop here anymore. The station is nothing more than a rotting wood platform, partially covered by a sagging wood roof which now has many large holes and missing boards, and a small ticket office. The rusted old padlock barely holds the door closed, its old screws sagging loosely in the worn wood.

Two men wait in front of the old ticket office, though no train will ever come again. They are men, barely, just starting out their adult lives.

Pacing restlessly, Ian scuffs his toes against the rotting timber of the platform, silently hoping it does not give way beneath his weight.

David is sitting calmly on one end of the wooden bench. The other end looks like it had been chewed off by rot; the half-seated frame looking soft, cracked, and unlikely to hold a man's weight. He watches his younger brother pace.

"They're building homes up there on the old Mill Road," Ian says. "A whole development."

He turns and looks at David, his expression grim.

David looks at him with a surprised look.

"Wow," he says, "I'd forgotten."

"Yeah, me too. It's been a lot of years."

David shakes his head, amused. He chuckles.

"Man, were we dumb," he says.

"Uh-huh. Bunch of dumb kids." Ian doesn't look amused. "They'll find it you know."

"So?" David has a half smirk, unconcerned over the possibility of their childhood secret being discovered.

"What if they figure out we were there?" Ian's forehead crinkles with the worry plaguing him. He can't help it. He grew up scared of being blamed for it. The memory of it tormenting his sleep, turning dreams into nightmares.

"What if they think we had something to do with it?" he asks.

"We didn't. We were just a bunch of kids. Nobody would suspect kids." David shrugs and sighs. "Besides, they don't throw kids in jail."

Ian chuckles. It is an unsure and nervous sound. "Yeah, but we sure thought they would."

"Yeah."

Ian looks at his brother with a dark look. "But they could now, couldn't they?"

"They wouldn't. We were just kids then. Besides we didn't do anything. We just found it."

"Yeah, but it could have been us," Ian presses. He just can't shake the hollow fear that filled him the moment he saw that billboard sign near the entrance to the old Mill Road announcing the coming new development.

"It could have been anybody," David says. He doesn't want to talk about this anymore. He wishes Ian would just drop it.

"We were there. We didn't tell anyone." Ian looks tired, almost sick. "Hell man, it was just a kid."

They are interrupted by a crashing through the bush. Both men turn to look in the direction of the noise.

Ian looks startled, like he might flee at any moment.

"They're here," David says.

Ian shakes his head, a puzzled look on his face.

"It's the wrong direction. Why would they be coming through the woods?"

4 - Nick's Return

The deafening growl of the large machines scraping away at the raw open wounds in the earth do not drown out the sharp cracks of trees being violently crushed and their sturdy trunks snapping as they are torn down by heavy machinery. Their large treads leave deep patterns in the damp hard-packed mud as they trundle about, unstoppable. The background noise of chainsaws and large mallets used to cut taller trees down can barely be heard in the cacophony.

A dented white trailer sits parked haphazardly on the grass at the edge of the black scraped ground. A hastily crafted makeshift boardwalk lies mud-spattered across the black expanse of raw mud extending from the trailer to a grassy area populated by thin mostly dead trampled long grass where an assortment of trucks and cars are parked.

On the edge of this parking area a group of middle-aged and greying suited men stand around looking important, waving and pointing at the construction area with what looks like rolled plans and blueprints in their hands. A couple of them are even wearing hard hats, an unnecessary accessory since they won't get close enough to dirty their nicely pressed suits and fine leather dress shoes, let alone risk bumping their well-coiffed heads.

One of the suited men pauses, looking hard at a young man driving a bulldozer across the field. The machine lurches in jerking lumbering movements like the operator is drunk or a child is driving it.

"Say, isn't that Rueben's boy?" he asks no one in particular.

The man beside him stares at the driver, thinking.

"Yes. Yes, I think it is," he says. "What was his name again?"

"Wow, I haven't seen them in years," the first man says. "Nicholas or Nick, I think. They moved away didn't they?"

"Or ran away," the second man chortles. "I heard there were some problems with the wife's brother."

They are brought back to the conversation at hand by the others of their group, planning the construction of the new development on the old Mill Road.

The young man driving the bulldozer is completely unaware of the men's sudden interest in him. He keeps glancing at the woods bordering the field they are tearing apart.

"I never understood why my family hastily packed a few bags, jumped in the family car, and drove far away after a telephone call interrupted dinner that night long ago."

Nick focuses his attention back on the tractor, the engine growling and the gears grinding as he shifts them, changes direction, and presses forward with the bucket scraping a fresh raw wound into the ground. The top layer of grass and soil wrinkles and gives, being scooped into the tractor bucket. He looks at the woods again.

It had been a strange day.

He vaguely remembers discovering something bad in the woods with his sister and their friends as a kid. He doesn't remember what they found, but he does remember the police coming to the house, his dad yelling a lot at everybody, his mother crying, and his sister's very strange behavior.

"I can't explain why, but I don't think we ever told anyone what we found. I only remember that something happened, not what was said or what happened."

Nick's memory is more a grainy impression than a real memory, lost along with so many other memories to time and the confusion of a child's mind.

Even now, his dreams are haunted by hazy images that mean nothing to him; disgusting insects crawling through moss and dead leaves rotting in the dark woods, a face that looks strangely soft and putty-like; a face that is not really a face. A face that is not all there, like it was in the process of being made or un-made by an unskilled special effects creator. The face would call his name, its dead eyes weeping, mouth twisted in a grimace of pain and fear.

This is why Nick came back.

He stops the tractor, putting it in reverse, and turning it. The machine bounces and jogs over the rough ground made rougher by his inexperienced work. He stops the tractor, looking at his handiwork, the ruined ground ahead of him, hoping no one notices what a mess he's making of it.

The woods pull at his attention again.

"Something happened to my family that day; something that changed them forever. I'm not sure what, but I know something terrible lies hidden in the woods along the old Mill Road."

He vaguely remembers a silent pact of secrecy made by frightened children, a pact his sister's haunted eyes staring back at him every time he looked at her never let him forget. Whatever it was it had to remain a secret. He could not remember what that secret was and could never bring himself to ask Felicia. Whatever it was, it had tormented her every day since.

When he learned of the development being built in the area, he once again tossed a hastily packed bag in the car and drove. It was not hard to get a job on one of the work crews. Workers were being brought in from all over for this project. They did not even bother to check his background. Otherwise, they would have known he lied about his training and experience when they hired him. Harder, was trying to drive a bulldozer he lied about knowing how to drive.

He works the bucket, the bucket's awkward jerky motions making the whole tractor rock, positions it too high, and starts the forward motion again, doing a poor job of scraping away the top later of earth.

A man stands at the edge of the woods some distance away from where the heavy machinery is tearing the woods apart to make way for the development. He is worn and weathered looking, dressed in old clothing that are as old in style as they are in wear. He has the look of a grizzled man who has seen too much, his age lost somewhere in the years of unpleasant experiences. His long hair and beard only make him look more scruffy.

No one notices him standing in the shadows of the trees.

He watches the young man driving the bulldozer with obvious inexperience. He sees the two suited men take notice of the young man. He tenses as he watches them and knows they are talking about the young man. He relaxes when they return to their conversation with the other suited men, ignoring the young man again.

He backs away, melting into the woods, and vanishes.

5 - Something in the Woods

David and Ian run hard down the overgrown long unused road leading away from the old abandoned train station, their breath coming in ragged gasps, legs aching from the effort, faces pinched with strain and fear.

They are so absorbed in the effort of running that they do not notice the approaching car ahead of them.

It's an older car, well used, and looks filled to capacity with young men. Music blares from it and its tires crunch on the broken chunks cracked out of the old road that has not been maintained since the train station it serviced was abandoned. The car stops ahead of them and waits for the running men.

David and Ian almost run headlong into the front grill, Ian dodging it last minute while David puts his hands out and deflects off the hood. He gives the occupants a grin and raises his arms over his head in victory, pretending it was on purpose.

The men inside laugh uproariously at the two brothers.

"What are you running from?" the driver calls, leaning out his window to address the two out-of-breath men.

The brothers look at each other, trying to catch their breath. David leans on the car and Ian bends over and grasps his legs to keep himself standing.

"What (gasp) the hell (gasp) was that?" Ian asks between ragged gasps for air. You can hear the strain of fear in his voice, although he tried to hide it.

"Bear?" David gasps. His voice holds the tension of fear too, but not as much. He is not just older; he has always been braver than Ian too.

Ian shakes his head.

"That was no bear," he puffs.

"You being chased by monsters?" the driver laughs at them. The others in the car laugh too.

"Oooo, the old Mill Road Monster is going to get you," the driver moans in his best spooky voice.

This makes everyone in the car laugh harder.

The brothers give the driver an unimpressed look.

They have all heard the same tales as kids. Tales they told each other in the darkened corners of rotting abandoned outbuildings, trying to outdo scaring the wits out of each other.

There is one story that has been told for generations, of a strange and frightening creature living in the woods. Those woods border the old Mill Road for miles past the old mill that gave the road its unofficial name on one side and the train tracks and the abandoned train station's long unused road on another. This creature is rumored to be the cause of the occasional mysterious disappearance of pets, farm animals, backpackers, campers, and children.

Disappearances in the area are uncommon, but that did not stop the stories. One such story is that the strange creature and some rather brutal unexplained deaths at the mill at the end of the old Mill Road is the reason the mill was abandoned many years ago.

The rear car door nearest to David and Ian swings open with a grinding squeal and the young man who opened it leans out with a grin.

"You coming?" he asks.

These young men are who David and Ian were waiting for at the old train station. Men they grew up with. This is going to be a typical day in a small town with nothing better for the young men to do than hang out and maybe get into a little trouble.

The brothers get in, wedging themselves into the already overpopulated car, relieved to be getting out of there.

"So, where are we going?" David asks.

"Down to the old Mill Road," the driver calls back over his shoulder as he guns the engine, turning the car around too fast in the narrow roadway. "We're going to go check out the construction going on down there."

Ian looks back the way they came, still unnerved by the noises they heard in the woods.

6 - Suspicion

David and Ian sit together at a worn table in the dimly lit beer parlor, the only one in their little town. The place is a throwback to an earlier time, the décor having never been updated in the decades of its existence. Glasses of draft beer on the table between them catch the light, making it seem brighter within the confines of the golden liquid.

The group dispersed hours ago.

"I just can't believe it," Ian says, "little Nicky, here."

"And working at the site of the new development on the old Mill Road," David finishes for him.

They recognized Nick almost immediately when they saw him working at the construction site.

"Do you think he remembers?" Ian asks.

David shakes his head thoughtfully, his eyes lowered against his own memories trying to peer out through them.

"He was the youngest. Maybe. Probably not. They moved away. It's pretty easy to forget when you aren't around a thing."

"Do you think it's just a coincidence then?" Ian asks. "He suddenly shows up, there of all places, when they start tearing the woods apart?"

"I always wondered what happened to them," David says, his eyes getting a far away look.

"When did they move away?" Ian asks. He searches his memory, but cannot remember.

"That next night. The day after we found it in the woods," David says. He stares at his beer as if it somehow holds the past like a crystal ball. He remembers that hollow feeling of loss when he discovered his friends' house empty of all signs of life, and the sick feeling that something was terribly wrong, all those years ago.

His first thought was that whoever or whatever had done that to that kid saw them in the woods the day before. That he, or it or whatever it was, had gotten them and that he, Ian, and their family would be next.

In the weeks that followed, rumors flourished, but no one actually knew what happened to Felicia and Nick's family. They just vanished. They never came back for their belongings and, after a while, the house and its contents were quietly sold off.

At times over the years he even crazily thought that maybe the monster that was supposed to live in the woods down by the old mill is real. That it got Felicia and her family. Of course, it's not and it didn't. It's just old stories kids tell to scare each other like Scary Mary coming out of the mirror.

"She came to the house after school the day after we found it," David continues. "She had been crying. She said everyone in her house went crazy, that the cops were there. She was scared. They never came to school the next day."

His eyes look hollow now, as if he'd lost something from sight long ago and has been looking for it ever since.

It is a look Ian hasn't seen in his older brother's eyes in a long time. David is always so confident and unconcerned about everything, unlike himself who is a worrier and tends to second-guess everything.

David's reaction to thinking about Felicia makes Nick wonder if that confidence is nothing more than a shell David hides behind.

"I went to their house after school," David goes on, his voice almost catching as the emotion fills him like it is happening all over again, "they were gone. It was like they just vanished, or were taken or something. Dinner was still on the table." He pauses. "I remember that. I'll always remember that. Dinner was still on the table."

He looks up at Ian now and Ian can see the torment in his brother's eyes.

It's the same look he came home with as a boy when he walked into the house two days after their discovery in the woods, the day he learned Felicia and Nick's family left. David had just been really quiet and it scared Ian. Finally, that night he told Ian what was wrong, about Felicia and Ian's house and how it seemed as if they had just been suddenly taken by aliens. Vanished in the middle of living.

They both thought immediately of their secret then, the thing in the woods, but did not say so to each other.

They never said so to each other, but they just knew; they had a pact of secrecy never to talk about it, not even to each other. And they never did, until now.

David and Ian both look down at their beers, needing to look away from each other.

"I always thought you'd marry her when we grew up," Ian says.

They both lapse into silence.

Someone enters the bar. The brothers look up to see who it is. Their faces change, brightening somewhat, when they recognize the face that has changed so much over the years and yet stayed much the same.

"Hey! Nicky! Nick!" David calls, waving him over.

The young man turns, squinting to see who is calling him, his eyes not yet adjusted to the dim interior after the bright sun.

"Hey," he calls back, waving back at them, approaching uncertainly.

These guys seem to know him, but Nick does not know who they are. It is that awkward moment when you know the other expects you to remember them, but your mind just draws a complete blank.

"Come, sit down," David waves him to sit. "What brought you back after all these years?" Something in David's friendly expression is off, guarded.

"Work," Nick says as he joins them.

He tries to place their faces, their voices. A sense of familiarity is coming to him. The hair color of the one who called him over, his lazy half grin that suggests he is up for getting into any kind of trouble. The familial resemblance between the two and the other's quiet observation of everything around him like he prefers to thoughtfully observe rather than actively participate, teases at his memory.

David looks around, catches the waitress's eye, and signals her to bring another round of draughts for the table.

"Just going where the work is, eh?" David says.

"That's about it," Nick answers, studying his long ago friend as if his face might give up some deep secret.

Too many years have passed. Nick was too young and the years and his mind's need to protect itself had melted away too many of his childhood memories. He just is not breaking through that barrier to place who these two men are.

Nick was the youngest of the group, him and Ian playing together while his sister Felicia and David were friends. Felicia and David's was that complicated kind of friendship of the older siblings, pushed together to keep an eye on their younger brothers, finally becoming friends and confidants, while David secretly crushed on Felicia and she wisely ignored her knowledge of that crush.

Forced together, all four had become friends despite the age difference that is small now that they have finally breached that barrier into adulthood, but seemed like an enormous gulf of time as kids.

"Hey, look who's here," a voice calls from across the room. All three young men turn to look at a figure shuffling towards them from the shadows beyond the end of the bar lined with bar stools. It's an older man, obviously accustomed to spending a great deal of time here and somewhat inebriated.

"Little Nick," he slurs, clapping the young man loudly on the back. He cocks his head at him. "You're not old enough to drink, are you?" he slurs with a wink, whispering too loudly.

Nick glances quickly at the waitress as if she might actually kick him out if she overheard. It would not have mattered if he was under the legal age. This is Dusty's and it has always been well known they do not kick out paying customers, even if they are under-aged. Nick heard as much from a few of the work crew at the construction site, but was skeptical of its truth.

"Your family move back?" the drunk asks.

"No, I'm just here for work. Got a job on that construction project up the old Mill Road, then I'll be moving on."

"Un," the drunk grunts. "Always wondered what happened to the lot of you after that trouble with your uncle. What was his name?"

"Harvey."

"Yeah, ol' Uncle Harvey."

"What trouble?" David asks, his expression unreadable.

Nick shakes his head, holding his silence.

"He just got out of jail back then, s'what I heard," the drunk tells them. "Killed some kid. Got off light because they couldn't prove it wasn't an accident. But we all know he did it. Didn't get enough time for it s'far as I'm concerned." He glares around the room as if Uncle Harvey might appear at any moment.

"Heard he was skulking around your house, making some trouble. Ol' Joe said he hit your mom, threatened her or somethin' the night your family packed up and left."

David studies Nick's face, watching it work.

Nick's face twitches with the effort of holding something back.

David exchanges a meaningful glance with Ian, a look that Nick catches and is not happy about. He wonders what they know that he does not.

Nick is stunned by the old drunk's revelation. His uncle Harvey killed a kid? Uncle Harvey always terrified him. He is a bad man, volatile and dangerous. But to kill a kid? Is it true? If it is, this is the first he heard of it.

There has always been rumors about Uncle Harvey. He was more than the black sheep of the family. He was the wolf in sheep's clothing. Hushed whispers were exchanged in quiet corners when those sharing secrets thought no one was around to hear. It has always been thought in the family that there was something wrong inside of Uncle Harvey. Something broken and sick in a way that he was not to be pitied like you are supposed to with the mentally ill, but that he was to be despised and avoided.

"No, I don't believe it," Nick thinks. He cannot let himself believe it. "Even crazy Uncle Harvey could not be that bad." That would mean he is related to a child killer. What would that say about him?

Nick turns his attention to his two new acquaintances.

"These men know me, but I don't know who they are. They look the right ages, so I probably went to school with them, maybe even played and hung out with them. These two know something they are not saying, and I'm pretty sure it's about me and my family."

Suddenly the familiarity of these two comes into focus and some broken memories come back to him, memories of playing with a friend, Felicia following along grudgingly and angry about always having to watch him, and the other boy who hung around with them. He was older and hung out more with his sister than with him.

He looks at the brothers and finally sees the resemblance to those boys in the young men. Their names come to him, Ian and David, but it comes with a feeling of unease.

"They never left, so maybe they know the secret that haunted Felicia all these years and made my family move so suddenly we didn't even take time to pack. Maybe they know the secret in the woods." He looks down, keeping these thoughts to himself. "Maybe they were the other kids in the pact of secrecy I only vaguely remember."

"Look," Nick says, jumping up hurriedly from his chair, "I've got to go."

"We'll come with you," David says, getting up to follow.

Nick is not happy about this. He will have to talk to these guys if he is going to learn anything, but right now he needs to be alone. He needs to digest everything.

Nick walks out without waiting, hoping David and Ian will just let him go. David follows on his heels. Ian jogs to catch up after hurriedly tossing some money on the table to pay the bill.

David catches up to Nick before he reaches the door and follows him out.

He comes in close to Nick as soon as they are outside, putting himself into Nick's space, slinging one arm around Nick's neck in a rough familiar hug and pulling him closer, dragging him along with him as he walks at a fast pace to put off Ian catching up to them.

The rough gesture makes Nick feel threatened.

"Do you remember?" David whispers harshly to Nick, putting his mouth next to his ear so not even Ian would hear as he tries to catch up to them.

"What?" Nick pulls back, trying unsuccessfully to pull free without making a scene.

David holds him firm.

"You know what," he hisses. David is not buying Nick's confusion. "That day in the woods off the old Mill Road."

David releases him and they stop and stare at each other, a stare-down to see who will win where there can be no winner.

Ian catches up to them, immediately sensing the tension between them. He stands back a few paces uncertainly, watching the tense standoff and wondering what is going on.

"I don't know what you're talking about," Nick insists.

"It's no coincidence you suddenly appear when they start digging up the woods, and working on the job site." David's stance is accusing.

"What are you here for?" he demands. "Are you trying to find it?" He stares at Nick, feeling that he is keeping something very important a secret. "To expose your uncle or to protect him?"

"You don't know anything," Nick mutters, angry.

"Exactly what is David accusing me of?" he wonders.

"No I don't," David spits. "All I know is that my friend and her family vanish after we find a dead kid in the woods, nobody would tell me anything, and suddenly you come back years later when the body is sure to be found." He glares at the younger man, breathing heavily, ready to pounce on him and pound the answers out of him.

The anger over the pain and feeling of abandonment so long ago comes rushing back over David. They did not even take time to pack, to sell the house ... to say goodbye.

Nick's mind whirls at breakneck speed. He tries to see the memory that David's words should have brought, but cannot.

Was that what we found in the woods? A dead kid? We found a dead kid? Is that what the old drunk was talking about? But my uncle was in jail then, wasn't he? He was released after we moved, wasn't he?

He feels the urge to shake his head to clear the confusion and fights it.

Didn't the drunk say Uncle Harvey had just gotten out of jail for killing a kid? If that's what we found in the woods, it could not have been the same kid that my uncle was accused of killing.

David is pressing him for an answer and not allowing him time to think. He needs to think, to process this. He has no idea what to say.

"Fine!" Nick snaps at him, blurting it out without knowing what is going to come out of his mouth. "Yes, I'm here to find the body before anyone else does. I'm here to find it and get rid of it. Maybe if I get rid of it everything will be ok again. It has never been okay; nothing has been okay since that day."

Nick's mind keeps working wildly. He has no idea what he just said, his mind caught up in trying to remember something, anything, about what happened so long ago.

A body? We found a body in the woods and that was the secret that haunted Felicia all these years?

What did David mean when he asked 'Are you trying to find it'? Does that mean whatever we found then is still there? That we left it hidden in the woods that fateful day?

I've always known Felicia knew more about whatever happened than she let on, although she always denied it, saying she didn't remember or that nothing happened. But I always knew she knew more. It was in her eyes.

After a while, Nick gave up asking and could only watch her suffer in silence.

David stares at him in a mixture of contempt and need.

"Felicia," David asks, "how does she feel about all this?"

Nick shifts his stance as if getting ready to make a break for freedom. He looks at David again, trying to figure out what he just said. He didn't quite hear the question.

"I've always wondered all these years," David continues, his anger melting away to leave him feeling suddenly exhausted at the thought of Felicia. "She took it harder than all of us when we found the body. Where is she? How is she doing?"

He studies Nick, noting how edgy he is.

Now Nick knows what David asked. He was asking about Felicia.

"She's fine. She's around, not here." Nick's eyes shift as if he is worried someone might overhear them.

"What happened?" David presses. He feels the need to know like a physical force.

"All those years ago, when your family disappeared, where'd you go? Why?"

"We just moved, that's it, we moved." Nick is being defensive, secretive. He is on edge and becoming more so with the questioning.

A group of young men passing by them stops and calls out to them.

"Hey, did you hear?"

"What?" David turns to them, calling back.

"A body's just been found up at the old Mill Road construction site, a kid or something."

Nick's face pales.

Ian blanches, turning to David for support.

David clenches his jaw, thinking.

David and Ian are thinking the same thing, "Is it THE body?"

Nick is unable to think at this point. He is still trying to process and make sense of what he just learned and the passer by's words have not sunk in yet.

News in small towns travels faster than the news happens. At that moment, a police cruiser pulls up beside them. The driver's window rolls down and the occupant leans out casually.

"Hey, you're Nick, right? Know where your uncle is?" he asks Nick, "Your Uncle Harvey?"

"Why?" Nick asks with a tremor in his voice.

"No reason," the officer says, "just looking for him."

The officer does not have to tell him. He knows.

The words do not sink in; they come crashing down on him.

"A body's just been found up at the old Mill Road construction site, a kid or something."

Nick knows they would have found something incriminating with the body. Either that or they suspect Uncle Harvey just because he is Uncle Harvey. He remembers Uncle Harvey well, although he has not seen him in years. He still scares him after all these years. But why is the officer asking as if he might have seen him? Is it a dig? Why would they think Uncle Harvey would have come back here with him? Why would they think he would come back at all? This is the last place his uncle would ever go if he went to jail for killing a kid. Everyone knows your face in a small community.

People never forgive child killers.

The cruiser's radio crackles to life with the news that Harvey has been located and brought in for questioning. The low volume is audible only to the officer in the car, not to the men standing outside it.

"I'll see you boys around," the officer says meaningfully, staring directly at Nick. He put the car into gear and drives away.

David turns back to Nick, studying him.

"So, old Uncle Harv maybe is the one that killed that kid we found all those years ago," David says to him. The statement is so loaded it is dripping with unsaid meaning.

There is something in Nick's look that tells David he is hiding something about his Uncle Harvey. As kids, Nick never could keep a secret. His face always gave him away. Apparently it still does.

"What are you hiding?" David wonders.

"Look, I really have to go," Nick says. He turns and walks away, ignoring their calls to come back.

"He's hiding something," David says to his brother. "He knows something he's not telling us."

Ian shrugs. He doesn't understand why this is bothering David so much, why he feels so compelled to dig it all up again. Ian wants it to stay buried and not have to think about it.

"I'm going to find out what it is," David declares.

"Well, I'll see you later," Ian says and turns to go home.

"Later." David just stands there watching Nick go.

7 - Memory Lane

Nick is torn. A part of him is telling him to go back. David and Ian have answers. But he does not even know what questions to ask.

He walks fast, thinking, not paying attention to where he is going. The only thing he knows is that he does not want to go home.

Home is not even a home.

His childhood home here had been sold years ago.

For now, with nowhere to go and little money, he is sleeping in his car. Even that feels like a safe refuge right now.

It is also utterly depressing, isolating.

"I wonder what the house looks like," Nick thinks.

Without thought to where he's going or his intentions, he finds himself taking a walk down memory lane. He wanders the town with an address in his head until he finds it, his old childhood home.

He had to look up the address before coming because he did not remember it.

Finding the address, Nick stops and stares at the house. Nothing about it is familiar. It jogs no memories.

He tries his best to remember what happened when he was just a little kid. Nothing comes.

"Is it the right house? 32 Galving Road. Yes, the address is right. Is the house wrong? The house is brown. Should it be blue?"

A memory teases at the back of him mind, but will not come.

"Wasn't there a swing set?"

He walks around the sidewalk, bringing the backyard into view and sees only a tired looking birdbath and a bunch of tall flowering plants that look more like weeds gone wild than flowers to him.

Nick walks up to the house. He feels in the back of his mind that this might not be the right thing to do, that whoever lives here now might be creeped out by this.

It does not stop him.

He looks in the window. Nothing inside looks familiar, but why should it? After all these years, the house must have gone through at least one family. They would have changed the wallpaper, the furniture. He moves on to another window and then another. Nothing he can see inside stirs any feelings of familiarity.

Nick moves on, wandering the neighborhood.

The neighborhood itself and the old schoolhouse bring back some fuzzy memories, but mostly just a vague sense that it should be more familiar than it is. The main street changed some over the years, but most of the buildings have the same sense of vague familiarity as the school.

After wandering for a while, Nick finds himself walking down the old Mill Road towards the construction site.

When he gets there, he sees the ruined raw wounds the tractors made clearing the field and the trees. The broken trees are piled along one side, twisted and mangled, like a giant beaver dam.

Nick stays back, backing into the shadows of the trees at the edge of the woods at the entrance to the site.

Police tape marks off an area at the edge of the woods across the field where the tractors had last been tearing the trees down.

A police car sits silently, the occupant guarding the site.

"That must be where the body was found. Whatever was there has been removed by now. What are they guarding then?

There were no police when I left work. Whatever happened, however the discovery was made, it must have happened after the job site closed for the day."

His attention is drawn to the police car and back to the yellow tape flapping in the wind.

"Who would have been digging around in the woods at the edge of the site to make the discovery?"

He looks up the road, its destination vanishing as it winds between trees on both sides. If he keeps going along that road eventually Nick will reach whatever is left of the old abandoned mill.

He turns around instead, heading back the other way. He wanders back through town, trying to find any familiarity in anything.

Nick finally stops when he finds himself at the old abandoned train station.

"There sure is a lot of old abandoned places. This town was dying before I was born."

He mounts the platform and sits on the partially rot-eaten bench in front of the ticket office. He just stares off into nothing, as though waiting for that long ago train that will never come again.

In the woods beyond the train station, the dry timber of the branches of a fallen tree crackles as something moves, stepping on the branches and moving over the fallen tree.

Nick hears the cracking of branches but takes no notice, his thoughts elsewhere.

"I have to tell Felicia about the kid they found." Nick mulls it over uncertainly, reconsidering.

"Should I tell her? How will she take it? No, maybe I shouldn't.

It might make her come back here, and that is the last thing she should do. This place is poison to her. She has a right to know. But will it only make her worse? Will it only destroy her more; bring old horrors back to life for her?

Definitely, I shouldn't tell her."

He is torn between needing to learn more, knowing his sister knows more than she would probably ever tell, and wanting to protect her. He sees her tormented eyes before him, the sadness that never leaves the curve of her mouth.

"I should tell her."

8 - Uncle Harvey

Harvey's motionless prone form on the metal bed of the holding cell belies the anxiety and turmoil that fills him. His eyes are open just a crack, enough to see but give anyone who looks at him the impression he is sleeping.

Harvey looks worn and weathered, dressed in old out-of-style clothing. His scruffy hair and long beard add to his worn image. He has the ageless look of a grizzled man who has seen too much, lived through too many unpleasant experiences, and does not fit in well with civilization.

That impression is fitting for the man who seldom leaves the woods where he lives alone in a small cabin that looks as derelict as the man.

Harvey is a bit of an odd bird who is not generally comfortable in the company of other people, something of a reclusive oddity, and a man of unnerving silence.

There is not a person alive who knew Harvey that did not harbor some fear of the man, even if only because they did not know how to break through that shell to the man inside.

Harvey listens to the sounds of the building beyond his cell. The officer who brought him in is out of sight in the area beyond the holding cells. He hears the squeak of his chair and his footsteps as he walks to the coffee station. The gurgle of him filling his coffee cup and his footsteps back to his desk. His chair squeaks again as he sits down to drink his coffee and wait.

The officer is impatient. The chair shifts and squeaks again and his footsteps come towards the holding cells.

Harvey does not open his eyes or move a muscle, continuing the charade that he is sleeping.

He hears the officer's uniform fabric rustle, his footsteps come to a stop, and the soft rustle of the uniform and a tired sigh as the man leans against the wall.

"Are you sure you don't want a lawyer?" the officer asks, his voice exasperated and bored at once.

"No, I'm good," Harvey says without moving anything but his mouth or opening his eyes.

His unconcerned casual attitude only serves to aggravate the officer more. He bristles.

"Twice in the history of this town a child's body has turned up in the woods, and both times you just happen to have come back to town around that time," the officer says. "With your past, aren't you even a little concerned about going to prison? You know what the other inmates will do to you. Even they don't like child killers." He sneers at this, trying to get under Harvey's skin.

"I didn't do it," Harvey says calmly, still not moving or opening his eyes.

The officer steps forward, whipping out and extending his baton in one swift stroke, banging it on the holding cell bars loudly. The sound can be heard through the whole building.

Harvey casually opens his eyes and looks up at him.

The officer glares down at him hatefully. He has no doubt the man in the cage killed this child and the other one found years ago in the same area.

Harvey moves slowly, swinging his legs around and sitting up on the hard bunk.

"The first one they determined an animal was responsible. This time…" Harvey shrugs, "they'll figure it out soon enough and you will have to let me go."

The officer's stance shifts menacingly. He grips the baton as if he might beat the prisoner senseless if not for the bars between them. Child deaths and child killers always hit the officers hard. In that moment, the officer wishes he is the kind of man who could beat a sick bastard like this to death. He tightens his grip on the baton in frustration, feeling useless. It would not bring the child back even if he had been that kind of man.

"Cut him loose," a voice behind the officer interrupts.

The officer and Harvey both turn to see a man wearing a suit minus the tie standing at the entrance to the holding cells area. The officer gives him a cold look.

"Are you his lawyer?"

"Detective Liam Tobin." He doesn't bother to flash his badge, expecting his sense of authority to be authority enough. "I've been put on this case."

The officer considers demanding to see his badge.

"He called in the feds?" he asks, referring to his boss.

The unfamiliar detective nods. "He did. He had to."

"We picked him up on suspicion he has something to do with the kid in the woods."

"We're letting him go," the Detective pushes. "We are not filing charges. Yet."

After giving the detective a sour look clearly signaling his feelings about it, the officer grudgingly puts his baton away and turns to unlock the cell door. Opening the door, he stands aside, holding it open.

Harvey bows to him graciously as he exits the cell, careful to keep his distance from the officer. He does not want to give him any justification to grab him and slam him down on the ground like he knows he is itching to do.

The officer only glowers at him, keeping himself in check. As much as he wants to beat this child killer, he will not touch him without cause.

Harvey walks out of the holding cells area past the detective without a glance back.

"Don't leave town," Detective Tobin says. "We will want to talk to you again."

Harvey gives him a wave without turning and heads for the building exit.

"Why the Hell are we letting him go?" the officer growls. "We haven't maxed out the time we can hold him without charging him."

"Just giving him a little rope to hang himself with," Detective Tobin says with a grin, watching Harvey leave.

9 - David

David cannot stop thinking about Felicia. What does she look like now? He is sitting on the couch in his living room brooding over it. If Nick came back, does that mean she will too?

Ian comes in and sees the troubled look on David's face. He sits in the chair across from him, studying him.

"You really think Nick came back to make trouble?" Ian asks, thinking that is what David is dwelling on.

David looks up at him.

"What? No. I mean yes, but that's not it," he says.

"Do you think they found it this time?" Ian asks.

"They must have," David says. "I haven't heard of any kids going missing. Have you?"

Ian shakes his head no.

"So, if they found a kid, it has to be the one we found back then. You aren't still worried they will put us in jail, are you? We were only kids back then and all we did was find it. They wouldn't even know we found it. How would they?"

Ian pales at the thought, looking guilty.

"What? David asks, catching the sick look of guilt.

Ian swallows, trying to think of how to say it.

"What did you do?" David's tone sounds like a father trying to coax a confession from a child that he knows is guilty of the crime, but wants to hear him say it.

Ian reluctantly meets his eyes with his own.

"I kind of left something behind with the body," Ian says weakly. His knees feel like they will crumple beneath him at any moment.

David's expression hardens. He is more angry than shocked.

"You just figured this out now? All these years, how did you just decide now that you left something behind? How do you even know?"

"I always knew," Ian says guiltily.

David glares at him.

"Why didn't you say something back then? You knew we were all freaked about getting caught. We could have gone back for it."

"You would have made me go back. I was scared."

"And all these years," David persists, "all these years and you never said anything, never went back for it. You left evidence that we were there and you didn't do anything about it."

"You said kids can't go to jail," Ian says defensively. "You said they would never think we did it because we were kids. I was afraid to go back. I didn't even think I'd be able to find the place again."

Ian stops talking, out of excuses. He hangs his head in shame.

"I lied," David snaps. "Kids have killed kids before. We were there. They could have suspected we did it."

He glowers at Ian, who just looks back guiltily.

Finally, David sighs. There is nothing they can do about it now. Maybe whatever it was is not even there anymore.

After so many years, it is a shock to think that there could be anything left of the remains to be found, that they had not been eaten by scavengers or rotted to nothing in the damp undergrowth of the woods.

"So what was it?" David asks. "What did you leave behind?"

Ian looks down, suddenly feeling embarrassed.

"A toy," Ian says.

"A toy." David's expression is a mix of relief and concern. "What kind of toy?"

"An action figure," Ian says.

David can't help it. He bursts out laughing so hard tears come to his eyes and he doubles over.

When he is finally able to get control of himself again, he straightens up and looks at Ian with that lopsided half smirk of his that is a sure sign he is plotting mischief.

"An action figure. How do you know you left it?" he asks. "I mean, how sure are you?"

Ian shrugs.

"I realized it was missing the next day. I was playing with it when we went to the woods. I stuck it in my pocket. The next day I couldn't find it."

"So, you don't even know where you lost it," David says. "We were all over the place. You could have lost it anywhere."

He bursts into a new round of uncontrollable laughter.

Ian just stands there looking at him.

10 - Felicia

It is dusk and the shadows are deepening across everything. It is that time at the end of the day when frayed nerves might jump at nothing and an overwrought mind plays tricks.

David wanders the edge of the woods just beyond where the now idle heavy equipment was clearing brush. Yellow police tape ruffles in the breeze, draped and ugly, marking off the area. No one is guarding the scene now. He knows he won't find anything, but he needs to look anyway.

His eyes scan the area, seeing trees, rocks, and brush that are no longer there, replaced by the ugly black scar and heavy machine tracks where the brush had been torn out and the ground scraped flat. He sees the rise and fall of the uneven ground, the shadows cast in the late afternoon sun of many years ago.

On the edge of one side of the cleared area, the mangled trees and bushes are piled up like a freak show dam built by an insane giant beaver.

Slowly walking across the area, eyes studying what is no longer there, he stops with a sharp intake of breath.

It's there. Just beyond the edge of ruined ground and a little ways in, there will be a slight hollow beneath the shelter of a downed rotting tree that had not yet been dug up. The body would be nothing more than sun-bleached bones scattered by animals if it were still there at all, still exposed to the sky as they left it so many years ago.

David ducks under the police tape and enters the darker shadows of the trees that have not yet been cleared.

Not far in, he spots it, the rotting remains of a large tree melting into the ground where it lays, ferns and other undergrowth devouring it as they grow in its place. The branches are mostly gone now; just a few rough stumps sticking out where the largest branches once extended from the trunk. The tree once lay straight, partially leaning and not quite touching the ground except at its base. It lay across the top of two large rocks, rough ground, and other fallen deadwood, and was partially caught up in the branches of other trees as though they had reached out to catch their fallen brethren, snagging its branches with their own and forever frozen in time in that position.

Now the tree lies on the ground, their hold finally released, limp and sagging with the rise and fall of ground and rocks beneath it. The top side looks chewed down and soft with the rot as it slowly melts back into the ground it once grew from.

With a nervous swallow, David walks around the tree to the other side. Although the tree partially sags into it, the hollow is still there. That spot where they found the body.

He knows without a doubt it is the right place. He has seen the image in his mind every day. It is burned into his memory as fresh as that first day they saw it.

There is nothing here now, but he can see the body in his mind's eye as if it is still present and preserved exactly as they found it. The face of the child stares back at him, not all there, soft skin covering a section from the nose down on one side of the slack jaw. The rest is part flesh covered, part pale bone, as if the skin and tissue were slowly melting away like an ice cube left in the hot sun. The rest of the body is lost in the dimness of childhood memory, only the grisly face staring at him, clear and accusing. He can't tell if it was a boy or girl.

"It's been a long time," a soft female voice comes from the shadows.

Startled, David spins around. He stands motionlessly staring, silent, and his mouth open with surprise.

He stiffens, trying to place the voice, knowing immediately who it belongs to, yet somehow disbelieving it.

She steps from the shadows.

His eyes roam over her, absorbing her. She looks even more beautiful to him than he imagined she would.

She is an older version of the Felicia he crushed on as a kid. More mature, curvy, somehow softer. Her eyes hold the aged look of someone who has lived a hundred years and seen too much trauma, the lines of her mouth an indefinable subtle sadness.

"Felicia," David whispers.

"What are you doing here in the woods?" she asks, her voice soft, undemanding.

"I-I'm," he stammers.

"Looking for something?" she asks as she closes the distance between them.

He can smell her now; her perfume is perfect for her. She is perfect. He never forgot her in all those years. There had always been something special between them, something that told him they were meant for more, to be more than just friends.

"What are you looking for David?" His name almost caresses off her tongue. "The body? It's gone. Are you scared? Worried? Worried they'll find out we found it all those years ago and kept it a secret?"

He swallows hard, his throat a large dry knot. He can hardly breathe; it feels like he will choke on his own throat.

"Are you scared they will find out what we did?"

"We-we didn't do anything," he gasps.

"Are you sure? Do you remember? Who do you think killed that poor boy?" She blinks at him. Her eyes locked onto his, drawing them, trapping them, trapping his stuttering heart.

She moves, walking around him, stopping behind him, so close he can feel her presence although he can no longer see her.

David is spellbound, unable to move. He swallows.

"Old Uncle Harvey?" she whispers softly, her breath tickling his neck with her closeness. "Bad bad Uncle Harvey? Do you think he did it? Do you think you'll find something after all this time to incriminate him? We all knew he was a bad man, that he did bad things, didn't we? Everyone in town said so."

Her body barely brushes against his as she circles him, her perfume wrapping him in its heady blanket. She stops in front of him, looking at him with her head slightly tilted as if he were some odd bird she is trying to think what it might be.

She walks again, stopping behind him once more.

It is pure torture for him every time she moves from sight. He wants to turn, to keep her in view, but is afraid to move. If he moves she might be gone, nothing more than a whisper, his imagination playing with him.

A part of him keeps harping deep inside that she is not there, not real, that he is dreaming her.

David shakes his head, unable to think. His heart cries out for her, his hands want to reach for her. His lips want to ask her a million questions.

Felicia takes his headshake as a 'no', that he does not think Harvey murdered the child. Her eyes narrow as she studies him.

"So, you don't remember much from that day?" she asks.

David's mind can only focus on one thing, Felicia. The rest of that day does not exist, just her.

"I remember we found it. We were all scared and decided to keep it a secret. You came to my house. You'd been crying. Then you were gone …" he trails off.

"Gone. Weren't we all gone that day, one way or another?" Felicia asks.

Her hands are on his shoulders now, her body not quite touching his as she stands behind him, whispering softly close to his ear.

David feels tingly and weak at her nearness, numb. His body feels like it is melting to soft goo. He is exhilarated and terrified all at once. It is what he has dreamed of all these years, only he wishes she would stop talking about the dead kid. It's ruining the moment, making it feel too surreal, and wrapping them in a dark blanket of anxiety.

"You remember, don't you," she pauses, "what we did, what we all did that day?"

"We did nothing," he stiffens, confused.

"We … did … NOTHING!" she starts softly then screeches.

She is on top of him now, shrieking, her nails raking at him, fists pounding on him, attacking him in a vicious wild frenzy. He shakes her off, turning to look at her, stunned by her unprovoked attack.

Something hits him in the side of the head, hard. His head swims, dizzy, his eyes becoming unfocussed. Pain crashes through his head with a second blow. He staggers; falls to his knees, trying to stay upright. He can't see, just a wild blur, but he can feel the dripping wet of blood flowing from his head.

"I DID IT!" She screams at him. Even in her fury, her voice is beautiful to him. He blinks, trying to look past the fuzz at his long lost friend and first and only love. Yes, even at such a young age, unknowledgeable about love, all those years ago he'd known that he loved her.

David falls forward, unable to keep himself upright on his knees, on his hands and knees now. His arms are strangely weak. He struggles to keep his head up, to keep looking at her, his eyes focusing in and out of the haze that is pressing in around him.

Felicia's voice comes at him, sharp, angry, accusing.

"I did it! I killed the boy! It was all my fault!" Her voice rises in pitch as she shrieks at him, her small fists frantically reining blows on him.

Finally the attack stops. David feels dazed, in mind and heart. He doesn't know what to think, what he knows.

He manages to pull himself upright again, still on his knees. Standing is too much for him right now. He looks around for her, but his eyes are unable to focus. His head feels so very heavy.

Something bites at him, biting him in the back with a searing pain as he wobbles there on his knees. It bites again and he cries out with it. He can hear her, see the blurry image of her circling around, stopping in front of him. He looks up at her, pleading with his eyes. It bites at him again. This time from in front, and again and again, searing pain shooting through him each time. He falls backwards, lying on the ground. He can feel a sticky wetness on his back and chest.

She stands over him, staring down at him.

"Don't you get it?" she demands quietly. "Uncle Harvey was scary, but not a bad man. He was never a bad man. Poor strange and frightening Uncle Harvey. He went to jail already you know, before the boy in the woods, for killing a kid. But he didn't do it. He went to jail so no one would find out it was my fault, it was all me. That was the first time. Now he's going to go to jail again, for this child, to protect me."

She sobs.

His heart beats, he feels just that one lub-dub, tries to look at her. His lips move, trying to talk to her.

She looks down at him, calm now, sad. Tears roll down her cheeks.

"Why David, why?" she whispers. He is dying. She knows it and he knows it.

"Felicia," he whispers her name.

"It's ok," she whispers. "Uncle Harvey will look after me again. Look." She shows him the weapon in her hand.

The knife and her hands are covered with his blood. Her hands are trembling.

"This is his," she says. "They'll think he did it. He'll go to jail for your death too."

"No!" David's mind cries out. His lips try to cry out too, but they are breathless, dying.

She thinks Harvey will take the fall for his death too. She does not know Uncle Harvey is sitting in a jail cell, having been arrested for that long ago murder. He knows. He wants to tell her, aches to tell her.

He wants to save her from this. Protect her. His Felicia.

His mind races, a million questions running through it, playing back the memories even as the blackness engulfs him. The blackness and the cold. Uncle Harvey, in jail for killing this child long ago, covering for Felicia. But, did she really do it? Or is she covering up for her younger brother Nick?

Ian steps out from behind the looming bulk of a bulldozer.

"You shouldn't have done that," Ian says.

Felicia spins and glares at him.

"He was going to find out," she says.

"Old Uncle Harvey is in jail, you know. They picked him up this afternoon for killing the boy in the woods."

Her eyes widen, realization dawning.

"What do we do now?" she asks.

END

Other books by L.V. Gaudet:

<u>The McAllister Series:</u>

Where the Bodies Are

Are you ready to step into the twisted mind of a killer? What kind of dark secret pushes a man to commit the unimaginable, even as he is sickened by his own actions?

A young woman is found discarded with the trash, left for dead. More bodies begin to appear.

The killer's reality blurs between past and present with a compulsion driven by a dark secret locked in a fractured mind. Overcome by a blind rage that leaves him wallowing in remorse with the bodies of victim after victim, he is desperate to stop killing.

The search for the killer will lead to his dark secret buried in the past.

The McAllister Farm

Take a step back in time to meet the boy who created the killer and learn the secret behind the bodies in Where the Bodies Are.

William McAllister is a private man who does not like to have attention on his family. His family history is as dark as the secret hiding in the woods.

Just as he begins to bring his troubled son into the family business, a serial killer starts preying on local young women. The McAllisters quickly find themselves drawn into the spotlight when the town decides William McAllister is the killer.

The attention is a threat to both William McAllister's profession and his family. He has no choice but to find the killer himself.

He might not like what he learns.

Hunting Michael Underwood

Step deeper into the twisted mind of a killer as he slips further into madness.

Hunting Michael Underwood follows on the heels of book one, Where the Bodies Are, bringing the first two stories and their characters together as the search for the killer continues.

Michael Underwood has vanished and Detective Jim McNelly will not stop until he finds him. Working with the detective, Lawrence Hawkworth is still chasing the bigger story he knows is behind the bodies.

Jason McAllister knows he must stop the killer he created before he goes too far. He may be the only one who can stop him.

Unable to let go of his barely remembered past and the search for his sister, the killer goes looking for Jason McAllister's past and his family.

Killing David McAllister

Sometimes the only way to stop a monster is to kill it. He has gone by many names, but he was raised as David McAllister, and finding what he is looking for is not enough to quiet the darkness inside him.

Other Books:

Garden Grove

Who wants to stop construction at the new Garden Grove residential development? Garden Grove is a hotbed of complications from costly mistakes and vandalism to sabotage and the poisoning of the work crew.

While the construction crew struggles to stay on schedule, they face growing problems and, with them, a growing sense of unease.

A group of local housewives drawn into the growing mystery uncover a secret that brings Garden Grove deeper into a new mystery connecting all the suspects.

The mystery deepens with the discovery of old human remains that have their own dark past recently planted at the jobsite.

When all attempts to shut the site down permanently fail, two long time elderly residents step up their own efforts. Each with their own family secrets, the pair of quirky old birds are pitted against each other and their longstanding family feud is brought to the boiling point.

The Gypsy Queen
(1952)

When a young man with an enthusiasm for get rich quick schemes discovers a rotting abandoned paddle wheel river boat, he has dreams of the riches and glamour she will bring rebuilt as a floating casino. His best friend and unwilling business partner sees only rot, decay, and their ruination in the old boat.

Struggling to rebuild her, they are pitted against everyone from the Shipbuilders' Union to the local casino boss. Meanwhile, strange accidents and a sense of dread falls on those who enter the boat as she awakens with a hunger for her ounce of blood.

The Gypsy Queen's dark past will not be forgotten.

Old Mill Road

Twelve years ago four kids found something in the woods that tore their innocence away. They made a vow to keep it secret. Now, impossibly, someone found it again.

The abandoned mill off the old Mill Road has a dark history that has been told for generations, a story about something sinister haunting the woods.

Unable to remember the events of twelve years ago and troubled by the haunted look he sees every time he looks at his sister's eyes, Nick has returned to learn what happened when they were kids.

Still obsessed with Felicia and Nick's family suddenly vanishing in the night after their childhood discovery, David is determined to get answers from Nick, while his brother Ian tries to temper his obsession.

Felicia's return to help Nick will trigger new revelations about the mummified bodies of children appearing in the woods decades apart.

About the Author

L.V. Gaudet is a Canadian author, a member of the Manitoba Writers' Guild, the Horror Writers Association, and Authors of Manitoba.

L.V. grew up with a love of the darker side; sneaking down to the basement at night to watch the old horror B movies, Vincent Price being a favorite; devouring books by Stephen King, Dean Koontz, and other horror authors; and has had a passion for books and the idea of creating stories and worlds a person can get lost in since reading that first novel.

This love of storytelling has this author working writing and editing into a busy life that includes work, family, and supporting the writing community. L. V. Gaudet volunteers with the Manitoba Writers' Guild, is the editor of the MWG newsletter, proofreads for the HWA newsletter, and visits schools for I Love to Read month.

L.V. Gaudet currently lives in Manitoba with two rescue dogs, spouse, and kids.

Follow L. V. Gaudet:

Facebook: https://www.facebook.com/LVGaudet.Author/
Instagram: lv_gaudet
Twitter: @lvgaudet
Wordpress: https://lvgaudet.wordpress.com

Garden Grove

Strange Events are happening at the new Garden Grove residential development in a small bedroom community outside the city. Garden Grove is a hotbed of complications from costly mistakes and petty vandalism to outright sabotage of the equipment.

Bruce Copeland, owner of the construction company building the community, suspects his biggest business rival Vern Lezkowitz is behind the vandalism and sabotage. His two most trusted employees Stanley Rutthers and Dave McCormack have their own suspicions.

When the work crew is poisoned by treats brought by Mrs. Crampchet, one of the elderly locals, it puts them further behind schedule. While the construction crew struggles to stay on schedule, they face growing problems and, with them, an increasing sense of unease.

A group of local housewives drawn into the growing mystery uncover a secret that brings Garden Grove deeper into a new mystery connecting all the suspects.

In the meantime, an explosion at the Anc-Chor Project Bruce Copeland's company also has the contract for has Bruce looking more closely at both the man behind it, Mr. Chornelhus, CEO of the Chornel Corporation and his business rival Vern Lezkowitz.

When all attempts to have the site shut down permanently fail, two local elderly residents, Mrs. Crampchet and Rusty Plowshare, step up their own efforts. Each with their own family secrets, the pair of quirky old birds are pitted against each other and their longstanding family feud is brought to a boiling point.

The mystery deepens with the discovery of old human remains that have their own dark past recently planted at the jobsite.

During all this someone, or something, is watching.